HEART OF DARKNESS

Book Eight of Dark Secrets

~Book Eight of Dark Secrets~

Editor: John Edmunds

www.angelamhudson.com

ISBN/SKU: 9780648525837
ISBN Complete: 9780648525837

OTHER TITLES IN THIS SERIES

(SHOULD BE READ IN ORDER)

Dark Secrets
The Heart's Ashes
Mark of Betrayal
Lies in Blood
Echoes & Silence: Part One
Echoes & Silence: Part Two
Bound by Secrets
Heart of Darkness
Underworld

ALSO BY THIS AUTHOR

Bound Series Book 1

Bound Series Book 2

In Another life 1

In Another life 2

In Another life 3

In My Blood

The Legend of the Raven Wolf

BEST READING ORDER FOR DARK SECRETS

Dark Secrets

The Heart's Ashes

Mark of Betrayal

Lies in Blood

Echoes & Silence: Part One

Echoes & Silence: Part Two

Bound Series Book 1

Bound Series Book 2

Bound by Secrets

In Another life 1

In Another life 2

In Another life 3

In My Blood

Heart of Darkness

Underworld

AUBREY

For those of you who don't know me, my name is Aubrey Knight. I'll eventually be a Lilithian vampire—a what? I'll get to that—but I was born with an ability to lift dead souls from the Other Side and bring them to life again.

Necromancy?

That's not a word I like to use, but my family did once refer to me as The Daughter of the Phoenix—a child conceived from one reborn in fire. That was my mom, if you're wondering. She's a bicentennial ruler of the entire supernatural community.

Well, she was, until the other rulers had a messy divorce that caused a permanent division in our family. Which, you know, eventually led to the downfall of the entire Knight monarchy.

If you're new to this world, to my world, none of that made sense, I guess, because you may not know that my dad and my Uncle Jason were the kings—yes, two kings; each one getting 100 years to rule before passing the baton—and that my mom and Aunt Lily were the queens. They all have a complicated history. You could practically fill an entire novel with the stuff that went down between them. And when I say complicated, I mean *really* complicated. Like, my mom is only alive because Aunt Lily gave her half of her soul. And my mom and Uncle Jason were in love once but now he's with Lily. Actually, I think Mom still loves him—because it's a forever kind of love—but since they're soul mates, and since my dad is also her soul mate, Mom had to decide to "commit" to my dad or end up feeling lost for the rest of eternity, pulled between two hearts who owned her equally. Confused yet?

Don't worry. You'll catch on as we go along. Although, the real story I need to tell you is what comes after we found my mother and my baby brother on the beach. One dead, the other alive, the murderer having escaped just moments before, taking my father with her.

But we'll get to that.

Because, if you keep reading, you're about to see just how complicated *my* life is going to get. All because I grew up in a generation of kids who fight for what they believe in, for what they want.

And what do I want?

I want to be powerful. I want to say I have a talent that no one else does. And I want to be damn good at it. But how can I become everything I'm supposed to be if I'm not allowed to use my abilities? Not even to practice.

People die every day. I get that there has to be balance, but once they've died, why shouldn't they come back to life? They did their time, right? And since I can bring them back, I don't see why I shouldn't. It's not that complicated.

Unless you ask my parents.

And that brings me back to them and their story. You see, everything that happened, it can't just be told by one person, from one perspective, because so many threads came together to bring you this epic tale of the fall of an empire, but there was so much I didn't know about until now. Until I was looking back. So, I'm gonna go ahead and give you the side notes as we go along—my parents' story, and my Uncle Jason's—because, otherwise, you can't really get the complete picture. And I'll probably have to write it all down in more than one journal, because there's too many pages of madness and chaos to fit in this one.

So, get comfy, friends, because your journey begins here.

Do you believe in magic? I hope so. Because everything, from the moment you turn this page, is about to change.

Even for you.

See you on the Other Side…

ARA

Aubrey slammed her door.

Sighing heavily, I glanced over at David, who slowly placed his morning coffee on the lamp table and stood up. "I'll deal with her."

"Don't worry about it," I told him. "She just has to accept it."

"I won't have her disrespecting you, or slamming her door," he demanded softly, moving toward the stairs. "I don't care how angry she is. If she wakes Daniel, I'll ship her off to Elysium to live with her grandfather."

Another heavy sigh pushed my shoulders down as he walked away. Once, I might have laughed at that statement, but this morning, it just dredged up the many ways our lives had changed since we found Jason. After he went missing for two years, following a devastating event, he'd come back with a fiancé, divided the supernatural world again, and seen our once dear sister Lily become an outsider to the family. Our world was in a state of unrest, and it was all for love.

Because of love.

In spite of love.

Now, with Aubrey stamping her feet about a total ban on using her abilities, I felt like I was being pulled in all directions. Add to it that I had a headstrong two year old—unplanned—and that Jase and his fiancé Jules were coming to Perth in a few days, and it just seemed like I was in a blender, being crunched up into a recipe for the most soul-tiring situation a person could be in.

Rubbing my face firmly, I pushed my hair back and prepared myself for another long day, looking up as the front door opened.

"Morning," Elora chimed as she came through, always just that bit too cheery for my liking. "Uncle Mike sent me to get those bedsheets for Jules and Jase."

Without a word, I aimed a finger at the stack by the door.

"Ooh," she trilled, "nice thread-count."

"Nothing but the best for the former king of the people."

"And his new fiancé," she added.

"Yes. That, too."

Elora placed the sheets back down then and swept over to sit on the coffee table in front of me, the high white walls going up around her like she was a snow queen in an ice castle, graceful and elegant as a vampire, but as alive and thriving as a human. "What's wrong, Mom?"

"It's nothing."

"Is Aubrey being a brat again? Because I can talk some sense into her—"

"It's not that. We have her under control. She hasn't lifted a soul from the Other Side for over a month now, but she's arguing about it constantly—says they won't leave her alone."

Elora's gaze fixed on my face, and she reached over to touch my arm. "But it's not that, is it, Mom? That's not what's bothering you."

I sighed, rubbing my face again. "I'm just tired, that's all."

Her eyes narrowed at me, boring inside my soul to read the energy imprint that I, stupidly, had taught her how to read. "It's Uncle Jase," she said, curious. "Why are you dreading him coming to stay? He's not staying *here*."

"I know." I sunk back in the lounge chair. "It's not that."

Elora jumped up and came to sit beside me, head on my shoulder. "Is it… do you still love him?"

"Not in that way." I laughed, shaking my head, trying to think of a way to put this. "But things… have been complicated since the vision."

"The one Drake showed you *three years ago*?" she confirmed, voice lifting upward on the end. "The other life?"

I nodded.

"How is that still an issue? I thought you and Dad went out to Loslilian to talk it out with Uncle Jase and Lily."

"We did, but…" My eyes drifted across the room, thoughts going back to that night—the night that started this entire mess:

"Happy New Year." Drake hugged me, stepping back to allow Jase in. I hugged him tight, opening my arm then for David to join the huddle. I hadn't seen Jase and Lily in a little over three years now, but I'd missed him a lot. Missed the dynamic between us all.

"Happy New Year, guys."

They both kissed my cheek and turned to hug Lily, while the rest of the family exchanged sentiments of joy and good tidings. I stood back with my arms folded and watched the others, all smiling and laughing, gathered in a room equipped to host fourteen but, over the years, having multiplied so much that I thought about moving to a bigger house—if it weren't for the fact that I'd never want to be anywhere but across the road from Mike and Em. Especially now, with the trouble they were going through. Neither had admitted it, but it was obvious enough just looking at them—they hadn't even hugged—that things were rocky. And with my ability to feel their energies, I knew it went a little deeper than that. I could almost hear the words 'divorce' in their thoughts.

Drake moved in beside me and watched on. "They don't look happy. Mike and Emily."

"They'll be okay. It's just a rough patch. Love like theirs doesn't die, Dad—"

"Love like theirs?" He scoffed, folding his arms. "I wouldn't say they're in love, Amara. And if they were, it is certainly not some great love."

I glared at him. "What do you mean?"

"Mike has never loved her in the way he should. He held on to her because he was under your curse and needed something, somewhere to place all that love that had nowhere to go. And were it not for the fact that they had a child literally the day you broke the curse, I think Mike would have come to realize that much sooner."

My jaw dropped. "What a horrid thing to say!"

He shrugged unapologetically, looking a little bit human when he did. "I've seen alternate futures for them—"

"You have?"

Drake nodded, watching them. "This is the only one in which they ended up together."

"Why? When did you see these alternate futures?"

"When you were younger, I concocted a potion that would give me the gift of foresight, like my father, but only for the length of time that the potion ran through my veins. And I saw some… interesting things in those alternate lives."

"Like what?"

"For one, I saw a future where you married Mike."

"For real?"

"Yes. And you had a number of soulless babes that died soon after birth. It tore you both apart, but you were happy to begin with."

I glanced over at Mike. "And what about him? Who else did you see him with?"

"I saw a path where he ended up with Morgana, and I almost took steps to see it come to fruition, were it not for the fact that the very path that saw her happiness also saw the resurrection of Anandene in her witch form."

"And chaos ensued?" I said with a smirk.

"It did."

"Wow. And… what, you were just going to… choose it? Choose a path?"

He nodded once, moving his eyes across the room to Jason. "I saw many paths in those weeks, Amara—"

"Why were you looking at alternate paths?"

"To see if there was a way around Safia's demands," he said. "I needed to know if I could spare you the horror that awaited you at her hands, and I feel, despite all you suffered to get here, I chose the best path possible for you."

"Chose!" My arms dropped to my sides and I moved around to stand right in front of him. "You chose *my path for me?"*

He nodded again, unfazed, even though my entire head and chest were boiling with the rage of ultimate violation.

"You can't just go around choosing people's lives, Drake. How do you even know you chose the right path?"

From across the room, David looked up, casting his eyes in our direction.

Drake smiled softly. "You have such little faith in me—"

"Yes, because I went through hell, Drake! And you chose that for me?"

Now, everyone was looking. Drake stood taller, exhaling. "Yes. And I did so, knowing it was the best path."

"How so? What were the other choices?"

"It's irrelevant now."

"The hell it is. I have a right to at least know what my life might *have been—"*

"Very well then. You ended up with Jason." He smirked, taking a sip of his drink to wash it down. "In every other conceivable path I could have taken."

The air squeezed out of my lungs, making my stomach sink. "What?"

"Still think I chose the wrong path for you?"

I just wanted to smack his smug face. David moved over then.

"Show me," I demanded.

"Out of the question."

"Why?"

"Because it will tear open old wounds, Amara—"

"No, it won't."

"It will, because these visions are as real as life itself. You will feel, at the end, as though you lived it. You will make connections with people you have no feelings for in this life, and it will *alter you. I have no doubt in my mind."*

"Mom," Elora said, moving over to me, her eyes locked to the mirrored necklace she wore that helped clarify the energies she could see in a person's soul—energies that could map out pathways, futures. "You don't want to see it. Trust me."

"I need to," I insisted. "I want to know what life you thought was so much worse than this, enough that you took steps *to* choose *a path that put me through torture, that—"*

"You must trust that I have only ever done what's right for you—"

"I can decide that for myself—"

"I'm warning you, daughter. It will do you more harm than good—"

"I'm willing to take the risk—"

"Show me," David offered, laughing at me as he peeled me out of Drake's bubble. "I'll tell you if he chose the right path or not."

My jaw set hard, feet edging along the rocky ledge of middle ground. David and I were like one person these days, so connected, so close that I trusted him to know whether or not I should see the vision. "Fine. But if he's lying, if it was a better path, then I want to see, so I can hate him for the rest of my days."

"It wasn't a better path, Amara," Drake assured, laughing softly with the rest of the family.

"Just... show me." David sat down on the couch, the family moving in around him to watch on as Drake sat beside him, and David put his hands on Drake's head, taking the memory.

"Get settled in," Drake said. "This will take until morning."

I snapped out of the past, eyes glazed, and looked at my daughter. I'd made so many friends, so many enemies, in that alternate life, and looking back on it, it sometimes hurt when I realized that some of the people I'd loved were never a part of this life. Elias Davenport—the London Set Leader; the intense relationship with Arthur that I could never have imagined in this life; my love for Falcon; the cruel side to David that I was glad I'd never met. And... the powerful, untouchable King Jason.

But, the simple act of seeing that alternate life *had* torn open the old wound. It was a shock to my system coming up out of that vision, having been so intensely in love with Jason in it, that, for a moment, I wanted to go back. But I got over it. And yet... Jason didn't. And it was the decision to show him the vision as well that triggered a string of events which led to Lily and Jason divorcing, and me giving birth to a son.

"What happened between you and my uncle after that vision?" Elora prompted, eyes narrowed at my face as if to read me.

"Nothing. We talked. We sat up all night talking. And then he went home to Loslilian. It wasn't until a few weeks went by that Lily asked us to come out there—said Jason was depressed, wasn't himself."

"So you went? Then what?"

"Dad talked to him, and everything was okay after that. On our last night there, we all sat in the library with a few bottles of wine, like the way it used to be. But…"

"But not for Uncle Jase, right? He wasn't okay?"

"No. But not because of the vision."

"Was it because of Lily? Because of the fact that she was abusing him and he couldn't tell you?" Elora asked, and I stood up, suddenly in need of a cold drink. "Mom?"

Elora followed me into the kitchen, where I pulled the giant fridge open and grabbed the juice. "It's a long story, Lors."

"And I think maybe you should tell me, because we all know something went wrong that week—"

"It wasn't Jason's fault. Any of it."

"What wasn't?" She stepped in to the island counter and leaned on it, bringing her eager ear forward, her wavering form reflecting off the glossy marble surface.

I ran my eyes along the back windows and looked out at the big eucalyptus tree by the pool, seeing the toddler's swim vest, the high chair by the dining table behind Elora, and the den full of toys beyond that, thinking about how much my life had changed. Thinking about the ways Jase's had.

"They just lost their baby, Lors," I said, a shake in my voice.

"Jules and Jase. And when he comes here tomorrow, it's going to be obvious. He'll know, the second he looks at him. He'll know."

"Know what?" she prompted impatiently.

Just then, Daniel woke with a mighty scream. I heard David end his lecture with Aubrey and close her door, releasing a somewhat jaded sigh as he headed in to Danny's room. Then I looked back at Elora.

"He'll know Daniel's his son."

Her eyes widened and she looked at the walkway leading through to the lounge, as though she might see Danny from here and compare the similarities. But what was there to compare, because Danny's biological father was the exact genetic copy of his dad. No one but me, and David, would ever know. Unless Jason laid eyes on that baby.

"Mom? How did this happen?" she asked, eyes welling.

With another long sigh, the hundredth for today and it was only eight in the morning, I sat down on the stool at the counter beside her. "We didn't know it then, but we were under the spell of the same potion that made you and Falcon have sex."

"How? And who would poison you with that? Did Jason?"

"No, Elora." I laughed grimly. "He would never do that. You know that."

"Then… who would do such a thing?"

"We had our theories, believe me," I said sadly, looking off into the past, but when I thought about the way David reacted, I smiled. "We didn't know it then, but it was Lily."

Elora nodded, sitting down on a stool too. After everything she'd seen this past year with Jase and Jules, the nightmare Lily put them through, and all the truths that came out, I knew she didn't need any further explanation. Lily's illusion of the perfect, sweet soul had been cracked wide open. We'd all seen right through her. We all knew the truth now.

"Why did she do that? She's so possessive over Uncle Jase? It doesn't make sense. And how come you never told me?" Elora asked.

"I didn't want anyone to know. And I wasn't sure we'd ever see Jason again after it, so..."

"So that's why you fought so hard to find him when he went away? You wanted him to know he had a son?"

"Somewhat. But I also thought I was helping him, helping Lily. We didn't know what she'd done to him back then, remember. Dad and I didn't even know it was her that drugged us until after everything went down in New York."

Elora nodded again, seeming to wake then to the situation, with all its deeper meaning, and closed her hand around mine. "I'm so sorry, Mom. I can't even imagine how you must be feeling right now. Especially since Jules just lost the baby. I mean,"—she covered her mouth, sinking back a bit—"poor Uncle Jason. That's the second baby he's lost before it was born. And he's coming back here to be with family *because* of it, and..." Her head turned in the direction of Danny's cries. I knew she understood why I was so worried about Jason coming home. This would kill him. It would kill Jules. And the fact that both Jason and I had lied to Jules about our past—telling her we hadn't had sex again since I threw myself off the lighthouse—made matters even worse. I only lied because I couldn't class it as sex. It wasn't real. It was the potion, and I knew Jules couldn't possibly understand that.

My thoughts strayed then to the agonizing phone call I got from Jo—Jules's best friend—the morning the happy couple woke in a pool of blood, the life within her no longer there. I thought I'd sensed it that night as I left them in New York, but I was so tired and there was so much confusion and grief that I hadn't been certain. Now, I wished I'd said something to Jason.

He'd been through too much. And baby Daniel might just be the final straw that unravels them. Yet, I couldn't tell them not to come. They needed their family right now. Jules had given up everything she fought for in New York—her stage career, her apartment, her life—because she just needed to shut down in the loving arms of family.

"You're worrying about Jules, aren't you?" Lors asked.

"I don't think she can take much more, you know. I think she's just so broken right now that it will take the smallest, simplest thing to shatter her. And Daniel is no small thing, Lors. He's an apocalypse."

Elora laughed. "Yeah, but a damn cute apocalypse," she offered, standing up as David walked in with the red-faced baby. His soft brown hair had curled around his brow with the heat of the morning, and his round emerald eyes shone like gems beneath those fluffy lashes. He was instantly lovable, with chubby, pinchable cheeks, and no matter how much hell he put me through, it was never enough that his beautiful face couldn't make me smile.

"He wanted to get up now," David advised, handing him to his big sister.

"But he was up *all night*." I sighed, dropping my head into my hands and then turning it to smile softly at David.

He took me in with a look of pity, coming over to kiss my brow. "You okay?"

"You just need this over with," Elora offered, sending a wave of supernatural calm over Daniel to make him quiet. "Once you've broken it to Uncle Jase, you'll feel better."

"Not if it destroys his relationship with Jules," David told her.

"If that can destroy them, then they weren't made for each other." Elora turned away and put Daniel down in his high chair.

David and I exchanged smiles.

"She has a point," he said.

"I know. But Jason's lost too much. I don't want to be the person who presses the proverbial red button, because if he loses Jules now..."

"He can hold on for his son." David swept my hair back and kissed my head again, sending a memory into my brain—one of Jase and I speaking after I'd seen that vision, the final piece, where we'd had a son.

"We had a beautiful baby," Jase had said, voice deep with eternal regret.

"And we both have beautiful babies now, Jase. In this life."

"I know. But they're not yours-and-mine. And as much as I love Lily, I know you understand how much that would have meant to me—for us to have a son."

The memory ended, and I nodded at David to say I understood.

"One look into those almond-shaped eyes," David added, "and my brother will never run away again."

"I guess." I nodded, not really feeling any better though. Because he might not run away from us again, but Jules wasn't bound by the same ties. If she left, and he stayed, it wouldn't be enough just to have him in our lives anymore, because he'd be destroyed in the process. All I ever wanted was for Jason to find his one true love. I had mine, I was happy, but because Jason was also my soul mate, a part of me felt like I had no right to be happy until he was.

"So, Dad?" Elora took the bib I handed her and placed it on Danny. "How did you react to Mom sleeping with Uncle Jase?"

His eyes flicked off to the memory, heart and brain painting a scene in the front of his mind, and I went back there with him:

Shaking, I walked the corridors of Loslilian to the Queen's cham-

bers—to Lily. I had to tell her I was sorry, that I didn't taste the potion in the drink, didn't realize what had happened until I woke beside Jason, naked.

But David opened her bedroom door instead, wearing nothing but a sheet and the same haunted expression as me.

No words were needed in that moment.

He knew from the smell, from the guilt, the shame. And I knew too. I knew he'd done with Lily what I'd just done with Jason.

But he didn't cringe and turn away. His eyes didn't darken and make him cold. He swept in and closed his arms around me, catching me where my legs buckled.

It was the potion, he'd said. We can't blame ourselves.

It seems we've all fallen victim to some cruel, heartless act, Lily offered, coming up behind David in just a dressing gown, her eyes puffy and red with tears. I will find out who did this, my darling sister. And I will kill them…

"I know my wife," David said, waking me to the present. "I knew she wouldn't do that of her own volition. And, for a moment, I thought my brother had drugged her—out of desperation to be with her. But—"

"But he wouldn't do that," Lors reminded him.

"No. He has too much honor. But he was very broken after Drake showed him that vision. He wasn't the same. He felt the promise of a life with your mother and he couldn't let it go, and… for a moment, I did blame him."

"Did you punch him?"

"No." He smiled to himself, eyes shrinking, dimple pressing in sharply in that almost secret smile I hadn't seen in years. "I would have, but he was gone before any of us could wash off the stench of the nightmare. And we didn't see him again until he'd already met Jules."

Elora's eyes widened. "So that's the real reason he left?"

"It was a contributing factor."

"A major one, I'd say," Elora scoffed, walking over to the fridge to get Daniel's breakfast. "I bet he ran so Lily wouldn't kill him."

"Probably," I offered. "Then again, he was conflicted by *many* things at that time." But I knew the truth. He wanted to leave because Lily was abusing him, and because she lied about the children being his, refused to let him see them. Yet Jason doesn't step out on commitment. He'd have stayed if we hadn't ended up having sex. It was the triggering event. And for a moment, I let myself go back there—to remember it and feel the agony in my soul. I'd shut it out all these years, desperate to move on, but it would forever haunt me.

Not even the fact that David had sex with Lily that night tormented me as much as my night with Jase; it hadn't left my soul yet. It still hurt. Still scared me. I still felt sometimes like I was going to wake up and lose David because of it.

Somehow, my act didn't compare to his, as if he'd never slept with Lily at all, even though this entire nightmare began because she wanted David for herself.

And to think I comforted her after that! She was the one who set this in motion. She was responsible for me now having another loved but *very* untimely child, and for David having to raise one that wasn't his. Even though he would never look at it that way.

It wasn't fair.

Coming back, as David and Elora carried on a conversation I'd missed entirely, I felt suddenly ill and overwhelmed. David stopped talking mid-sentence and pressed a hand to my back as I stood up.

"Ara?"

"I need a rest," I said, steadying myself with a hand to the counter. "Just look after Daniel for a bit."

"Okay." David walked me to the stairs, sliding his hand down my arm then as I walked up, not letting go until I smiled back to say I was okay.

AUBREY

Who are you when you close your eyes at night—above all else, when it's just you and no one else?

Are you evil?

Inherently good?

Or are you a cold person trying to be charitable, when all you really want is to hide in a dark room and do nothing to fix the world?

That's the question I need to answer. I know who my parents want me to be. I know who I have to be, for the sake of the world. And yet, at just seventeen years old, I already know it's not who I *want* to be.

But, then, who am I if I'm not their version of me *or* my version of me?

Does that mean I'm stuck in some halfway-middle-ground; not human and not yet, maybe never will be, Lilithian; not witch nor seer. Neither good, nor bad.

They don't have a name for me, for what I can do. So they

try to make me human. Suppress it. Lock it away. Force me to hide it because it's a dangerous skill if anyone were to know.

But that's just it, isn't it? I have a skill that's burning inside of me; fighting to emerge and take me down a path that I'm supposed to walk. Danger, isolation, fear. None of it scares me, because this is my fate. So, I decided to practice, learn, and develop my abilities in secret. And that attitude just wasn't conducive to the vision my parents had for me, which is why Dad was yelling at me right now.

"Even if you don't agree, you will obey. Not just for your own safety, Aubrey, but for the sake of your mother," he demanded, blocking my doorway and blinding me where the sun blast through the stairwell window behind him, framing him with bright white light. "She's fragile right now," he added, "you know that, and..." Blah, blah, blah...

I knew Mom was fragile, did I? Sure. I also knew why. I knew he'd shut her down at the dinner table last night and completely invalidated her, and her worth, and that she'd just sat there and absorbed that message like it was gospel. That's the real reason she was fragile, admit it, Dad. Mom isn't depressed. She's miserable because you're a prick to her. Say it. Go on, say it. I dare you.

What's that? You won't admit it? No, of course not. You'd rather yell at me and make it all my fault that Mom's lost the will to go on.

Fury and frustration rose up in me like fire when I checked my watch then. Late. I actually had things to do this morning before school, and now I'd have to skip class because of him.

I nodded across to the corner of my room, and a second later, Dad sighed heavily and ended the lecture at the demand of my baby brother's screams. I felt bad for Danny, but Dad forced my hand. He wasn't backing down, and with a bunch of unfinished assignments, problems with friends, as well as my own teen journey of self-discovery, the last thing I needed was to sit in here listening to him force his opinion down my throat until I missed roll call.

As he tried, in vain, to shush my brother back to sleep for the sake of my always-depressed mother, I smiled at the ghost beside me, her ethereal form wavering like heat bounding off hot pavement.

"One crying baby, as you requested," she said.

"Thanks." I smiled, sitting down in front of my mirror to finish my hair. "While you're at it, go down and see what my mom is saying to my sister. I heard Uncle Jason mentioned."

"What's wrong with that?"

"I think I heard her say she had sex with him, but my dad deliberately spoke over that bit." I turned to the mirror and swept my dark auburn waves into a ponytail. "I want the truth."

"Aubrey, this isn't right," she advised. "It's one thing to wake your brother to get you out of a lecture but… spying…"

"Do you want passage back to the living realm or not?" I snapped, piercing her ethereal form with a sharp stink-eye. "Go down there and find out what they're saying!"

The ghost evaporated, so I went back to my mirror, brushing on a layer of mascara and some shiny red lip gloss. I didn't need a lot of beauty-accentuation, since Dad passed on his thick lashes and curvy lips, and Mom gave me her gem-like blue eyes, but it didn't hurt to feel fab either.

When the ghost appeared again a few minutes later, it was with a somber expression.

"What?" I prompted. "What did you find out?"

"Apparently, your baby brother is more like your brousin."

"Brousin?"

"Brother-slash-cousin."

"What?" I stood up, gliding over to my ghost. "What do you mean?"

"Your mother was under a spell and she had a child with your uncle."

I sunk back on my heels, a wash of white dread flooding me from head to toe. "My Uncle Jason?"

"Yes."

Holy cow! Daniel was Uncle Jase's? I wanted to laugh—to call Uncle Jase and see if he knew! "Does my uncle know?"

"Not as far as I could tell. I couldn't stay long, because your sister sensed me. She'll make me cross over to the spirit realm if she sees me."

Huffing out my frustration, I grabbed my school bag and opened my door. "She won't see you. She can only *sense* spirits in your domain, not see them. So, linger some more. See what else you can learn," I said, feeling my mother's presence as she came up stairs. I ducked back into my room and hid for a second until she passed, lingering then at the top of the stairs to see if anyone divulged more information. But, after a moment of listening to my big sister goo and ga over our baby brother, I realized they were all done sharing for the day, so I darted out the front door, eager to get to school and tell Mia all about it.

In the crowded school yard, I found Mia with the lanky and tragically-nerdy BS—so-titled that today because he was lingering like a bad smell. She squeaked in surprise when I hauled her away from the conversation and dragged her off to the wall, putting my hand up to stop BS from following. "Girls only, Tom," I snapped, and he humbly stepped back, glancing around the yard like he didn't know what to do when he wasn't hanging off of us.

Mia bent her head in a conspiratorial lean, her short blonde curls meeting the curtain of my hair as we closed the circle of trust.

"Is it bad news or good?" she asked, her caramel eyes reading my face.

"Mia, I've known you my entire life. You can't tell with just one look?"

"That's just it: I normally can, but you're kind of both excited and upset."

I squeezed her hands excitedly. Not excited because Danny was only my half-brother, but excited because she was the only person who would fully appreciate the juiciness of this gossip. "Danny isn't Dad's."

"What?" The shock threw her away from the huddle for a moment. "What do you mean? How do you know?"

"My mom had sex with Uncle Jase—a few years ago."

"What!" Mia belched. "When? How? Why? Does your dad know?" Her eyes widened on that last question, because we all knew how fiercely protective, maybe even controlling, my dad was of my mom.

"He knows." I grinned, feeling a sparkle of scandal flare within my eyes. "But Uncle Jase doesn't know. And—"

"Oh my gosh." Hand over mouth, she spun away and faced the wall, hunched slightly. "Aubrey, when he arrives tomorrow…" Mia looked at me again, tears in her eyes. "If he finds out… especially right after…"

"Aunt Jules lost the baby, yeah." I nodded, glancing back to see Tom look away, hands in his pockets like he was just hanging out casually in the middle of the yard. Alone.

"How could your dad forgive your mom for that?" she asked,

leaning on the wall. "He must have been so hurt."

"I don't know." I dropped my bag and leaned on the wall beside her. "They did promise each other forever: nothing do them part. Maybe that counts for infidelity?" I shrugged.

"Maybe. Or maybe it's just that he makes allowances for their love—for hers and Jason's—you know, since they were designed for each other."

I nodded, thinking that over. My mom had always loved Uncle Jase. That was evident to me even in my earliest memories. She always hugged him just a little too long, placed her hand over his when they talked, leaned in to him when she laughed at something he'd said. And my dad was always right there beside her, a part of it, not so much on the outside. Maybe they had some kind of agreement that Mom could unburden herself of that pressure, that immense torture she felt around Uncle Jase, every few years. Dad clearly didn't hate her for either sleeping with Uncle Jase, or for loving him. Maybe they were some sick kind of threesome.

"My dad said she chose him," Mia offered, passing me my bag as the bell rung.

"Huh?" We started walking.

"Dad said that she would always love King Jason—"

"He's not the king anymore. Not since the divorce, remember—"

"Sorry, force of habit." She smiled sheepishly into her hair, the cute freckles across her nose turning pink for a second. "But… my dad also told me that your mom would eternally love both of them," Mia said sadly. "That must be excruciating."

"Tell me about it." I actually felt kind of sorry for my mom then. Just for a moment. "I kind of understand how hard that would be, though."

"What do you mean?"

"You know how it is with me and Uncle Jase. He's always been like a dad to me, and I love him like he's my own father. *As much as* my own father. But I can't even imagine loving two guys in the capacity my mom does."

"Can't you?" She raised a blonde brow at me, nodding in the direction of Sawyer. "I know you can at least imagine what it's like to really want someone and not be able to have them."

"I don't like *him*." I threw my bag over my shoulder. "He's cute. But he's a bad-boy. So not my type."

"He's not a bad boy," she scoffed. "He's just not a sheep, like the rest of them."

"Who's not a sheep?" Tom asked, joining the gang again.

"Girl talk, Tom," I said coldly, taking off then at a different speed, as if to make it to class on time, flicking them both a smile as I left. But I didn't head to class. Straight after roll call, I jumped over the gate and headed to the beach. I'd made an agreement with a certain ghost, and it was time to pay up.

AT THE EDGE OF AUSTRALIA, ON A COAST THAT COULD BE seen for miles in either direction, I climbed and balanced my way over half a kilometer of limestone rocks to the secret cave. Several warning signs, rooted randomly and tipped sideways, gave me a stern reminder that limestone wasn't to be trusted and that this hollow could cave in at any time. But this was the only place that was really private enough to do this. Private enough that my parents' spies wouldn't see.

The quiet waves that rolled on freely to this one part of the coastline smacked at the rocks, but the force disintegrated even more by the time the water reached the back of the dark cavern, lending it more of a lazy slap.

I set myself up on a rock and dug through my bag for the matches to light the lantern. The ghost was there when I looked up again, her expression lit, expectant, as though she'd hoped to scare me. But I didn't scare easy.

"So you understand the arrangement?" I asked.

"Never speak of this to anyone; never visit my old family, or my old life; and if I'm found, I lie about who I am and what I know."

"Right." I looked her dead in the eye. "Or else the cult I belong to will hunt you down and kill you again, and my mother, the Queen of Purgatory, will lock you in a dark place for eternity."

The ghost nodded.

"And if you try to kill me, hurt me, or threaten me when I bring you back, I will leave you trapped in this cave. I'm the only one that knows the way out. Got it?"

She nodded again, humbled.

"Now, once you've been brought back to human form, my brother will turn you into a vampire. That takes care of the new identity, since, to become a vampire, you would've had to die in your old life. The Order won't even ask you about who you are."

"But what about… you said a person had to have approval to become a vampire."

"They do."

"But… I don't."

"You were turned by a rogue. You don't know who."

"As with all your other resurrections?" she asked.

"Not all of them. Only four have been turned to vampire. You make five."

"How many have you brought back?" she asked nervously.

"After you… six."

"And… how do you know I won't die… or… worse?"

"My uncle. Well, great uncle, Arthur. He was the first one I brought back—when I was seven. He's still alive and well."

The ghost nodded, visibly relieved.

"So, where will you go?" I asked her.

"Anywhere."

"What will you do?"

"Live. Eat. Enjoy the times."

I took more notice of her dress then. Since button dresses were in fashion right now, it never occurred to me that it might have been of the era of its design. Souls didn't literally carry their clothes over from death, but I had learned over the years that they were more like projections; tiny clues about their past-selves. When I pulled them onto this side, brought them to the living realm, I wasn't sure why those clothes followed them then. I had theories, like maybe I could manifest the clothes as well as the living, but that seemed insane and really didn't make much sense. There was a lot I hadn't made sense of, hadn't figured out, but doing it, bringing them back, was really the only way to even start understanding my abilities. Few ghosts ever slipped between the living realm and the Other Side, so there weren't many opportunities over the years to learn much about it, but I knew they came from this place between here and there, and nowhere, a middle ground. A kind of crawlspace. My mom couldn't see them once they slipped into this place, and neither could my sister Elora; she could only sense them. Mom had once said that the goddess Lilith might know more, but my parents, my very uncool, overprotective parents, said I had to be immortal before they'd let me speak with her. And don't get me wrong, I wouldn't normally let that stop me but, sadly, the only place where anyone had ever been able to summon Lilith was in the supposedly enchanted forest on the island of Loslilian. However, my Aunt Lily currently reigned over that domain and she'd iced my family out. My *entire* family. So, all I could do to help myself was to keep bringing back souls as they found me, and just hope I learned something in the process.

"Do you remember your old life?" I asked.

Her hazel eyes drifted away as she tried to think back. "I remember music. And what it felt like to love. But I don't remember who I was or what I did."

"What you did?"

"What I stood for, I suppose."

I nodded. "Well, you look like a good person. And I can sense that in your soul. That's the only way I allow a spirit to come back."

"You can sense what's in a person's soul?"

"Yes."

"Even the living?"

I had to think about that, but… "Yes," I said, brushing away the tightness that answer gave me in my chest when I realized what that truly meant—what I'd sensed in certain people and never wanted to admit.

"Have you ever had requests for life from bad souls?"

"A few. But I threaten to send them to Hell, and they go away pretty quick."

"Is there a Hell?"

"No." I stood up. "Not that I know of. Now, let's get this over with."

Sweeping her pretty blonde hair out of her ethereal face, the ghost stood, and I could see her mentally preparing herself. When she reached out, I grabbed her hand and tried to imagine it was real. As I gave it a little tug, she stumbled forward for a moment and then gasped for air, clutching her chest. It was that simple.

"Holy Lord!" she breathed, folding over.

I let go of her hand, but she tried to hold on, as if she might slip back into oblivion without my touch.

"It's okay," I told her, placing a comforting touch to her shoulder. "You won't vanish."

The woman let go and straightened herself, her skin luminescent even in the darkness of the cave. She was much prettier in person than she was as a ghost, and I knew she'd be fine. She'd leave here and get on with her new life, and never look back.

"I'm remembering things," she said, reaching for a necklace at her chest that was no longer there. "I died." Her hands went to her belly, pressing in. "I was pregnant."

My eyes widened, landing on her hands. I'd never brought back a pregnant person before. Did the soul of the babe stay within her and cross to this side when I pulled her out, or did it wander away on its own after her death?

"Okay, come on," I said, taking her arm.

"Where are we going?"

"To my brother. He'll be the one turning you, but he can also sense if there's a baby there."

"It might still be there?" she asked, hands going across her belly again.

"I don't know. But we won't know if we don't ask. Come on."

Harry's house sat humbly at the center of an acreage, surrounded by dense Australian bushland. He'd bought an apartment when he moved out of home, but since he preferred to make his dinner scream before eating it, and because he liked loud music, he had to move. But he didn't live too far away; only ten minutes outside of my town, where a lot of the old farmland was being bought up for new estates. Because of that, he was far enough out that no one could hear the screams but close enough that he was only fifteen minutes from our house. He even had a pet goat and a few chickens with ridiculous names.

I turned off the highway and up the gravel drive, following the passage of gumtrees toward the farmhouse. Even with my windows rolled up and the air-conditioner on, I could hear his amp blasting out the baseline of a Foo Fighters song.

Beside me in the passenger's seat, the new human, who still didn't know her name, sat with her hands closed around her belly, probably wondering if she'd made a mistake coming back to this world.

Her red-and-white polka dot dress was really wicked, and I kind of wanted to ask if I could have it before she left for her new life. But she was at least a size smaller than me. I didn't get Mom's petite frame. I was taller, sturdy, and had curves in all the right places, just the way I liked it. Which was great but also sucked when it came to borrowing clothes from the stick figures in my family.

"Are you scared?" I asked.

"Of what?"

"My brother, since he's a vampire? Sometimes my resurrections are a bit intimidated."

"A little." She smiled sweetly, moving her hands away from her belly with quite a bit of effort. "Is he immortal?"

"Yes."

"And… you said there were two kinds of vampire. Ones that drink human blood and ones that drink vampire blood—"

"He's the human-killing kind."

"Killing?" Her eyes widened and the blood left her face.

"Mm-hm." I nodded casually.

"Is he... old?"

"Old?" I laughed. "No. Why would he be old?"

"If he's a vampire..."

"He's a new vampire. He made the change at twenty, much to my parents' disgust. They were pissed at him for a really long time."

"Made the change?"

"We're originals, which means our vampirism is triggered when we drink blood. He's a hybrid, and when it came time for him to change, he could choose between vampire or human blood—basically choose whether to be Lilithian or vampire. He chose vampire," I said proudly, knowing I'd choose the same if I weren't a stinky pureblood Lilithian, thanks to my dad being human when he made me. Mia was also Lilithian, so I wasn't alone at least, but she was so much softer at heart than I was—more like a true Lilithian—whereas I had the nature of a vampire.

The woman's eyes went to my hands then as the car steered itself into its usual parking spot outside my brother's house.

"How are you doing that?"

"It's autonomous driving, meaning these cars drive themselves. They passed the law six years ago that allows them to travel on the road without a driver."

"Incredible."

"Not really. It's just technology. I mean, I shouldn't be behind the wheel, because I'm still on my learner's permit until next month, but if I don't make any mistakes then no one will ever know."

Her eyes widened and she moved them onto the house, her age-old-brain just too challenged by the idea of a self-driving vehicle.

We climbed out of the car and Harry met us at the porch,

stamping out a cigarette as he flipped his chin in our direction. “Skipping school again, little sis?”

Harry had such an easy smile. It was big and open and welcomed everyone he met as an immediate friend. He was tall, with dark hair like my dad, and the most sparkling blue eyes I'd ever seen on a guy, set into a slender face that narrowed at the chin and seemed to pull his youthful skin down into two neat and adorable indents on either side of his sharp grin. And the woman beside me had an odd reaction. She took the stairs up the porch a little faster than me, angling her head as though she meant to put her eyes right on his and stare deeply into them.

“Who are you?” she asked, meeting him face to face. She was a full head shorter than him, but at least the same age. “I know your face.”

“Not possible, love.” He winked at her, leading the way inside. “You've been dead since before I was born.”

“But...” She followed us inside, her eyes wide like a scared rabbit. “You look so familiar.”

“Don't know what to tell ya. Maybe you're imprinting.” Harry shrugged, bouncing down into the big green armchair by the bookshelf. His house was neat but in an orderly-chaos-kind-of-way. There was a piano by the window, drums in the corner, surrounded by books in tall but categorized piles, and a dozen-or-so really expensive guitars on stands or pinned to the walls. All of them bought with the money he made writing songs. He never played the songs, didn't do shows or tours—aside from open mic night at the jetty cafe down the beach every Thursday—because he didn't want to be famous for his voice. He wanted to be famous for his words.

My ghost, who really, at this point, needed a name, scooped her dress under her bottom with both hands and sat down on the sofa across from Harry. “Imprinting?” she queried.

"I'm one of the first people you've seen since you came back to life. Your brain is searching for familiarity in any place it can find it," he offered, coming forward on his seat a little and closing his hands together between his knees. "It'll wear off in a few weeks."

"So, do you remember your name?" I asked. "Because my inner voice-over can't keep calling you 'Ghost Girl'."

She gave me a look like I was completely insane. "Inner…? Never mind. I probably don't want to know."

"Aubrey's a storyteller," Harry advised. "She internalizes her day and then writes it all down in her journal every night."

"Oh." Ghost Girl nodded, but when she looked at Harry again and a bright smile forced its way to her lips, she hid it, averting her eyes shyly. Her cheeks even went kinda pink. And I was like, whoah! Revelation. She was totally crushing on my big brother!

"So, what can I do for you, Aubs?" Harry stood up, clearly uncomfortable when he realized that too. He was cute, cool, and confident, but he was all mush and sentiment when it came to girls, which had seen him being single for just a little too long. Girls just didn't like sweet boys.

"Ghost Girl here can't remember her name, but she does remember she was pregnant when she died."

Harry looked at her belly, then at her hand, as if looking for a ring. "You want me to see if she still is, now that she's alive again?"

I nodded, sitting down beside Ghost Girl.

Harry knelt in front of her, and his expression changed, as though he was listening for something. Then he shook his head apologetically.

"Nothing there now," he said, and Ghost Girl cried.

Neither of us knew what to do. In our family, Mom was the

compassionate one—enough for every man and his dog… and his cat, his fish, or pet rock. We'd never needed to show any. We were both a bit more like Dad in that sense, standing on the sidelines and waiting until Mom fixed everything.

"I'm… sorry," Harry mumbled, not sure what else to say.

"Look, I gotta get back to school before lunch." I stood up, eager to be away from the emotion. "Here's some clothes and stuff for her."

Harry stood and took the bag, coated in awkwardness, his big blue eyes begging me not to leave him with Crying Ghost girl. But I just smiled, spun on my heel, and left him with it. It was our agreement, after all: he turned my "ghosurrections" to vampires, sent them to the right people for processing and ID, and I didn't tell Mom about his pile of bodies under the house.

When I made it back to the car, I'd never been so happy to breathe fresh air. Emotions like that, heavy emotions, did unnatural things to my soul. Mom thrived on it, understood all the levels of energies like they were just numbers on a page, but I felt weighed down and suffocated by it. And so did Harry. But I smiled as I pulled away, because that was his problem. Maybe he shouldn't have illegally fed on so many people. Damn serial killer!

I shut the car door and pressed the button to turn the car on, telling it to drive me back to school.

"Hello there," said a man beside me.

I squealed, laughing when I realized it was just another ghost. He had a thick black beard and squinty aqua eyes, and though he was older and probably from a time when kilts were common attire, he was actually not too bad-looking, if a little on the skinny side. "You can't sneak up on people like that!"

"Didn't seem to bother you with the others."

"Others?" I halted the car halfway down my brother's gravel driveway and turned to look at him. "You've been watching me?"

"Only long enough to know what you can do—and that you use my kind for your own juvenile tasks before you allow us to come back."

Oh, if he wanted me to bring him back, he just went the wrong way about it. "That's my prerogative. If they want something from me, they can do me a favor first."

"Does that make you an opportunist, or a little bitch?" he mused, then he reached for my hand and tried to bring himself back! I whipped it away, but my hand went right through his anyway.

"Ha!" I barked. "Nice try, dickhead. But it doesn't work like that. Only I have the power to bring someone back. And you"—I pressed the button on the screen at the center of the dashboard to open his door as a metaphorical get-the-hell-out—"will never get my help now."

"Don't be so sure," he demanded, floating out of the car. "I have ways of getting what I want."

With a haughty huff, I pressed the button to close the door, wishing it would slam to drive my point home. What that ghost didn't realize is that *I* held all the power. I didn't need to slam the door, because my refusal now to grant him any attention would essentially get the same point across.

When I activated the car to drive away, nothing happened. I issued the command again, but the car wasn't having any of it. It was like the battery had been disconnected. Electric cars were quiet, so it was sometimes hard to tell if they were even on, but this was like flicking a light switch and having no light.

"We can do this the hard way or the easy way," said the ghost, his voice strangely not muffled by his position outside the car.

"Fine!" I challenged, knowing he had no power here. "I'll take the hard way, you dress-wearing beanpole."

The screen came alive again on the dash then, and the wheels spun, throwing me back in my seat and taking me down the driveway faster than a self-driving car would ever go. I squealed, pressing every button and stomping my foot down on the pedal, but the car reached the road before I got control, snaking suddenly and bursting out into oncoming traffic before righting itself and then cruising along at an acceptable speed, as if nothing had happened.

Breathless and shaking, I put both hands on the wheel for some semblance of control, letting my heart thump in my throat and fill me with rage.

When I arrived back at school, the rage had turned to shock. No ghost had ever been that powerful before. I still hadn't shaken it off by the time I met Mia in the lunchroom, so she pulled me away from the group, all the way to the girls' bathrooms, and locked the door.

"What happened? Did you have a Consequence?"

Consequence: the word given to a side-effect or ripple-effect of using certain abilities. Mom had suffered some in leaving the Lost to walk the Fog of Purgatory for too long, and Elora often got exhausted when helping ghosts cross over, but, so far, I hadn't had any for bringing people back from beneath the veil. It was an ever-constant concern for Mia, who was spiritual and earthly, and spent too much time talking with my big sister's witchy friend Ali.

"No. But I had a kind of… like… malevolent spirit," I told her, hiding the emotion. "He manipulated my car—made it go fast. Really fast."

Mia's freckles darkened along her nose as her face paled. "I didn't think ghosts could do that."

"Neither did I," I said, moving over to the mirror to look at myself. My eyes were too wide right now, encasing the deep fear I'd carried all the way back from Harry's. I was adept at hiding my emotions, but this was giving way too much away. "I don't know what to do, Mia."

"You have to tell your mom."

"I can't—"

"Don't tell her you've been bringing people back. Just tell her you have a ghost hassling you."

"And she'll use that to support her idea that my powers are dangerous and that I shouldn't use them. No," I said decisively, turning the faucet to wet my hands. "I'll shake this off, and next time, I'll be ready. But there is no way in hell this ghost is going to scare me into running to my mommy and daddy."

"What if it hurts you?" Mia said, grabbing my arm as I bent to wet my face.

"I have Harry. He can protect me."

"You better hope so," she advised gravely, "because we don't know anything about your abilities, Aubrey. This could be really dangerous."

"Then bring it on," I said, water dripping from my face. "I'm in the living world, and that douchebag is dead. Far as I'm concerned"—I dried my face on some paper towel—"I have the upper hand."

"You hope."

I looked into the mirror, fixing my bold blue eyes with determination. Nothing had ever bested me before. I wasn't about to let it now. "Watch this space, Mia," I said, pushing out of the bathroom. "That ghost is gonna get his ass handed to him."

ARA

"Aubrey, is that you?" I called, hearing the front door open and then close again with a rattle. Upstairs, her bedroom door slammed and a blast of bass came through the floor from her speakers. "Looks like big sister is annoyed at Mommy again," I told Daniel, plucking my phone from my back pocket when it rang.

"He's here," Mike said down the line. "And what happened at school today—with the girls?"

"I don't know. Why?"

"Mia came home with that worried expression—"

"The one she has when my daughter is up to something and she's promised not to tell her parents?" I said, folding my arm in, eyes narrowing with fury in the direction of Aubrey's room.

"That's the one."

Exhaling, I moved over to the high chair to pick up the sandwich Danny threw on the floor. "How's Jase?"

"Tired."

"That's to be expected, I guess." Although, vampires didn't

tire from travel, so we both knew it was the other kind of tired; the kind that affected the soul when the weight of too much grief bore down on it for too long.

"I think he needs to see you."

"That's the last thing he needs, Mike," I demanded, lifting Daniel from his chair.

"He loves you, Ara. You're the only thing that can bring light back to his soul right now—"

"No, his fiancé can do that—"

"His fiancé can barely look him in the eye—since it was his ex-wife that killed their child," he said firmly. "I know it's not right. I know he needs to build his relationship with her so he can forget about you, but he also needs to survive this, and… right now… I'm not sure he will."

"What makes you say that?"

"When David was human, when he was depressed and suicidal, he had this look in his eye." I knew the look. "I saw it on Jason's face. He lost two kids, Ar—"

"I know."

"You're his soul mate, like it or not. He needs you."

"Jules is his soul mate too. Morgana saw it."

"And even if she is one of his soul mates, that has no bearing on what you mean to him, and you know it. You're being selfish by distancing yourself."

But Mike could just never understand why it was more important that I kept my distance right now.

"Is Em coming by your house today—"

"Em can't fix him either, Ara. And she doesn't care. You know she doesn't subscribe to the family drama since she moved out—"

"What about Aubrey? They've always been so close—"

"A kid can't fix this either. He needs you."

“Okay, but…” I sighed, watching Daniel as he toddled into the toy room behind the kitchen. “No one’s here to look after Danny, and I can’t bring him with me. Jase doesn’t even know I had another child.”

“True. Guess it’s not a good idea for either of them to see a baby right now.”

Especially not since that baby was Jason’s.

Mike groaned. “I’ll come by and—”

“I can watch him,” Aubrey offered, appearing in the doorway.

“Hang on, Mike,” I said, nodding at her, shocked that she’d even surfaced from her room let alone offered to look after her brother. “Aubrey will watch him.”

“Okay, and ask her what happened at school.”

“I will. After.”

Desperate for some relief from the exhaustion of the twenty-four-seven demands of motherhood, I smiled as I handed Danny’s snack to Aubrey. But when I heard a solid rap on my front door, a rolling pulse of dread washed over me with an energy signal I hadn’t felt since New York.

“Mike?” I said, my voice panicky. “You better get over here.”

“Why?”

“Jase is at my door.”

Jules looked gray. She’d lost a lot of weight in the last three weeks, lost that healthy round figure she had when I was in New York with her, leaving behind sallow cheeks and thin hair hanging over hollow eyes. She hugged herself inside a long gray cardigan, in the middle of summer, standing just slightly behind Jason as he opened himself with a huge smile.

I stepped outside and hugged him, ending it before I wanted to, then gently reached out to touch Jules.

"Hey."

"Hi," she said, trying hard to be her best-self right now.

Mike casually trotted across the road and up the driveway then, his eyes round with concern, but he played it off well and omitted a friendly greeting.

"Hey, guys, thought you were resting," he said cheerfully.

"Jase needed to see Ara," Jules advised.

We all looked at him.

"Not for any reason," she added, tightening the hold of her cardigan. "He just needed to see her."

We all knew what she meant—that she was saying the same thing Mike had said moments ago. I knew she was aware of the eternal connection Jase and I shared but I never imagined she'd openly seek it out for him if he was suffering. She was good like that, but she wasn't okay with it, anyone could see that. Yet, Jules was just so beaten down by the world that one more knife in the wound couldn't possibly hurt her anymore. She sensed that he needed me, and she marched him over here to take his medicine and to sit by and watch as it cut her deeper.

"Come inside," I offered, hoping Aubrey had managed to get Daniel out in time. But my eyes closed in defeat when I heard the subtle tones of her negotiating with a headstrong toddler, and Jase heard it too.

"Who had a baby?" he asked, pushing past me.

I followed him in to the kitchen, and Mike shut the door, coming in behind Jules. I could only hope right now that he wouldn't ask; that he wouldn't put two and two together—the child's age and the act we committed almost three years ago—because I would not lie to him. It was one thing for him to assume it was David's baby—for now—but another to lie to him.

Jason bent at the knee and came down in front of our son, his head whipping up at the hammering of my heart in my chest. It was all he needed, and I wished so badly that I could have controlled my heart in that moment, as he laid eyes upon the baby for the first time.

"His name is Daniel," I offered, moving over.

Jase covered his mouth, closing his eyes slowly. As he recalled the moments we shared following the vision that started all of this, his words slipped past his lips when they would have been better shared between thought. "After the baby in the vision."

I nodded.

"What vision?" Jules asked, stepping in defensively.

Jason couldn't answer her. I knew the state he'd slipped into after seeing his child for the first time. He wasn't aware of anyone else in the room right now.

Two marble-like green eyes gawked up at him, seeing what he thought was his daddy's face there but with several years atop it, confusing the young mind. And even though Jase and David were twins, and Daniel had always looked like David's son, there was something undeniable in the tilt of both of their heads, the expression in their gentle eyes, that screamed the truth between them like a sudden burst of familial connection.

Jase reached out and placed his hands under Daniel's arms, drawing him to his chest. And Daniel didn't fight or protest. He watched on with interest, reaching up to touch the unfamiliar stubble on Jason's jaw, because David rarely ever walked around without a clean-shaven face.

And Jules knew. The moment Jason set his brow to the baby's, and cried, she knew. Mike chased after her when she turned and darted out the front door, but she was gone, with vampire speed, before any of us could stop her.

"What the fuck, Ara?" Mike said.

"It's a long story," I advised.

"That's *Jason's* baby? Are you fucking kidding me?"

I shook my head, looking back at Jase.

"Why didn't you tell me?" Jase asked, his voice barely a whisper. He gave Daniel one more soft squeeze, inhaling him as though it was the first breath he'd taken, and put the angel down on the rug, handing him a toy hammer.

"I wanted to. But when I came to you that day—outside the university—I saw what was in your heart, Jase," I explained softly, apologetically. "I saw Jules there and I couldn't do it. I had to let you go—to at least have a chance to be happy."

He stood up, wiping a hand down his face, but he couldn't take his eyes off the little boy at his feet. "He's beautiful. He's so… *so* beautiful."

"I know." I swept in and put my arm around Jase's waist, resting my head to his shoulder.

"Were you ever going to tell me?"

"Yes. But it wasn't the right time."

Jason nodded, understanding every single angle to every thought I'd had in coming to that decision. He turned to me then, placing his hands on my upper arms and fixing my gaze. I was vaguely aware of Aubrey standing in the corner, having just heard this for the first time, and I wanted to explain. But she didn't seem upset, or even surprised, now that I thought of it. Not like Mike, whose energy could be cut by a knife, made worse by me ignoring him right now.

You know what this means to me, Jase said in thought, keeping it just between us.

I do.

I've dreamed of being a father ever since Rochelle died, taking our baby with her. And… when the truth came out that Lily's children weren't mine, then… now… with Jules…

I know. I touched his hand.

But for this, Ara… for you and me to have… you know what this means to me…

I slipped back into the vision then, replaying the moment he found out we were pregnant in that other life:

"We're in this together, Jase. All the way," I'd said to him then. *"We didn't plan this. But we both want it. So stop being scared that everything you love is going to fall apart around you, and just get used to being happy."*

"How does one get used to being happy, exactly?" he challenged.

"One day at a time." I stepped closer. "Every time you feel yourself expecting the worst, you move your mind onto something else and be thankful for it all for a moment. That's how. And it takes time. But it has to be okay, Jase, because you're going to be happy now for a very, very long time, and if you fight it, you'll be the only one destroying anything."

Jase let my words sink in before he closed his eyes, reaching one hand out to pull me closer. He pressed me into him and kissed my head. "I never told anyone this, Ara, but I always wanted to be a father. Ever since my own father failed me terribly. I just wanted a chance to prove to that abused, neglected little boy that not all fathers are like that."

"Well"—I took his hand and placed it on my belly—"now you're gonna get your chance."

"And it's only taken a hundred-and-fifty years."

I smiled. "Better late than never."

I know, I said in thought, smiling at him as I slipped out of the memory and came back to the present, where that life was only a dream.

What did my brother say?

What could he say? It wasn't our fault.

But he didn't know about the potion then. He would have thought you did it of your own volition.

He never thought that. He knows me better than that.

Jase nodded. It was all he needed to do to convey his full understanding. *I hope Jules will have the same compassion for me.*

She will, I promised, certain of it.

She doesn't know, he said. *I never told her the reason I left my life behind—not the real reason. I told her about Lily and the abuse. But I didn't tell her about you. About us. In fact, I lied about us.*

I nodded. *She'll understand. And if she doesn't, then you have to let her go, Jase. If she comes back—*

I know. Then she's truly mine. He rolled his eyes, looking so human and young with the gesture, but also just so agitated and fed up with the world. *But haven't Jules and I been down that road? Haven't we tested our love—*

It never stops being tested. You know that. Look and David and me.

Jason sighed, glancing over his shoulder at Aubrey. His eyes narrowed and came back to me then. *Looks like our little Aubrey knew, even though you kept it from her.*

How?

She's using ghosts to spy on people.

The shock opened my eyes and filled me with blind fury. And Jase just laughed, leaning in to kiss my brow.

"I have to find Jules. I'll check back in with you later."

"Wait." I grabbed his sleeve. *There's something else.*

He stepped back beside me.

When Lily drugged us, she drugged David too.

I saw it cross his expression, darken his eyes. He understood then: it was David she wanted all along, from their earliest days together, before I woke from the dead. And if she hadn't wanted David, she would never have drugged him, which means she wouldn't have drugged Jason and I to avoid looking suspicious. *I'm so sorry, Ara.*

I tried to smile to say it was okay. But it wasn't, and only Jason, of all the people in this entire world, truly understood that.

I wish I could stay—spend time with you, and my son. He grinned hugely, all the light and joy of that little boy igniting his soul. *But...*

I know. Go find Jules. We'll talk later. I reached up to touch his face, holding him there for a moment before we parted. He squatted down then and brushed his long, beautiful fingers through Daniel's soft brown hair, igniting a fatherly connection between them with no more effort than a sweeping smile.

"How can I love him already, when I don't even know him?"

"Same way you loved each of your children when they were born, and all your nieces and your nephew."

"I guess." Jase pressed his lips into a line of consideration, his eyes carrying decades of love and fatherly affection as he glanced back at Aubrey, and she returned his smile. Then he stood up and walked away, leaving me in the aftermath of a suddenly altered life.

NIGHT FELL, AND JASE STILL HADN'T FOUND JULES. SO HE called me. I didn't want to be the first one to find her, but when I followed her energy signature to a rocky outlet by the lake, I knew instantly that I couldn't call Jase. He was the last person she needed to see right now. Elora would have been a better option, given that they were friends, but action needed to be taken now. This girl was in true pain.

She sensed me as I approached but didn't look up. Her entire body was shaking, hands closed tightly around her stomach as she leaned into her grief, kneeling there on the rocks. I came down beside her and carefully moved her hair back to reveal her face.

"I've lost him now, haven't I?" she cried, barely able to breathe.

"Is that what you want?"

"No," she whispered, fat tears dripping from her chin. "I need him, Ara. I just don't know how… to…"

"Compete with me?" I suggested.

She looked up at me, her brown eyes red and puffy. "You have his baby. Something I couldn't even give him—"

"Hey, don't be unfair to yourself, Jules," I demanded, closing my hands around her cheeks and turning her eyes to me. "You did not lose that baby. It was taken from you when his ex-wife killed you."

"But it doesn't matter, because it's gone. It doesn't matter who was at fault. I'll have this hole in me now for the rest of forever and I…" She looked away, sinking down on her knees. "I don't know if I can live with it. I don't know if I can live in your shadow."

"You don't live in my shadow," I explained. "Jase and I have a connection that will never go away, but it's not like we hold onto it, welcome it. Both of us would rather it vanished and that we never had to feel like this again. It's agony."

"Then why not just give in to it? Why not just be together?"

"Because I may love Jase, feel connected to him, but I love David too. I chose him. And when you're immortal, you can't just go around following your heart everywhere it wants to take you—"

"But that's just it," she said, her lashes pushing the tears out. "You want him, and he wants you."

"It's not like that." I sighed, sitting down on my butt with my legs crossed. "Look, immortal relationships go through *so* many stages over the centuries. When a person promises forever —promises to love no matter what comes between you—it's a promise that's made because *everything* will. You can be as solid a couple as you want, and you can love each other more than air itself, but you *will* come to a time when that's not enough; when the heart wants something else for a while; when the promise of eternity is all that holds those threads together," I explained. "That's it: just a promise and nothing more."

"Then why? Why hold on if there's nothing but a promise between you?"

"Because, otherwise, you'll end up alone. All relationships are the same thing on repeat. You can find somebody new, but the same issues will always arise eventually. Forever. It has to be a commitment—"

"Even if you're not happy?"

"No one is ever happy all the time. That's an impossible expectation to place on a relationship. It's a pipe dream."

"But you should be happy some of the time, at least."

"Yes, but who's not happy?"

"Jason's not—"

"You think he's not happy with you?" I scoffed. "Because I've never seen him happy like this, Jules—"

"It's different now. I'm not the same person I was before—"

"And you won't be for a really long time, or maybe ever again. But… when you live for hundreds of years, you change a lot in that time. If he can't love you changed by what life throws at you, then he doesn't deserve to love you at all, and you'd be better off without him."

She turned her head and allowed a soft smile. "I know you just want him to be happy, but just be straight with me, 'kay?"

"Okay."

"Do you love him like you love David?"

"Yes."

"Does he love you that way?"

"I think so."

"Do you wish that I'd just go away, that David would just vanish, and that you could be with him?"

I had to really think about that before I answered because, the truth was, I did sometimes think of a world where Jase and I were together. But if that world also had David in it, then… no. I wouldn't want that. The vision my father showed me opened my eyes to the truth I was denying in my heart for the last forty years. In some other life, Jase and I would be together, and I could blow the world away until there was nothing left but us two. But…

"I made a choice, Jules. I chose David. And I will always choose David. Nothing has ever brought that in to question—"

"See, you say nothing, but you fucked Jason. Three years ago. That's a pretty huge fucking question if you ask me."

I laughed softly to myself. This girl did still have that fight in her that I loved. Looking off at the horizon, I prepared myself for an explanation. "Jase and I were drugged."

"Drugged?"

"We didn't know Lily was working against us then, so we didn't know she'd laced our drinks with just a few drops of this noxious potion—same one that saw my daughter sleep with a man she'd always considered her uncle," I explained.

"Elora?"

"Yes. And it crushed them both, like it did to Jason and I. Lily only needed a few drops, tasteless drops, and it was enough to tap into the already burning tension between us and... Daniel happened."

Jules nodded, sitting down on her butt as well, her eyes out to sea. "So... without that—"

"It just would never have happened, Jules. You know that. Everyone knows that."

"Wouldn't it?"

"I wouldn't do that to David."

"But Jase would," she demanded. "He did it to Lily—with me. And he would have run away with you if he could—"

"Yes, before he met you. And what you have to understand, coming in to this family, is that the burden of our connection will always be there. You either love him as who he is, connection and all, or you get up and leave his life now. You and I had a conversation just like this, a few months ago, Jules. We've been through this—"

"But I didn't have all the facts then."

"You have them now." I stood up. "I love Jase. I always will, and I'm sorry for that. But both he and I need to make a life away from each other. He will never stop loving me, Jules, but he will never commit to me, just as I'll never commit to him. And that is what matters. You can never own all of someone's heart. Not ever. No matter who you, or who they are. And you'll only get hurt if you try."

"You own all of David's," she challenged.

I smiled to myself, nodding, because I'd never admitted this to anyone before. "That's not entirely true."

"What do you mean?"

"He loved Lily—before all of this nonsense. And he often

had thoughts about a life with her. He just refused to admit that to himself."

"How do you know?"

"A woman knows," I said with a nod, because she understood that, whether she wanted to admit it or not. "You're not alone in this, Jules. We all suffer for this stupid magical bond, but you don't have to suffer alone."

"I'll keep it in mind," she said dismissively, casting her eyes back out to sea.

AUBREY

"Hey, Harry. What's up?" I asked, walking faster to get out of the spring rain.

"Um… so… Ghost Girl, she's refusing to become a vampire."

"Why?" I screeched, ducking under a tree as I skipped off the sidewalk and into Uncle Mike's café, feeling the call of the beach across the road, willing me to its shores, but ignoring it for the sake of responsibility.

"She says she has a strong aversion to vampires. I dunno. Maybe one killed her. But, weird thing: she woke up this morning with a French accent."

"For real?"

"Yeah. So, I'm googling around a bit, looking at the era she was alive, to see if I can find out anything about her death—"

"Why are you going to so much trouble for this, Harry? You hate being involved in my schemes."

There was a pause. "What can I say?" he chimed in a playful tone. "I'm a sucker for blondes."

"Yeah, well, she's still human, you just remember that. Because if you suck her neck, I will kill you myself. Then I'll tell Mom about your compost heap."

"Relax. I'm not gonna kill her."

"See that you don't." I hung up, stuffing my phone in my black jeans so I could tie my apron around my waist.

"Hurry up, kiddo." Eric winked at me, passing like a rushing car, two trays in hand. "You're ten minutes late."

"On it." Patting the sprays of rain from my hair, I glanced longingly at the rolling blue ocean again. I just wanted to be out there, even in the rain, as if maybe it could ease all the tingling and the tightness in my blood today. But, lame as it is, responsibility called.

"Hey Aubrey," Mia chimed, gliding out of the kitchen with a tray of drinks. "Uncanny rain, huh?"

"My mom's sad," I explained. "I kinda figured this might happen once Uncle Jase arrived."

"Does he know about Danny yet?"

"Yeah." I bit my lip, leaning against one of the overstuffed bookshelves, where an old man sat in the leather armchair with a pair of headphones keeping him out of this conversation. "Jules was with him when he found out."

"So that's why my dad was in a funny mood last night."

I nodded, walking over to the stage between the high windows and the wall that backed on to the bathroom, and fixed up the "Open Mic Thursdays" sign where it slipped down from the urban-style brick wall. "Aunt Jules ran off. My mom found her though, but I don't know if she plans to stay."

"She's gonna go home?"

"She doesn't have a home to go to, really. She gave up her apartment and her career in The Big Apple. She's got nothing now."

Mia leaned on the bar, moving aside to let Eric out with a tray of drinks. "Poor Jules."

"Poor Jason." I hopped down off the stage, the sign fixed in place, and dusted my hands off. "My parents act like they have it all together, but their entire life is a hot mess, and it's dragging everyone else down too."

"At least they're not divorced, like my parents."

"Sometimes I think it'd be better that way," I noted.

"Why?"

"Mia, my mom…" I stuffed my hands under my apron and into my pockets, drawing on the rich smell of coffee behind me and the ocean across the road to ground me so I wouldn't show emotion. "I love my mom. You know I do."

She nodded.

"But I think she's stupid. This whole… *choice* thing. My dad… he…"

"He what?"

I couldn't tell her. Mom and Dad had this perfect relationship—in everyone else's eyes. No one else saw the things I saw, or they didn't think anything of it. I loved my dad, but if anyone treated me the way he treats my mom—controlled me, manipulated me, but equally loved me—I don't think I'd be with them. Not by choice. At least, I hoped I wouldn't.

"Mia!" Elora called across from the bar. "Back to work. And Aubrey, stop gossiping and get started."

Mia pouted, turning away then to deliver the drinks.

Beside her, the same hairy-faced, dark-eyed ghost that tried to haunt me the other day appeared, like wavering fog. I rolled my eyes, pushing past the crowds in line to clear a random table.

"Go away."

"Make me," he teased.

"You don't scare me, prick. And after that stunt you pulled, there's no way I'm helping you now," I whispered, hiding my moving lips in my shoulder.

"Then I guess I'll have to resort to Plan B."

"Go ahead." I flipped him off as I backed into the kitchen, knowing no one around would ask who I was talking to. "It won't change anything."

"We'll see," he said, fading away.

I dumped the plates I was carrying on the counter behind Uncle Mike, and he turned to smile and point out two orders that were up.

"On it." I reached across for the plates and ticket, checking which item was for which table, just as Uncle Mike roared in agony. The sudden restart of my heart made the plates jump onto the floor, and I looked over as he pushed back from the stove, hands covering his face. "What happened?"

Three other people came in as I rushed to him, watching in horror as his skin bubbled and bled across his face.

"Pot exploded," he yelled, ducking away from human eyes before his skin could heal. We all looked over at the bubbling pot, its clear steaming liquid splashed up the walls and all over the floor.

"I'll get him to the hospital," I said, moving to follow Uncle Mike into the staff room, but Elora pushed past with a towel in hand.

"I got this, baby sis, you take care of things round here."

Her husband Eric touched my shoulder, giving an encouraging nod as Elora led Mike through the kitchen, towel over face, and out through the side door by the bar.

"Come on, Aubs. We got people waiting."

"Do you think he'll be okay?" I asked. I knew he was Lilithian, could heal fast, but that looked bad.

"He'll be fine." He patted my arm and then squatted down to start cleaning up the food I'd dropped.

Something caught my eye then. I looked over to see the malevolent ghost I'd just flipped off sitting by the stove, a cruel look in his eye. I narrowed mine at him to ask if this was his handiwork, so he shrugged, winking at me.

Inside my mouth, my teeth crunched, and my jaw set so tight it popped. But beneath the anger was a hollowing pit of fear. Mom always said ghosts couldn't hurt people. What was so different about this one that he could?

As he faded away, he lifted his wrist to tap an imaginary watch, shaking his hand out and putting it to his ear as if the watch had died. And suddenly, my determination to leave him in the spirit world started to wane. I'd need to come up with a plan, fast.

HARRY STOOD ON HIS PORCH WHILE I IMPATIENTLY WAITED for the car to pull over and turn off. I watched his hand go to his mouth, a flicker of light flaring there a moment later in the dark. He was smoking again. Another useful bit of info I could use against him. I mean, it's not like smoking could kill him, but Mom thought it made him look cheap. Even though Uncle Jase smoked for years and she never said anything. I always got the sense that she found it oddly sexy, and yet she wouldn't let Harry smoke. But, hey, her double standards worked in my favor.

As I climbed the stairs, untying my black apron, Harry stamped out the butt. "I heard about Uncle Mike. 'S he okay?"

"He's fine. But he can't be seen in public now for a few weeks, until the burns heal," I said, with air quotes.

"Sucks." He picked up the butt and tossed it into a trashcan down on the ground below his porch. "What brings you here so late—and without pizza?"

"I need to talk to you. About Uncle Mike's accident."

Harry stepped back and offered the way inside, following. But I stopped dead when a woman looked up at me from a book, all snuggled down in Harry's cozy green armchair. His favorite, do-not-sit-in-unless-you-want-me-to-fart-on-you chair.

"What the hell is she still doing here? And"—I stormed over to her, sniffing the air—"is she still human?"

"Okay, first of all"—Harry grabbed my arm and drew me out of her territorial bubble—"you're not a vampire yet, so you can't just sniff the air and expect to know what species a person is. And second—"

"I don't care about second. We had an agreement, Harry! She could get me into trouble."

"You could get *yourself* into trouble," he said casually, always that easy, carefree mannerism, like nothing fazed him. He sat down on the sofa and picked up his guitar. "You're the one bringing people back from the dead. It's not Rochelle's fault—"

"Rochelle?" I gawked at her. "So it has a name now! You're naming it." I sat down on the sofa beside him. "Once you name it, you get attached to it."

Harry just laughed, smiling over at it. "Told ya."

It smiled to itself, looking back down at the book.

"Told ya what?" I demanded, suddenly feeling like the outsider in my own brother's life.

"You're a firecracker—so much like Mom. I knew you'd go off your chops when you found out."

"Found. Out. What?" I said each word through caged teeth.

"Rochelle's not going anywhere." He put his feet up on the table. "She wants to stay human. I'll arrange her some new ID—through a mate of mine in the US—so you don't have to worry about people finding out she's come back from the dead."

I sunk back, exhaling to release some of the fury. "Are you sleeping with it?"

Harry just grinned, and I rolled my eyes, while the it blushed.

It was hard to stay mad at Harry, though; he had that same thing my dad and Uncle Jase had. It was this smile they'd give you when they'd been a shithead; it was like they knew it, but they also knew their shenanigans were somewhat endearing and, before you'd even let it go, they knew you would.

"So, what's this problem you came to see me for?" Harry asked, walking in to the kitchen. "Anyone want a Coke?"

"Yes please," It said, her thick French accent suddenly apparent.

"Yes," I called. "And why does she suddenly have an accent? She sounded Australian when she was a ghost."

Harry placed a Coke in Its hand and threw one at me, sitting down heavily beside me again, as though he had no respect for the springs in this sofa. "Far as I can discern, since we know nothing about the place they come from between worlds, and we know nothing about your powers, is that, since only you can hear them, they must be speaking telepathically to you. When thoughts come through"—he tapped his head, because he was the expert on this, since he was a super-clever telekinetic mind-reader—"voices from the mind don't come through with an accent. So, you're not actually hearing them talk—at all. It's why no one else can hear them. They're speaking to your mind."

"Oh." I opened my can and took a sip. "But she wasn't speaking like that when she was pulled out."

"I dunno." Harry shrugged. "It might just be that they *take on* an accent—like they remember words, sentences, and how to talk and walk—but the accent doesn't come back unless they remember who they were."

Which made sense. An accent was learned. If they had no memory of their old life, how could they remember learning an accent? I looked at Rochelle. "So you remember now?"

"I remember pieces. I remember the war—"

"Which war?"

"World War Two," Harry said, completely impressed, and I could tell immediately that they'd talked at length about history; one of Harry's favorite topics.

"But I don't remember much after, so I can only surmise that I must have died in the war," Rochelle offered.

I shrugged, bringing my legs up under me on the sofa. "So, I need your help," I told Harry. "There's this ghost who saw what I can do, and he's been threatening me."

"How so?" Harry slid forward, putting his can on the coffee table.

"Uncle Mike's face… the burns, the ghost did that. Made a pot explode."

"What?" I watched as several realizations turned to concern in Harry's blue eyes. "But ghosts can't hurt you. Mom says—"

"Mom's wrong. This one can."

"But how?" He came a little further out to the edge of his seat, completely invested.

"I don't know. I mean, we don't really even know much about the spirit world. Everything we know has been passed on from Mom. I know that she calls The Fog 'Purgatory', but I don't think it is—"

"It's not," Harry said. "It's more like fog of *a* purgatory but it's not the only one. Well, not for mortal souls—"

"Mortal souls?" Rochelle said, putting her book down and sitting up straight.

"Mortal souls are those in humans," Harry explained. "They die, and they usually cross over, which is another way of saying they walk through the Rivers of Life to a new existence."

"Reincarnation?" Rochelle asked.

"Yes."

"But what about God?"

"My mom's been to The Other Side many times," I snapped. "She never met God."

"But she never said there is no God, my iconoclastic little sister," Harry said kindly. "Lilith, the First Woman, directly said there *is* a God, so don't spit on Rochelle's faith just because you're jaded, Aubs."

"Argh, Fine." I sat back, folding my arms.

"Anyway," he went on to explain, "when a person becomes immortal, their souls become… kind of… marked. Changed. And we refer to them as 'immortal souls' even though, technically, all souls are immortal. It's just that these souls don't cross over naturally. They become bound to the mortal plane when they're changed. So, when their bodies die, they go to this halfway world, the fog between, you might say, because they're no longer natural and so Nature doesn't really know how to sort them, categorize them."

"That's where our mother comes in," I added.

"She has to walk the fog every few years and help them find the light, which just means walking them to the river, because they can't find it alone."

"What about Heaven?" Rochelle asked.

"Mom says there's this place there on the Other Side—a silver city. She's been there a few times. She thinks that's what people mean when they talk of Heaven," Harry offered. "Mortal souls, or those that are free of the fog, they can decide not to cross over—to go to the city instead and remain there. Forever, if they like."

Rochelle smiled, but then her expression changed. "Why did I end up wandering the earth for so long then?"

"That's the mystery." Harry shrugged, both hands out, and he looked just like the little kid I'd seen growing up in family movies. "I mean, it's no mystery how ghosts end up wandering but we don't know how you get to where you were—where my eldest sister can no longer see you, only sense you."

"Sense me?"

"Elora can see them on the earthy plane, and she helps them cross over—"

"She's like your mother?"

"No. She can't walk on the Other Side. She basically just opens the doorway to the Other Side."

"She's a gatekeeper," I offered. "There aren't many gateways to the Spirit Realm, but she can create them—"

"Yeah, we once thought she was sending the ghosts to Heaven or maybe to another life, because she gets a great feeling of peace when she helps one, but she's actually just opening the door or, I guess, lifting the veil to the Other Side," Harry added. "And there, if they're mortal or 'natural souls', they can either cross over or go to the silver city."

"And if they're not?" Rochelle asked, deeply invested in this.

"The Fog usually consumes them."

Rochelle nodded. "Why do souls stay on the earthly plane?"

"If they don't cross over soon after death, they get stuck," I told her. "It's like they forget what they are, who they are, and why they're here."

"Oh." Her eyes darkened, searching inside for some spark within a memory.

"Harry can see them here too, like my mom and Elora. It's

an inherited gift—passed along in our genes," I added, and she looked up at me. "But I don't see them. I only see the ones that get *stuck*, I guess." I placed both palms together and then separated them to create a small pocket of air between my hands. "It's like the crawlspace between the walls. I don't know how they get there, but there's some reason, maybe it's like they're halfway between dead and alive, and I can reach them—pull them out."

"My theory is violent deaths," Harry added.

"Why?" I asked.

"Because I spoke with every ghost you brought me to turn. Only one hasn't remembered her death"—he nodded at Rochelle—"and the others are all violent deaths, or they experienced violence leading up to their death, like Uncle Arthur."

"Arthur?" Rochelle sat forward on her chair. "I knew an Arthur."

"That's good." Harry turned his body to face her. "Can you remember anything else—maybe try to remember his face?"

"No." She shook her head. "I don't know. I think I'm imprinting your face onto these memories, because I keep seeing you. Only… you were older. Darker"—she pointed to her hair—"And your eyes were green."

Harry and I exchanged glances. Was it possible Rochelle was a victim of Arthur's, or maybe my dad's, or even Jason's? Harry was the image of Dad, but with electric blue eyes. And Arthur's were blue also. So it wasn't like she meant him. But placing green eyes on Harry's face, that was something. That could mean she knew my dad.

Harry turned to me. *If she was a victim of Dad's, we can't tell her,* he said in thought, sending it to me, since I didn't have the ability to read it.

Why?

Because I like her, Aubs. I like her a lot. There's literally no other girl on the planet like her. She's from a different time. She's not a vampire who was born and then changed over the years. She just stepped right out of that time. I'll never find another girl like her, and she actually likes me back! I don't want her to hate me if it was my dad that killed her.

I sighed, looking around his farmhouse, thinking about how far out he lived from everyone else. Everyone assumed it was purely because he had a preference for the taste of fear and trauma in the blood, liked to make them scream and beg for mercy, but I knew my big brother better than they did. I knew he liked to get away because he hated the sound of the world at night when he'd close his eyes; when his guard was down and he couldn't control the thoughts he'd hear: nightmares, worries, sexual thoughts from people he loves and knows well. It was too much for him. And I think, because of that, he felt somewhat isolated.

"Fine," I breathed. "So, what are we doing about this malevolent spirit?"

"Well, first we need to figure out how it's able to bring harm."

"Think about it: if it's halfway between the living and the dead, then the veil is thinner," I mused. "It wouldn't be that hard to learn how to reach out."

"But then why can't he pull himself out?"

"It doesn't work that way." I folded my arms, bopping my head a little with offense. "The veil isn't something they can walk away from. It takes power. *My* power. And he tried to just grab me and pull himself out, but that didn't work either. I have to draw him out with the intention of bringing him to life."

"Right, so he can't come until you say he can?"

"Something like that."

"Good." He leaned back, hands behind his head, looking so

much like Uncle Jase as he did. "Then tell him he wins. Tell him you'll bring him back, turn him into a vampire, and send him on his way. And when you bring him here, I'll kill him. He'll hopefully cross over—"

"Or end up back in the thin veil," I pointed out.

"Maybe. But probably not for a while."

I sighed, exhausted and heavy. Taking on extra work tonight and staying until close really took it out of me.

"You okay, sis?" Harry asked, tugging my hair affectionately. "You look tired."

"I am." I stood up. "I should go home."

"Say hi to Mom and Dad for me."

"Can't," I said, walking away. "They'll ask why I came to visit you, and if I try to lie, Mom's magic energy-sensor will see it."

Harry laughed.

"Energy sensor?" Rochelle asked.

"Our mother can read energies. She can even find a person by following their signature," Harry informed.

"And she can pulse people," I added. "Like she sends a signal to them if she needs them. It's very annoying."

"Yerp, especially when you come running because you think something's up, and all she wants is for you to do the dishes." Harry laughed.

"She sounds wonderful," Rochelle hummed dreamily.

"She is," I muttered. So wonderful her own daughter wanted to grow up to be *anything but* her. "Bye, Harry."

"Bye, sis."

Since Mia was born in November the year before me,

and my cousin Evie was born a month after me, we were all the same age at one point in the year. If only for a few months. But since the cut-off age for a new school year in Australia was June—and our school year ran from January to December instead of August to September, like America—Mia was a grade above Evie and me, and she'd graduate this year. It sucked. I loved Evie, but Mia was my best friend. Forever. I spent most of my life across the road at her house ever since I was born, so Uncle Mike—her dad—was like a second father to me. Well, third, really, because, if anything, Uncle Jase was more like my second dad. But Uncle Mike was around a lot more than my own father, since he worked all the time, which meant I was closer with Mia and her dad than I was with my own family. Which made me wish I'd been born just a few months earlier so we could have been in the same grade.

I left class beside Evie but intended to break away and sit with Mia at lunch. It was just easier. Evie had that same gorgeous blonde hair my sister Elora had, all long and wavy, intense green eyes—signs of the immortal blood running through her veins—and legs all the way to the sky. She was well-liked, fit in easy, but her conversations were somewhat hollow, and it was often exhausting fitting in with her group.

"Hey, Aubs," Evie whispered, leaning in. "I need blood. Can you oblige?"

"Mom says I'm not allowed to."

"I know. But I'm just getting tired of eating Dad's leftovers. I don't like them once they're running thin."

"Well, unlike you, my dad was human when mom conceived me, so I'm not immortal yet, Evie. If you get carried away again..."

"I won't. I promise." She extended her hand and offered me her pinkie.

"Argh, fine." I huffed, linking mine over hers. "Let me just text Mia and tell her I'll be late."

"Aren't you sitting with us today?"

We started walking toward the bathrooms. "I'm just tired, Evie," I explained. "It uses a lot of energy sitting with those girls, pretending to be nice, when all I wanna do is tell them they're all shallow bitches with no aspirations."

Evie laughed, pushing the bathroom door open. "You're snappier than usual. Are you sure you're not starting to change?"

I walked over to the basin and looked in the mirror. My eyes were dark and my cheeks sallow. I did look a bit like my mom did when she was blood-starved. But I hadn't begun the change yet. Evie was a different species to any Vampire or Lilithian in existence. Born of Elora's mixed immortal blood, and the blood of her vampire father Eric, she'd needed to drink human blood since she was born. Unlike me, her change needed no trigger. But I had never even touched a drop of blood, and yet my body was acting as though I was blood-starved: the exhaustion, moodiness, losing weight.

"It's okay." I smiled encouragingly. "People will just think I'm anorexic."

"That's not a good thing, Aubs." Evie leaned on the basin beside me. "I can't drink from you when you're like this. It'll make you weak."

"Yeah, you're probably right. What me to get Mia?"

"No. God, no." She moved away from the basin. "She'll rat me out, like she always does. And I hope you haven't told her about bringing those ghosts back, because she *will* tell her dad, and you know Uncle Mike…"

"He tells Mom everything." I rolled my eyes, because he and mom were so lame. But, then, Mia and I would be the same. What I didn't tell Evie is that I did bring Mia into our circle of secrets. And she hadn't told Uncle Mike. But she also didn't want anyone to know she knew, plausible deniability and all. I was happy to oblige.

"So, where will you get blood then?" I asked.

"I don't know. Maybe we should tell Tom what I am—what you are. Then we can use him as our blood bag."

"You can," I scoffed. "He's human. He can never feed me. And I would never drink from him, even if he was a vampire."

"Why not? He's kinda cute."

"In a dorky-John-Mayer kind of way. No thanks. Give me Sawyer any day!"

"Why not ask him out then—to the dance next week?"

"Why?"

"Because you like him," she scoffed, widening her eyes. "Duh."

"Are you kidding? I'm not telling him that. I wouldn't give him the satisfaction."

"Of what?"

"Of knowing I like him. He's cute, but he's scum."

"Scum? How so?"

"He's an asshat. He thinks he's all that—"

"Remind you of anyone?" she said smugly, raising a brow at me.

"Knowing I think he's hot will only fuel it," I said, as if she hadn't just insulted me.

"Why?"

"Because I've been mean to him since kindergarten. He'll think it was because I've always liked him—deep down inside, or some bull shit like that."

"He might not." Evie shrugged. "You're mean to everyone."

"Yeah, well, I don't want him thinking he's anything special."

"But he is to you, since you like him."

"Not enough to want him in my life. And when you start having friendships or relationships with people, they get in your life, Evie," I professed, casting my eyes down to my phone so she wouldn't see the emotions behind them. "You know that."

"Are you scared he'll die? Because of the family we come from?"

"No," I lied. But it all went back to Gregory Tailor, my eighth-grade love. He'd come to my house to hang out one afternoon, and Mom didn't know we had a guest. She drank from my dad in the kitchen and Greg saw it. They had to erase his mind, and they told me I couldn't be friends with him after that. Humans brought complications to our lives, and I was better off sticking with family.

I sighed, skulking out of the bathroom, with Evie on my trail. "So, I'll see you at dance class this afternoon?" she called.

"No," I called back, pocketing my phone. "I'm too tired."

"But…" she said, calling louder when she realized I was still walking away. "You're never too tired for dance."

EVEN THOUGH I WAS PALE, SHAKY, AND SO EXHAUSTED I could sleep for a year, Mom made me go to dance. Practically kicked me out the door, affirming that I should put my iPad down earlier at night if I was tired. She was right. I had been staying up later than usual. But this exhaustion didn't feel like tiredness; it couldn't be slept away.

"Aubrey," the teacher called across the room. "Hold your shoulders back."

I rearranged my position and took a graceful leap across the floor, coming down into a hard slam.

"Light-footed please, girls," she said, aiming that at me. "We don't want to watch a clan of elephants racing around stage next month."

Groaning to myself, I joined the cue and went around for another leap, smiling at Evie as she landed like a butterfly and glided past me, her skinny arms fluttering. Why did some people have to be so effortlessly perfect?

As I stepped in to the middle of the floor and flexed my ankles to take a leap, the malevolent ghost appeared again, jerking toward me. I immediately faltered and hit the ground with one leg sliding out and taking me into a painful, unintentional split. A tight band of pressure circled my back shin and a mighty crack made all hands fly to mouths, some of the girls turning away. The sharp rod of deep pain became apparent in my knee then, so I rolled onto my back and brought my leg up to my chest, clutching it tightly.

"Shit!" I winced, feeling down to see if the bone had come through the flesh. It hadn't, but something was definitely broken because there was a searing jab radiating out from that one spot and pulsing agony throughout every other limb like an alien death ray.

"Aubrey, are you alright?" Miss Maree landed beside me, as graceful as a damn fairy, while I lay rolling from side to side, trying to breathe but too afraid to in case I ended up crying in front of the evil ghost.

He stood above me, black hair falling over his eerie aqua eyes.

"You didn't land wrong, if that's what you're thinking," he said in a voice that carried with a sleazy lilt. "You landed perfectly. I just..." He lifted his foot and stomped down hard on the ground. "Helped it along."

I squeezed my shin, caging my teeth to keep in the sobs.

"Ready to bring me back now?" he asked, reaching down for my hand.

"Go to hell," I muttered.

"Aubrey," Miss Maree gasped.

"Not you." I held my breath for a moment. "I meant him."

"Who is she talking to?" Miss Maree asked.

"She's delusional," Evie offered, helping me to sit up. The teacher grabbed her phone when one of the girls handed it to her, and I just wanted to die—to shrink away and hide from the shame, the drama. Everyone in the room had huddled around me, probably reveling in my suffering.

When my dad came through the door less than five minutes later, it was like all my pain just went away. He scooped me up in his arms and kissed my head.

"You okay, sweetheart?"

"No." I closed my arms around his neck and held on tight, knowing I was safe with him.

Six hours and a special boot thing on my leg later, I was finally laid in my cozy bed. Dad pulled the covers up to my chin and kissed my brow, and Mom swept my hair back, smiling into me like nothing bad had ever happened. And I almost felt guilty for not telling them about the ghost. Almost.

"Love you guys," I said.

"Love you too, baby girl," Mom said, closing my door. "Sleep tight."

I shut my eyes, opening them again in the darkness, just to make sure the ghost wasn't lingering in the corner, watching me.

When the school bell tolled, I picked up my crutches and threw my bag over my shoulders—both of them—

and got to my feet. If I were immortal already, a dose of blood could have fixed this. But my stupid parents wanted me to look older before they'd allow me to trigger the change. Which meant four weeks walking around on stupid crutches.

"What's the matter, Red?" Sawyer asked, breaking from his group of testosterone-in-jackets. "Kick someone too hard?"

"Shut up, or I'll break my other foot on your jaw."

He laughed, hanging back while his friends walked on. "Seriously though, what'd you do?"

"Snapped it in dance class."

"Dance class?"

"Yeah. I take dance. What's it to you?"

"What kind?" He walked at my pace for a moment, hands in his pockets, way too cute.

"Ballet and modern alternative," I grunted, trying to ignore the blistering ache of the impressions on my underarms from these stupid walking aids.

"Nice."

"It's fun. That's what counts."

"Do you perform? Like, could I come see you in a show sometime?"

I glared at him, but he seemed genuinely impressed, so I simmered down and kind of mellowed out a bit, melting slightly under those dimples. "If you're that bored, I guess."

He smiled, and the rest of the school yard blurred out of focus behind those igniting eyes. "Hey… are you going to the school dance next week?"

I rolled my eyes. "No."

"Why? Haven't got a date?"

"What's it to you?"

"Just curious." He looked at his phone, but I think he only did that as a distraction because he was scared of me. "I was just gonna say that if you didn't have one, I might be free. I could probably take you."

I stopped hobbling and gawked up at him, a hateful look burning a hole in his soul. "Did you just ask me to the dance?"

"At risk of dying young, yeah." He laughed, hands going into his pockets. "What d'ya think? Wanna come?"

Yes. Of course. Absolutely. "No. I have something on that night."

"Sweet. I'll pick you up at seven."

"I said no, dickhead," I called, but he just waved over his shoulder, and I figured then that I'd be going to this stupid dance after all.

I smiled to myself as I hobbled to class.

MIA CLEARED AWAY THE EMPTY MILKSHAKE GLASSES, AND I readjusted my leg on the seat across from me, the gray sky looming over the ocean at Evie's back. She busied herself painting my lone toenail sticking out from the giant boot I now had to wear, and I watched people riding and jogging past on the sidewalk across the street, wishing I was over there.

On my shoulders right now, I had too much weight, and because of who my parents were, I couldn't talk to anyone about it. I'd usually sit by the ocean, wait until no one was around, and then tell the waves. It was stupid, I knew that, but I somehow always felt better after I'd sent my problems out to sea.

Evie was family, so was Mia, and if we were normal human beings then I should have been able to talk to them about Mom and Dad, but there had always been this line—clear and defined by their royal titles—and no one crossed it. They were the bicentennial rulers of the entire immortal world, and our family business had to remain within the small circle of our immediate family. Non-negotiable. Out of respect. So, with my leg in a boot, and no hope of getting to the ocean alone for a chat, I had to bottle it all up and try to drink it down with an afternoon of strawberry milkshakes.

"So, how's the healing going?" Evie asked.

I looked down at my broken leg. Still broken. "Mom says I need another few sessions. She wants to heal it gradually because I'm human and still growing."

"But still faster than if she didn't use her freaky Cerulean Magic."

"Yeah. I'll have to wear the boot out in public for at least four weeks, she says. But I'll be healed in two. And it doesn't hurt as much now."

Evie smiled, screwing the lid back on the nail-polish and then standing up. "I better go. I'm going shopping with Dad to get a dress for the dance."

I smiled as Eric came over. "It's so adorable that your dad takes you shopping."

"Yours would too—if you asked him."

"Oh, you mean while he's working twenty hours a day, or do you mean if I could actually pry him out of my mother's shadow for two seconds?"

She smiled sympathetically at me. "Why not ask Jason?"

"Maybe."

"Is that how you really feel, Aubs?" Eric asked, messing up his wild blonde hair as he sat down in Evie's seat, uninvited.

"About what?"

"David. Your dad."

I refolded my arms again for good measure, determined to hold this secret inside. "I don't wanna talk about it, Ric. But I appreciate the concern."

Elora came over then, taking off her apron and, catching on to the tone, sat down, reaching across for my hand. "What's up, Aubs?"

"Nothing." My eyes shifted sideways onto Evie's face as I swallowed the hard lump in my throat. No one ever saw me cry. No one ever saw me even get emotional. I wasn't about to let it all out now. So I caged it down and unleashed my inner-smart-ass. "Guess I'm just wondering how I'll coordinate pretty with inconvenience." I nodded to the boot. "I got a date for this stupid dance, much to my disgust."

Elora smiled, turning her head then to give Eric a "look". He took that to mean exactly what it was, and Evie waved as they left us to a sisterly chat.

With a face full of sympathy, Elora cast a look of solidarity onto me. "Okay, now let's have the truth."

"What?" I shrugged. "That was the truth. I need a dress, and I don't think anything will match this stupid boot."

"And you want *Dad* to take you shopping?" She raised a brow at me. "When you and I both know it's never been that way with you two."

I lowered my foot from the chair and sat up, glancing around to see how close other people were and, when I'd successfully cleared the sheen of tears from my eyes, set them on hers. "I think he hit Mom."

"What?" She shot forward, face open as if to absorb the words through it.

"I was high on drugs the first night I did this." I tapped my knee. "But I woke up to a really strange sound and they had another argument."

"What about?"

"Mom had just got Danny back down to sleep and then Dad's phone rang. Loudly. And it woke him. And she got mad."

"And?"

"I heard Dad say *It's not my damn fault.*" I said it in his cold, commanding voice. "And then I heard Mom… like, it was the same sound that woke me in the first place."

"What sound?"

"She made this…" I coughed the sound out to show her. "Like, it sounded like when you get hit and you let the air out real quick."

Elora smiled. "Dad wouldn't hit her, Aubrey."

"Wouldn't he?" I shot her a smug look. "Because I've seen him, Lors. I've seen him manhandle her. I've seen him tower over her, grab her."

"Yes, he's always been like that, but he wouldn't hit her."

Clearly, Elora had no idea who our father really was. I looked off to nothing, blinking back tears. It humiliated me when I had to sit there and watch him belittle her, or tell her she was wrong about something in that brusque, assholey way, like when he'd lecture me and didn't let me defend myself. And yet he'd do that to Mom in a room full of people we know, people we love, and no one, not even Uncle Mike, ever batted an eyelid. I was starting to think I was the one who was wrong, that maybe this was normal, and yet I'd feel crushed if any of my friends treated me that way, let alone my husband.

"I hate her, Lors." I crossed my arms tightly over my body and spoke to the view on the other side of the road. "I hate the way she just accepts that. If any guy grabbed my arm… I mean… has Ric ever grabbed you like that?"

"No, but—"

"Because if I saw him do that, I'd kick him," I demanded, meeting her wide eyes with a fierce, assertive glare. "And I think you would too. It's not right, Elora."

"What did you see, Aubrey?" She shuffled a little closer. "This clearly isn't just about some noise you heard."

"Why does she allow it?" I wiped the corner of my eye. "Why doesn't she leave him?"

"I don't think…" Elora exhaled, stuck for words. "Aubrey, I think maybe you've got it wrong. Dad loves Mom. He'd literally die for her, and if he does anything she doesn't like, she pulls him up on it. She is not a victim. She never has been."

"You don't see what I see."

"Look, she has great empathy, which means that, sometimes, she lets him get away with things I might not let Ric get away with, but that's just because she understands why he feels that way, why he's doing it."

I felt suddenly very sick. "So you're justifying the abuse?"

"It's not abuse." She laughed.

"It is! If it were *anyone* else, we'd call it abuse."

Elora's gaze drifted down to her hands, sweeping the area and landing on Mia, where she cleared tables by the edge of the road. "Okay, look… I only say this because you're my sister and I have a duty to teach you right from wrong, and to make sure you never end up in that kind of relationship but… yes… by my standards, Dad can sometimes be a bit abusive. But—"

"See, and that's just it," I said, breathless from the emotion. "She disgusts me, Elora. I can't respect her. I can't even look at her sometimes—"

"So you're victim-blaming?"

"Yes!" I slapped the table top. "You said it yourself, she's not a victim. She can stand up for herself, but she doesn't—"

"Aubrey. Just stop." Elora shut her eyes for a moment, her throat making a sound as she swallowed. "Look, I know our parents, okay. And I've seen some things in the past. I've seen Dad at his worst, and I've seen Mom stand up to him when he's like that. But… she's not the kind of woman to ever just sit by and let someone abuse her. I need you to tell me what you saw, what's made you so upset, because I think you need me to translate for you."

"*Translate*?" I raised a brow at her, sipping some water to shove down the lump. "Like you can explain it all away, make sense of it so I no longer see what my mother suffers as abuse?"

"You just have to understand their past to understand the way they interact with each other. But… growing up, I never saw Dad mistreat her. Ever."

"Aside from the arm-grabbing, the manipulation, shutting her down—"

"That's just who he is."

"But it's gotten worse," I said. "Ever since…" Shut up, Aubrey.

"Ever since what?"

She already knew about Daniel being Uncle Jase's baby. I'd kept that secret from Harry, but I knew I could speak to Elora about it. I had to, because I was worried it had set Dad off, made him hate her, and that's why he was being so mean. I couldn't think of a time—before she came home and said they were expecting another baby—where Dad was like this. I'd seen small things, but this was constant now, like he hated her. And it all started after she got pregnant.

"Does he hate her for sleeping with Uncle Jason?" I asked.

Elora was taken aback.

"I know Danny isn't Dad's," I added.

"How do you know?"

"I… overheard you and Mom talking," I lied.

"Aw, Aubs." She stood up for a moment to hug me, bending awkwardly over the table between us. When she sat back down, there were tears in her eyes. "I'm sorry you found out that way. I think Mom planned to take it to her grave, you know—"

"So that it didn't hurt Jules. I get it. But… how can Dad stay with her after that—"

"You didn't hear that bit?"

"What bit?"

"Dad slept with Lily that night too, Aubs—"

"What!"

"They were drugged." She sighed and leaned back, letting her hands fall loosely into her lap. "Look, big family secret: Aunt Morgana created this awful potion a long, long time ago. And if you drink it, you will literally sleep with anything in the room. Even two girls will get it on. Or guys."

"For real?"

"Yeah." She nodded, something cold and serious flashing in her eyes for a moment—something like regret. "So, Mom didn't cheat on Dad. And he didn't cheat on her. They love each other, Aubs. And I know Dad can be a first-class asshole sometimes, I've seen it, but Mom pulls him up on it. Always."

I took a deep breath, thinking about it all. "It was just really confronting, I guess."

"What was?"

"I came down this morning, and I heard that same noise. It sounded like he slapped her. And when I walked into the kitchen, he had his forehead against hers, holding her cheeks. When they saw me, Mom pulled away quickly and I saw blood. As she wiped her lip, I saw blood."

"Sure she wasn't just feeding off him?" Elora smirked.

I nodded, certain of it.

"Normally, I'd say we have a duty to investigate," Elora said with a sigh, as if she really didn't want to be having this conversation. "Because cases of abuse can come from the most unlikely situations. But Mom isn't an abused wife, Aubrey. She can defend herself. She *does* defend herself. And I'll be honest with you, Dad would be abusive if she let him. It's in his nature. He just doesn't see it as abuse, more like discipline. And from the era he was born, that's not that unusual and it wasn't as frowned upon, but—"

"But you don't think it's the case right now," I said, feeling the lump in my throat tighten. "No matter what I say, no matter what I saw, you think I'm blowing this out of proportion?"

"I do, because you don't know their history—"

"Fine. Forget it!" I stood up, grabbing my crutches.

"Aubrey…"

"No, you're right. What would I know? Why should I trust my own two eyes, my gut? If Mom is pathetic enough to put up with that, and you're too naïve to care, then I'm done," I stated, hobbling away. "She can suffer."

"Aubrey, come back," Elora called gently. "Come on, sis. It's really not like that."

But it was, and she was just living the lie right along with them.

JULES

I lost my baby. I never even wanted a baby, so the fact that I was now grieving something I never asked for was just… really fucking unfair.

Jase came into my life, messed it up, made me fall in love with him, and now I was immortal. For a moment, it was all for the better. And then I died. I got engaged on the same day and woke the next morning to find that the life that had been growing inside me at the time was now gone. It just didn't survive Jason's bitch ex-wife trying to wipe me off the earth—all out of insane jealousy and some pathological need to own him.

Now, sitting here at his brother's best friend's house, in my once dream-destination, Australia, I couldn't believe how stupid I was to come. Lily, his ex, was still out there. She was still the queen of the immortals, still raising his kids. How could a psychopathic bitch like that be allowed to walk around in the free world, run a monarchy? Or shape tomorrow's minds!

All this, she got all this—kids, a crown, a life—while I sat here mourning a baby I'd never even asked for, in a house I wasn't familiar with. No family left. No life left. All because of these vampires I was still, even after everything, hanging around. Like a stupid idiot.

I should run. I should jump on the first plane and get away. I loved Jase; loved him more than anything in this world, but I wasn't blinded by love. Not even a little bit. And I knew, even now, that I'd made the wrong decision coming here with him. As long as I was a part of this messed-up family, I'd never be safe. There would always be drama. How long would it be before Queen Bitch herself came after me again?

We'd never be allowed to live in peace, and I just wasn't sure any love was strong enough to make me want to live my life that way.

I glanced over at Ara—the incomparably exquisite immortal, who could do no wrong in my fiancé's eyes—as she moved across the room to answer her phone. She was the hub of all my worldly problems: Jason's soul mate; designed for him; a structural component in the greater universe that would attract havoc like a magnet until the two fractured pieces—her and Jason—were unified as one and slotted perfectly into the little hole they'd left in the natural order of things. I couldn't help but to think that nothing would ever go right for me and Jase while those two defied nature.

And it wasn't even Jason's fault. He'd have Ara in a heartbeat. But she refused to have him. I liked Ara, but she was stubborn and stupid. And I just wasn't sure I could be second to her anymore. I felt like I deserved better.

Felt like I was *worth more than that.*

She told me I had to accept Jase *with* his connection to her, or not at all. The connection is a part of who he is and if I can't love him that way, then I don't really love him.

Well, guess what, Ara? Maybe I'm not okay with that. Maybe

I'm not okay with being a substitute. Maybe your little pep-talk was just sound advice: I should get out now, no matter how much I love Jase, because choosing to stay with him was not "choosing to love him no matter what", like she seemed to think; it was *settling*. And, as I established a moment ago, I deserved better.

"What?" Ara screeched, sitting down on the couch beside me, her phone tucked into her shoulder. "Why would she think David hit me?"

I could hear Elora on the other end of the line, explaining that Aubrey had talked to her today about something she'd seen in the kitchen that morning.

"Oh, that." Ara shrunk, casting her eyes sideways at me. "No. He was spinning Danny around and his foot flew out and hit me in the lip."

Elora didn't catch it down the phone line, but I did. I wasn't even an empath and I saw the truth. A child's foot wouldn't break the lip of a Lilithian. Aubrey was right. David had hit her. But why? I thought they were some great love.

Ara laughed and said goodbye to Elora, who seemed content with that explanation, then hung up the phone and looked at me.

"So he hit you?" I said boldly, both brows pushing up on my head, challenging her to even attempt a lie. It wouldn't get past *me*.

She sighed. "I said something I shouldn't have."

I laughed derisively, sitting taller. "Are you kidding me?"

"You don't get it." Ara stood up. "David's not abusive. He's really not," she added when I scoffed. "You just don't know him. It takes a lot for him to react the way he did this morning, and he was immediately sorry."

"Welp, I guess that makes it okay then," I huffed sardonically.

"You just don't understand."

I brought my knees up to hug them. "How many times?"

She didn't even need to ask me to clarify my meaning, because any woman who'd been hit would know. With a sigh, she sat down on the sofa. "I'm not being abused. He lashed out, but we've been under a lot of pressure—"

"How many?"

"It's just a bump," she advised. "He's not always like this, and he'll stop. He just…"

"How. Many," I reaffirmed.

Ara couldn't say a damn thing. David was an ass. She loved him anyway, and she wasn't going to leave him. She'd be more the type to help him learn from his ways—expect she could change him. But Jason had told me about this guy. He'd told me stories of the way he'd treated Ara over the years, but she never saw it as abuse. The arm-grabbing, gaslighting, the way he ordered her around and she just obeyed without even realizing. Had she become so accustomed to it now that she thought that was normal?

Would the same happen to me if I stayed in this family—enough that I'd advise someone to stay and love a man who would never love her back with all of his heart?

When did this become normal?

"Okay, fine, don't answer me," I said. "But just tell me… if Ric was doing that to Elora, would you be okay with it?"

"I'm not arguing with you about this, and I don't need to defend my relationship with David. He's not an abusive man. He made a mistake. And I'm sorry you don't understand that, but stop thinking I'm a helpless victim."

I shook my head, biting my tongue. This entire family was so fucked up.

"Yes, we are." She stood up, calm and serene, having stolen my thought. "But when you love someone eternally, you don't leave them just because they go through a phase—"

"Abuse is not a phase."

"And David is not always like that."

As if that made it okay.

"You will understand one day," she reaffirmed.

"Fine, let's say I do." I folded my arms. "Let's say I totally get it. Why did he hit you? What did you do wrong?"

Ara sat down again, her lips pressing in as if she were searching for a way to explain this. "I told you he was drugged—to sleep with Lily."

I nodded, turning slightly to face her and invest myself in the conversation more so she felt supported.

"He always had feelings for her. I knew that from the moment I got my memories back. And I catch him thinking about her sometimes. And the truth of it is, he would never leave me. He loves me more than he would ever love her, but he's not as sorry for that night as I am. He doesn't regret it in the ways that I do. And I've never once told him I know how he feels about it." Her voice cracked. It was the first time I'd really seen her so vulnerable. "But when I came in this morning and he was at the table, drinking coffee, he was thinking about her. And… I just… I didn't want to see that."

"Thinking about her in what way?"

"Remembering that night," she explained to her lap, keeping her eyes there. "It hurt me to see him thinking about it."

"I don't blame you."

"It's just… she shared our marital bed, as did Jason, I guess," she said humbly, smoothing the front of her dress down. "And I get that David is only human. We all are. And we all think about other people in that way from time to time, even if it's just a celebrity or a book character. But I don't want her to share space in his thoughts with me. I didn't need to see that before my coffee—"

"You shouldn't even be *speaking* before your coffee, from what Jase tells me."

Ara smiled. "And that didn't help, believe me."

"Do you think he wants to be with her?"

"No." Ara shook her head, certain of that. "That's why he got so angry with me. I accused him of it. It was petty, because I know better. And he just didn't know how to get his point across. He felt the world shift out from under him in that moment, thinking I'd made my mind up—that I would never believe he didn't want her—and he just… in a single moment of desperation, he just reached across and slapped me when I…"

"When you what?" I leaned over and touched her wrist in a show of support, pushing aside the slight pinch of jealousy at her silky warm skin.

"I said he should just go fuck the baby-killer, since he was just as bad."

My hand flung back to my own body and covered my mouth, feeling the full weight of that on David's behalf. "How could you say that?"

"I hate her, Jules. I hate what she did to you, but… David did that to Rochelle, and I… forgave him, and so did Jase, so I had no right to bring it up. But… we hate Lily." She touched a hand to her chest, a thin line of tears slipping down her pore-free cheeks. "She's been cast-out from the family, and I *feel her pain.* I am her. I have her soul. So I feel how alone she is, and I don't care, trust me. At least, I don't want to care. But we tossed her aside for what she did, and yet…"

"David did the same thing, and he's the one you fall asleep beside every night."

Ara nodded. "I was angry. Overtired, and… I'm only human, I guess. I didn't mean it—"

"But you also did."

Her eyes landed on me, filled with tears. "I'm just so mad, Jules—for what's happen to you and Jase. You don't know, none of you can *ever* understand how happy I was for him when he found you. And now I'm just so mad and hurt and..."

I felt the knot in my throat thicken, a fat line of tears slipping out past my own lashes now, even though I fought to hold them back.

"And he isn't…" Ara continued, wiping her cheeks. "He sat there, and he thought about Lily that way—after all she's done. I just wanted to hurt him. I wanted to hit him and throw him on the floor and scream in his face that he's no better if he can actually still have feelings for her. But then, the truth is, he's not any better. And sometimes...." She sniffled, composing herself.

"You just want to punch him?" I said, and Ara laughed.

"Yes. But—"

"You wouldn't because that's spousal abuse." Point made.

Ara nodded. I had her there. What could she say? "Yes. He can be abusive sometimes. But it's not him, Jules. And you have no idea how sorry he is…"

"Guess that makes it okay then." I dried the rest of my face, glad to feel angry for her so it took away some of the agony of my own tragic life.

"We're eternal, David and I," she said weakly, standing up. "If I cast him out every time he does something stupid…"

"You'd be happier," I offered.

"That's just it, I wouldn't." The broken, dejected woman walked away then, and I felt an eternal and deep sadness for her.

What a life! To actually believe that she couldn't be happy without that controlling prick. David was gorgeous, in truth, and could be a real sweetheart at times, but fuck… he was a narcissistic bastard at the best of them, and she was completely under his spell.

Part of me wondered then if I should take my own advice and leave Jason now. Ever since he told me that he was designed for Ara—that the universe would keep pulling her and David apart until the order of the world was right, and that Lilith had *told* Ara this and yet they defied Nature anyway—I kept wondering if everything that went wrong, all the shit, even losing the baby, was because of that. And if that was the case, what else could we stand to lose if we stayed together?

Mike waltzed in then in his usual spritely manner and slumped down heavily on the couch, making me bounce up a little. He didn't say anything, as usual, even as I made a point of glaring at him for his annoying ways. He just sat in the same space as me, open to talk but not openly inviting it, and propped his feet up on the table with a book in hand. I bent slightly to look at the title.

"Hitchhiker's Guide to the Galaxy?" I said.

"Ever read it?"

"No." I smiled, facing the front. I came in here to be alone but, so far, with this family and all their love floating around the space—casually coming in and out of the room all day—I hadn't been. Not once.

"Want me to read it to you?" he asked, offering the book.

"That's okay," I said softly, resting my cheek on my knee. I'd feel silly having someone read aloud to me like I was a little kid.

He settled down into a lazy slump then and brought his ankle across his knee, resting the book there, and cleared his throat. And even though I said no, that I didn't want him to read to me, he flipped back to the beginning of the book, moving his bookmark from the middle to the front page, and started reading.

The soothing, deep voice, with that almost cute Australian accent, carried the words on the quiet afternoon then, as I sat and listened to what was probably the funniest book I'd ever read. And after a while, I realized I hadn't cried since he came in. And there was peace in that—in feeling like maybe I could move on, even if it was just for a moment.

I glanced over at him—this big hulk of a guy, with kind warm eyes and an air about him that made everything okay—and I wanted to thank him. But I felt like that was silly. How could you thank someone just for knowing how to make you feel better?

"You've done this before, haven't you?" I asked, cutting in to the story.

"Done what?" He looked up at me.

"Brought someone back from the brink."

His eyes darkened with a memory, but he smiled and pushed it away, reading the words again as if they were a spell to cure any suffering.

And maybe they were.

ARA

The soothing tones of Mike's voice carried up the stairs as he sat with Jules, reading away her troubles, just like he'd done with me all those years ago, when the very man who I was looking at right now had kidnapped and tortured me at a masquerade.

I smiled over at Jason and he sent one back, but I'd never seen that kind of smile before. Danny was so busy with his coloring, sitting there at Harry's old desk in his old childhood bedroom, that he didn't notice his dad stop coloring and move away.

"I feel complete," Jase said, but he said it quietly, as though he didn't trust anyone else with that admission.

"What do you mean?"

"You and I…" He pushed out a hard breath and sat down on the bed. "It was always going to leave a hole, but… with Danny, it feels like I own a part of you that I didn't before. And it… some of the longing…" he explained, touching his chest. He couldn't put it into words, but I knew what he meant. I knew that he never stopped wishing for us to be together, even when he found Jules. He'd told her that—that her love changed him—but it was a lie. It would always be a lie.

But Danny—a part of him and me combined—it was as if it merged us both in ways we never could have in this life, and it made the fact that we would never be together a little less painful for him.

"He's beautiful, Ara," he said, glancing over at the bright little boy. "I know you were worried that this would break me apart after I just lost… the baby. But it gives me a reason to go on, when I really thought there was none."

I sat down beside him on the bed.

"I was listening just now—to you and Jules," he confessed. "And… she had a thought—about that notion that the universe will always pull against us until you and I… until we're set right."

"And?"

"Do you think this sets it right, in some way?" he asked, nodding at Danny. "Like maybe this will appease it and give it cause to leave us all alone? Because I can't take anymore, Ara. I'm tired of playing a game that I'm never gonna win at. The odds are stacked against us, against *me* mainly, and they always will be—"

"I don't believe that."

"Really?" His voice rose incredulously. "After everything we've been through."

I smiled softly at him, rubbing his arm. "I'm sorry, Jase."

"What for?"

"I feel like it's almost selfish of me to love David the way I do—"

He laughed out a short, breathy sound, cutting me off. "It's not. And I get it. If you loved me, then the universe might stop punishing us, and I might have even a single hope of ever being happy, but… you're not selfish. You belong with David. Light and dark, balancing the universe in some way, I'm sure. And I have Danny now." He shook his head, smiling over at the little boy like he just couldn't believe it. "I think we'll all be okay now."

"Me too," I said, resting my head on his shoulder. "And what about you and Jules? Is she gonna be okay?"

"She's smart," he said. "She sees things for what they are."

"And?" That sounded awfully final.

"I think she just doesn't see a path where she and I can ever be happy. Jules doesn't want to live in your shadow, and she thinks it will always be that way."

"Is she planning on leaving?"

Jason shook his head, ears lifting as if listening for something, maybe her thoughts. "I think she needs us right now. But I don't think she sees a future with me."

"How do you feel about that?"

"Honestly?" The top half of his body withered with a dispirited breath. "I'm not okay. I'm really not. If we didn't have Danny, I'd…" Seven layers of hopelessness and regret drowned him, and I saw a flash in his mind of a vial in his nightstand, filled with venom that could, *would*, kill him.

I bit my lip, closing my eyes slowly. "I'm sorry, Jason."

"Me too." He put his arm around me, kissing my head, as if I was the one that he needed to feel sorry for. "So, I spoke to David last night."

I smiled, nodding as I let him move us off the topic of love. "He was upset that he wasn't there to tell you about Danny himself."

"He regrets it, you know," Jase offered.

"Regrets what?"

"Lily," he said, but he didn't need to say anything else. I

knew he meant David regretted sleeping with her. I knew he'd been listening to that entire conversation with Jules.

"I know."

"And he doesn't think about her that often. You caught him in a fleeting thought—"

"I know." I smiled. He didn't need to tell me that. "I just couldn't explain that to Jules. She can't possibly comprehend the relationship David and I have—"

"But I do." He squeezed me closer, rubbing my arm as if to say it would all be okay. And I believed him. "I'll punch him—for hitting you. He's not getting away with that."

"Thanks," I said, laughing to myself.

"But I kind of owe him, so it won't be a hard punch."

"Why do you owe him?"

Jase nodded at Danny, the obvious. "He raised my son—"

"It's his son too."

"I know. And I'd never deny him that right. But… he's a good man. To take this on without a second thought."

"He is a good man, yes. I just wish I could explain that to Jules. She hates him."

"Sounds like Aubrey does too."

My heart doubled in on itself, seeing a world of new problems arising from this single realization. "How can I make her understand?"

"You can't," he said, nailing the coffin of dread shut. "Because, the fact is, David *is* abusive and controlling—"

"But it's the hex, Jase—"

"Even if that's true, I wouldn't wish your relationship dynamic on anyone. Your love doesn't outweigh the shit, in my opinion, but I know you're okay." His jaw set hard and his eyes fixed on the wall, but he shook it off and softened his voice. "I know that not being with him is worse than suffering the occasional darkness he gets lost in. And I know you accepted that as a part of him—that you love his darkness as much as his light—but just... do me a favor?"

"Okay."

Jase turned slightly to look right at me. "If the darkness ever outweighs the light, if he ever stays in that... if he's ever the bitter, cruel man longer than he's the loving one, promise you'll walk away. I don't want that life for you. Or for Danny. And the kids see it, Ara, even if you hide it from them. They can feel it."

I nodded, holding back the urge to roll my eyes. "It won't come to that, Jason. It can't."

He exhaled, resting his head on mine. "Do you really think this is because of the hex? Because your single moment of unguarded thought downstairs makes me think otherwise."

"What do you mean?"

"This abuse... it started after we had sex. And knowing the way he reacted last time..."

"He gets a look in his eye," I assured him. "When the hex surges, it's this particular look. And I can't really describe it, but I know the difference. And every time he's been a prick, or hurt me, it's definitely been under the surge but, in truth, it *is a lot* worse since you and I slept together."

"Do you think his resentment is amplifying it?"

"He doesn't resent me."

"Ara, he probably does but he won't say it. And if that's the case, then it could be the reason why he's gotten so much worse since then." Jase groaned then, rubbing the bridge of his nose. "I should have stepped in."

"What do you mean?"

"I've always known about this, you know. I didn't know it was the remnants of that hex. I just thought it was his arrogant personality mixing with all that darkness—"

"All the darkness of Man in one soul," I said with a smirk.

"Yes, and I've known since the early days when I returned to the vampire world that he was cruel to you sometimes, but I thought you had it under control—"

"I did. I do," I corrected, smoothing my skirt down my legs.

"But you should have had more help. The whole family should be working on some kind of… I don't know, cure, maybe…"

"Morgana's tried, Jase. There's nothing anyone can do once a curse is set in someone's bones."

He nodded. "I know, but I don't think, as a family, we can just sit by and allow this any longer. Not now that I know for certain. And not if he's progressed to hitting you."

"He doesn't want anyone to know—"

"But we *need* to. Mike needs to. Aubrey needs to. Because we need to watch it carefully, we need to step in, and we need to protect you when he's having a… what do you call it, a surge?"

"Yes, but, trust me, stepping in will only make matters worse. Drake tried, and we decided it was best to just stop."

"How the hell can that be best?"

"I don't want to talk about it, Jase. Not in front of Daniel."

"Well, I can't just sit here staring at a fucking wall when I know he's over there hitting you."

"It's not like that." I laughed, shaking my head. "Wow, you've really blown this way out of proportion. This is David were talking about, Jase. David! He's the sweetest, most gorgeous person in the world. And those surges cut him up like he's in a blender, okay, so he doesn't need to walk around with a steaming hot pile of shame on top of it. So let it go. David's fine. I'm fine."

"Try convincing your daughter of that then."

He was right. I couldn't. She would say that a hex is no excuse, because no one but me knew the real David—the one I fell in love with before Morgana cursed him to hate me, before the curse took root and set within his bones.

How could I possibly hate him when he was a victim himself? He'd be so alone. He'd lose me, when he'd never done anything to deserve any of this.

"I know." Jason put his hand over mine, giving it a gentle squeeze. "Maybe one day we can make her understand."

"Or she'll end up hating me—resenting me."

"If I know my Aubrey," he said, "and she got to the point where she actually opened up and talked to someone, then she probably already does."

"Do you really believe that?"

"I'm sorry, Ara." Jason nodded, resting his head on top of mine, sucking all hope out of the room with the silence that followed.

AUBREY

The school dance was lame. Mostly, it was packed with kids whose parents had made them come, and some who'd come willingly but couldn't manage to sneak alcohol in and were now sulking in corners. I had one dance with Sawyer, but my leg hurt too much, so we ended up sitting down at our table until about eight o'clock, when Evie and her shallow followers came around announcing that there'd be a party at Point Peron, with alcohol, if anyone wanted to ditch the dance.

"You keen?" Sawyer asked.

"Yes. But take me home first. I want to get out of this stupid dress."

"I can take you out of it," he suggested with a wink.

"Nice try. But if you like your dick, keep it away from me."

"Why?" He laughed. "You got an STD?"

"No." I stood up. "My dad will cut it off if it gets in me."

He laughed louder, standing up to hand me my crutches.

"Take me home. I'll meet you at the party later," I said in a kinder voice than before. I liked that he laughed at the idea of my scary father. It made it all seem more likely that this friendship—maybe more—could survive my screwed-up family.

"Suit yourself." He offered his hand, which I happily took—as a means to hobble past the chairs without falling over and not because I wanted to hold his hand—but he didn't let go as we got clear of the tables, so I relaxed into it a little, opening the proverbial door that I'd slammed shut when I lost my first human boyfriend.

After getting changed and calling Mia to tell her about the party, I climbed in the car and reversed down the drive just as Mia came out of hers across the road. We waved excitedly at each other, and as the car took the next turn, I flashed my high beams at her a few times. She stuck her finger up at me.

"Miss me," said a voice from the backseat.

I squealed, really glad the car was driving itself—even if I was in the driver's seat—and attached my hand to my chest to steady my heart.

"What happened to not scaring so easy?" Malevolent Ghost asked.

"Get out of my car."

He appeared in the front seat. "Make me."

I groaned. "Okay, fine, you want to come back? Meet me at my brother's house after the party tonight. I'll free you—"

"Yeah, or you'll free me and then have your brother kill me," he said, and all my plans went right out the window, deflating me. "I'm a ghost. I hear things."

Even though it wasn't a requirement these days for hands to be on the wheel of autonomous cars, I just needed a sense of control, so I gripped it tightly, steering the car myself.

"I tell ya what," the ghost said. "Bring me back, right now, and I won't kill your friend."

"What friend?"

He nodded ahead of us at Mia's car, just as it turned onto the freeway toward the beachfront.

"Late night," he said. "What's this… hundred kilometers per hour, that's… sixty-two miles, right?"

I nodded, my knuckles going white with the squeeze of my hands.

"Dark stranger appears suddenly out of nowhere," he added.

"She won't be able to see you?"

"Are you sure of that then, Conduit? Because ghosts can't break legs either, can they?"

My jaw tightened. "Go ahead. She's in a Tesla. You'll probably do more damage to the road than you will Mia."

"Only one way to find out," he said, but as he shifted to move, I reached out and grabbed his wrist. I had no intention of bringing him back to life, but the simple act of reaching out to stop him going anywhere was enough to do just that.

My car screeched to a halt in the middle of the empty road and I pressed the button to open the door, my face hot with fury. The ghost laughed madly, looking down at his solid arms.

"That was easier than I thought."

"Get out!" I yelled, on the brink of hysterics. "Now."

"No way. I'm human now. You need to get me a new identity and—" He didn't get to finish that sentence. I lifted my good leg over and booted him out the door. He fell heavily, grabbing at the sides of the car as I pressed my foot on the pedal and shot away, not really caring if I ran him over in the process.

I wanted to speed the whole way there; I wanted to do handbrake turns and rev my engine; but the stupid car didn't have an engine and it wouldn't let me drive like a maniac. It forced me to adhere to the speed limit for each area and responded to take control when I tried to hook the corners too fast. It was an excruciatingly perfect drive all the way out to the rocks, leaving my rage with nowhere to go.

I got out, and when I tried to slam the door, the hinges took over and closed it softly into place, so I hit the side of it with my crutches.

"Whoah." Sawyer laughed from behind me. "What'd the car do to you?"

"It won't let me express my anger!" I stormed past him, hobbling as fast as I could on these stupid walking sticks. "And if you're smart, you'll stay away from me until I cool down."

"You don't scare me. I like fiery red-heads," he said, grabbing my arm. But as I placed my hand over his to shove him off, his eyes went wide and he held his breath. For a moment, I thought the ghost was behind me, until I remembered he wasn't a ghost anymore. He was human.

When I looked back at Sawyer, he dropped down heavily on his knees, gagging on air.

"Sawyer." I dropped my crutches, reaching for his shoulder but his mouth fell open and my eyes grew wide, reeling back as his cheeks sunk into the shape of his teeth and his skin sucked inward around his bones, drying as it tightened all over him.

"Sawyer!" I cried, not sure where to touch him or what to do. "Help me!" I screamed. "Help me, please! There's something wrong with him."

Several people came racing from the shadows all around the beach, screaming when they caught sight of their classmate mummifying before their eyes. No one knew what to do. No one took any action. We all just stood there, screaming and crying as Sawyer decayed.

"Aubrey." Mia grabbed my shoulder and spun me around. "What happened?"

"I don't know," I wailed, hiding my face in her chest as

Sawyer hurled his final breath and fell flat to the ground, igniting terror from the innocent minds around him. “I don't know.”

“I’m calling Dad.” Mia took her phone out.

“No,” Evie said, getting hers instead. “Your dad’s burnt, remember. I’ll call my grandfather.”

My dad arrived at the same time as the police. No one knew what had happened to Sawyer, and once a coroner from the Vampire Order was called in to cover up what was very clearly some kind of supernatural death, no one, but us, would be any the wiser. Liam Sawyer choked to death as a result of an allergic reaction to some alcohol he’d had. And it was safe to say that no one at my school would probably ever drink again.

But I wasn’t getting off so easy. I was the last person to touch Sawyer, and that could only mean one thing.

When the dust settled and Mom and Dad returned home from the red-tape nightmare, it was with that look in their eyes —the one that meant everything had changed. The last time I saw that look was when I brought back my first ghost—Uncle Arthur.

“It was my fault, wasn’t it?” I said to Mom, fighting to keep the emotion out of my voice as my own father, who was supposed to love me no matter what, walked right past me and into the kitchen without a word.

Mom sat beside me on the couch, nodding. “We think so, honey. We just don't know why.”

But I did. I’d brought back a malevolent spirt. That had to carry some kind of detrimental consequence.

“You did what?” Mom shrieked, standing up.

Oh crap. My mouth dropped as I realized how much trouble I was in. Stupid mind-reading parents!

“How many have you brought back, Aubrey?” she demanded so loudly that my dad popped his head in. When he’d read enough of the situation to know what was going on, he stepped into the room with his arms folded, and I knew the gig was up. I'd be grounded for the rest of my life—if he didn't send me to the torture chambers first.

"Only four that you didn't know about..."

"Four?" Mom screeched. "When? And where are these people now?"

"I took care of it, Mom. You know why?" I stood up to make myself the same height as her. "Because I'm resourceful and a hell of a lot more capable of things than you and Dad think I am!"

"Right, so capable that you killed a boy!" she yelled. "Do you even know why? Or how?"

"No," I muttered under my breath, dying a little inside as the raw truth of that killed a small piece of my soul.

"This is a mess." She brushed her hands over her head and sat down, and my father, ever the knight to her rescue, was there beside her before her butt even touched the seat. "I don't know how to deal with this, David. With the lies, the disobedience—the death."

Dad looked over at me with an expression that sliced a thousand wounds into my heart. She was the most precious thing in the world to him; to upset her was to offend him in the most heinous, serious way possible. There was no coming back from this. I'd royally screwed-up and there would never be a way to make it right.

"You know, for what it's worth, I'm not sorry," I announced, digging my hole even deeper. "I will forever regret Sawyer's death, but I don't regret bringing those people back. They had a right to live. If there is a way possible in this world to bring people back, then why should it be such a crime to do it? You used to do it all the time, Mom—before I came along. I've heard the stories—"

"That's bringing people back from the brink, Aubrey—healing them with *natural* Cerulean Magic and guiding their souls back to their body. Not picking long-dead souls from the Other Side; souls who should be at rest—"

"But they're not at rest!" I yelled, as if the volume could get it through her thick skull. "They're lost. Confused. Alone. Why is it so wrong if I give them peace?"

"We've talked about this," she said, standing up. "It's dangerous because it puts you at risk of being kidnapped, used as a tool for other people's gains. And we don't know anything about your powers. What if this boy's death is a consequence—balance, maybe? What then?"

"Then it makes it my fault," I said, voice quivering, "and I will have to live with that for the rest of my days. But I'd rather do more damage for trying than to sit around and do nothing with what God gave me."

"God didn't give you this power. It's not a blessing—"

"But you would say that, wouldn't you? I—"

"I mean it, Aubrey. You weren't born to this; it wasn't passed on in your genes. It's witchcraft! The result of a heinous and violent spell that my sister cast on me."

My entire argument fell out of my mouth and died on the floor. "What?"

"I was resurrected from flames," she explained. "Your Aunt Morgana murdered me—burned me alive—as a part of a spell to give my child the ability to bring souls back from beyond the veil. She did it purely so you could bring her mother back for her. It's not natural, and that's why I don't want you using it."

"You never told me that." I sat down hard, the air straining from my lungs until I felt weak, using the crinkle of the leather under my hands to ground me. "Why didn't you ever tell me that?"

"Because I didn't want you to know about some of the dark things in our family's history, honey. It's haunting and scary, and you're just a child."

"I'm not a child, Mom. I'm almost—"

"Honey." She laughed, shaking her head. "You will never be younger than you are right now. You just don't understand how much of the world you don't know about because you haven't lived long enough to understand that there are things you can't possibly understand."

"What the hell does that even mean?" I shot to my feet again, ready to storm up to my room.

"It means I love you. And it's easy to make mistakes when you're young—to feel like the adults in your life are trying to control, not protect you," she reasoned, her tone soft, a white flag that just came off as patronizing. "So I'm not punishing you for making a mistake, or for killing that boy. But I am punishing you for lying to me, and for going against my wishes."

Uh-oh. Mom had that look. The same look she'd get when she talked about Court—about the old days—and some of the sentences she dished out. This was bad. Really bad.

"I'm sending you to live with your grandfather—"

"What?" Both my dad and I said together.

"He understands everything about magic, Aubrey. And my sister Morgana won't be far away either. I need you to go there and learn what you can about your abilities, and maybe, just maybe, he can teach you a little respect while you're there," she said, breaking to tears as she left the room.

I looked at Dad with pleading eyes, hoping he'd say something to sway her, but he just shook his head at me, cold as ice, and followed Mom.

"Fine, go ahead," I cried. "Run after her, Dad, as always, even though she's wrong and you know it!"

He stopped as my voice hit hysterics. I controlled it quickly, hellbent on keeping the truth of how much this hurt me buried deep down. "Aubrey, I support your mother's decision because—"

"Because you have to suck up to her so she won't leave you for beating her up all the time!"

Dad's core imploded, making his vampire face pale.

"Yeah, that's right, I saw it," I probed, pushing my knife deeper. This was justified now. If they could just so easily hurt me, then I had no problems returning the favor and casting the light on everything heinous about them. "And I stole Mom's journal. I read it, Dad. I know what you did to her. I know how you hit her—hard enough to make her hit the ground, to bleed. That small, innocent woman up there, who loves you no matter what. How could you?"

He pointed at me then, so enraged he was breathless, deep voice trembling. "You know nothing about that, Aubrey Knight."

"I know everything about it," I demanded. "I know you're sick and twisted and you enjoy it. I see the look in your eye when you're gunning for an argument."

"If you truly had read your mother's journal, we wouldn't be having this discussion."

"What the hell is that supposed to mean?" My lip lifted in disgust because I couldn't let it tremble with the whirling vortex of pity I had inside for Mom. "You know what, it doesn't even matter. I hate you. Both of you."

"Then I suppose it's a good thing you're going to live at Elysium."

"Yeah, I guess it is!" I yelled.

As he walked away though, straight spine, stiff legs, he left behind a chill that would stay with me for the rest of my life. I could feel it.

Over on the mantle, the old clock behind a picture Harry drew when he was younger ticked loudly, counting down the seconds around me as my entire life expanded and then shrunk back in, changing forever.

I didn't know it then, but the moment I'd brought back that malevolent ghost was the domino that triggered the unraveling of this entire family. And I was the moron that kicked it over.

ARA

"Calm down," David muttered softly.

Since I'd been sitting here reading my book for the past two hours, the evening light making the room almost too dark now, I wasn't sure what he meant. I looked up at him where he sat on the bed across from my arm chair.

"What do you mean?" I asked.

"Two words," he clarified. "Two simple words that give me all the power I need over you."

"David, I don't understand." I sat up a little more and put my book down between my leg and the arm of the chair.

"That's why I should leave, Ara." He looked at the closed bedroom door and then back at me, his squared green eyes liquid with hurt. "That's why this can't work between us anymore."

"Why?"

"I do this. We get into a disagreement about something stupid. And you're so calm, so measured in your responses, and I can't rile you up." He stood and walked over to the window, looking down on the descending night. "So, I wait. I look for a moment when I'm losing an argument against your rationale, and I slip those words in and you"—he shook his head, shutting his eyes regretfully—"you get so mad. And I know you will before I even say it. You *react* then. You're no longer calm, you're suddenly so angry that you say something provocative, something without thought, and that's what I'm waiting for. That's the moment when I'm justified to do anything to you that I want."

I stood up, my nightgown falling in silky layers around my legs as I wandered over and stood beside him, seeing the warm house across the road light up as Mike arrived home.

"And that's why this needs to end, my love," David continued, "because it's never going to get any better. I've told you this over the years, told you all the ways I manipulate you into an argument in the hopes that you might get better at it, that you might find new ways to avoid it and be safe. But you don't."

"David, I—"

"Every single time." He looked at me, wetting his lips as the regret ate his hard exterior. "I aim for an argument and I pull you in every time, no matter how often I give you insights to my methods, you—"

"I'm trying."

"You're not trying hard enough," he demanded, voice getting louder. "You're becoming more and more submissive, less defensive, every year that goes by and it's disgusting, Ara. I hate seeing my once powerful, untouchable wife shrink when I speak, or cower when I strike. And that only makes me want to do it more."

"Are you saying this is my fault?"

"Yes! Because we've talked about this. Like telling you about the words 'calm down' just now, I have told you time and time again how to avoid an argument with me, and you still can't—"

"I walk away, and you chase after me. I refuse to argue about something, even if I'm right, and you find a way to get my mouth moving," I said, thrusting myself forward in defense. "I go to bed, roll over to go to sleep, and you will wake me, rip me from my dreams to argue with me about how loudly I'm breathing."

David turned away, shaking his head derisively.

"I do everything I can to avoid it, David. I am always on my toes, thinking, calculating, choosing my words so carefully so it won't provoke you. But there's no avoiding it sometimes, and I'm not to blame." I started crying because I couldn't make him believe me, and I knew that. "You can't blame me because you hit me—"

"I can. And I do. You're a smart girl. Look at this." He presented me, my misery. "Look at us now. Can't you see? This is a surge. This is me provoking an argument and you walked right into it!"

"This isn't a surge," I said, coming down from my anger. "You can never acknowledge the hex during a surge, you can't even call it that in those moments because you think you're so justified."

"But you see, don't you?" He stepped closer, fixing my gaze with a sense of urgency. "This, right here, this argument is the same way it happens every time and you fall for it, because how can you not? I bait you. I pull you in because you love me. And it will always happen."

"I know," I said, shoulders sinking heavily with a forlorn sigh. "But what choice do we have? We tried to undo the last remnants of the hex. We tried everything in every single spell book ever written. We tried dark magic, David. What else can we do?"

"Split up."

"You don't want that," I stated. "And I don't want it."

"Well I don't want the guilt!" he yelled, pressing his hand to his chest. "I fell in love with you, Ara—this sweet innocent girl on the driveway in a yellow dress. And I can't stand to see her cry every time I hit her. And it's not because you're bruised. It's not the cuts or the broken bones. It's the hurt." My David, my broken, hurt David rubbed his chest, making a point of it, his own eyes liquid with that pain. "I can't bear to see you so hurt. I want to protect you with everything in me, but I'm the one hurting you."

"David." I moved in to stand beside him as he pressed his hands to the windowsill and leaned into them, sobbing. "Are you seriously trying to ask me to leave you?"

"I am *begging* you, Ara," he cried, shoulders shaking.

I touched his back, feeling nothing but love for him beneath it all. "I'm just not ready to lose you yet—"

"Only because of Daniel," he said, taking a few jagged breaths. "If we hadn't had Daniel, you'd have left. But you can't do it alone. You're so run down by the world that you can't face raising him alone, but you'd be okay," he insisted, wiping his nose. "Once you're free of my abuse, you'd find the strength, the will to want to go on again. And the girls, Lors, Aubs, even Harry, they'll help. They'll support you—"

"It doesn't work like that, David! I can't just watch you pack a bag and walk out that door and never come back. We're forever! We. Are. For. Ever," I demanded, making him stand up and face me. "We don't get to break up. We don't get to go our separate ways. I will be lost without you. Eternally miserable and longing. It's not that fucking simple and you damn-well know it!"

"Well, I don't know what else to do," he said, thrusting his hands out in question. "Do you think I want this?"

"No." I sat down heavily on the arm chair, head in my hands.

"And here we are again, at the start of the same circle we go around every time you come out from a surge."

David sat in front of me on the footstool, closing us in with the way he leaned in and brought his hands to mine. "It will never end, Ara. The cycle. I'll slip into a surge, start being vile, until eventually it blows up and I hit you. And then I'll be sorry, I'll beg you to leave and you won't. And then I'll get mad that you keep putting me through this. Never mind the fact that I could leave if I wanted to, but don't, because I need to place the blame on you since I'm not strong enough to walk away. I'm not strong enough to end this. And that's not your fault," he cried, using my hand to wipe his chin. "But I will blame you. And I will hate you after I hit you because it's your fault that I can't leave."

I leaned down and laughed into the back of my hand, but it broke then and turned into tears. David cupped his palm over my knee, saying nothing as the hope died just a little bit more between us.

I went back in my mind then to the morning after Morgaine had lifted the hex off David. I'd lured him into the forest that night, where her dark magic would have no hold, and when the curse was absent within that single space, my David had returned to me. He'd been so blood-starved from the effects of the hex that he'd drank from me and, in the end, killed me. Bled me out until I was dead. Then, he ran in search of help, but found only agony outside the forest border. The hex took hold again and I'd woken back to life to find him torn and bloody on the ground, having ripped at the marks on his back, the binds of the curse.

But when Morgana finally drew the hex from within his blood and broke the news that it had taken hold—that some of the black, the dirt, the tainted blood would always remain—I hadn't realized it then. I had ignored the truth and brushed it away with hope. But this was the truth, cold and hard and evident in every single day of our lives since then: there was no undoing it, and this was us now. This was our love now. So strong that we would live through this abuse, both of us, because we had no choice.

What would it take? How many more of these conversations would we have before one of us was strong enough to walk away?

I knew the truth. I hated myself for it. But I knew the truth was that I would never leave him. Everything that happened, every hit, every argument that left him feeling like this, it was my fault because I was too weak and too stupid to leave him.

And he would always hate me for that.

"Ara, calm down, sweetheart," David said with a laugh, taking the turn up Harry's long gravel driveway. "Aubrey admitted to blackmailing him into helping her. It's not his fault."

"Yes, but what did he do that was so bad she *could* blackmail him to begin with?" I demanded. "Whatever it is, she thought it was severe enough not to rat him out even now, but I will have the truth!"

He just smiled and looked back at the road.

"What?" I said, sensing his smug gratification.

"I love it when you get all fired up like this." David reached across and patted my leg.

With a huff, I folded my arms and looked up at Harry's house, just about ready to strangle someone today. The car stopped, and David came around to open my door, keeping hold of my hand as we walked up the porch steps, as if I might charge ahead and make a scene.

"Door's open," Harry called from somewhere in the house.

"Just in the John. Be out in a sec."

Inside, the living room was cleaner than usual, and there was a lingering scent of honey and vanilla. And cookies. I looked at David, who frowned, his ears inching up slightly as he listened, trying to discern the cause of the sudden change.

"What?" I said.

"Something… smells familiar."

"Oh, hello!" chimed a high, pretty voice, and David went sheet-white. Seventy years of regret slapped him hard in the gut and caved his chest. My eyes followed his to the woman across the room, and a moment of my past—of a terrified young girl at a masquerade, looking in on a memory that didn't belong to her —came rushing up from the depths of my deeply suppressed past.

I shot backward with a hard breath. "Rochelle!"

"You know me?" She looked more closely at our faces, dropping the tray of cookies then as her eyes darted around the room for a path of escape. When Harry came up behind her, she folded into his arms, sobbing loudly, her knuckles red where she clenched his shirt.

"Shhh," he soothed, stroking her wispy blonde hair. It was immediately apparent what had happened between them. He'd had her in ways that only his Uncle Jason had in the past. I didn't know what to say or do. And clearly, David didn't either.

Heavy, looking weak in the knees, David sat down on the sofa and pinched the bridge of his nose.

"What's the deal, guys?" Harry asked.

"Rochelle just remembered her death," David said, voice deep and penitent.

Harry's eyes widened then as he made a few connections. We rarely ever talked about our family history, but Harry knew a little, mostly from his early days of learning to read minds, when he'd accidentally pick out pieces of information we'd never have willingly divulged to our children.

"She's the same Rochelle?" He drew her from his arms and looked her over. Small, her head only just meeting his chin, with big soulful eyes and fair skin, she still looked like a girl fresh out of the forties, even in modern jeans and a loose-fitted white top. Her hair was pulled back in that half-up, two-clip style they wore then, and she was pretty and classic. I could tell she was inherently sweet by nature, just the kind of girl a mother would want for her son. Just the kind of girl Harry had always turned his head for.

"Please don't give me to him," she cried, truly believing he would. "Please—"

"Shh, it's okay." Harry drew her close again, rubbing her back in gentle, loving circles. "I won't. I promise. You're safe with me. I swore that to you, and I meant it."

"But so did Jason," she wailed, drawing nothing but pity from me.

I moved over and stood close to them, waiting for her to look at me. "Rochelle, I'm Ara. I'm a friend of Jason's—your Jason."

"He's still alive?" She looked up, her eyes glassy with tears.

"Yes." I nodded. "And I know you remember David as the cruel, heartless vampire that killed you, and that Jase wasn't there to save you, but that's an act that David has regretted every single day."

Rochelle looked over at him, and even though David didn't show emotion very often, that fact was evident in his posture and the deep, brooding agony in his eye.

"He will not harm you again, you have my word as well, as a queen of the Lilithian vampires and the heir to the Drakarian Throne."

Her eyes widened. "Queen?"

"Yes."

She moved to curtsy, but Harry stopped her, laughing. "We don't do that around here. At Loslilian, yes, but not around here."

Rochelle nodded, smiling sheepishly. Then she looked at Harry. "May I please be excused?"

"You don't have to ask, love," he said sweetly, making David and I exchange looks. "You go. I'll come in later."

Rochelle's wide, haunted eyes took us in again, her polite upbringing prompting her to say farewell but her grief, anger and fear making her leave without doing so.

I sat down beside David, worrying suddenly about how this would affect Jules and Jason's already fragile engagement. "Is this what Aubrey was blackmailing you with?"

Harry's head pushed forward on his neck. "She didn't tell you?"

"She's a girl of her word," I said, presenting her father, because he was exactly the same.

"I take it Aubrey brought Rochelle back?" David surmised.

"Yes, but we didn't know who she was." Harry sat down on the coffee table in front of us, leaning forward in that way he did, which could bring an entire room into a conversation. "What's happened? I can tell there's something up. What is it?"

"Aubrey killed a boy—"

"What?" He stood, as if to rush to her defense.

"It was an accident," I said, tugging his hand to make him sit. "We don't know how it happened. She thinks it's a consequence, for bringing back a malevolent spirit—"

"What?" His clear blue eyes fixed mine. "She brought it back? But we… we were going to kill him." He let out a deep, agitated moan and linked his fingers behind his head. "How did she end up bringing it back?"

"What do you know about it?" David asked calmly, from one man to another. "Because Aubrey won't say anything."

"I know it had the ability to cause harm," he explained, hands falling lazily back down into his lap. "It burned Uncle Mike's face—"

"How can it do that?"

"I don't know. But it also broke Aubrey's leg."

"What?"

"Her fall at dance class, that wasn't just a fall, Ma."

I closed my eyes, suddenly feeling like the worst mother in the world. David put his hand over mine and squeezed tightly.

"I punished her for bringing it back," I said, going over every mean word I said. "I didn't realize the ghost was taunting her…"

"Yeah, well, it was a pretty tricky spirit. It must have done something awful to have made her bring it back without me there. She was terrified, Mom. She wouldn't show it, because Aubrey doesn't do emotion, but she was scared."

David squeezed my hand a little tighter.

"So… how did she end up killing someone?" Harry asked, resting his forearm to his thigh.

"We don't know, as I said. She says she just touched the boy, right after she brought that ghost back, and the kid died. Mummified, to be exact."

Harry's brows slowly pinched, indicating a ticking brain. "What is that, like, a life for a life? Or years for years? Do you think maybe it took the exact years off the kid that the ghost had been dead?"

"Maybe. But why didn't it happen after she brought the others back?"

Harry looked in the direction of his bedroom, eyes narrowing. "I don't know. I mean, it was malevolent, right? So maybe that's it?"

"I don't have the energy for this right now." I sat back a little, so conflicted with so many worries that I didn't know which one to address first. "David, do we tell Jason—about Rochelle?"

David looked up from the ground and over at the wall backing on to Harry's bedroom. "I don't think that's a good idea right now—for either of them."

"And no," Harry added, having just read my mind, "I don't think Dad should go in there and apologize to her, Mom. She doesn't want your pity or apologies, and I'm not sure she ever will."

"Yes, but—"

"Sorry, Mom," he said as kindly as he could, ever the diplomatic little boy. "But he killed her. And until she's ready to forgive, you guys don't get to make yourselves feel better by trying to tell her you regret it."

I nodded. He was right. I wanted to make her understand how sorry David was, but that wouldn't help *her* healing. It would only serve to help him. "Do you love her?"

"Not yet," he said, but he grinned as he said it. "Might be hard not to though—eventually."

David and I understood the gravity of this. We both knew how bad it would be for Jules, who'd lost her baby and discovered Jason had one with me. And for Jason, who had finally put Rochelle's death behind him. Would he forbid Harry to be with her because she was once his greatest love?

"Don't worry for me, Ma," Harry said, cupping my shoulder firmly and fixing my gaze like a middle-aged man in a young adult's body. "If that's what happens, I'll be okay. Knowing who she is now, I'm expecting a bit of upheaval. But Uncle Jason has a right to know about her."

"You're right," I said, patting his hand. "And please stay out of my head, Harry."

He flashed that cheeky grin and put his hands in his lap. "So, who wants to be the one to break the news?"

"Let me do it," I said.

"No." David stood slowly. "I should be the one. Since it was I who killed her."

I stood too, dragging up the weight of all our dread as I did. "We'll go and let you and Rochelle talk. She…" I cast my eyes away as the moment of her death played out, and Harry sighed, getting up off the table.

"I know," he said. "She's been through hell. But she's alive now. That's what counts."

"Not always, son," David said, drawing that statement from a century-worth of experience. "Not always."

When we pulled up outside home, David stared over at Mike's house for a long time, and I knew his mind was changing. Over the years, he'd developed a much closer relationship with Jason, but whether he wanted to admit it or not, the fact that Jason had been out of our lives for three years, and that I'd had a child with him, had wedged a rift there between them. He didn't know how to break the news to Jason about Rochelle any more than he knew how to tell him he still loved him after everything.

I placed my hand on David's. "Want me to tell him?"

"Do you think me weak?" he asked softly. "Should this be coming from me?"

"I don't think it matters much either way. If anything, it might be better coming from me, because I'll know how to break it to him more gently."

David dropped his shield, turning his hand over in mine and giving it a gentle squeeze. "What would I do without you?"

"You can thank me later with a back massage." I winked at him, hopping out of the car. "I'll just stop by Mike's to check on Danny first."

"Want me to do it? I can bring him home?"

"No." I listened carefully to the feel of the day. "He's napping. So I'll just check in and then pop down to see Jason."

"Pop down?" David looked over at Mike's house. "Where is he?"

"At the lake." I nodded in the direction I could feel Jase's energy signature. He was in a calm, if not contemplative mood. It would be okay to break this news to him now without destroying him in the process.

David nodded, carrying the weight of it all like a physical barb, and headed up to the house. I darted across the street and stepped through the front door, feeling that ever-present absence here without Emily and Vicki. Vicki had moved two blocks away with her new husband about ten years ago, and Emily was happy now, with a man who deserved her, while Mike was happy being on his own. He had Mia, and Em took their youngest daughter Scarlett, since she was still too young to leave her mother when they divorced, and it left the road ahead for Mike wide open. Without my curse—the First Woman's Curse—holding him hostage, he was finally free to fall in love. He just… never had.

Hearing the piano in the den, I crept down the short corridor and fixed my shoulder to the doorway, watching as Mike played and Jules, to my great shock and awe, sung along with him. As they finished the song, Mike applauded loudly, and Jules took a theatrical bow.

"Damn, girl," he said. "You got a set'a pipes on ya."

Jules took the compliment in her usual confident stride,

drawing a deep breath through a smile. "I forgot how good it feels to sing."

"Wanna do another one?" Mike offered.

Jules turned her head and glanced back at me. "You here to get Danny?"

"I know he's sleeping," I advised softly. "I just wanted to check in and make sure he didn't give you guys too much hell."

Mike smiled, his eyes glinting. "He's got your spirit," he said, "I'll give him that."

"By spirit, are you saying my son is a handful?" I teased.

"He's too smart for his own good," Mike said with a laugh. "He unlocked my phone with the passcode and purchased a new skin for his game. I never taught him the passcode."

"He takes after his father." I laughed absently, choking on the words as they came out, because they all knew now that he was Jason's, so saying that in a room with his fiancé after they just lost their baby was incredibly insensitive and stupid. "Shit. I'm sorry, Jules—"

"It's okay. You're right. He is super smart, just like Jason," she offered, and I appreciated that. It must have been hard for her to be here today while Mike babysat Jase's son. "He's on the jetty at the lake, by the way," she added, "if that's who you were looking for."

"How'd you know I was looking for him?"

"You have that look in your eye," she said, and Mike nodded, both of them exchanging the same glance.

"What's happened?" Mike asked. "Bad news?"

"Yes. And no. It's good news that will likely… upset him."

"What is it?" Jules asked.

I looked past her to Mike. "Aubrey brought someone back. Someone Jase knew."

"It's not Arietta, is it?" He stood up.

"No," I said sadly, wishing it was, even though Arthur was happy now without her. "It's Rochelle."

Mike's jaw dropped, and Jules sprung forward a little, stopping herself mid-step. "You're kidding me, right?"

"No."

She broke down then, sitting on the couch with her head in her hands. Mike gawked at me with an open mouth, not sure what to do or say, clearly. He opted for sitting beside the sobbing girl and patting her back.

"You okay?" he asked softly.

"This is a joke, isn't it?" she cried. "I was right. The universe is doing everything it can to tear us apart, and now I know I made the right decision…"

Mike glanced back at me, and I gave an apologetic wince. He nodded to say he'd handle it, so I backed from the room and walked out of the house and across the street to the bushland, like I was dragging sandbags behind me.

Down a wide dirt track, with the hot spring sun beating the shade from the trees and making the cicadas here sing louder, I wandered toward the large body of water. Black swans and pelicans lazily bobbed about on its surface, while dragonflies darted in and out of the brush at the water's edge.

I spotted Jason on the low jetty, leaning on the railing, his thoughts all the way across the other side of the wetlands. He looked glorious out there, with a pelican sitting on the rail right by him, and I knew that meant he hadn't moved for the longest time. For a wild bird to come so close, he must have been standing there like that for hours.

It gawked at me as I started up the long path out over the water, reeds and grasses lining the wooden planks, and then flew away when I met Jase at the railing. He turned his head and smiled at me, and I kept my thoughts covered in case he took a stroll inside my mind.

"You okay, Jase?"

"I'm pulled in two directions," he said.

"Which are?"

"My life is falling apart. Jules gave this back." He showed me the small diamond ring in his hand. I closed my eyes to cover the pain. "And I just want to check out now," he admitted. "I don't want to live in a world where the pain just never stops—"

"Jase." I put my hand on his arm.

"But"—he tucked the ring into his back pocket—"at the same time, I've never felt more complete, you know, because of Daniel. And that makes me want to live. It's just… what kind of life am I ever going to live? I'll be here for Danny, but I'll be alone. Miserable."

"Or maybe you can find happiness in—"

"Don't finish that sentence, Ara. Come on." He sighed, shaking his head and turning back to rest his forearms on the rail. "Every relationship I've ever tried to have has fallen apart due to circumstances outside of my control. And you know me: I'm the kind of guy who needs a partner. A person to love. I don't think I'll ever be happy on my own."

I didn't think he would either, kinda like me. I leaned over and rested my head on his shoulder, not sure what to say or do. He smelled like soap and vanilla, all clean and pressed, and he was so warm from where the sun had been beating down on his long sleeve all this time. I could feel he was at peace right now, which made it so much harder to find the words that would break the ice.

"You came out here to tell me something," he stated, angling his head down to look at my face, his pointed nose almost touching mine. "What is it?"

"Harry… I think he's maybe falling in love."

"Really?" Jase stood taller, so I did too, turning to face him.

"I saw in his thoughts… he… you know, his killing style, even though I've never mentioned to him that I know this, but… he's a lot like you."

"Likes to make them scream, huh?" he said with a nod, casting his eyes out to the lake again.

"Yes. And since he met this girl…"

"So she's human?"

"Yes."

"And he's struggling to kill now?"

I nodded, smiling, because I was really happy for Harry, but I knew the next bit would cut Jason up. Maybe forever. "I just need you to think about that when I tell you the next bit."

Jase looked worried. "He's not in love with Jules, is he?"

"No."

He turned slightly and leaned his elbow on the railing, reaching across to rub my arm. "It's okay, Ara. You can tell me."

My throat made a crass sound as I swallowed. "Aubrey… she brought someone back."

Jason stiffened then, turning instantly to face the lake and bury his head against his arms on the cold paint-chipped bar. I knew he caught the thought, but I had to say it aloud anyway.

"Rochelle."

He coughed out then and leaned deep down into his hands for a moment before jerking back, shaking his head as he walked away and sat on the bench just behind us. The sun hovered overhead with a heat that wouldn't let up, and though I was Lilithian and had every reason to be sweating, Jason didn't. Which is why I covered my mouth, crying into my hand a little when I saw the beads of moisture across his vampire brow.

"The baby?" he asked, as though he was afraid of the answer. "I mean, I think I saw that—in your thoughts, but…"

"I'm sorry," I said, sitting down beside him, "the baby didn't come through."

Jase cried harder then, losing that baby all over again and spiraling back down into the heavy weeks that had passed since he and Jules lost theirs. It wasn't fair. I just wanted to absorb him into me and make him okay again, as if his soul couldn't be right until it'd touched mine. And that probably was the case—in the same way that passionate sex, connecting, always helped when David was hurting—but I couldn't ease Jase's pain that way.

He turned his knees and put his hand on my shoulder. "I'm okay, Ara."

"I'm so sorry, Jase." I wiped my cheeks, reaching over then to dry his sweat away with my hands. "I can't even imagine how this must feel—"

"I had so many instant thoughts, I couldn't even begin to say which one was my first." He sat back, running both hands over his sunlit dark hair. "I want to see her. I want to tell her I'm sorry. And yet so much time has passed for me that I don't feel like those words, those feelings, have a place anymore."

"So you don't still want her?"

He laughed to himself, wiping his chin dry on the back of his wrist. "No. And I know that was a big concern for you—that it would cause a rift between me and Harry—but even if I feel anything when I see her again, Rochelle needs to be ancient history, Ara."

"Why?"

"For one, Harry likes her—has probably slept with her, if I know my nephew."

My lashes widened and I pressed my lips together to indicate the truth. Jase groaned, closing his eyes slowly until he finished lamenting.

"Also, it could never work out with her," he said. "Look what's happened. Look what happened to Jules. The baby. Every time I try to go against Nature and be happy, terrible things happen. I will never again try to love someone, Ara, because it'll end in misery."

"You don't know that for sure."

"What's the definition of insanity?"

"You're a scientist, Jase. You don't believe that. Trying things over and over and expecting different results is what you do."

"With variations, Ara—"

"And Jules is a variation—"

"She's not. She's a future, a wife, kids, all packaged up in a different woman. Same results. I'll never trust that things can work out. Ever again." He rubbed his chin, shaking his head. "This is insane, you know that, right—Rochelle being alive?"

I nodded, sitting back and casting my eyes out ahead of me. "Jules knows."

Jase nodded too, accepting whatever ramifications would come from that. "Just one more reason for her to leave, I guess."

"Do you want her to leave?"

"I want her to be happy. And I can't make her happy. I'm too damaged. I thought I could but…" He tried to smile but he was in too much pain. "I need to be happy first, and that will never happen while the universe keeps fucking things up for me."

"I'm sorry." I put my hand on his, wishing I could make it all better.

"And you…" He seemed to hesitate, focusing on my touch. "My first concern, right now… with this news of Rochelle, is that…" His voice quivered, and he looked right into me with those soulful green eyes. "I tortured you. I hurt you because of what happened to her, and now she's here, alive, as if I did all of that for nothing."

What could I say to that? He still carried so much guilt for what he did, even though none of it was his fault; even though Greg Thompson planted the idea for him to get revenge, which eventually led to him kidnapping and hurting me. Looking at him now, he wasn't the formidable king he'd become; the untouchable, unquestionable man who ran an order and a family. He was that scared kid who'd broken something precious and didn't know how to take it back.

I bit my lip, and just nodded instead. "Yeah. That sucks."

Jase laughed, coming back down from the proverbial ledge. "Does it make you hate me now?"

This time, I laughed. "Am I even capable of hating you, do you think?" I asked, genuinely curious.

With a long exhale, he moved his eyes back out to the birds in the water. "So, I take it Harry knows who she is."

"He does. Now. He didn't know until David and I walked in there an hour ago and dropped that bomb."

Jason nodded, clearly having seen it all in my thoughts just then as I recalled it. "If only we'd known back then what we know now."

"You might not have tortured me."

He smiled to himself, but it slipped off his face a second later. "I'm afraid to see her."

"You don't have to."

"I don't think I can stop myself though," he said. "She was the love of my life—the girl I compared all others to."

"Then go see her."

He sat quietly for almost five full minutes then, and when he spoke again, he needed a long, deep breath first. "What did my brother say?"

"He said the same things as you, really. He's actually annoyed, because all this was put to rest, and now it's dredged up the emotions and the drama again."

Jason nodded, laughing derisively, as though he completely understood that sentiment.

"And he's kind of angry that he has to apologize to her. You know…" I hesitated, searching for words. Because David was just so honest about this. Anyone would expect him to feel remorse and be begging Rochelle's forgiveness, but he didn't need it. Not David. He didn't even want it because he wasn't that kind of man. He felt bad for killing her because Jason had loved her. But she really was just a human who was breaking vampire law when he did that. "He feels sorry," I went on, hoping Jase understood. "He *is* sorry. But he hates that he's got to be the bad guy again when this was all put behind him."

"I understand that, believe it or not."

I nodded. "He doesn't want to deal with it. He doesn't want to look at her or talk to her. And the fact that Harry likes her complicates things."

"Why?"

"What if she becomes our daughter-in-law?"

Jase laughed, hanging his head for a moment. "This family is really fucked up."

I laughed too. "I know."

The energy changed then. It was like discussing a lack of funds and then suddenly deciding to talk about food for a party. I went with it, understanding that Jase had said all he wanted to say on that matter for now.

"Ah, so… what do you think the chances are that Elora will let me stay with them for a bit?" he asked.

"She wouldn't mind. Why?"

"Jules needs space." He faced the front again, rubbing the

heels of his palms along the tops of his blue jeans. "She can't have me there—with Danny. It's too much. But she has nowhere else to go. Jo's trying to finish college and there's nothing left there for Jules now. Nothing but reminders of everything she lost, everything she was."

"You don't think she'll go back to the theatre?"

"No. She fulfilled that dream and I think it was enough for her," he explained, his voice deep and soft, and almost out of place here by the hot lakeside. "She needs to stay here, and I think it may be permanent, which means I need to move on."

"You can stay with us," I offered. "You know David wouldn't have it any other way."

"I don't think that's right," he said. "Danny's my son, and he's also David's. It's too conflicting having two fathers, with opposing values, under the one roof. Trust me, I know from experience—from when Lily married Beth's father."

I nodded, wishing I could've been there for Jase in that entire year of emotional torture he had to endure. Lily didn't tell anyone else that the children weren't Jason's, but when she took Beth's real father as a second husband, I know it made Jason feel like he was an unwelcome third wheel in everyone's lives. And thinking back on it all, I just wanted to hug him. He'd had a shit life. It wasn't fair.

"You're right," he said, taking my thought and a deep breath. "But, you know what?"

"What?"

"It's my life now. I'm free of Lily after nearly twenty years. I just… Jules and I came back here for a holiday," he said. "We needed a break, and it was always the intention to go back to New York. But…"

"But?"

"She's staying. And I'm staying too. I can't leave Danny. I

won't."

"So, what are you saying?"

"I'm going out to buy a house." He nodded, drumming his palms on his thighs once. "Today. Is Falcon's old house still up for sale?"

"Yes, it is," I said excitedly.

"Come on then." He jerked his head toward land. "Let's go call him. I'm gonna buy it."

DAVID WALKED OVER WITH TWO CUPS FROM HUDSON'S Coffee Shop and handed one to me, smiling into his own as our daughter jabbed him with a hateful glare. He was trying to take it lightly that she hated us right now, but he was cut deeply. Something she'd said to him the other day had stayed with him, and he wasn't the same since then.

"You know, you don't have to stay here," she snapped. "I can wait for the damn plane on my own."

"We have to sign off the flight," David informed. "You're not eighteen yet and you need an adult to authorize a private charter—"

"Uncle Jason offered to bring me—"

"Uncle Jason is not your father," David snapped gruffly.

Aubrey folded her arms, jaw tight. "He was a better father to me than you ever were."

"Aubrey," I started, but David shook his head.

"Say what you like, Aubrey. You're just showing your maturity—"

"No I'm not. I'm trying to make you see that I don't need you. I don't want you here. You're both sending me off to live in an ugly old castle for the rest of my childhood, so clearly, I don't need parents anymore and I don't need you to sign off the private charter either. I can do that myself. And if you don't want me to, then you should have sent Uncle Jason, or Uncle Mike. They've both been around a lot more than you ever have, and since Uncle Jase was missing for the last three years," she said sassily, folding her arms in and jutting her chin out slightly, "I think that's a statement in and of itself."

David rarely showed emotion around the kids, especially not that kind of emotion. He looked down over the fold of our daughter's arms to her cold, hate-filled glare, and nodded, backing away.

He didn't reprimand her, he didn't hide the break in his heart, he just walked away.

My entire chest swelled with despair for him. Not because he was hurt by her anger, but because he realized she meant what she said. He realized there was validity to her statement. He had worked all the time over the last three years. He'd been busier with cases than he ever had before, taking on difficult clients whose cases took years to resolve. He hadn't been there, and he hadn't listened when I'd begged him to see that Aubrey was distancing herself, and now he regretted it. Our little girl was being sent away for her own good, and she was leaving without any love in her heart for us.

She turned her hate on me next, but I had thicker armor than David. I straightened my shoulders and took a subtle step inward, daring her to test me. "How could you do that to your own father?"

"How do I even know he's my father?" she snapped. "For all I know, you probably fucked Uncle Jason when I was conceived, or Uncle Mike—" Her words ended short as I used the energy around us to mute her voice. With wide eyes, both hands came up to her throat and she gawked at me, shocked.

"This is the point where any other parent would slap you across your face, Aubrey. You are way out of line and I will not tolerate it. Do I make myself clear?"

She nodded, but I could see her hatred for me was only growing. I released her voice and she cleared her throat, rubbing under her chin.

Both of us looked over then as the pilot approached David with an iPad and the pencil, and he signed off the flight for our daughter. From here, she'd follow him out to the private jet and arrive at Elysium in the capable hands of my father and, later this week, Morgana. We didn't know how long she'd been gone, or if there was anything either Drake or my sister could do to help, so it left me feeling raw and bloody in my chest when Aubrey bent down, hoisted up her bag, and pushed past me to follow the pilot without saying goodbye.

I looked over at David, and he just lowered his head, his shoulders sinking.

"Aubrey?" I called, determined not to let this end on such a bad note.

She spun around, her auburn hair flicking with the motion. "What?"

"I love you," I said, even if she didn't want to hear it. "And Dad loves you too."

Her lip lifted in disgust, eyes moving on to him. "He knows what I think of *him*," she said, and walked away.

David's lips parted and his eyes closed, the energy radiating off him like flesh cut with glass. I moved over and put my hand to his arm.

"What did she say to you that day?"

"It doesn't matter," he said, turning away. "She's right. About all of it."

AUBREY

I'd been to the castle twice in my lifetime. It was the main home of the Drakarian king—my grandfather—who now reigned as overlord to all vampires, Lilithians, and witches who chose to belong under the protection of his Set.

At home, when he'd come for Christmas or to spend some time with family, he was warm and kind, very human, but when I'd seen him in this castle, he was a very different man. He had to be. I knew that. But I wasn't really looking forward to spending an undesignated amount of time with him—away from my friends.

On the bright side, maybe I'd have a half a chance in hell of seeing my cousin Beth here. Ever since Lily tried to kill Aunt Jules, our families had been estranged, and it killed me not to see Beth anymore. When it all went down, my two biggest concerns were Beth and Uncle Jase. She was like my sister, and he was like the dad that mine hadn't been—warm and loving and playful. I missed Beth like crazy, and I really hoped she'd come to see me here.

My grandfather met me at the giant creaky doors to the castle and watched on as I walked the ten wide stone steps to the entrance, hauling my suitcase along beside me.

"Seventeen years you've been a member of this immortal world," he said firmly as I stopped in front of him, his sky-blue eyes icy. "Seventeen years, you have known that even if you do not understand our reasons, our ways, you must follow our rules."

I looked him firmly in the eye, jaw in a determined set. "Your rules don't know me, or what I'm capable of."

"Murder, it seems—of an innocent human boy."

"It wasn't murder. If anything, it was manslaughter."

"A crime that would see you imprisoned in the human world and, for that matter, in ours. Alas"—he turned away—"you are royal, and therefore, are offered, at our discretion, certain allowances, which should not be abused."

"I didn't abuse those allowances," I demanded, following him into the cold, murky castle. "I have a right to understand my abilities, Drake—"

"King Drake." He wheeled around, invoking the mighty vampire within, but I did not flinch of falter. "While you are under my roof, you will address me with respect."

"I'm here by force. And I don't respect people who treat me unfairly."

"Unfairly?" He moved a little closer, sort of floating like he didn't have feet beneath his ridiculous cloak, and towered over me. "And how is it that you are being treated unfairly?"

"Shipped off here for the simple crime of practicing my abilities against my parents' wishes?" I put my bag down. "How is that *not* unfair?"

"Did you or did you not kill someone as a result of going against your parents' wishes?"

"I killed someone as a result of not understanding these powers yet—something that might not have happened if they'd helped me!" I stood straight when I realized I was leaning in. "My brother's just as guilty as I am, but they didn't even lecture him."

"Harry is a man of his word. A good man. He does not do stupid things, and your parents know that. They would have no need to lecture him for helping you, when you admitted to blackmailing him." Drake walked away again. "You have a string of offenses ten pages long, Aubrey Knight, and if you're not careful, you will find yourself down a path that will be very hard to come back from."

"What path?" I spat haughtily, challenging him to support his own melodramatic claim.

"Darkness, my dear. Great, miserable darkness."

I dragged my eyes upward in a slow, agitated roll, following him up an ugly gothic staircase, being stared down by silver armor and ancient weapons on the walls. When we reached a big wooden door, set deeply into the gray stone, Drake stopped me and placed a heavy brass key in my hand.

"You are headstrong, like your mother," he said, which I knew was his deranged version of a white flag.

"I'm nothing like her," I snapped, burning his flag. "She's weak and old and tired, and lives in the permanent shadow of my dad's desires—even if that desire is to hurt her. And right now, I hate her."

Drake smiled, but it wasn't a happy kind. "And yet, you are more like her than you will ever realize. But while you have her gumption and determination, you have none of her empathy, compassion, light. And yet you have all of your father's darkness." He pinched my chin, angling my head up until I shoved his hand away. "There is danger in you, my girl, and you can hate your mother until your dying day for sending you to me, but it is that decision which has probably saved you from a life of shadows."

One of my eyes narrowed, my lip lifting with the deepest, most heinous expression of detest. "Are you always so dramatic?"

"Only on Saturdays and Thursdays, especially over summer," he said, sweeping away.

"What the hell is that supposed to mean?"

"Theatre, my dear. Theatre."

His shadow bent around the corner up ahead and his footfalls faded beyond that. I stood looking at the behemoth key, then at the door. This wasn't the nursery room I'd stayed in with Harry and Evie when we were younger. This room seemed cold and there was no light coming from under the door. Given the eerie appeal of this castle, it really wouldn't surprise me if this were a cell.

It took some jiggling of the lock, but the door eventually gave way, creaking slowly open and exhaling a breath of musty air into my face to greet me. I coughed, waving a hand as I entered and went straight across the room to push the curtains apart. Light meandered in cautiously, as though it hadn't done in twenty years, illuminating all the dust and cobwebs. There was no light switch, that I could see, and the bed clearly wasn't made up fresh. Whoever had lived here before hadn't left the room; they'd abandoned it.

Above me, a round iron sconce clutched at half-melted candles, and a giant stone wall opened out around a rectangle where a fire could be lit. There was a heavy box at the foot of the four-poster bed—probably the original bed from when the castle was built—and a door near the fireplace that was hopefully a bathroom.

I dumped my bag and sat down in the leather armchair,

facing the stone hearth. They sent me here to learn about my abilities, with the help of Drake and my Aunt Morgana, but I'd make them pay for sending me away. My words hadn't done anything to wound them at the airport. It was like they didn't even care if I hated them. So, I'd do the worst thing Mom could imagine: find a vampire, drink his blood, and become immortal. Then, I could live at Loslilian University—on my own terms—and I'd never have to speak to any of them ever again; never have to be under their control.

THIS BIG OLD BED WAS BROWN AND UGLY, BUT UP CLOSE, lying on my back and looking up at the headboard, it actually had very intricate details carved into it. Yeah, the super-gothic-medieval style was bulky and hideous, but at least it was well-crafted. Having such an ancient father had given me an appreciation for the way things were made in the past, and for some reason, this bed made me think of him—made me think about the things I'd said to him. I still felt the thumping beat of justification pumping blood through my veins and, if anything, spending the entire day cleaning and dusting my room, with all that time to think, had only cemented that. I was right to stand up for my mom when I yelled at him for hitting her. I was right to hate him if she couldn't do it herself, and my only hope now was that I'd hurt him deeply and that maybe, just maybe, he might find some cause to change from it.

Mom, on the other hand, didn't deserve the way I treated her at the airport, and I did feel awful. Like, it actually hurt in my chest when I thought about the look on her face. I was just so mad at her for sending me away. It was like she just didn't care about me anymore, all because I dared to speak up to my father.

I sat up then and spent the next few hours of my day looking out the window at the beautiful castle gardens, sprawling like widespread arms with lush grass and leafy autumn trees. There were sheep out there, and a giant wall that you could only see between gaps in the trees, shutting us away from the modern world. When that got boring, I paced the room, carefully eyeing the painting on the wall. It was a house with a white picket fence, and it wasn't until I randomly looked down at the artist's signature that I realized it was one of my Uncle Jason's paintings. He and Uncle Cal were infuriatingly good at stuff like that, and it made me wish I'd let Cal teach me to paint when he offered once.

I sat on the bed again, facing the painting, and thought about Jason for a while. I felt bad that I'd brought back his dead girlfriend—the one Dad had killed—and I wondered if that would create a rift between him and Aunt Jules, or if enough time had passed now that he could let Rochelle go. And I wondered if Harry and Uncle Jason might fight now because Harry was walking around with Jason's leftovers on his arm… and in his bed. Gross. But, because of how much I loved my uncle, I just couldn't side with anyone else on this. If Jason wanted Harry to break up with Rochelle, I'd support that. And if he wanted to dump Jules and run away with the dead girl, I'd be totally cool with that too. I caused all of this, and though I didn't feel bad for bringing a ghost back, I did feel bad that it was his ghost. He was honestly the last person in this entire world that I'd want to hurt.

My phone buzzed then, so I rolled across the bed and grabbed it off the nightstand. When I accepted the call, Mia's face appeared on the screen.

"Hey you," she chimed.

"Hey." I looked at my watch. It was half-past-six in the morning there now. "How's the other side of the world?"

"What are you talking about?" She laughed. "You're the one on the other side of the world."

"Um… Mia… you know what, never mind." I shook my head, trying not to laugh. "So, what've you been up to? I need all the goss. How's John Mayer Junior?"

Her cheeks changed color in a sudden flash of shyness. "He's okay, I guess. Um… so have you seen Morgana yet?"

"Not yet. I only arrived this morning. Been in my room all day, cleaning."

"Seen Lily?"

"No. Why?"

"I heard Dad telling Jules that Lily's at the castle right now—for the summit. He wasn't sure if he should maybe tell your mom."

"We won't cross paths. Drake will see to that. He knows how my mom feels. And if it's the Three World Summit, which"—I looked at the date on my watch—"it is, then Mom knows she's here. She used to attend that herself, remember."

"I guess. I just…"

"What?"

"Beth is there too."

My stomach did a flip. I hadn't seen Beth in four years. Hadn't even spoken to her. I wasn't sure what I'd say now. I mean, so much had happened. Her dad was now the father of my baby brother, and she wasn't at all blood related to him. But we were still cousins, because her mom and my mom were blood descendants, split souls. That had to matter, right?

"I really miss her," I said.

"Me too. If you see her, give her a hug for me."

"I will. Hey, is that Uncle Jase I can hear in the background?"

"Um, yeah, why?"

"What's he doing there so early in the morning? I thought he was moving to Elora's until the sale on his house went through."

"He is. He's just packing and heading over there now. Falcon said he can live in the house now if he wants, but Jason's going to stay with Elora until he finds furniture and gets it all delivered."

"Oh, right." I nodded, biting my lip. "Hey, can you put him on for me?"

"Uh… sure…" She hopped up off her bed and the screen turned pink against her pajamas as she walked down the hall toward Uncle Jase's voice.

"Huh?" I heard him say. "Oh, sure."

He appeared in front of the screen then, his hair a mess and his eyes dark in the shadows of dawn. "Hey you, how's castle life?"

"It sucks." I groaned, rolling up to stand with the painting at my back. "Recognize this?"

His face lit up. "I do. I must have done that painting over a hundred years ago."

"That's so cool," I remarked, shaking my head at just how awesome that truly was. "So… um, I actually wanted to talk to you about something. Are you alone?"

"Uh…" His eyes drifted sideways, and I watched as the den became the corridor and then everything blurred until he closed a door and I saw the bookshelf from the guest room behind him. "I am now, what's up?"

I sighed, sitting down on the bed again. "Uncle Jase… I'm so sorry about Rochelle—"

"Aw, Aubs, don't be. It's okay—"

"No, it's not. I feel really awful. I didn't know who she was, and I know it's caused all this trouble now, and I feel really, *really* bad."

He smiled, his eyes lighting up in the corners. He had this smile that he'd always give my mom, and one that he'd always give Beth, but this was my smile. This was the clear and obvious love he had for my mother shining out in the love he had for me, for her daughter, for a living, breathing part of her. "Thanks, sweet girl. You know that means a lot to me. But I am okay, I want you to know that. This thing with Rochelle is pretty ancient history, and I'm okay with Harry falling for her as well, in case you were worried about that."

"Really?"

"Yes."

"How can you be? It—"

"It was a very long time ago, Aubs. And time changes hearts. It really does." He nodded, his expression soft with both empathy and understanding.

I pouted thoughtfully, accepting that. "Are you okay, like… really? Because I know how much you love Aunt Jules, and—"

"It's going to be a long road ahead." His eyes drifted across the room and his expression changed then, melding away to a soft smile. "Mia wants the phone back."

"Okay, bye. Love you, Uncle Jase."

"Love you too, sweet girl. Be good, okay? And don't backtalk your grandfather." He winked at me. "He's not as tolerant as your own father."

"I'll keep it in mind." I flashed him a grin, kissing the screen then as he handed the phone back to Mia.

"Hey." She carried me away, flicking her hair. "So Dad says I have to get ready for school now and I need my phone to call Tom. He's driving me today."

"Replacing me already?" I muttered sarcastically, looking at my door then as it opened and Drake stood, expectant. "Uh, I gotta go too, Mia. I'll call you tomorrow?"

"Yep. Sounds good. Bye."

I hung up and rolled off the bed to stand.

"You will dine in the Great Hall tonight with our guests, as a representative of the Knight family," Drake said firmly.

"The hell I will." I folded my arms, lifting my chin defiantly. "I—"

"We can do this the easy way, or we can do this the hard way." Drake stepped into my room, his electric eyes shooting warnings into my soul. "Your choice."

I threw my hands up. "Fine. What time?"

"Six. I will have a guard walk you down."

"Do I have to dress up? 'Cause I don't have anything fancy."

Drake's eyes moved across the room to a blank wall. His body followed, and he pushed on it, revealing a hidden door. "This was your mother's room when she stayed with me before Elora was born. And your father's before that."

"For real?" I said, sweeping over to him.

"There should still be some clothes—oh, perhaps not." He shut the wardrobe. "She was pregnant at the time."

"So, what do I wear?"

"I will have something sent up. Be ready on time, or you will be eating your meals in the tombs for the next fortnight. Do I make myself clear?"

"Crystal," I said, saluting him.

He groaned to himself and sauntered away, closing the door. I went for a shower and did my hair while I waited for my clothes to arrive, coming out in a towel when a vampire—a pretty cute one, with dark shaved hair and dark eyes, and the round stockiness you'd see on rugby players—stepped in with a garment bag over his arms and a shoebox on top.

"King Drake sent these up for you," he announced, looking away from my towel-covered body.

"Ta. Just pop it on the bed there." I aimed my finger to it. "Also, I'm parched," I lied. "Mind giving me a few drops of your blood?"

He froze on the spot, jaw dropped, not sure what to say. "You're Lilithian?"

"Yes," I lied, hands on my hips, hair still dripping down my arms a little. "So? Can you spare some blood?"

"Not sure I'm allowed—"

"I say you are, and my farther is the bicentennial ruler—"

"In that case, I am *definitely* not allowed." The vampire laughed, taking a step closer to examine my face, hands in pockets. "Who are you? Are you Beth?"

"No. I'm Aubrey."

He rose from his slight lean inward. "David's daughter?"

"Do you know my dad?"

"Yeah." His mouth split into a super-massive grin. "He turned me—back in the day."

"Cool. What's your name?"

"Nate."

I nodded, moving over to see what my grandfather had sent up for me. It was an emerald green silk dress—perfect for both my milk skin and red hair—and a pair of slinky black heels.

"So… if you're Aubrey, then you're only seventeen, right?"

"Yep."

"How did you end up making the change so young? Your parents—"

"They don't know," I lied. But Nate was too smart for that. He just grinned again, nodding to himself. Clearly, his schoolboy charm and boyish smirk were just a mask that disguised the wiser, bolder vampire beneath.

"You know, if you trick some poor sod into triggering your change, Drake will kill them—just in case you care," he advised.

I didn't, actually. Not really. If they were stupid enough to fall for that, then that was their problem. "If *you* care about some poor sod, then you should give me your blood, because this is happening, and I don't really care who I take down. But you clearly do."

"Well, I don't exactly wanna go down for it either. I'm not even under Drake's reign. I'm under Queen Lilith." He stuffed his hands in his pockets. "I'm guessing I only got sent up here because I can be trusted not to hurt you—or feed you."

"Probably."

Nate folded his arms, leaning on the end post. "Drake clearly knows what a pain in the ass you are."

I smirked. "If he's smart, he does, yeah. So… who do you hate then? Who should I force to feed me?"

"No one, Aubrey." He narrowed one eye at me, raising a brow. "What's this about? Why do you wanna become a vampire now?"

"I wanna leave this place. I'm seventeen now, old enough to be on my own. I'm tired of my parents trying to control me all the time."

"You really should trust them when they say what's best for you," he said softly. "They know shit."

I laughed, leaning on the bed post across from him. "They don't know shit, actually, and if you'd been around them for the last seventeen years, you'd understand that."

"Say no more." He raised both hands and started backing out of the room. "Just… if you're edging to mess up your own life, don't take anyone else down with you."

"I can do what I want."

"Yes, and even that has consequences. Action-reaction, if you get my drift," he said smugly and walked away.

"Could have closed the door on your way out!" I called,

stomping over to slam it. Unlike my dad's Tesla, castle doors made a remarkable and very satisfyingly loud bang when slammed properly. I turned, dusting my hands off, feeling so much better already.

EVEN THOUGH I WAS ONLY SEVENTEEN, I LOOKED OLDER. And in this green dress, fitting me in all the right ways, with my long auburn hair down to my butt, I immediately caught the attention of a much older man when I stepped in to the Great Hall.

My eyes quickly swept away from him to the exposed beams atop the stone walls, and then moved down the long oak table with high-backed chairs, landing, in the end, on my grandfather.

He stood when he saw me and ushered me to his side. Thankfully, he showed me to a seat at least fifteen away from the old guy who was still staring at me, his mouth slightly agape.

The summit, which was held every five years, entitled leaders under the Lilithian and Drakarian rules, as well as coven leaders and the politicians from the human faction, to meet here at Drake's castle and discuss all matters of politics, security, and a whole lot of other boring stuff. But it meant that, even though I was thousands of miles from home, there were a few familiar faces here.

Aunt Lily deliberately avoided my gaze, casting her attention to the person next to her, while Beth kept her eyes on her phone. I looked to the New England High Councilor, Falcon, but, like Blade, who was the New York leader, I knew them by face and name but knew nothing of them personally. Well, I knew that Falcon was once close to my family—before I was born—but he'd never been a part of my life, and yet it was still nice to see someone familiar. They helped warm the ice-cold shoulder Lily was giving me.

Beside Drake, a woman with short dark hair moved her black eyes onto me as I sat, then she smiled sweetly, raising her glass.

My own eyes narrowed, and my head tilted contemplatively to one side. I'd met her once, but even if I hadn't, the resemblance to my mother and to Drake was as plain as the pointed nose on her face. That was Aunt Morgana. Witchy and dark, with a dangerous, mischievous glint in her eye, I knew instantly that we'd get along. It was like I could tell she didn't walk to the same beat as my goody-two-shoes mother, and that made me feel more comfortable already because I didn't feel like she'd judge everything I did.

The woman next to her, with springy red curls and too many freckles, leaned in to say something, and when Morgana nodded, the girl's eyes widened and landed right on me, her mouth forming an open smile.

"Hey you." A very familiar pair of arms came down around my neck then, and Ali's face appeared beside mine, distracting me before Shirley Temple could loop me into an over-eager conversation.

"Hey!" I spun in my seat, hugging her properly. "What are you doing here?"

"I come every year," she said, sitting down beside me. My face lit up and I hugged Quaid as he sat down on my other side. "Quaid's the London leader of the Lilithian Set, remember?"

"Right, yeah, I forgot about that since you guys don't live in London anymore," I mused. In my family, kids were kept pretty distant from the politics of the monarchy, so it never occurred to me that Ali and Quaid would come to this summit.

"And that guy, who hasn't stopped looking at you," Quaid

said, leaning in to keep it between us, "he's the Vampire Set Leader."

"The London one?" I asked, tuning my ear to the noise around the room as the waitstaff began serving dinner.

"Yep. Have you heard of him?"

"I've heard Mom and Dad mention him once or twice," I said. My eyes moved down the table then to look at the older guy, and he quickly averted his, joining a conversation at random. "What's his problem? Did I kick him in a former life or something?"

"You must have," Ali whispered. "Because I have no idea why he's staring at you otherwise. That's not like him at all."

"Then what's the deal?"

"I think he's hot for you," Quaid said, laughing to himself.

"He doesn't strike me as the kind of guy to gawk at a child," Ali stated. "In that vision Drake showed your mom and dad, Elias was this apparently super-honorable man."

"And that makes him impervious to the lure of hot teenage girls?" I snorted.

"You would think." She flicked her blue hair from her face, and it snagged in her nose ring for a second before she discreetly plucked it out, casting her gaze back down the table at Morgana, who had hers squarely fixed on Elias. The man glared back at Aunt Morgana, challenging her stare, and I got the sense that something larger was at play here.

So I looked at Drake to see if he was acting weird, but instead, he was smiling in my direction.

What? I mouthed at him, hands out.

He laughed and nodded down at Elias. The man had gone back to his conversations now and was no longer staring at me, but I figured Drake saw the whole thing.

As we ate, I kept trying to catch Lily's gaze, or even Beth's, but neither of them would look at me, and they both made very deliberate efforts to look away if ever our gazes crossed for a moment. It hurt, and it made me actually want to cry. Which made me want to punch them both. But what did I care? If they wanted to be stupid, then they could be stupid. I didn't need them.

After dinner, people left the table and moved about the room, forming clusters for conversation that didn't appear to discriminate breed or race. Witches talked with vampires; vampires with Lilithians, and even the humans mingled equally, without fear. It was pretty awesome, and it made me think—just a tiny, tiny bit—that my parents had achieved something pretty cool here. I knew a lot about Vampire and Lilithian history but seeing the peace among them, first-hand, really put things into perspective for me. Made me think maybe my dad wasn't such a closed-off prick after all.

Drake glided over to me then and leaned in, a playful grin on his face. "I noticed you turned a few heads when you walked in."

"One in particular," I scoffed, sipping my soda. It was in a wine glass, which made me feel all grown up.

Drake laughed. "Are you offended?"

"Um…" Was I? "No. I just… why was he staring? Did I meet him as a baby or something, or does my dad or my mom know him?"

"They know *of* him. But they're not closely-acquainted," he advised, leaning in with his hands behind his back and a bright, honest smile. "He was staring because you're beautiful, Aubrey. And though that doesn't give a man the right to follow you with his eyes, I know it took a great amount of control for Elias to draw them away." He leaned away again, casting his eyes across the room. "You affected something in him, I would say."

I snorted, feeling a bit awkward and also kind of beautiful.

"Elias is a good friend," Drake explained. "A worthy suitor. After the vision I saw of him, the way he protected your mother, I would not have objections toward this union—"

"Whoa!"

"However," he added, as I freaked out, "I have informed him that you are only seventeen, and he was quite taken aback by that. He has no interest in a child."

"Good."

"Although, I've not known of Elias taking an interest in a woman ever, except for in that vision. So, if you can find it in your heart to, perhaps, establish a friendship with him, I would not frown upon it."

"Um... he's like, thirty. I really don't think we'd have anything in common."

"Aubrey, my dear." Drake laughed loudly. "He is much, much older than thirty."

"How old?" I asked, following him as he walked away.

"He's one of my oldest council leaders. Comparable only to your uncle, Arthur."

"Wow." My eyes popped, moving across the room then to find him. Okay, so in human years, he was too old for me. In vampire years, he was too old for my grandmother. And yet that somehow made him so much more fascinating. "What century was he born in?"

"If you would like to know him, my darling, ask him yourself." He glided away, turning back to throw me a grin, and I smiled into my glass. I wouldn't go talk to him. I wasn't interested at all. I only wanted to know how old he was.

Across the room, I spotted Morgana speaking with Lily—what looked like a heated discussion—so I shifted my eyes along the walls to see if Beth was still here. Maybe if I could get her alone, she might talk to me. But, instead, I found Elias glancing my way again. He smiled at me, so I raised my glass at him, smiling back.

Then I turned away. He was cute, for an old guy. Okay, so he wasn't that old, if I was honest. He was tall—really tall—with neat sandy hair and eyes that stood out, light blue, even from across the room. He wore an expensive dark-blue suit and his shoulders were broad, so he looked like a gladiator at a business meeting, as if he was almost out of place. And yet, beneath all of that, he also looked like a super sweet guy.

Maybe I *would* strike up a friendship. After all, he was a vampire. I could probably trick him, or even seduce him, in to triggering my change.

"Aubrey Knight," trilled a high voice from behind. I turned to see Morgana coming at me with open arms. "I've been trying to get away to come see you all evening."

I put my glass down on a table and hugged her as she hugged me, her silky hair smelling like melon as it brushed my nose. "I'd say it's nice to meet you, but I'm not sure about that yet."

"What do you mean?" She held back a smile.

"Mom says you created me with witchcraft." I got straight to it. "And everything I know about you so far is only bad."

"What do you know?" she asked, folding her arms in as she cocked her head.

"Only what Mia told me. My parents don't tell us anything."

Morgana smiled to herself, looking kind of evil when she did.

"I know you killed my mom so that she'd have me. And you were burned, like she was, and came back without memories too—"

"That's right."

"But you got your memories back?"

"Yes."

My mind flashed back then to when I first saw Morgana—

the day I pulled a thin, olive-skinned woman through the veil at my parents' behest. "And that woman that I brought back, like... five years ago..."

"That was my mother," she said, her eyes shadowing with concern. "I'm surprised you remember. I thought David erased that."

"Erased it?" I frowned at her. "Why would he do that?"

"Because they didn't want you to know anything about me, or my family. Or your own abilities."

"Yeah, well, now they *do* want me to—I mean, to at least learn about how I killed that guy. And they said you and Drake could help me. So." I shrugged, folding my arms after. "When can we get started?"

Morgana looked up then as Shirley Temple bounded over. "Hi!"

"Hi." I tried not to frown and lean back in outrage, but she was way too bouncy and enthusiastic.

"I'm Eva. Lilith's first daughter."

I looked down over her red hair, freckled nose and kind eyes. "My parents told me about you."

"All good, I hope."

"Well, nothing bad, if that counts."

She seemed disappointed. But she perked herself up and elbowed my arm gently, standing beside me to look across the room. "So, Elias Davenport, huh?"

"Not interested."

"He's too old for you. And too important." Morgana steered my shoulders away from him.

"Too important how?"

"He's a World Council Leader. If he's to take an interest in anyone, it should be someone with as high a stand-in as—"

"The princess?" I offered, presenting myself, a little insulted that she was about to say *I* wasn't good enough for him, even though I didn't even want him.

Morgana laughed. "You're not here to fraternize with the opposite sex, Aubrey. You're here to figure out how you killed a boy with one touch. What if that touch can kill a vampire?"

I never thought of that. And now it made sense. Elias was important. If we became friends, and I killed him, it would cause a few big problems in the Set. And probably royally piss off my grandfather.

"So, where do we start?" I asked her. "In figuring my abilities out, that is?"

"Well, I already know a few things that can help. For one, I know that you can see souls that have slipped through fissures in the veil."

"Fissures?"

"There are these tears, like… if the earth and its magic is made up of both dark and light, positive and negative, good and evil, if you will, then when a tragedy occurs—something that goes so far against the laws of nature, like a violent murder, for example—it creates fractures or fissures in the energy that shrouds the mortal realm: the veil. And so—"

"So, the ghosts I see are ones who died tragic deaths?"

"Yes. They're neither a ghost nor the living, because, when they tried to walk through the Rivers of Life, the hold of that tragedy stopped them from passing through, and they got stuck halfway between life and death."

"Which is why that ghost could manipulate things in the living world?"

"Right, because he wasn't quite dead. Wasn't quite in or out of the living world."

"That makes so much sense." I stared off at nothing, realizing my mom was probably right to have sent me here, even if I'd never admit that. "So how come no other ghost has ever done that before?"

"I guess you were just lucky." She shrugged. "But your ability to resurrect isn't what worries me. It's this touch of death."

"Do you think it's a consequence?"

"No," both her and Eva said.

"It's some kind of gift," Morgana added.

"But we don't really know what it is, or why it surfaces," Eva said, "and it's also really weird that your gifts are surfacing before you've been made immortal."

"So you two are working on this together?" I asked, wondering why Eva knew so much.

"Mm-hm." They nodded.

"I was a student of Jason Knight's—your uncle's—for many years," Eva told me. "I'm the science in this team, and Morgana's the magic. Drake can help us too, but he'll be busy with the summit for the first few weeks."

Weeks? Argh. I sighed, shrinking, ready to go home already.

"So, is it true?" Morgana asked. "Is Danny Jason's baby?"

"Where did you hear that?" I looked around for Aunt Lily, not sure if she knew yet.

"She doesn't know," Eva said, turning my attention back to her with a sense of urgency. "And it's probably a good idea if we don't tell her."

"Why?"

"She can be really petty," Eva advised. "Especially when she gets jealous."

I nodded, hugging myself. "So, who told you? Because the only people that know are those involved, and me. And Elora."

"Lily just told me that Jason cheated on her with your mother," Morgana said. "And I put two and two together pretty quickly."

"What? She's spreading lies about my mom!"

"Yes," Morgana said pragmatically. "And there's nothing you can do about it, so don't go storming over there trying to shut it down."

"But—"

"Look, we know she drugged them," Eva said softly. "And—"

"How do you know that?" I asked.

"I'd replicated Morgana's Passion Potion, and there was some missing. So, I figured the only way Jason would do that is if he was drugged. He's just not that kinda guy, you know? I knew him for ten years."

"But other people don't know that," I said, feeling a panicky rise of anxiety. Lily couldn't just walk around spreading bad stories about my mom. I wouldn't let her!

"They don't need to know that," Eva reassured me. "Everyone who knows your mom and dad know that they're an unbreakable force, Aubrey. A love like no one has ever known, and not one person, in their right mind, would ever believe that Ara would cheat on David. Not even with Jason."

I nodded, exhaling the panic, because she was right. My mom wouldn't even leave my dad after he hit her, so there's no way anyone could rightly believe she'd cheat of her own volition. Mom seriously, pathetically and determinedly, loved my dad just way too much. "So what gave it away about the baby being Jason's then?"

"Come on, Aubrey. The two-and-two on this one is as obvious as Lily is bitchy." Morgana tapped her head, and I laughed. "Daniel is the exact age that corresponds with the time when everything went down. I just can't believe Lily hasn't figured it out."

"Guess it's hard since Dad and Uncle Jase are twins."

"Probably. Anyway, you look tired." Morgana turned me

toward the door, glancing over her shoulder as Elias Davenport moved our way. "Go up to bed and I'll come get you in the morning. We can have a chat and see if we can figure out this dangerous ability of yours."

"I'm not ready for bed—"

"Then go for a wander through the castle, but don't be standing here when Elias finishes his walk through the blathering mob of seizers."

My head jerked back in confusion, making my chin double for a moment. "Blathering mob of Caesars—as in the Roman emperors?"

"No, as in seize. To grab."

I glanced at a woman who moved her hand out as Elias passed—plucking, or… seizing him to a stop—so she could blather his ear off, when all he wanted was to get five steps through the crowd without being talked at. He waited politely though, giving no indication that he was desperate to move on, and offered an expression of genuine interest as she droned on. I laughed. "Blathering mob of seizers. That's pretty good."

"Yes, and it's given you the perfect moment to escape. Now get going," Morgana insisted. "If he comes over here, he will charm the pants off you, and I will have to kill him. I won't have my niece ending up with a man who's a few centuries older."

"Why not? My dad was a hundred years older than my mom," I teased.

"Your mom wasn't a baby I once held in my arms, or I might have put a stop to their relationship too. Now go." She gave me a little push.

I laughed. "Okay, night."

"Nice meeting you," Eva called.

I waved back without turning around, and followed my guard up toward my room.

JULES

Mia made a word on the game board that I was certain no dictionary had ever recorded. I smirked at her tiles. "You sure that's a word?"

"Positive." Mia seemed so confident that I considered letting it slide, then thought better of it and grabbed the dictionary. "Ha!" I exclaimed, and she started moving the tiles before I even showed her proof.

"Okay, okay." She got up then and headed into the kitchen. "Want a drink?"

"Please."

"What would you like?"

"That red soda stuff."

"The Bundaberg?"

"Yeah, thanks," I said absently, planning my next word on the board. I felt so comfortable here. I liked this big house, with its homey smell of bread, squishy sofas, and the giant square dining table, made of solid wood, kind of like the foundations of this family—not the greater family, with Ara and Jason and all that—but the family residing within these walls. Mia was a great kid, and she'd been so welcoming of me, even babysitting me, keeping me company when she should have been hanging out with her friends. They'd both gone to such great lengths to make sure I felt at home here and yet, with Jason staying at Elora's now, I felt like maybe it was time for me to leave too.

Mia came back in and placed the drink on a coaster in front of me, scrutinizing my word. When she decided it was acceptable, she sat down, pulling her chair in with her ankles.

"So, how's life now without Aubrey at school?" I probed. I knew this had been a real sore spot for her.

"It's okay." She shrugged shyly, hiding her emotions behind a half smile. "I have JM Junior."

"Who's that?"

"Tom. Aside from the secret nickname of BS—*Bad Smell*—Aubrey always called him John Mayer Junior—"

"Let me guess, because he looks like John Mayer?"

Mia smiled. She was a really simple, really kind girl, with curly blond hair and warm eyes like her dad. I could see why she had so many friends. But none of them would ever measure up to the friendship she had with Aubrey. A sisterly one.

"She'll be back, right? Aubrey?" I asked.

"Yeah, when Aunt Ara cools down, I guess."

"She's just worried," I said, arranging my tiles on the stand. "It's pretty scary that Aubrey killed someone, Mia."

"I know. I mean… I was there. I just…"

"Miss her?"

"Yeah." Mia looked up then as Mike came through the front door, calling out hello.

"We're in here, Dad."

"Hey." He grinned, moving over to kiss her head on his way to the kitchen. "So, Mom called. She wants to know if you can look after Scarlett tonight. Said she'll buy pizza."

Mia's eyes lit up. "Do you think she'll mind if I bring a friend?"

"Is that friend a boy or a girl?" Mike asked, leaning around from the kitchen.

Mia looked guiltily at me, pleading for help.

"It's a boy," I told him, "but it's as platonic as it can be. He looks like John Mayer." Both Mia and I screwed our noses up for good measure.

Mike nodded, falling for it. "That's fine then. Just… stay in the lounge room."

"We will." She grinned, hopping up to start packing the game away.

"I got it," I offered, taking over.

"Thanks." Mia burst from the room and up the stairs, leaving behind an almost awkward silence then as Mike came back in, not realizing she'd left. He stood for a moment, and the silence swelled.

"Hungry?" he said.

"Starving. Want me to cook something?"

"Uh…" He laughed to himself. "Let's keep my kitchen safe for the night, and maybe eat out, since it's just us two."

I nodded. I hadn't been out anywhere since I got here. Not the beach, the supermarket. The only place I'd visited was Ara's house and the lake across the road. I hadn't even seen Mike's cafe. If he was forcing the issue, trying to get me to go out, was this just a step toward asking me to leave? I mean, it was pretty weird me staying here. It was okay while I was with Jason, but… now that we'd broken up, I wasn't Mike's family anymore. I had no place here.

"Um… I…"

"What's wrong?" Mike sat across from me in Mia's chair.

"Should I leave…? I mean…"

"Why would you leave?"

"It's just… I'm not your family, and I'm taking up a room—"

Mike laughed, cutting me off. "Jules, like it or not, you're family. Even if you break up with the person who brought you in to the family. Do you think Em stopped being family just because we divorced?"

"That's different. You were married?"

"The bonds are still there. And it's those bonds that make family, not the promise in ink, kiddo," he explained. "You are welcome here for the rest of your days. After everything this supernatural world has done to your life, you will always have a place here with us."

I hid my smile in the tilt of my head.

"Besides, it's just me and Mia here now," he exclaimed. "This is literally the emptiest this house has ever been. And I've got six vacant bedrooms up there. Seven if you leave, so do me and my house a favor, and just stay. M'kay?"

"Okay." I tried to fight my goofy grin back, but he was just a really nice person and it made me want to laugh. I appreciated that. Because I really had nowhere else to go. "Are you sure I'm not a burden though? I mean, you barely even know me—"

"No living creature can ever be a burden to another," he stated. "I don't know where people get that idea."

My mouth popped a little, a short breath huffing out. "Wow, Mike. You're…" I shook my head, smiling into my lap. "Way too nice."

"I wouldn't say that." He shrugged. "I just have a set of beliefs that differ to the consensus, I guess."

"Differ greatly," I scoffed.

Mike laughed, and it was warm and honest and surprisingly cute. "Come on," he said, standing up. "Leave the game. We'll pack it up later. Let's get you out of the house for a while."

"Yeah." I stood, mentally preparing myself. "Sounds great."

ARA

"So... Drake says Aubrey's settled in well," David said with a giant smirk.

"And what else did he say?" I probed, pushing Danny's stroller up the curb toward the beach. "From the look on your face, I'd say she's giving him hell."

"Yes, but that's not all. He made her attend the summit welcoming dinner."

"So she's seen Falcon then, and Morgana—"

"And someone took an interest in her, before he knew who she was, or how old she was."

"Who?" I asked, on the edge of my proverbial seat. Danny pointed at the playground as we neared it, calling out, "Play. Want play, Mommy."

"Not now, Danny," I said quickly, prompting David to go on.

"Mommy, play," Danny insisted.

"It's home-time, baby." I looked at David. "Who?"

"Davenport."

"What!" I screeched. "Did he know she was our daughter?"

"Not that it would matter, but no. And he doesn't know about the relationship you had in your other life, remember."

I nodded, realizing that. "She's not… Aubrey isn't interested in him, is she?"

David laughed, pushing his hands into his pockets. "From what Drake told me, she was very intimidated and a bit put-off by it. And—"

"Elias knows now, right? He won't go near a child—"

"Do you think he would?"

"For the man I knew in that other life… no, but—"

"It's fine. Stop worrying." David stepped around to the front of the stroller as we stopped, and shushed Daniel, who'd worked himself up over not being allowed to play. "I asked Falcon to hang back for a few days after the summit and make sure she settles in, but he said he'd ask Nate to stay. Apparently, she met him already and they bonded."

"Bonded how?" I asked, leaning on the park bench, while David strapped the wriggling Danny tightly into his seat. We both just tuned the crying and whining out.

"He delivered her dress for Drake, and they chatted for a bit. On her way back to her room that night, Nate passed her in the halls and asked if she wanted to come hang out and play video games."

"That's good." I nodded. "I trust Nate."

"Yeah." David stood with the wriggling Danny in his arms.

"Did you ask Drake to hide your journals and your dead bodies?"

"No. Why?"

"Because he put her in your old room, and our inquisitive, headstrong daughter will find them."

"Don't see what it matters." David showed Danny the big waves and the seagulls, and he stopped whining, pointing things out and talking about them as we carried on our conversation over the noise. "She hates me now anyway."

"She doesn't hate you," I assured him, agreeing with Danny that the bird was 'Laridae' at the same time, whatever that meant.

"You didn't see the way she looked at me, Ara—when she accused me of beating you."

"I'm sorry," I said, because there was nothing else to say. "I'll talk to her—explain about the hex."

David just nodded, which crushed me, because he'd never once agreed to tell anyone about the hex. It meant he was desperate for her to understand. But in telling Aubrey about the hex, it would, consequently, bring the truth to light that we buried all these years. Our closed doors would be thrown wide open and scrutiny would wash in over all that aired laundry. He didn't want to be "that guy". He didn't deserve to be, and yet everyone would look at him that way. It wasn't fair. But it would be worse if they all just believed he was abusive and cruel without reason, when he was so far from that kind of man. My David. My sweet, honorable, law-abiding David now had to face the people he loved and show them the truth, when it wasn't really a truth at all.

"David—"

"Do you trust Morgana with her?" he asked, changing the subject and needing no elaboration about all the reasons we might not trust my sister.

"Drake's going to watch closely."

"So, no… you don't trust her?" He laughed gently.

"I don't think I ever will, rightly so."

David nodded, putting Danny down as he struggled to get

free. He ran straight for the playground and we both rolled our eyes, too tired to argue with a two-year-old right now. "Give him fifteen minutes—"

"But it's past his bed time. And we said no," I advised. "We're just teaching him that no means yes if we let him—"

"He'll be fine. Just give him a quick play. We don't have to get up to take Aubrey to school tomorrow."

"We? You mean *me*, since you have to go to work."

David shook his head. "Nope."

"Nope what?"

"Nope, I'm not going."

"Why?"

"I've given my cases to Cal, Ara. I need some time off. And you need me to take some time off."

"Really?" I said, stars in my eyes, as I looped my arms around his waist.

He rubbed my back, kissing my head with his warm, wet lips. "Yeah. I'm taking a month, and we can reassess after that."

I hugged him a little bit tighter then, having one of those moments where you step back and appreciate everything your life is. And I appreciated him, his love, his warmth, and how much I needed him—that needing him, knowing he could be there to make it all better, would fix everything. Because it always had.

We watched Danny play, walking up the stairs and going down the slide on repeat, until a blonde-haired pair caught both of our attention at the same time, strolling down the sidewalk across the road by the cafes and restaurants.

I was about to suggest flagging them down, until I read Mike's body language. "Uh-oh."

David nodded, catching on. "Shoulders high, hands in pockets. Leaning slightly."

"Big smile."

"It's not unreciprocated," David noted, nodding at Jules.

"Do you think she's rebounding?"

"I think she's clasping for anything to make her want to hold on right now, Ara. I don't think it's necessarily a bad thing, either."

"Do you think Jason will feel that way?"

"Jason wants her to be happy. He knows he can't make her happy, so if another man can, especially if that man is Mike, then I don't think he'd stand in the way of that."

"I guess."

"And it's not like they're gonna get married or anything. I doubt they'll let anyone catch on that there's sparks, if they even figure it out for themselves."

We both laughed.

"It'll probably just be a quick fling—help them both move past their tragic love lives—and that'll be that. None of us will be any the wiser."

I nodded, hugging David a little closer. "Should we warn Jason?"

His hand pressed firmly into my ribcage and he hugged me tight. "I think he's had enough shocking news for one month, my love."

"But it's worse if he finds out—"

"Mike won't allow it to go too far. Not yet. You know him. They're cutesy with each other right now, flirting, but he won't touch her. He's too honorable for that."

"Yeah, I guess."

"Just let it be what it needs to be for now. I really don't think they'll progress things past friends, maybe touchy-feely friends."

I laughed hard. "It sounds so weird when you say touchy-feely. And cutesy, for that matter."

"Why?"

"Because you're so... old-world. It's not right."

David threw his head back, his fangs gleaming in the streetlight as he laughed. "I love that you still love that about me."

"I love everything about you."

"Not everything," he said gravely. "And I know you don't want to keep talking about it—that you hate it when I bring it up—but I can feel it, Ara. I don't think you can take much more."

I sighed. "Look, it might just mean we need some..."

"Time apart," he said regretfully, nodding, because we both knew I was tired and jaded, and I couldn't handle another surge right now. I just couldn't.

"No. Not time apart. But... just... maybe a few more good days than bad ones."

He forced a smile, drawing me close again. "I'm sorry, Ara."

"Me too."

"Do you want *me* to leave for a while?"

"Not yet." I pressed my ear to his empty chest and praised the sound of his working lungs. "Let's just get through this surge and we can talk about it the next time it comes around."

"You always say that." He kissed my head, wiping away the memory of the first cut he'd given me on my cheek, watching it play out as that same cut had been etched in again and again over the years. "It comes around more often than it used to."

Only over the last three years, but I just couldn't say that to him. I cupped his hand, wishing I was brave enough to ask him if he resented me for sleeping with Jason and having his baby—if that was the reason it was worse than ever before—but all I could muster was, "I know."

"If I were any decent kind of a man, I'd leave now—stop putting you through this."

"Let's not talk about it, okay."

"Okay." He nodded, casting his eyes out to sea, while I walked over and watched Daniel on the slide.

JULES

Mike sat down on the bench, with the café strip at our backs and the ocean in front of us. He slurped a melted line of ice-cream from his cone and smiled at me as I sat beside him, doing the same.

Out on the water, orange and yellow lights blinked as the dying day settled into a purple-and-black hue along the horizon and, behind me, couples and families walked along the path that cut through the grassy picnic spots, enjoying the calm evening. I glanced along the sand and noted the space between each settlement of swimmers or sunset-seekers, not sure I'd ever seen a less crowded beach. There was something special about this town, like it was a secret no one else had figured out, and between the amazing Italian food we just had at the local kitchen behind us, and the company of a man who was becoming a good friend, I was starting to fall just a little bit more in love with this place.

"So, you wanna talk about that argument you and Jason had the other day?" Mike asked, his deep, heavy voice taking on a slightly playful lilt. "I don't think I've ever really heard him yell before."

I laughed to myself. "He's usually pretty guarded and steady, isn't he?"

Mike nodded, slurping his ice cream. "So what happened?"

"He's lost hope," I told him, taking a deep breath because it felt like I'd been holding it. "He gave me back his aunt's ring and told me to keep it even though I'm not marrying him."

"Weird."

"Not really," I assured him. "He said he kept it all these years for when he met someone he truly believed in, and now he's pretty certain that *that* life will never happen for him. He wanted me to keep it because it needed a new life—something better than what he can offer it—just like I did."

"So you kept it?" He nodded at my right hand.

"I did, out of respect for him and his long-dead aunt, but you know what it means, right?"

"Nope." His lips turned down in thought and he shrugged.

I shook my head. Typical guys. "He's giving up, Mike. I don't think he intends to stay around much longer."

"As in… death?"

"Maybe."

"Nah." He sat back, tossing a corner of his cone to a nearby seagull, who squawked loud enough that fifty of his friends descended upon us. "He's got Danny. He won't do that."

I sat back too, thinking about that argument and phasing out as I wandered through my own thoughts.

"We had it all figured out," I'd said to Jase that day, sitting down on the lounge, his aunt's ring the center of my focus between my fingertips. "I thought we were so in love and that nothing could break us apart."

"I thought so too." He sat down on the chair across from me, pressing his chin to his hand where he leaned on the armrest.

"You know, when you proposed to me, I actually had this idea in my head that you loved me more than you'd ever loved anyone," I said sadly, thinking back to how naïve and blind I was and how, until yesterday, I'd still been wearing one of the matching woven bracelets Morgana had given us to shield our whereabouts from Lily. Jase took his off weeks ago. That, in my opinion, said it all.

"Jules—" he started.

"No, it's okay. That's what every girl tells herself when she gets engaged. Otherwise, why would you ever say yes. But..." I considered the ring—once a symbol of our future, now, a symbol of starting anew. "For what it's worth, and as corny as this will sound, I think we were to each other exactly what we were meant to be. Nothing more, in the end."

"Meaning?"

"I don't know." I sat back and slipped the ring onto my right index finger. "Maybe we were supposed to learn something important about ourselves, which we did. Both of us. Or maybe I was just meant to meet you so I could become a vampire."

"Maybe. Or maybe we were naturally drawn to each other through the soul connection and weren't actually all that compatible," he advised.

"If we are soul mates, shouldn't that make us instantly compatible?" I challenged.

"Who knows? And who knows if we even are soul mates. It was Morgana who said it—"

"And we don't trust her," I noted.

"No. But even then, from what Ara says, soul mates, or soul connections can result in great friendships just as easily as great love."

"True, I guess." I sighed, regretting all of this as deeply as I regretted nothing. I'd miss Jase. He was an amazing guy and we could have been great together, but the truth of it was, I'd never be the girl he didn't go to the lab for and that, in itself, made me glad I was ending this now.

"What does that mean?" Jason asked, pressing a hand into the arm of his chair to sit taller.

I looked up, caught off guard. "Huh?"

"The girl I wouldn't go to the lab for?" he repeated my thought. "What did you mean?"

"Would you stay out of my head?"

"After you tell me what you meant."

"I meant…" I huffed. What *did* I mean? "When you get an idea or something, some theory you want to test out, you run off to the lab and there's no bringing you back until you've got it all out of your system."

"And?"

"And you'll know when you've found the right girl on the day you decide that you'd rather be with her than your lab."

"I stayed with you after the scar serum cured your scars," he reminded me.

"And you spent all day jotting down notes. You weren't really with me that day, Jase, and you know it."

He smiled, his expression changing as his thoughts went back to that. He knew I was right.

"You know, you promised me," I said, and he looked over at me. "You promised me that Ara didn't even take up half of the space in your heart that she used to."

"She doesn't."

"She does," I said to the ground, cut by the lie in those well-rehearsed and overly-repeated words. Cut, because he believed that lie and he'd never be free of it.

"She really doesn't, Jules. She's not the reason we're breaking up—"

"She's one of them. One of *my* reasons."

He scratched his neck, closing his eyes slowly. "I'm sorry. I'm sorry you see it that way."

"But you don't see it that way?"

"No. I got over her. I will always love her, always wish things had been different—"

"And that's just it." I stood up. "You won't always wish that was the case with me."

He sighed. "Jules—"

"Why did you really give this back to me, Jase?" I asked, holding up my ring finger. "You want it to have a new life, but it can do that when you give it to someone else—"

"Give someone else an engagement ring?" he scoffed. "Jules, that will never happen. That part of my life is over—"

"What part? Trying to be happy?"

Jason just sighed again, leaning forward to press his elbows onto his thighs. "There's no point anymore. I have Danny, and that's what my life has to be about now."

"A kid. You're living for a kid and nothing else?"

He nodded.

"So, what, you're breaking up with me so you can go off and be miserable alone?"

"I'm not breaking up with you. This is mutual—"

"That's not the point. The point is that while a normal person would go off and find someone else to love, you're planning to spend eternity on your own. For what? Some sick, twisted idea that the universe is somehow responsible for all your troubles?"

"Yes." He stood up, his voice pitching with his stance. "Because it's true—"

"Maybe it is, maybe it isn't. But if you want to blame someone then blame someone tangible, Jase! Blame *Ara*." I pointed off at the blank space that symbolically represented her, or her unending presence, the elephant in every room he was in. "Blame Lily, because, so far, they're the only two people that have anything to do with our relationship falling apart."

Jase sighed and sat back down.

"You're so messed up, Jase. And I love you. I always will. But this, right here, this is why I can't be with you. I *won't* be with you." I looked down at him with disdain, cutting the air with the hand of finality. "You need to grow up. You and Ara and that asshat David. You all need to sit down in a room and, I don't know, have a fucking orgy or something and get it out of your system—"

"This isn't about Ara!" He stood up again, his eyes cold and his lips like stone. "This is about Fate, about a plan someone I can't control has in place for me, and the many ways that my life has failed because of that. You don't have to believe in it, Jules. But you don't get to judge me or mock me because of the love I had for Ara. That's not fair."

"What's not fair is that you've given up on living *because* of it, Jason," I countered. "You're actually an amazing guy. Smart. Talented. A fucking great painter, and a clever, compassionate man. Worthy of Ara a hundred times over," I yelled. "But as long as you keep looking in the mirror and seeing a lesser man, your life will always be a mess, because the problem isn't Fate, it isn't Nature or its plan: it's your love for her. It always has been, always will be. It's the elephant in the fucking room."

I snapped out of the memory and looked a Mike, who'd been patiently waiting for my train of thought to end. "We had to fight so hard to move past this Ara thing," I said, swallowing hard. "When Jason and I first started falling in love, she was a pretty evident wedge there right from the start. And it took so much, so many talks and so many promises to convince me that she was out of his heart, but she never was. And even though he will never be with her, she will always be there with him." I pressed my hand to my chest. "In here. I can't compete with that. I don't even want to."

"Ah, yes, the ever-long issue of Ara's unchangeable heart," Mike said with a hard breath, lopping his arm over the back of the seat behind me. "You and I are kindred spirits, my friend."

"What do you mean?"

"I've been down that road before."

"With Jason?"

"With Ara." He laughed, wiping his hand firmly down his jeans to expel the obvious tension. "She left me at the altar."

My jaw dropped and I scuffled forward on the seat, turning to face him. "Seriously? You were going to marry her?"

"I loved her before David ever even came on the scene, so, yeah." He nodded, smiling at a distant memory as though it was the most ludicrous thing. "Once that happened, I'd lost her long before I was even aware of it, and no one has had her heart since."

"Wow." I shuffled down in the seat and put the last of my ice cream cone in my mouth, much to the seagull's disappointment. "Does she have a golden vagina or something?"

"No, it's just circumstantial, really. I loved her because I grew up with her."

"And David?"

"David loves her because she changed him—made him more human."

"And Jason?"

"He probably loves her because she was designed for him."

"So it's eternal, you think?" I asked, realizing this went so much deeper than I ever imagined. "Neither of them, no matter what she does, will ever love anyone else?"

He exhaled through his nose, pressing his lips into a tight line. "If you think about it, with that whole twin-soul-split thing —David and him being one soul that split in two—"

"One with all the good and one with all the light?" I smirked.

"Yeah, but… see, Ara's the same, so—"

"What do you mean?"

"When Lily gave up half of her soul for Ara to live, I think she gave up the good. Or, I don't know, maybe Ara's blood or just her consciousness makes that part of the soul good."

"And Lily's is bad?"

"Wouldn't you think that's the case? Given what she's done to you?"

I nodded, overly accentuating the gesture. "And what does Ara's soul have to do with the twins?"

"I guess those two parts speak to the different parts of the twins in ways that normal girls don't."

"Normal girls?" Both brows moved up on my head.

"Girls who weren't specially designed for them with an evil spell," he noted. "Ara was designed for Jason. Fated to him. And that has to pull at them. It has to," he reasoned. "But if you take the fact that she's inherently good—to her core—then maybe David's darkness calls to that, for balance, and Jason's light is drawn to it."

"But he isn't drawn to Lily's darkness."

"How can he be?" he said. "Something like Jason—someone who's all the light of bloody Man, I doubt he's gonna be drawn to something dark."

"But Ara is. She's light, and yet she's drawn to David."

"She's not all the light of Man," he reminded me.

My jaw came forward in thought, eyes moving along the darkening horizon to the blinking lights of the ships out there. Maybe Jason was right. Maybe this was outside of his control after all. "So he doesn't love her—Jason? He's just drawn to her?"

"No. He loves her. He always has. *And* he's drawn to her. Of course, it helps that she's uniquely beautiful and also one of the sweetest, kindest people I know," Mike added. "That's a pretty likeable combination. Golden vagina aside."

"You wanna go fuck her then?" I joked, laughing.

"Hell no," he said, certain of that. "My days of loving her that way are done. Have been for a long time."

"You think?"

"No. I *know.* Because I don't say that in the way Jason says it —like he's trying to convince himself. That whole three-way dynamic between them is completely fucked-up, like an unsolvable puzzle, where someone just has to be the loser," he said, wiping a hand across his jaw and shaking his head. "I say it more in the capacity of a dog who stuck its snout in an electric fence and just knows now, beyond a shadow of a doubt, not to go near it ever again."

I laughed loudly, feeling a warm pull, a tingle in the air that made me feel like I was sitting a bit closer to him than I actually was. I looked up from his chest into his kind, fall-leaf eyes, and saw the truth there. Solid, dependable, honest Mike. He was the best of this immortal world, and if it weren't for him, I probably would be on a plane right now, heading back to live with Jo. But this beach, that house, Mia, and even Mike, were all reasons I wanted to stay. It's just that his honesty and his friendship made it all feel like home. Made me feel like I could trust this life and fall safely in love with it.

AUBREY

I grabbed the morning paper, sifted through to find the comics, and dumped the rest of it back on the silver tray as I walked into the dining hall. There were only a few people in here this morning, but the table was laid out to feed a hundred, with all manner of yummy breakfast foods to choose from.

Drake looked up as I sat down adjacent to him, and nodded a quick good morning, going back to his conversation with Falcon after.

"That line was broken," Falcon said. "But it's only a rumor at this point."

"What is?" I asked, knowing how much my grandfather hated it when someone entered a conversation uninvited. He didn't scold me though, just groaned to himself, probably logging it as a lesson to teach me later—in private—and sat back, taking his coffee cup with him.

"The Blackwell bloodline," Falcon said. "An old witch bloodline."

"So what's the big deal?" I asked, grabbing some toast.

"They were as powerful as the Blackworth Coven—opposing families, now I think of it," Falcon advised in a teacher-like voice. "But, in fact, they were all the same bloodline. It's just that the Blackwells were from Ireland and the Blackworths migrated to England and changed their name."

"Cool." I started spreading my toast. "So the bloodline survived—in secret?"

"Apparently, since the Blackwell castle in England has been claimed by an heir."

"Is it… do they know what they are, do you think, or was that history lost?" I asked, intrigued by the idea of someone learning that they were a witch later in life.

"That history is deep within the roots of our society," said a bold, very fancy voice. Elias Davenport took a newspaper from the silver tray and entered the room and the conversation, sitting himself beside Falcon. I found myself wishing I'd put on some mascara before I came down, even though I wasn't the tiniest bit interested in this guy. "Anyone who has lived in London in the last two thousand years knows the legends of those witches," Elias finished.

I nodded, biting into my toast.

"Do we believe this person to be a threat?" Drake asked Elias.

"I will look into it when I return to London Castle." Elias gently and gracefully laid his napkin across his lap, quickly looking away from me as though we'd had a dirty night of dark secrets together.

He was in a white button shirt today, the sleeves rolled up, and I'd noticed as he walked in that he was wearing gray slacks and a shiny brown belt and shoes. He had style, this guy. He dressed like my dad, but it looked good on him with that big muscled chest, like a Viking in a suit. I must have been half his size in width and at least two heads shorter, which wasn't common for me. I was taller than my mom, at least a size bigger, and that had always been the case with my friends too. I sort of understood then how Mom could say she felt precious in Dad's arms. I never even wanted to feel that way about anyone. I wanted to feel powerful and strong, like I could hold my own, but I also understood that feeling now because of Elias, and I thought I might like it. Maybe. A little.

When Elias looked up and caught me gawking at him, I blushed. And I only know that because I felt my entire face and cheeks heat up and then rush with cold when I realized what had happened. Drake and Falcon were too invested in their conversation to notice, but Elias did, because his eyes warmed first, then sharpened, and his lips pulled outward into a lovely smile.

He wiped it away then, turning his head to join the Blackwell discussion again as though nothing had happened. Because it hadn't. I wasn't affected by him. At all!

I grabbed an apple and stood up, storming off. There was no way I was gonna come here to learn about my powers and end up falling for a guy that was probably, like, two thousand years older than me instead. Gross!

In a library that looked like every other castle library I'd ever been in, with high walls, old hard books, and deep wooden desks down the middle of the room, I dropped my head onto a smelly old page and sighed. Morgana and Eva couldn't agree on anything. My kill-touch was "The Touch of Death". It was a curse. A gift. A defense mechanism that needed training. A consequence. An inherited skill. They couldn't quite decide what it was, and so they couldn't tell me how to recreate it or prevent it. And nothing, in any of the fifty books I'd flipped through today, could either.

I was tired, I'd missed lunch and afternoon tea, and I had another stupid formal dinner to get through, with the Norse god staring at me, making me think I liked him even though I didn't know anything about him.

"I say we get her to bring a few souls back," Eva said. "Have her touch a human in between each one and see if we can recreate the scenario."

"And make me kill another innocent human?" I said, lifting my head. "Out of the question."

"It might be our only option, Aubrey," Morgana explained. "It could be a lot worse if you killed someone you care about."

For some reason, Elias flashed into my mind. I quickly brushed that aside. "What if it was anger? Or maybe shock?" I suggested. "I was pretty pissed about that ghost forcing me to bring him back—"

Morgana scoffed out a loud, throaty laugh. "Just like your mother," she said. "I bet you hate being told what to do, don't you? Hate being controlled?"

I sat a little taller in my chair, straightening my shoulders.

Morgana just laughed again, slapping the table. "Oh, you are so much like her—"

"I am not!"

"See, that." She pointed at me, and Eva laughed too. "Like a cat in a cage, about to strike a hand."

"I am nothing like her," I demanded, standing up. "She's weak and stupid, and I have way more self-respect than she ever will."

"Good," Morgana said, appearing suddenly behind me with the librarian. She shoved her into me, and as I caught her by the shoulders, Morg and Eva took a breath. I realized instantly what she was doing.

"Oh my god!" I rolled away from the girl, who was lucky to be alive right now, since she was human and very clearly Morgana's test subject! "That was a really shitty thing to do."

"Well, at least now we know it's not triggered by your temper." She wrote something down in her book. "Like your mother's light was."

"More proof that I am nothing like her," I said through my teeth.

"And yet you are," Morg said offhandedly. I just wanted to slap her.

"She lets my dad hit her, did you know that?" I probed, hands on my hips, as the librarian scuffled away, clearly happy to be alive.

Morgana didn't even look up, just kept on writing in that stupid book. "I hexed him," she said simply. "He always will."

"What do you mean?"

"You may have been told that I hexed your father to make him hate Ara, back in the days when she first became queen?" Now, she looked up. "It was a billion years ago, but I did warn her then that it had taken root."

I sat down on the chair, sweeping my skirt under my butt. "So?"

"So, I couldn't clear it all out," she said casually. "He will get surges from time to time, where he hates your mother, and he has to fight them. They strip away the love that makes him a better man, Aubrey, and what you see when he mistreats my sister is the impurity of all Man in one soul, fueled by the hex that makes him justify it to himself."

"So..." I felt a hot, unwelcome rush of liquid in the corners of my eyes. "He'll always abuse her? And she'll always have to accept it?"

"If she loves him enough to stay with him, yeah. But it doesn't happen that often."

"Yes it does," I insisted. "It was happening almost every day when I was at home."

Morgana's eyes darkened and her brow furrowed with concern. "I wonder why."

"Is that bad? Does that mean something's happened?"

"No. It's fine. I'll check in with them, okay? But just so you know, it kills him—David. He's a mess every time he surges. So I hope you didn't say anything nasty to him when you found out."

"They didn't tell me any of that," I mumbled, eyes wide with worry. "I *was* really mean to him."

Morgana shrugged. "He'll get over it."

But he wouldn't. To say that, it just meant she didn't know my dad very well. And then I took a moment to imagine how that must be for Mom. I mean, for me, if I loved someone and yet they were under a curse—something they had no control over—and that meant they hurt me sometimes, I wasn't sure I'd stay. But if I loved them like my mom loves Dad… I wouldn't know what to do.

"It's all right." Morgana patted my shoulder. "Your mom and dad don't live in the misery of the hex, Aubrey. They're happy."

I nodded, trying to believe that.

"Come on." She pulled my arm to make me stand. "That's enough for today. We need to do one more round of healing on that leg, and then we have to get ready for dinner."

I looked down at my leg, glad it was healed enough now to walk on and that I didn't have to wear the boot here to keep up human appearances. Also thinking about the malevolent ghost and wondering where he might be now—hopefully flat on the road where I left him.

Mom and Dad had sent the proverbial dogs after him when they found out, but it was too late. He was long gone. But I just wanted to find him… and kill him for everything he'd cost me.

By the time the dinner bell gonged, calling us to attend, Drake had stocked my wardrobe for me, even left a little note to advise me of the perfect dress to wear for tonight's event.

Dearest Aubrey,

I trust you had an insightful day of education with Morgana and Eva. Tonight, we celebrate the official commencement of the summit, as the leaders of each branch of the Four Cores meet tomorrow to discuss our future. With this in mind, this evening will be slightly more formal, and there will be dancing. So please wear comfortable shoes. May I suggest the cream dress.

Love, Grandfather.

I put the note down with a shiver of dread at the idea of having to dance at this thing, and pushed my secret wardrobe door open. There, on a mannequin in the center of the space, was a shimmering cream ball gown. It was strapless, fitted all the way down the body, aside from a longer tail and a puffier bit about halfway down the skirt, where it flared slightly. There was a fine layer of stiff organza over the top, dotted with what must be thousands of tiny sparkling sequins, making the whole dress look like sun on water.

My eyes widened and I immediately undressed, thinking better of it and opting for a quick shower first. With my hair pulled into a neat roll at the back, showing my neckline, and a few wispy hairs left down, I zipped the dress up, slipped on some silk flats, and left the room, feeling magnificent.

Being sent away really sucked. Missing my friends, even my annoying brother, sucked, but living this life did have its perks, especially not having to attend school anymore. And being given expensive clothes really didn't suck too much either.

When I reached the ballroom, Drake met me at the large open doorway and bent to kiss my cheek. "You look stunning."

"Thanks. I scrub up pretty nice, don't I?" I leaned back and inspected his get-up, nodding with approval. My grandfather scrubbed up all right too. With his thick black hair swept back, revealing more of his face than usual, and a white bow tie and shirt beneath a black coat with tails, he looked more like a hot guy at a party than an ancient and cunning vampire grandfather. "Lookin' good, Gramps," I joked.

He smiled affectionately, balancing my wrist against the top of his arm like we were in some cheesy Jane Austen film. "Shall we go in?"

"Beats standing here all night, I guess."

As we entered, a feeling of space opened up around me, dwarfing us beneath the grandeur of the room. The high white walls gave way to stone pillars that supported an arched ceiling, accents of gold framing the rectangle panels marked out on each wall. Women in cream, white, or gold gowns danced under the warm glow of crystal chandeliers with men in white bowties and black tails, while a gathering of musicians played the strings and piano softly to their steps.

We walked across the room then, well, glided, actually, and I realized only in that moment that dinner was more like hors d'oeuvres and wine, and that the *entire* night would be filled with dancing and socializing. I just wanted to turn around and go to bed now.

Drake swept me into position among the swirling crowd, without even asking if I'd like to dance. I didn't feel awkward or out of place though, like I thought I would. I knew all of these dances, from the years of standing on my dad's toes doing all the steps, so as long as I didn't have to dance with anyone weird or really creepy, it might actually be an okay night.

"Do you like the ballroom?" Drake asked.

My eyes went to the gilded gold mirrors on every wall panel and the giant paintings of naked women with cloths wrapped around them. "It's… um… grand?"

"We finished the renovation last month," he said proudly, eyes following the room as we turned. "Transformed it from something quite medieval to a more Victorian style, like the tea rooms."

I could tell he was proud of it, even though I didn't really care, so I put my best efforts in to sounding genuine. "It's really cool."

"I'm glad you approve." Drake laughed to himself, hopefully knowing I meant well.

When the song ended, he bowed to thank me, and a tall guy with sandy hair and broad shoulders stepped in, his thick hand taking mine before I realized the long warm fingers belonged to Falcon. He smiled down at me as I relinquished my freedom to yet another dance. "You look so much like your mother."

"People keep saying that."

He laughed, his sharp fangs so perfectly white beneath a set of dark but thin lips. "And you sound like her too."

I rolled my eyes. Was there no escape from her? "Well, I'm my own person."

"I don't doubt that." He drew me a little closer then, in an almost protective way, and I looked up at him to see his gaze on Elias across the room. "He's going to ask you to dance. Are you comfortable with that?"

I glanced over my shoulder at him as we passed. He stood by the edge of the dance floor, his two big hands clasped at his front, watching the people swirl past him with interest. His white vest, tie, and shirt was exactly the same as what every other man was wearing here tonight, but, somehow, it's like the suit had been cut just right, just for him, making his shoulders look straight, his legs long, and his chest firm and maybe even smooth beneath all that fabric, like a place to rest my head. "Not really."

"I can speak to Drake—"

"No, it's okay. I'll just dance with him," I insisted, seeing him smile warmly at someone and wave. "Maybe I can step on his toes and show him how annoying I really am."

Falcon laughed, and it was warm and honest, not holding anything back. I decided that I liked his laugh. If I had a friend with a laugh like that, I'd make them laugh all the time just to hear it.

"What?" he said.

"You laugh nice."

He did it again. "I laugh nice, huh?"

"Yeah. Hey"—I folded his hand down a little so I could look at it—"how come you never got married or fell in love?"

"I did." He squeezed my hand a little. "I just fell in love with the wrong person."

"My mom?"

"For one, yeah." He nodded.

"Wasn't that the curse though?"

"Some of it, maybe."

"And the rest?"

"She was just really easy to love."

"So you still love her?"

"I don't think anyone that loved your mom can ever fall out of love with her," he advised.

"So… you're just alone. Forever?"

"I love my job, Aubrey. It's the only other thing that makes me feel complete. I'm happy that way."

"Are you though?" I scrutinized him.

He smiled, with a glint of sincerity in his eyes. And I believed it. "I'm immortal," he said. "I don't doubt that I'll one day find love."

"Or are you holding out for my mom to leave my dad?" I teased. "Like maybe the abuse will get too much, and she'll dump him."

Falcon's eyes darkened and he lowered his head regretfully. "You shouldn't talk about that here—so openly. There are only three people in the world that know about that, and you make four."

"So you're number three?"

"I was her righthand man for a very long time, Aubrey—"

A stiffening ripple of rage rushed through my core. "Then why didn't you do anything to stop it?"

"She didn't want me to know. I tried to acknowledge it once and she shut me down and threatened to transfer me, so I watched carefully, from afar. But it wasn't bad," he advised, and I rolled my eyes. "She told me that you know about it—"

"And wants you to downplay it?"

"No. She wants me to convey to you that she's not *beaten*," he said firmly, with an air of authority, and intense eyes to match, that made me just shut up and listen to him. "David, despite the hex, still has a lot of control, which… if you knew what that hex did to him in the past, then the fact that he's only hit her a handful of times in forty years is actually somewhat of a miracle."

"Do you think she'll leave him?"

He laughed loudly, shaking his head. "No. I once asked Elora to look at all possible outcomes for the future—"

"But she's unreliable. Her visions are garbage—"

"Yes." He laughed, but it was unexpected enough that he had to wipe the corner of his lip on the back of his wrist after. "Which is why she refused. But she did a tarot reading instead and she said there wasn't one conceivable outcome where she left him because of the abuse. So, no. She won't."

I nodded, relieved. The only thing worse than my mom being abused by my dad would, in all honesty, be if she had to live without him. "Elora said she didn't know about the abuse," I said sadly. "When I told her about it, she said she didn't know."

"She didn't. Not about the hex," he advised. "I went to her after your father had given Ara a particularly brutal beating while he was still human—when she didn't have her memories."

"What happened?"

"He went psychotic. Tried to beat the old version of her to the surface. So I asked Elora if Ara would leave him because of that—when she got her memories back."

Oh boy. His intentions in that act were written all over his cute face. "Is that because you wanted to swoop in?"

"Yes."

I nodded, grateful for his honesty. "So what do we do?"

"We help them. We talk to Mike so he can step in if David's having a surge. He can protect them both."

"So you're not just waiting on the sidelines anymore, hoping she'll leave him?"

"Aubrey, she would never be okay if she left him. She can handle this, handle the hex, the surge, but she can't handle life without him." Falcon lifted his chin and stood taller, looking dead ahead. "And I would be wasting my time hoping for it."

"Wow." I snorted, seeing how deeply in love he was with her that, even though he knew that, he *was* still waiting for her, deny it as he might. "She really messed you up good, didn't she?"

He laughed again, slowing our steps as the song ended. "I'm sure you'll do the same." He nodded in the direction of Elias, headed this way. "I think it's in your blood."

I grimaced, trying to prepare myself and plan out some ways I'd show Elias that I wasn't anything he wanted to waste his time on. I could be annoying. Bratty. Bitchy. I'd show him all my worst qualities in the short three minutes he'd have me in his arms, and by the end of the song, he'd be convinced I was just a pain in the ass. I even started mustering up a big, obnoxious burp to let out.

He and Falcon exchanged a polite bow, and Elias turned to me.

"May I?" he asked, offering his hand. I was shocked a bit by his accent then. I'd forgotten about it since breakfast, and as I laid my hand in his, a small shiver of something oddly warm went through me from the place where we touched. Elias looked down at our hands, spreading his fingers as it sparked in him too, and we closed them together in a non-traditional way, interlaced.

When I stepped into his arms and the music began, we didn't move in time. Each step we took ended for a moment, a breath, as Elias seemed to read and pause, unsure what it meant, unsure what to do next. After a moment, he found the rhythm, brushing off whatever it was that confused him a moment ago, and we glided around in time with the music, like the rest of the guests.

"I feel I must apologize," Elias said softly.

"What for?" I asked, too afraid to look up and meet those

pretty blue eyes because, suddenly, I couldn't remember all the snarky things I had planned to turn him against me.

"I've made you uncomfortable—with my staring."

I smiled to myself, letting out a small chuckle. "I'm just not to use to it. I thought maybe I had something on my face."

"If that were the case, I would not have stared. I'd have"—he removed his hand from the small of my back and dipped his head sheepishly, scratching at a spot on his cheek as if to indicate something on mine.

I nodded, looking away again with a smile that I didn't even need to force.

"Please understand, it is not my intention to make you uncomfortable, nor is it my intention to court you, being so young," he advised. "I wasn't aware of your age when I first saw you but…"

"But?" I prompted.

"I am not too man to admit that… I was *struck* by you, Aubrey. And I cannot rightly say that has ever happened to me before."

Okay, that was kind of lame but also kind of sweet, because I knew he actually meant it. And suddenly, the idea of a millennial-old vampire didn't seem so bad. He was at least way more mature than the boys at school. And for some reason, I actually couldn't find it in my heart to be mean to Elias. It normally came easy for me. I didn't care if I hurt their feelings, as long as it deflected the attention off the fact that I liked them. But… this guy, I couldn't even make myself step on his toes.

"Drake tells me you have a rare skill," Elias offered.

"He told you about that?" I rolled my head up to look at him, instantly regretting it as the kindness in his eyes struck me, changing my opinion of him entirely. "That's my family's best-kept secret."

"I believe he told me as a warning," he said, smiling to himself. "I have a… let us say, deep aversion to the spirit form, and I assume he meant for me to run the other way, so to speak."

I laughed up a crass grumble of mockery in the back of my throat. "You're afraid of ghosts?"

"Deathly."

I laughed again. Boy, he picked the wrong person to hang around then. "Well, you should be. The ghosts I've met can hurt you."

"One hurt you?"

"He broke my leg." I nodded.

Elias's eyes went down my body, coming back up in surprise. "Do you have a manor with which to defend yourself?"

"Nope." I shrugged. "That's kinda why I'm here. Aunt Morgana is helping me find a way to defend myself and also…" I didn't want to tell him the next bit.

"A cure for the touch of death," he said with a nod.

"So Drake told you that too, huh?"

"He did." His hand very gently squeezed mine, as if maybe to test out the cursed touch or maybe, just maybe, to comfort me because of it. "I'm sorry, that must have been quite an ordeal."

Right there, in the middle of the dance floor, in a stranger's arms, I almost cried. There were just so many layers of understanding in his voice that I felt like he knew exactly how much that hurt me. "It was."

He sighed, and his hands came down from mine, pressing instead to the back of my head and my shoulder to hold me close to him. It felt weird, because it was like a hug, but I didn't know him at all. And yet, at the same time, as the music surrounded us and filled in the blank spaces through every corner of my soul, I felt okay with it. It was even kind of nice.

"Does it fill you up with guilt—this death?" Elias asked

softly, as though his voice might break through his chest and bust my ear if he spoke too loudly.

"Not like it should."

"In what way then?" He drew back, looking down at me.

Good question. The truth was, it filled me with exactly the kind of guilt that it should, yet I couldn't admit that. It would make me feel weak and vulnerable to tell him that I cried at night because Sawyer would never graduate, or have kids, or buy a house. He'd never do any of those things, and that was my fault.

"I was on a date with him when he died," I confessed, ignoring the stares of everyone nearby who was unimpressed about us just standing here in the middle of the dance floor. But they all blended away as a wash of sympathy softened Elias's eyes.

"And you were punished?" he asked.

"Sent away." I motioned around the room, giving a nonchalant shrug to hide the devastating sense of betrayal and sadness.

"I can see you cared for this boy," he offered with an empathetic tilt of his head. "I am sorry for your loss, Aubrey. If it is, at all, any consolation, I do understand completely how you feel."

"You do?"

We started dancing again as another song began and a few old men moved past us, clearing their throats suggestively.

"I became close with a woman once, and I killed her."

"Why?"

"I'm a vampire," he said simply. "I hadn't intended to kill her, but these things happen, and the guilt I suffered for that was immense."

I nodded, burying my own guilt a little bit deeper.

"You're not alone," he offered. "Almost every person in this room has killed someone they cared for, and we all feel guilt and shame. But please do not feel like a monster for that, Aubrey.

Because if you are, indeed, a monster, then you are in the company of many more just like you."

I felt warm all over my entire body then. That did make me feel better. A lot better. I hugged him again, just wanting to relive the way his big hard chest and strong arms made me feel a moment ago. "Thanks, Elias."

"You are most welcome." He drew a long breath and let it out slowly, his deep voice coming through his chest with the sound. "May I call on you in a year? Perhaps court you then?"

The teenage girl in me, who'd literally just left the modern world of high school and picking on boys all the time, wanted to laugh. She wanted to say no and tell him to go gain a few modern phrases and come back down to earth. But I couldn't say it.

I didn't mean for this, to feel like I was falling for him when I didn't even know his middle name. But something about dancing with him like this… it felt like I was falling *in* to him, like being breathed in, absorbed. And I'd never felt like that before.

What was it about this guy, no… this *man* that could make me feel this way?

"Um… yeah," I said instead, smiling to myself. "If you're still interested then."

The music stopped, and Elias stepped back, standing so tall and straight that it looked like he couldn't breathe. His eyes searched mine, fixing there for a moment, a thousand words exchanging between us without a thing being said. I knew he'd come to find me in a year. I knew he'd seen something in my eyes that he couldn't explain, and I knew that, because I'd seen it in his too.

He didn't say a word after that. He just bowed, his hand across his midsection, and left the room, grabbing a bottle of wine off a silver tray on the way out. And I stood in the middle of the dance floor, stunned into speechlessness, until I felt a pair of eyes on me.

"Beth," I called, darting after her. "Beth, wait."

Aunt Lily cut in front of me then, barring me from going any further. "Do not speak to my daughter," she warned.

"Please, Aunt Lily—"

"And do not address me as such. I am your queen, and you will respect me with my proper title."

"But—"

"Go." She aimed a finger across the room like I was a naughty puppy. "If you try to speak to her again, I will have you whipped."

My face tightened with rage. "And to think, everyone once thought you were so kind."

She didn't say anything as I walked away, and I refused to let it get to me. I'd speak to Beth if I damn-well wanted to, and nothing Lily said would stop me.

For breakfast the next morning, I actually put some effort into my appearance, knowing Elias would be down there. I sat at the table, eating fruit, but the only other person in here was Nate. He picked up his plate and walked the length of the table, coming to sit across from me where Elias had been yesterday.

"Where is everyone?" I asked, checking my watch. I wasn't early.

"The summit. Meetings began today."

A rolling wave of disappointment pushed over me. "Oh."

"Hoping to catch Elias, huh?" He winked at me.

"He's… kind of growing on me."

Nate's easy smile beamed. "I'm attending the weapons lecture this afternoon. I could slip him a message if you want."

"Nah." I grabbed my coffee and leaned back comfortably in my chair. "It's not like that. I kinda just wanted to chat casually with him over toast. I don't really wanna sneak around or whisper in corners just yet."

"Got it." Nate laughed. As he sipped his coffee and his eyes flicked absently across the room, they suddenly burst wide and he coughed the brown liquid out into his cup.

"What's wrong?" I asked.

He nodded to the giant entry doors, and my gaze followed. I could smell his cologne then as he entered the room—all fresh and showered, looking like a million dollars—a newspaper tucked under his arm.

"I thought you said he was at the meetings," I whispered through my teeth, shrinking down in my chair.

"He was. Maybe he got hungry, I dunno."

"Vampires don't get hungry," I pointed out.

Nate shushed me and smiled at Elias as he approached.

"Morning," Elias said.

"Morning." I glanced up at him, hoping he didn't sit beside me. He did.

I stared forward, catching Nate's gaze with a tiny hint of horror in mine, wondering if I had morning breath.

"Catch you later for a game of chess?" Nate said, standing up.

I tried to signal him not to leave, but I felt like Elias would see. "Um. Sure," I said instead. "Later."

Beside me, Elias opened his paper and shielded me comfortably from view. He leaned back and propped his long, outstretched legs on the support bar beneath the table, making no effort to talk. I felt like I couldn't even chew my food because it'd force an awkward bend into the silence between us.

We were the only two people left in the room, and I could suddenly hear my own heart beating, hear my stomach protesting everything I just ate, so it was a safe bet he could hear it too. And the nerves mixed with the undigested food in my gut, making me want to fart.

Slinking down further in my seat, I brought my feet onto the chair and tucked my knees up, resting my coffee on them. In the time that ticked on around us, I looked to my right and studied Elias's hand. His nails were clean, trimmed, and his fingers thick but also long and almost graceful, like he could swing a sword and, in the same moment, play piano. He had no wedding ring, thankfully, but did wear one on his pinkie and his index finger. I wondered what they meant to him.

He folded one corner of his paper down then and smiled at me over it. I looked away quickly, having been caught checking him out, and curled my shoulders around. When I sipped my coffee, it made a horrendous gulping sound as it went down my throat, and Elias laughed.

"Aubrey." He laid the paper aside then and sat forward to look right into my face. "Would you care to take a walk?"

"Don't you have meetings to go to?"

With a bit of hesitation, he nodded. "And still…"

I smiled. "Why though?"

"Why?"

"Yeah, I mean, you know I'm younger than you. What could we possibly have in common?"

"At my age, what could I possibly have in common with anyone, save for maybe… Arthur Knight?"

I nodded with consideration. "I guess."

"That's the point of conversation, I would say," he added. "We talk, we walk, we see if we get along."

My coffee steamed in my face as I lifted it up to my lips to hide my smile in. Elias stood then, offering his hand. "Shall we?"

I obliged, but didn't take his hand. That was just too weird. He drew it away, seemingly not offended, and as he took in my cute baggy white sweater and the black leggings, tucked into adorable gray boots, one corner of his lip pulled upward.

"So," he started, walking with his hands behind his back as we headed for the large glass doors that led to the gardens, "you live in Australia."

"Usually," I offered, "when I'm not being sent to ugly castles against my will."

Elias laughed, casting his eyes forward. "What are your plans… for when you're old enough to escape your parents' control?"

"I had planned to go to college and become a dance instructor."

"Dance?" He pushed his brows up, turning slightly to look at me.

"Yes."

We passed under the stone wall and into the clear cool air outside. Apples and cinnamon wafted on the breeze and brought me home to the days I'd spent at Loslilian as a kid. The same trees grew around the border of this castle and it made me miss that place and look forward to going there when I became a vampire.

"What kind of dancer are you?"

"Alternative, mostly."

He nodded, casting his gaze forward again. "I'd love to see you dance sometime."

“Not sure I ever will now. I mean, my plans have changed since coming here.”

“And what do you plan to do now?”

“Drink blood, become a Lilithian, and move out to Loslilian.”

“Your change will occur naturally, though—”

“Yes, but I want it now. Once a person becomes immortal, they’re no longer bound by the human conventions. I’d be declared an adult.”

“Are your parents really so terrible?”

“It’s not that,” I said, squinting in the sun as it blast its bright morning light down on the autumn leaves around the garden. “It’s that… I’m tired of being treated like a child. I tried to tell my mom that I needed to work on these abilities, and she wouldn’t listen. Now, someone is dead, and I’m living out here away from my friends.”

“That does seem incredibly unfair, to first create the monster and then punish it.”

“Exactly!” I skipped for a step, glad someone got it.

Elias laughed once to himself, and held my gaze with a very warm one of his own as we stepped down onto the grass beyond the stone path. “You could light up an entire room when you smile that way, Aubrey.”

And he could light up my entire soul when he said my name in that sexy posh accent. “So how did you end up on the council?” I asked, trying to take the focus off me, and also to learn a bit more about him. “You’re a World Council Leader, right? That’s pretty profound.”

“Yes, I am. Since the earliest days of the Sets.”

“Really? How did you end up a vampire?”

“I was sent by the king of my lands, at the time, to hunt

down and kill a godless creature, who sought to suck the life from innocent people by drinking their blood."

"A vampire?"

"Yes. And, in fact, it was King Drake himself who was my target, to be precise. As it stands, we instead became friends, and the rest is history. I was given a castle and asked to maintain order among vampires."

"Wow. That's pretty cool."

He laughed again, lowering his head as he did, as though he was shy about it. But he had nice straight teeth and cute indents beside his lips when he smiled, so I wasn't sure why he tried to hide it.

"Why do you do that?" I asked.

"Do what?"

"When you laugh, you, like…" I did it to show him.

His hand came up to his jaw, and he meshed his words around inside his mouth for a moment, lips moving in response. "I suppose… it's because I find you endearing. Perhaps, I hang my head so as not to admit that too openly and offend you."

"Oh." I looked forward and my mouth hung open a bit, until I realized and snapped it shut. Really tense, deeply-concerning silence hovered around us then. I was worried he'd realize we had nothing in common and then walk away, so I had to say something. "It's tricky for me," I confessed.

"What is?"

"I don't know what to talk to you about, because I'm so used to boys that talk about the latest Riverdale episode or which video game they're playing this afternoon. But I *want* to talk to you—"

"We don't need to have anything in common in order to get along," he stated. "And we needn't find words to fill the silence either."

"Sure you won't get uncomfortable and run away if I don't say anything?"

"I do not find silence to be uncomfortable," he said, his footfalls crunching over the dead leaves in the short silence he let hang. "It is merely a brief period of time where one reflects on thoughts and analyses the many possible angles of conversation before speaking."

"Not for me!" I said boldly. "I find it awful, awkward, and altogether a little bit damning."

Elias laughed loudly, bowing his head.

"And not once had I been analyzing *possible angles of conversation*," I added. "I was too busy grasping for anything intelligent to say."

"I love your honesty," he said, his laughter simmering. "It is endearingly refreshing."

Kind of like I found his old-guy mannerisms. I'd never been a fan of films like The Count of Monte Cristo or The Three Musketeers, but my mom loved them. Loved the charm. And I was starting to think I might check out Drake's DVD library and grab a copy of Kate & Leopold tomorrow.

"Perhaps we should discuss our values, core beliefs. And if they align, then there will be plenty to talk about," he said, his warm eyes shrinking with fondness.

"Okay, so how do we figure out if they align?"

Elias scratched the back of his neck, wincing. "I suppose we could speak in hypotheticals."

"Oh, like a 'what would you do if' game?"

"Precisely."

"Okay." I moved over to a bench beneath a big leafy tree and swiped the wet leaves aside before sitting down. Elias sat beside me, keeping a respectable distance. "I know a few. Should I start?"

"Be my guest."

"Um… so… there are two doors, one leading to heaven and one to hell. And of the two birds guarding each door, one bird lies and the other tells the truth," I said. "How do you know which door to take?"

Elias sat back, turning his head to look out over the grassy gardens in front of us. "Can I simply open each door and check before entering?"

"No, that would be too easy."

"Of course it would." He sniffed up a breath of humor, closing his big hands together with a pop. "So… one bird lies and the other tells the truth?" he said to himself. "Ah, I… would ask both birds what color my eyes are. One would say blue. The other would lie. Then, I would ask where the door led. And I would have my answer."

I burst out laughing, folding over a little. "Wow. That question took me a few *days* to answer!"

"And what had your answer been then?"

"That it wouldn't matter which door I took. If I was evil, I couldn't enter Heaven and if I was good, I couldn't enter Hell. I'd always end up exactly where I belonged, where I deserved to be."

One corner of his mouth quirked, revealing a thin dimple. "That's a rather enlightening response, Aubrey."

"What can I say?" I shrugged, hands out. "I'm full of surprises."

Elias's face lit up with a huge grin. "That you are."

Another moment of silence moved between us, but this time, it wasn't awkward. I found myself listening to the birds as they built their nests to prepare for the coming winter, and enjoying the icy breeze that moved my hair in soft tickles over my cheeks.

"I think I have one." Elias curled his fingers around his chin in thought. "Would…" he started, still thinking it over. "Would you rather forget who you are, or who everyone else is?"

"Easy. I'd rather forget who I am. Because I can learn that all over again, but learning who to trust, who to love, that's *not* easy."

Elias nodded. "I like that response."

"Why?"

"I think I feel the same. In my world, it has taken centuries for me to learn who can be trusted, and who cannot. To give that up would be… possibly very damaging," he finished with a laugh. I smiled at him.

"Okay, my turn to ask one," I said, really enjoying this, enough that I found myself looking over at the castle, half expecting someone to come and say he had to go to his meeting now, and I really didn't want that.

"The floor is yours," he said.

"Okay, let's see…" I cast my eyes around the yard, looking for inspiration. "Ooh, this is really relevant to you, I guess. Um… would you rather spend fifty years in total happiness or live out eternity being unhappy?"

"I suppose I've already answered that by being alive as long as I have," he stated. "No matter what has befallen me: happiness, grief, sadness, anger, I have never once wanted to end my existence here on this earth."

"So you don't really concern yourself too much with emotions then?" He did seem like the kind of guy who maybe found happiness within himself, not others.

"I wouldn't necessarily say that. But I suppose the underlying question really asks: is happiness more important to you, or time?"

"Wow, it's more profound when you put it that way," I said.

"I think so too."

"So... which is more important to you?" I asked. "Because, for me, it's happiness. But I have all the time in the world right now."

"For me, it is time. Because I've never been discontent living without the societal view of happiness."

"What about love then? What if you could have fifty years of love, or never have it?"

"Had you asked me that two days ago, I would have said I could live without it. I've never let my heart, the want of a woman, consume me." He scoffed then, wiping a hand across his jaw. "Until you entered the room."

"What do you mean?"

"I was ashamed," he confessed, hanging his head. "I couldn't, for all the acceptable social accords in the world, force myself to look away. I got this sense that I knew you somehow, or that I'd seen you before. And nothing rational went through my mind."

I felt kind of sorry for him then, instead of feeling awkward, like I might otherwise. He was, like, *genuinely* ashamed of himself.

"Would you rather get uglier or dumber?" I asked, moving on.

"Uh... well, I believe beauty is in the eye of the beholder, so... uglier. Because every man and woman should have their wits about them."

"Good answer."

"What about you?"

"Um... yeah, I'd rather get uglier, because I'd hate to be dumb. But," I said, raising a finger. "What if you were married? Would you rather your spouse got uglier or dumber?"

Elias looked me over, as if he were picturing me in that position. "Uglier. We all change so much over the years, even immortals change their appearance. Their views, opinions, moral core, that's where true beauty lies. But good conversation never makes one unattractive. What about you?"

"I'm with you on this one. You can't hold a conversation with *Pretty*."

Elias laughed, lifting his head back as he did. And I thought about his fangs. I knew that one day I'd be Lilithian, and I'd have a set of fangs in me from time to time, but it made me want them right now. And he felt the change in my energy. He didn't make it obvious, but it was there, like a lingering truth, between us.

"If a genie offered you three wishes, what would they be?" he asked, deflecting.

"Um…" I really had to think about that. "I'd wish…" I was a year older. Wow, really? I'd really wish that just because I liked this guy? What had gotten in to me? "I think I'd wish for… I don't know. I don't think I want anything badly enough that I couldn't go out and attain it for myself."

Elias's eyes lit up, and he nodded.

"What about you?" I asked.

"I have everything I desire, I believe. However, I did once wish for a family."

"How come you never had one?"

"I've been busy as a Set Leader. I enjoy my job, my people. I've never had time for love."

"Have you ever been married?"

"I've had several close relationships over the years. Some have died, others moved on, but never anything that lasted longer than a decade."

"Why?"

"I really can't say." He folded his arms, narrowing one eye in thought. "If I knew why it hadn't worked out, I might have done something to fix it. But… it just didn't."

"But, come on… everyone knows, right? In retrospect. Everyone can say where they went wrong."

Elias nodded, his jaw jutting out slightly. "Then, I suppose, there wasn't enough love, enough interest there to keep me. I would say I am to blame for each of my failed relationships, save for those that died, and I would have to mark that down as a lack of interest."

"Do you lose interest easily?"

"Not often." He unfolded his arms. "I think maybe I am not modern enough for most of the women I've dated, and that becomes tiresome for them. To which I respond with the same sentiment, and things slowly unravel."

"I'm modern," I pointed out. "If you want to 'court' me in a year, what then?"

"You mock me," he said playfully, aiming a finger at my raised brow. "I'm sorry if I do not adhere to the modern tongue, Aubrey, but it changes so often one cannot possibly keep up. I do not know a word other than 'courting' to explain the custom of getting to know a person with the intention of something deeper than friendship."

"I bet you also say me-me instead of meam," I teased, because that's how my dad had said 'meme' when he first saw the word.

He didn't admit it, but the way he wiped a hand down his smile and looked up at the tree said it all.

"And I bet it doesn't help that you live in a musty old castle in ancient London," I added. "Away from the 'modern tongue'."

"Well, London Castle isn't actually in London but, no, it doesn't help," he advised. "We are rather cut-off from the world there. And to answer your question about courting you as a 'modern woman'… I can't say. I don't know where things might go between us, but I'd like to find out." He cleared his throat. "When you're old enough."

I was old enough now, if you asked me. So what if I wasn't eighteen? "Cats or dogs?" I said, breaking the silence that had followed.

"Pardon?"

"Cats or dogs?"

"Cats," he said, without a moment's hesitation. "But I also like dogs."

"Do you have any pets?"

"I have two dogs—Scout and Monty—and a cat named Boris."

"Boris!" I laughed.

"Named for my father, thank you very much," he said, stern-faced.

"Oh. Sorry."

"It's okay." He leaned in a little. "I was joking."

I pushed him playfully with the back of my wrist. "You had me there."

"I think I had you at '*May I*.'"

I swallowed hard, realizing how much truth there was in that, going back to the moment we'd joined hands before we danced last night.

"What is this between us?" I asked, holding his gaze and letting myself slip all the way inside him, wrapped up warm in the budding of new emotions. "Why did it feel like that when we danced?"

"I wish I knew," he said softly, his voice taking on a deeper, more intimate tone.

"Do you think we're soulmates?"

Elias laughed to himself, nodding. "The thought had crossed my mind, yes."

"But?" I asked.

"No buts. I just… I don't want to admit that too openly for fear of frightening you away."

"That doesn't scare me," I said, sliding forward on the chair. "Strangely."

"It scares me," he admitted, facing the front, his arms folded. "You are infinitely too young for me, Aubrey Knight. I shouldn't even be sitting here with you like this."

I nodded. I didn't see it that way, but if I had a kid, I would. So I totally understood. "So, I guess, we can pick this up in a year?"

Elias reached over from the fold of his arms and put his hand on my shoulder, nodding. But he couldn't look at me. "I should go."

"Why?"

"Because it's clearly too easy to get lost in conversation with you and forget all of my worldly duties, and…" He studied me, his nostrils flaring as he exhaled. "Responsibilities."

"Okay. Well, maybe I'll see you around sometime."

"If I am as smart and noble a man as I like to think, I will make sure that is not the case—for at least another year." He got up then, and turned to bow at me once, before walking away.

After that, I sat and stared at the trees for a really long time. I could feel a change in me, a shift of some kind, and I liked it. I liked Elias. I liked the idea that maybe we were something more, before we were even friends first. I hated insta-love books and movies almost as much as I hated triangles, but I liked this. I had a feeling I wouldn't see him again until I was over eighteen, but I was also okay with that. It was kinda nice just feeling like this.

JASON

I never felt sorry for myself. But if my life were measured in comparison to others, I'd suffered more. Standing here now at the end of the long jetty, the ocean at my feet, a busy beachfront and café strip at my back, I couldn't find a reason why I shouldn't just jump into the deep water and let it carry me away.

Somewhere along the shore, the first girl I ever cared for was living a new life, falling in love with my nephew. And not far from her, the last girl I would ever try to love again was falling for one of my closest friends. There was something devastatingly isolating in that.

The only thing that kept me here was the small child I'd conceived with the only girl I would never have. And Daniel wasn't just my child; he wasn't just the only child that had survived; the only child whose life I was allowed to be a part of; he was *hers and my* son. A part of the woman who owned every piece of my soul, and forever would. And there was something in that—something larger than just having a son—because Daniel was my reason to live, my piece of Ara. I couldn't fill the hole that she'd left, but Daniel helped, for now.

The only trouble was, it fulfilled one of my wildest dreams so completely that I was afraid to lay eyes on Rochelle again. I should feel as though nothing in this world is more important than holding her. After more years mourning her than loving her, I should have been over at Harry's house the second I found out she was alive.

Yet, I couldn't, because she didn't matter to me, and I was afraid no one would understand. I was happy that she was alive, but so much time had passed since I met Ara—almost forty years —and I'd done a lot of healing in that. Rochelle was the first woman to make me feel like I mattered, but she wasn't the last, and since her, others had mattered more to me. What kind of a man was I if I showed up there without any emotion?

I had tried to say it to Ara the other day, and I knew she'd understand, but a part of me didn't want to explain it to anyone because I shouldn't have to. It wasn't natural. Rochelle shouldn't be alive, and I shouldn't be having to face these emotions. I'd buried her, and I'd buried my past with her in the years after I hurt Ara. And a part of me was mad—at Rochelle and at Aubrey —because I was forced to face this now. I was forced to face the fact that everything I suffered, everything Ara suffered, was all for nothing.

I completely appreciated my brother's stance on this, because I was right there beside him. And I was glad for that—to know I wasn't alone in feeling this way.

Behind me, Mike's Open Mic Night started up, and I turned around, with my back to the sea, to listen. Elora was playing right now, I'd recognize her style anywhere, and I had thought about attending. Ara would be there, but so would Jules. And Harry. Which meant Rochelle would be with him. And all I wanted was to be at home with Ara, snuggled up on the couch with Daniel sleeping peacefully in the room upstairs. I wanted to stir in her arms and get up in the cold to tend to him when he woke at night, because he was *still* waking up, even at two years old. I wanted to make her coffee and let her sleep-in while I got up to play with him and make breakfast. It was just so simple and yet, for me, it was the most unattainable thing in the world. I'd tried that with three girls in the past, and now I was grieving two children. If I couldn't have that life with Ara, with Daniel, then I would never have it. Not if the universe kept killing my unborn babies and pushing the people I love away.

"Jason?" a hesitant voice said.

I shut my eyes, recognizing it immediately. Her French accent had changed slightly in the time she'd been living with Harry, but the tones of her voice were just the same, and I went back more than seventy years, seeing her there as the same girl she was when she loved me.

"Hi," I said, not sure what else to say.

She swept forward and closed her arms around my neck. "You look older."

I laughed, hugging her gently. "I'm about ten years older."

"It looks good on you." She leaned back, pressing her hand to my stubbly cheek. "You're still so beautiful."

"I'm sorry, Rochelle," I said, looking down into those familiar eyes. "I should have been there—"

"You couldn't have been. Your brother made sure of that," she said, reliving her own death.

"I know. But I never stopped regretting it."

"Well"—she stepped back from me, hugging the light cardigan around her dress—"I give you permission to forgive yourself, Jason. I forgive you."

"Do you still hate me?" I asked. "For what I am?"

Her eyelids fluttered and she hung her head. "I wish I had never said that to you."

In my mind, I replayed the moment I told her I was a vampire—how she rejected this ungodly creature, and essentially set in motion the steps David took to erase her.

"I would have changed my mind," she offered. "With time. I was just scared—of what our child would be."

When I saw the agony in her eyes for that loss, a loss that was still raw to her, since she just woke up from it all, I moved in and gently touched her arm. "It wouldn't have survived," I told her.

"Why? Because it was a vampire?"

"No, because I have unnatural forces working against me—against everyone I will ever love."

"Why would you think that?"

I leaned on the railing, looking out to sea, and she came up beside me. "I was warned once—by a higher power—that I am destined to be with one person and that everything I do that goes against that also goes against the will of Nature."

"Like a curse?"

"In ways."

She nodded, understanding. "Is Harry cursed too?"

"No. Why?"

Rochelle tried to hide her smile, but I knew her too well. "He reminds me of you."

"He's a lot like me," I noted.

"He's gentle. And funny, and he makes a joke out of almost anything, even the most wildly inappropriate things."

I laughed, angling my head a little then, without making it obvious, to look at Harry down the end of the jetty. When he saw that she was with me, he waved and headed back in to the café. "He's a good man," I said. "I couldn't have chosen a better friend for you."

"I really like him." Rochelle looked out at sea. "And I like this modern world."

"What do you like about it?"

She smiled, taking a deep breath of the gentle sea breeze. "The food. The cars. The shopping centers. I like Australia." Her head bent in a nod to include the greater world outside of this jetty. "I like television and the internet—"

I laughed loudly.

"And I like that they have so many medicines—to cure almost anything."

I laughed again. "Be careful what you believe though—"

"Oh, don't worry. I am. *Now.* Harry has had to teach me a lot." She laughed too. "I think maybe I'll fall in love with him one day."

"That's good," I said, reaching over to cup her wrist, giving it a firm squeeze. It felt odd touching her. I expected to feel a connection, a longing. But it was akin to touching a friend. And I still felt a numb sense of resentment toward her for coming back after I'd spent so many years putting her to rest in my heart and my mind.

"I should get back," she said, glancing over her shoulder. "Harry might wonder where I am."

"Okay." I nodded once, feeling the lights from the shore reflect in my eyes.

Rochelle stood on her toes and cupped my cheek, kissing it softly. "I will always hold a special place in my heart for you, Jason."

I nodded, wishing I could say the same. But I couldn't.

When she walked away, I faced the ocean again and closed my hands together, resting my head on them.

AUBREY

Elias remained true to his vow—to back away for the better of us both. He finished out the summit, and not once crossed my path in that time, saying goodbye with a handwritten note.

Dear Aubrey,

Please forgive my poor manners. I felt it best if I did not say goodbye in person. If you sensed the energy between us when last we spoke, then I know you understand why.

I do not like to think of myself as a perverted man, but I do feel that entertaining affections for a girl so young is somewhat immoral and very ungentlemanly. Had we met in my era, it would not be an issue, but in this modern world, these feelings are unwelcome and ill-placed. Yet, since our walk in the garden, I have thought many times about requesting your company again.

I hope we can spend more time together discussing

hypotheticals when I see you again in a year. Until then, stay well, my lovely friend, and please do not drink vampire blood.

Yours, in friendship,
Elias

I'd read and re-read that letter a hundred times in the last few weeks, even tried sniffing it to see if it smelled like him. It didn't. It just smelled like ink. And I was starting to think the next year would go by very slowly.

A part of me wondered if I'd still feel this way after a few months, a year, but I was okay with it if the feelings died. It was nice in the now, you know, just feeling something like this. It made time pass quickly, and I didn't get as bored in the hours between dinner and breakfast as I might otherwise, having nothing to do.

When Morgana finally came back to the castle a few weeks after the summit, I was so ready to start investigating my powers again that I practically jumped on her back and rode her to the library.

"Have you been completely bored with no one here to talk to you?" Morgana asked as we strolled through the airy corridors, the ancient armor and shields not so gaudy and ugly to me now.

"A little. Nate hung back for the first week, but he had stuff going on, so he couldn't stay any longer." I shivered against the cold that breezed through the dim, candle-lit halls, taking in the smell of the odd singed flame as we passed. "I can't believe I've been here for four weeks already."

"Time flies?"

"Not really." I laughed, hugging my sweater around me. "Hey, you know my mom really well, right?"

"Uh… why?"

"Do you think she'll let me come home for Christmas?"

We stopped by the library door and Morgana hesitated before pushing it open. "Probably. But..."

"But?"

"I know Drake was looking forward to having you. He's throwing a ball."

"Really?"

"Yeah," she said, a glittering grin lighting up her eyes. "Elias will be there."

"Oh." I walked in behind her, standing in a flood of light as it poured through the high windows on the outer wall. "He won't come near me though."

"Why wouldn't he?"

"We went for a walk when he was here last, and we talked a bit."

"And?" she prompted, a rising air of curiosity lifting her voice.

I grinned. "Turns out we kind of get along really well, and I think he just wants to be careful not to stoke any feelings we have for each other."

"Look, I know I wasn't exactly an advocate for you two hanging out, but if you actually have feelings for him, then that changes things." She sighed. "I guess I can support it—"

"It doesn't matter anyway, I'm too young to date him. It's illegal."

"It's illegal to have sex," she stated, pulling out a chair. "You can date him."

"He thinks it makes him unworthy if he likes me—a creep, I guess. Not his word."

Morgana laughed. "Elias is, for lack of a better word, really honorable," she said, questioning it as though she wasn't sure she should use it. "Sorry, lame word, I know. But that's him. I really don't think his dating a seventeen-year-old is going to change that. Especially not when it was acceptable to marry girls at fourteen in his era."

"I know. But… it was pretty intense." I sat down on the chair across from hers, the big wooden table warmed slightly from the fireplace along the wall. "I don't know about getting to know him… I mean, I want to. And I think that will come naturally. But I kinda wanted to jump his bones"—Morgana laughed loudly when I said that—"like, right there in the garden."

"Oh, I like you, Aubrey," she said, sitting down. "You're fun."

I smiled.

"So, okay, you're both clearly attracted to each other, so why not just, you know"—she presented five fingers—"get one out before you see him? Ease the pressure."

"I guess." I toyed shyly with the wood grain on the table. "Or we could just keep morals out of the equation, and you could give us a dose of that wicked sex potion."

"Now, *that*," she said with a laugh, "my dear niece, would not be taking morals out of the equation at all. It'd be forcing Elias to do something he would deeply regret."

"I guess."

Morgana exhaled, pressing her mouth into a thoughtful slit around it. "So… your mom and Jason were drugged, huh?"

"Did you know about that before Eva mentioned it at the dinner?"

"No. I mean, yes, because I figured it was the case when Lily mentioned that they'd fucked." She smiled to herself. "My sister would never willingly cheat on David. But I'm glad it happened."

"Why?"

"Jason. That poor guy has suffered enough. He's lost two unborn babies, and Daniel will be his only one. Lily will never let him see her children again, so he's lost that, and the universe will never let him have a child with someone else."

"Why?"

"It's a part of its greater plan, I guess—that those two are supposed to be unified, for so many reasons other than just the fact that they're soul mates, designed for each other," she explained. "But, so far, it's Jason who's suffered the consequences of your mother's choice to love your dad, and Jason's too gentle a soul, Aubrey. He loves Daniel, clearly, but I know he thinks about taking the true death on an almost daily basis because he can't take the pain of being alone."

"How do you know that?"

"I have my ways." She tapped the side of her nose. "So, I'm just glad he at least got to have a son with the only woman he'll ever love before he dies."

"Poor Uncle Jase."

"No kidding." She laughed, raising her brows to express that sentiment. "So, did they ever tell you about the mischief I got up to in my early days—before I was resurrected?"

"No." I shuffled a little closer, grinning. "But please, do tell."

"That potion, I got a few people with it."

"Oooh, I love a bit of gossip." I closed my hands together on the table. "Who?"

"You wouldn't have met them, but I got one of your mother's House officials—Margret. Put her with the butler."

I laughed hard. "Oh my god, classic! I love it."

"I also got Falcon."

"Who with?" I leaned a little closer, knowing, from the look on her face, that this was juicy.

She couldn't say it without cracking up. She was laughing so hard that she folded her head down on the table and slapped it a few times. "Mike," she coughed, but I barely heard it.

"Did you just say Mike?" I stood slightly to lean over and tap her. "For real? Mike and Falcon?"

"Yes." Morg looked up, her face bright red with hilarity.

"Oh my god, but Mike isn't bisexual—"

"I know. He couldn't walk for a week!"

I folded down to laugh into the table then, trying to keep my voice low in the empty library, but I couldn't. I just couldn't laugh quietly while trying to picture Uncle Mike and Falcon butt-humping!

"Don't ever tell them you know though. They will take that to their graves," she warned. "Well, Mike will. Falcon wouldn't care."

"Was he hot for Uncle Mike? Is that why you did it?"

"No. I did it to get back at Mike. He… we were really close once, and he just turned on me. I was hurt, so I hurt him."

"Argh," I scoffed. "You sound like me."

"I think you and I are a lot alike," she noted, smiling at me in a way that drew me into her circle of friendship. "Wanna know who else I got?"

"Who?" My eyes widened with interest.

"Okay, so this one was an accident. And I do actually feel bad for it. I meant for Falcon to share that bottle with me, so we could… you know." She popped her index finger in and out of a circle on her other hand.

"What happened to morals?" I teased.

She shrugged. "I don't care much for them. But Elias does, that's why I won't let you do it to him. But… Falcon drank the bottle with Elora."

"My sister?"

She nodded.

"Did they…?"

"Yes."

"Oh my gosh!" I covered my mouth, all the blood rushing to my face as I laughed. "So is that why he left? Because he used to be a part of the family, you know. She still refers to him as her uncle—"

"No, he left because he was still in love with your mother after she broke the First Woman's Curse."

I nodded, taking that in.

"And then," she added, "after a few years running the New England set, he started operating solely out of Loslilian."

"Yeah, I heard about that. So why… I mean, why did he live there?"

"He'd started to get close to someone there."

"Who? Lily?"

"No." She smirked. "Jason."

"For real?"

"He never had a relationship with him. He just stayed close, you know. Sort of became a good friend."

"I never knew that."

"Jason keeps their friendship close to his heart, I think," she said. "Not many people actually know about it unless they lived at Loslilian then. But those two sat in the study every night and shared whiskey and *deep* conversation."

"In what way? Like… friends, or…"

"I think Jason's a bit like Falcon."

"Bisexual?"

"That's not what Falcon is. I mean, by today's standards, yeah, you might call it that. But sexuality is really more of a spectrum than an either or either. And it's just that Falcon loves outside of gender or race. He doesn't 'see' it, if you know what I mean."

"Like, he doesn't necessarily check guys out, or turn his head at a cute one, but he can fall in love with the *person,* even if they're a guy?"

"Exactly."

"And Jason's the same?"

"Not sure, since I never asked him. And it doesn't feel right to place labels on people in order to fit them into our box, but I know Jason hasn't had a problem blood-sharing with other guys, so I have to wonder which side of the fence he sits on."

"Hm… damn. Do they have sex when they share blood?"

"Who?"

"Guys, in general."

"Yeah. They do. And I've been with Jason and done that stuff too."

"Really? You and Jase?"

"Yeah. Pretty much everyone in the immortal world has been with everyone else after a few hundred years. It's actually very normal."

"Even guys with guys?"

"It's a long eternity. You gotta try new things."

"And you and Jason did it with a guy?"

She nodded, shrugging.

I looked up at the window and the gray sky, picturing that for a moment before I felt sick thinking about my beloved uncle naked. "Do you think Elias has been with a guy before?"

"Nope. Straight as ruler, that one." She laughed.

"What about my dad?"

"Okay, so maybe not all guys do that stuff. But I know your mom and dad shared blood with Jason once—a blood threesome."

"Did they have sex?"

"No."

"What about Falcon? Did he ever get with mom?"

"No."

"Did he ever have sex with Uncle Jase?"

She hesitated way too long, her face tight and her lips pressed into a hard line. "Jason… when it comes to things like sex these days, especially with guys… it's complicated for him now. I think, had he not been abducted and raped—"

"He was raped!"

"A long time ago."

"By a man?"

"Yes, a very sick, very twisted man. They extracted his semen to use in a spell, and the man took advantage of Jason's captivity many, many times over."

I covered my mouth, looking around for something to throw up in.

"So, after that, I think Jase found it hard. Before it, he'd actually talked to Falcon about a blood threesome. But… after it, he was never the same," she told me. "I think being around Falcon, thinking about that stuff with him, it brought back too many memories. 'Cause I don't think Jason is bisexual, per se, but I think maybe he loved Falcon for a while, and yet the abuse he suffered kind of ruined that for them."

"Wow. I had no idea." My eyes landed on her. "How do you know all this?"

"I stole Jason's journals." She smirked, leaning a little closer. "Wanna read 'em?"

"Yes!" I sat taller, shrinking then. "But… isn't that a little invasive? I mean, he's my uncle. Do I really wanna know this stuff?"

"You tell me," she challenged. And the truth was, *I did.* I wanted all the juice!

"Okay, give me the journals! I wanna read them."

"I'll have them sent over when I return home. Now"—she

stood—"let's find a ghost. I want you to bring one back and then touch a human. We'll see how many it takes before your touch of death surfaces."

My stomach did an uncomfortable flip and made my blood cold. "Morg, I can't kill a human. It isn't right."

"It might not even happen. But we have to test it, Aubrey. We can't just let you walk around with the power to kill at your hands." She grabbed my wrist and tugged me along in a sisterly way. "Just think of Elias as you do it. Imagine if it was him."

I groaned. "Argh. Fine. Let's go find a ghost."

"I'll summon one. I have my kit."

We walked across the room to a large wooden chest that had been left there, and she opened it, revealing a bunch of things like tarot cards, candles, salt, and other weird things.

"Go lock the doors," she said. "We can't have anyone entering while we do this, and I don't want any of your resurrections escaping once we bring them back."

"Why?"

"Because the kinds of ghosts that would linger here in this castle are not the kinds of people you want roaming around freely."

"Oh." Hesitantly, I locked all the doors around the room and came back to sit on the ground where Morgana had drawn a chalk pentagram and laid out five candles.

"Contrary to popular belief, this doesn't represent the devil." She tapped the pentagram. "It's a knot, for protection. All those religious nuts that get scared of these should actually be using them, because they're one of the things that *will* ward off those evil spirits they fear."

"I know." I grabbed the matches and lit a candle, the smoky scent of burnt wood igniting my senses, reminding me of

Christmas for a moment. "Elora and Ali are into all that witchy stuff."

"It's not just witchy stuff." She laughed. "Anyone can use a pentagram. And Ali was once my apprentice, you know, before she was my father's. I *taught* her most of that witchy stuff."

"Really?"

"Mm-hm." Morgana reached out for my hand then and I placed it in hers, straightening my spine and closing my eyes as she did the same. She started saying words in another language, and the mercury in the room dropped, the day going darker around us. I had to fight hard to resist the urge to open my eyes, sensing the many spirits around me. She'd said that I could see them when they slipped through the fissures, but it wasn't often that I ever came across one. But from what I could feel right now, she either opened a whole heap more fissures, or she just shone a light down on my location, attracting them all like flies to Uncle Mike's garden boots.

"Open your eyes very slowly," she said in a quiet, calm voice.

Her hands pulled away and I felt her energy change as she stood. When I opened my eyes, several columns of wavering light flickered around the room. I couldn't make out their form yet, until they were ready to reveal themselves to me, but I knew they were there.

"I didn't realize you'd be able to bring so many through."

"Stay here, okay," she said, backing away. "And please don't argue with me, or scream."

"Why?"

"I'm gonna bring in our test subject—"

"What!"

"Shhh." She pushed her finger to her lips. "Don't scare them off. They don't know why they're here."

I glanced back as she opened the door nearby and wheeled a chair in with a man tied to it, a gag in his mouth.

"Morg, I can't do this—"

"He's a heinous human being," she assured me. "He murdered his kids."

"For real?" My eyes landed on the prisoner. He looked so ordinary. Just a chubby man in jeans and a shirt, with short brown hair and sweaty white skin.

"Yes. I bought him from the human faction. So don't feel guilty if he dies. I'll be killing him when we're done either way—after I torture him for a bit."

The man sobbed to himself, but I didn't feel sorry for him at all. "How old were they? The kids. And do you have proof?"

Morgana sighed, digging out her phone as she walked over to me. After thumbing at it for a moment, she showed me the news report and the certificate for approval of brutal execution from the Drakarian Set, and I'd seen enough. "Okay. Fine. Let's get started."

Morgana stood back, offering me the floor, and I pushed my sleeves up. "I'm a conduit for the dead," I announced to the ghosts. "You can walk into the living realm through me."

One by one, each ghost came forward. It started with a giant blonde man, who's dumb expression made him look like a toddler, and as I pulled him through, Morgana gasped loudly.

"What?"

"Stand in the corner!" she demanded with a sharp, pointed finger, and the big man-baby moved over and huddled against the door.

"Why are you being so mean to him?" I asked.

"If you knew who he was, you'd be mean too." She gave him a vehement glare.

"Who was he?"

"Never mind. Here." The chubby child-killer came across the floorboards on his rolling chair with a giant push from Morgana, and when I touched him, nothing happened.

I looked at my aunt, confused. "He didn't die."

"Okay, pull another ghost free."

Holding my hand in spirit form and emerging as a human, shocked and crying, another ghost stepped into life, followed by another and another, and I touched the human to see if he'd die between each one, repeating it all six more times before I looked at Morgana again.

"Nothing. He's not dead yet."

"What's the most you ever brought back?"

"Ten."

"Including the malevolent spirit?"

"Yes."

"Then let's go to ten and see what happens," she advised.

I brought back a few more, directing each one to stand with the others, and after number ten came through, I turned, pressed my hand to the killer and… nothing.

"What does that mean?" I asked.

Morgana huffed. "It means your touch of death isn't likely related to your ability to resurrect."

"It's not a consequence?"

"I don't think so," she mused, looking me over. "A defense-mechanism, maybe. How do you feel—after so many resurrections?"

"I'm fine," I said, touching my stomach where it felt hollow. "I don't usually get tired until a few hours after I bring them back."

Morgana nodded. "So it may just hit you all at once?"

"It will. I've never done so many in one go before. I'm not sure what that will do."

"Okay, go and rest." She pointed off to the door, distracted by the mental list she was clearly making in her mind. "I'll come up in a few hours and bring this jerk with me. See if exhaustion triggers the death touch."

"Okay. What about them?" I nodded at the new humans.

"I'll relocate them." Her eyes scanned each face. "And feed some of them to a hungry vampire."

"Why?" I laughed, but a few of the humans cried.

"Some of them deserve it. And Drake will be interested to know one certain person is alive again."

"Okay." I spun on my toe and walked away, hugging my sweater to my ribs to get warm in the sudden cool. "I'll see ya later then."

ELORA

Uncle Mike handed me a coffee, passing one to Jules, as we both sat laughing and talking on the lounge in his cozy den. I loved this space, with the high white bookshelves all around the room, the fireplace and mantle with the picture frames of our lives, and the piano in the corner, where a lounge suite and two comfy armchairs watched on, making a home of the space. While this room held so many good memories, it also held one of my most painful ones—of the day my dad beat my mom out there in the courtyard—and yet it was still one of the only places on the planet that felt like home.

I'd spent so long living here since I was sixteen, falling in love with this house and with the lifestyle, that I could see why Jules was crushing so hard on it all. In the two months that had passed since she arrived, and with Jason now staying at my apartment, she was starting to come alive again. She smiled a lot, and the moments of sad reflection didn't seem to last so long.

Uncle Mike was a big part of her moving on, but I think it also helped to know that a lot of it was outside of her control. All of it, really. Because I was more and more sure every time I saw life fail for Jason that things *were* working against him. And Jules felt the same. I think she was grateful that their life hadn't gone too far along, making them think they could be happy, before crashing down. She could move past this, past a break-up, she was tough. And I was pretty sure she was crushing hard on Uncle Mike too. Maybe a rebound-guy thing, maybe not, but the energy between them was electric.

"So, on a more serious note," I said to Jules, waiting until Mike left the room. "How are things now? Are you finding it hard without Jason?"

"Sometimes." She nodded, sipping her coffee. "I thought we'd spend forever together, literally, so it's been an adjustment. But…" Her eyes flicked off to a picture of Mike on the mantle. "I almost feel like… what if I was meant to meet Jason just so I could meet Mike?"

My heart lifted at the notion of it. "Really?"

"Yeah." She wet her lips, frowning to herself. "I know that's corny as fuck, but—"

"Sure that's not just the grief talking?"

"Maybe. But… Jase and I weren't together that long, really. I was a year without him, remember, without any memory of him. And when he came back into my life, it really wasn't for that long. It was intense, but I never fell hard enough to want him at *any cost*, like Ara seemed to think I should."

"My mother has a unique way of loving a person."

Jules nodded. "I can't love like that, you know—to be with them even if they don't love me. I don't know how she does it."

"Does what?"

"Stays with David."

"Why wouldn't she? She loves him."

"I know. But… have you ever thought her love with Jason is

a bit more… intense?" she said.

"No," I snapped a little, not meaning to. "To say that just means you haven't been around her that much when she's with my dad."

"No, it's more because… when I first saw Ara, it was at the university, and she took Jason by surprise," she said. "And the connection I felt between them then was... like pure energy."

I nodded. I'd felt that too, on and off over the years. It wasn't always there but when it was, it was, by all definitions, very intense. "We all thought they'd just move on one day, but it's since become apparent, over the last thirty-five years, that none of them ever will."

"And what will that mean for Jason?"

"I don't know. I asked my dad the other day what he thought would happen from here, now that it's kind of clear that Jason will never be able to move on, and…" A dizzying wave of sadness rushed over me when I thought about that conversation.

"What did he say?"

"He said we might have to accept Jason's death." I looked into my coffee cup, swirling the brown liquid around. "Being Vampire, he can't just live out his life and wait for death. He has to choose it. They do this big ceremony and everything—"

"I won't let him do that."

"It might be cruel not to."

Jules nodded, obviously understanding the depth of Jason's despair like I did. "If I'd stayed with him, would it be different?"

"You can't blame yourself for this," I stated. "It would only have been a matter of time before you both realized that his love for my mother was a bigger ball and chain than you first understood and, by that time, a child might have been involved."

Jules nodded. "I'm glad I let him go."

"Yeah?"

"Yeah." She nodded, sipping her coffee. "I love and respect myself enough to want someone who loves me, and only me. And I think that's fair. I don't think I'm being unreasonable. And Mike says the same."

I grinned into my coffee. Of course he'd say that. He was hot for her, big time. "So you guys sit up late-night-talking, huh?"

Jules didn't miss the inflection in my tone, hiding her smile. "I think maybe he's my new best friend. We have a lot in common and he's super sweet, like, super super sweet." She laughed, her pretty smile so open and honest. "Jo thinks I'm falling for him."

"Oh?" I said, thinking about the sassy, pragmatic young woman I'd met in New York when I went to find Jules. Jo didn't mince words, and didn't make assumptions lightly. If she thought Jules was falling for Mike, then it was probably true.

"It's not that, though," Jules assured me with a wave of her hand. "It's probably just a rebound thing."

"Probably."

"But… I think it's okay, right? Because he's not attached, and if we end up having sex or something, it doesn't have to be anything."

"No. It doesn't, and I know Uncle Mike can keep sex and friendship separate. But just… don't make him fall in love with you if you're going to dump him, m'kay?"

"I won't hurt him. I promise."

I looked down absently at my mirrored necklace then, wondering about them—their closeness, their friendship. I wanted to look ahead and see where it went, but a small flicker of curiosity flared within my heart. I knew the feeling well. It was the 'tap' from my Seer's eye, telling me to look, so I looked. But I didn't look into their future or their past. It was an alternate path I saw, and I smiled.

"What is it?" Jules said.

"It's a vision," Mike advised, coming in to the room to sit down beside her. "She does that all the time."

"What was it? What did you see?" Jules asked, eyeing my mirror.

"She won't tell you," he added. "She doesn't like to tell people their future."

"Yeah, because I suck at foretelling. I'm *always* wrong," I announced, and Jules laughed. "But this wasn't a future. It was one of six possibilities."

"For what?"

"For how you two met," I said, sipping my coffee to deflect their shock.

"So we met in alternate paths?" Jules asked, smiling at Mike and elbowing him softly to get a reaction. But he just frowned, coming forward on his seat.

"Well, that was bound to happen if she knew Jason," he scoffed, downplaying it.

"Yeah," I said casually, "except this version, right now, is the *only* one where she met Jason first."

They both exchanged glances, mouths hanging open a little. And my work here was done. That pull I'd felt earlier, urging me here, that's what it was: I was supposed to set something in motion, and now that it was done, I felt complete. And I also felt the same old hunger—for ice-cream and vodka—that followed the completion of a pull.

I left the house with a bit of pep in my step and headed back home to hug Uncle Jason and tell him I was sorry. Tell him I couldn't imagine a world without him in it, and maybe even look in on his future, if he'd let me, and see if there was any conceivable possibility where he might one day be happy.

AUBREY

Drake came and went many times, as the sun fell and rose again around me. I couldn't move, couldn't speak. It felt like my body was in transition, and if I'd had blood, I'd be certain this was blood hunger. I heard them say it —say my body needed feeding, but they didn't know what it needed.

All I wanted was to sleep, but they kept waking me every time they came in to probe me and make sure I was alive. I heard my mom's voice on the phone a few times, but I barely had words to speak, and as the days passed, drawing us closer to December, I wasn't sure I'd ever be able to wake up. I felt stuck, lodged between worlds.

"Should we give her blood?" Morgana asked.

"Out of the question," Drake demanded, both of them standing above me. I opened my eyes for a moment and then rolled over, slipping back down into a deep sleep.

Elias was there in my dreams, as always, and even though I didn't know him, hadn't made any real friendship with him, I wished he was here in the real world, right beside me. I wished my mom was here. Or my dad. Or Mia.

"She took so many souls out," Morgana suggested, waking my mind again. "Do you think she needs to put some back?"

"Frankly, I don't know what she needs. If she doesn't start to recover soon, I may need to send her home. It's been eight days."

"She brought ten back," Morg advised. "Maybe give her ten days. It could be a day for a life."

"Very well. If she's not awake within the next two or three days, we will need to send her home. I can't have her die on me, Morgana. Her mother would never forgive me."

"It's *me* she'd never forgive, Father. I'm the one who did this to her."

"It won't matter if Ara can ever forgive either of us," he said, his voice coming now from near the door, "I will never forgive *myself.*"

Morgana sat down beside me on the bed, sweeping my hair back. "I'm so so sorry, little Aubrey. *So* sorry."

I fell back asleep, opening my eyes again in what seemed like two minutes. This time, I felt rested. Awake. I looked around the room at the dawn shadows, seeing someone asleep in the corner on an armchair, and rolled over to flex my body. The blankets were warm, even though the fire was out and the room was cold, and I could hear the subtle sounds of the birds outside beginning to wake the world.

Beside me, there was a handwritten note on yellowing paper. I picked it up and sniffed it, knowing instantly who it was from.

Aubrey, my dear friend,

I hope this letter finds you well. I have received word that you were weakened by your ability to transform spirits to the human form, and I want to assure you that I am doing my research as I write this.

However, in my ancient library, I have come across only legends of creatures whose myth appears to fit your abilities but not your nature: necromancers. I am at a loss, to be honest, but I will find a way to make you all right again, I swear this to you.

I had hoped to share one last dance with you at the Christmas ball before we part ways again until September 7 next year—my birthday—*so please, rest, recover, and be well, my darling friend, so that my wish may be fulfilled.*

I will see you again very soon, if you are well or not, and please know that you are in all of my thoughts. Until then, fondest regards.

Your friend, as always,
Elias

I pressed the note to my chest and let the goofiest grin consume my face, safe from judgement in the darkness of pre-dawn. He was so old-world and gentlemanly. My dad was like that too, and I guess they say girls fall for guys who are like their fathers. But Elias's old-world charm was really winning me over. He was way better than the turd boys I went to school with.

I sat up a little and looked at the person in the chair. Nate. When did he get back?

"Psst," I hissed, trying to wake him, but feeling bad about it, so not really wanting to just shout and say *wake up*! "Nate?" I whispered.

He shot up out of the chair and appeared beside me, rubbing a hand over his shaved head. "You're awake!"

"So are you." I laughed, rolling my covers back to get up.

"Whoa!" He tried to stop me. "You can't get up yet. You'll be too weak."

"I'm fine." I got up, spreading my arms to present my not-so-weak-self. He stood back but kept a hand nearby in case I fell over. "See?"

"Okay. How do you feel?"

I did a scan of my entire body, thinking about it. "Rested. But starving!"

"Good." He chuckled. "Come on. I'll ask the chef to make breakfast early."

"I don't wanna be any trouble."

"He won't mind." He grabbed my arm gently and dragged me along.

"So, when did the note come?" I nodded to it on the pillow. "How long was I out?"

"Eleven days," he said, handing me my dressing gown and kicking my slippers over as he opened the door. "Drake was getting real worried. And Morgana's beside herself."

"I'm okay though."

"I know. But they love you. They've been beating themselves up over this." He shut my door and locked it with the big key. "Morgana doesn't want to do anymore research on you for a while. She had to go back anyway. Back home."

"Why?"

"She's got a coven to run, remember?"

"Oh."

"I better text her though," he added. "She wants hourly updates on you."

"Oh."

He stopped for a moment and thumbed against his phone, while I put my hands in my dressing gown pockets and looked down the black corridor, seeing a man in the distance who was lighting the candles. The phone rang a second later, so Nate handed it to me.

"Hello," I said quietly in the early-morning darkness.

"Aubrey! I am so sorry!" she practically yelled. "I had no idea that would happen to you. I—"

"It's okay," I assured her. "I'm fine now. I just needed to sleep it off."

She exhaled. "You don't know how much relief I feel. I thought I'd killed you."

I laughed. "Maybe we'll keep the ghost resurrections down to one or two at a time from now on."

"Or none. Just… we know now, okay. We know you need a full day of rest for each ghost, and we know that neither your temper nor the resurrections trigger the touch of death, so I say we leave it at that for now. Go back home, live your life. Be a kid. We can figure the rest out when you're older."

"But—"

"Aubs," she said, and I knew I'd grown on her in my time here, because she'd never called me that before. "My biggest fear when I thought I'd killed you was that you haven't lived yet. You don't belong in a musty old castle. Go home. I mean it."

"But the ball. Elias will be—"

"Forget the ball. Forget Elias. Date some stupid young guys and get in to all kinds of trouble before you invest yourself in an eternal courtship—"

"Who says Elias is eternal?" I smirked.

"I read that letter he sent, Aubs. And I bet you gushed over it." She laughed. "It's eternal. Or at least very long-term."

I grinned, feeling the heat of that delicious uncertainty that came with new love push up into my cheeks and warm them. "Yeah, I think it could be too."

"So, go home, okay. Fall in love too quickly, have sex with a jerk, and get drunk from your parents' liquor cabinet, all right?"

"Okay," I said, handing the phone back to Nate as I muttered, "Right after the ball."

ALL DAY, AS I WAITED FOR THE TIME TO COME WHERE I could put on my ball gown, then, as I did my hair and put on some make-up, I couldn't stop my heart from flipping around in sudden and very rapid little fits of excitement. I'd waited so long here in the dingy castle to see Elias again, and even Beth would be here tonight, along with Falcon, and Nate. Everyone I either loved or was growing to love would be here and, for the first time since I arrived, almost three months ago, I wouldn't be alone.

Nate had been here on and off since I woke up from my really long nap, and Drake spent every Tuesday and Thursday with me, as I watched him rehearse for the upcoming theatre season—where he hosted a castle tour and vampire play—but most other days I'd been on my own, reading books, watching too much tv, or talking to Mia on the phone. I'd also written a few letters to Elias. Kept some, threw some out, but never sent any of them. I'd managed to read through most of the journals that Morgana sent me too, but hadn't yet got to the part where Jason and Falcon had been… 'close'. One thing I did know for sure was that Jason was a much darker person than I ever would have imagined. He kept that hidden, *really* hidden, but I could see why he made a good king. He was fair, generous, and loving, but… wow, he was a killer at heart, and he didn't stand back from this love he longed for with as much poise and grace as we all thought. I was actually surprised he hadn't killed my dad and run away with my mom. And what's worse: he wrote some of those journals while he was with Lily! No wonder she got so jealous.

Here, I'll show you a passage:

I know why he followed me here. After the First Woman's Curse was broken and Ara went back to her old life, to her husband, with her memories now restored, there was no place for Falcon there. He's an outsider to her heart, just as I am. And though I have Lily now, it eases none of the burden. Lily is my soul mate, and yet my love for Ara is so set in my bones that I can't let her go.

I never will.

I am now, and forever will hold out hope that there is a way to make her mine.

That's why Falcon came to Loslilian. We're kin, in that sense, and when we sit for these long hours, drinking whiskey by the fire, nothing ever need be said. We can talk about life, about politics, responsibilities, but we never talk about Ara, because everything that needs to be said is done so, better, in silence.

See what I mean? It's pretty messed-up. I love Uncle Jase, but I feel super sorry for him, and for Falcon. I wanted to call him and tell him I understood. I wanted to wish him, Mike, Harry, and Mia a happy Christmas, but I didn't want to talk to Mom and Dad. At all. So I had to play it like I'd just missed their calls, speak to no one so I wouldn't have to speak to those two. I would never forgive them for sending me away, didn't really even want to return home anymore. Even in my isolation, I liked it here and I liked hanging out with Drake and waiting around for moments when Elias might visit the castle. This is the life I wanted now, and it was their own fault for sending me here.

In a red dress, strapless, of course, that was fitted to the base of my ribs and then puffed into a gentle outward flow, I inspected myself in the full mirror. My eyes shone against this color, and with my hair up, exposing my neckline to entice the vampire, I felt like I'd turn all the right heads: all *one* of them: Elias's.

He wanted to wait until I was eighteen before we got closer, but I wanted to kiss him tonight. Just one kiss—maybe lasting a few hours. Just something to hold onto, dream about, over the next year. I was certain my parents would force me to come back home, back to school, to be a normal teenager for a while longer, and Drake would support them in that. But once I turned eighteen, I'd trade it all in for a life as a Lilithian and a trip to London to see where this friendship, this… *feeling* might go. It had only grown over the last three months, and so had I. I didn't feel like the same young, somewhat innocent and playful girl I was when I first arrived here, and I hoped Elias saw the differences tonight.

In my letters—the ones I never sent—I'd gone from writing 'Hey, Elias' to 'Dear Elias' and the common appearance of an 'LOL' here and there or an exclamation mark to support my excitement had reshaped instead to more mature, sentimental lines of text. I grew up in those letters to Elias, and I was ready for what came next, even though no one that loved me would allow it.

I opened my door and quickly slipped my hand into my bra to lift my boobs up and make them look fuller, then shut the door and headed down the corridor, grabbing Nate as my escort on the way in.

"You look pretty tonight," he noted.

"Thanks. So do you."

He straightened his red bowtie and then his dorky Christmas vest, winking at me. "This is my favorite season."

"Me too." I looked up at the festive splendor around the

ballroom as we entered. Drake really had gone all-out for this ball—to make it special for me—with garlands of lemon-scented pine, adorned with red baubles and holly, curled around almost every pillar. Little yellow fairy lights twinkled among the brush, while red-and-green candles marked every table or stood proudly in candelabras between chairs at the edge of the room. The dim light made the space more intimate, while a giant banquet table with glistening crystal glasses and polished silver invited us to be hungry by the hooked finger of wafting turkey and mince pies.

Nate walked me to my spot at the table, and I greeted everyone with a gentle nod, feeling Elias's eyes on me the second we walked in but refusing to look at him. I only had to look at Falcon's defensive glare, turned in that direction, to get a sense of what Elias thought. And I just felt so adored.

Nate sat me down and pushed my chair in, sitting beside me after. I nodded a greeting to my grandfather, who pressed a hand to his heart, shaking his head with an expression of complete awe.

Thanks, I mouthed, tipping my head to my shoulder as if to bashfully accept his praise when, in truth, I knew I looked perfect because I'd planned it that way.

Over by the windows, a man sat at a piano, a woman beside him with a violin, and they played gentle Christmas tunes to set the tone of the evening. Everyone laughed and talked as though there were no cares in the world, and as I let my eyes stray down toward Elias's seat, watching him tip his head back as he laughed at someone's joke, I wished I'd been sat there beside him. I got a sense then that I might always feel that way now.

After a seasonal toast from the King, and the best feast I'd ever had—even better, sorry Uncle Mike, than what I grew up with—people started moving to the dance floor. My heart hammered as Nate stood and offered his hand, wishing Elias had asked instead.

We only made it as far as the edge of the dance floor before Elias appeared, though, and 'politely' suggested to Nate that it was better for his wellbeing if he gave away the first dance with me.

Nate laughed, realizing he'd meant his comment playfully, and stepped away with a bow to his superior.

"Aubrey Knight," Elias said softly, and as he moved into me, all the little molecules of energy on the surface of my body reached out to him, even though I didn't move.

"Mr. Davenport." I greeted him with a bow of the head.

"I feel as if I don't know where to touch you." His eyes searched the bare skin along my shoulders and chest, making me feel ethereal. "Because if I place my hands anywhere on you right now, it would be an act of sin."

I laughed to hide the sudden rush of shyness that made me turn pink. "Then, maybe… just for tonight, we can pretend I'm eighteen."

"I wish I could." He brought his head down and rested it on mine, curling an arm round my ribs and holding me close. "But, on my honor, I could not rightly ask your father for your hand one day if I had touched you before it was appropriate."

"You want to ask my father for my hand?"

His wise eyes fixed curiously on mine. "Is that not the custom?"

"Um… when you know each other better." I laughed in the back of my throat because he was so ridiculously out of touch with the times, but it was also just so endearing. "But… we haven't even 'courted' yet."

"And yet my intentions for our future are clear, even then."

I wanted to be scared. It made sense to feel that way. I

wanted to tell him this was moving too fast. But, in his day, that was the way it was done. It was sweet. And scary. And… kind of okay with me. I smiled, trying really hard not to laugh like a giddy, stupid teenage girl.

In his big hand, he cradled mine against his solid chest, and it felt warm and soft and safe. I'd never needed anyone to make me feel safe before, and I didn't feel like I was in any danger right now, but somehow, I just felt safe anyway. And maybe it was in the sense that I felt like he 'got me', and that he'd always side with me, be my backup, my wingman, my go-to for when the world didn't make sense. And I liked that. The word 'safe' took on a new meaning for me.

I wriggled my fingers then to lay them flat against his chest, closed in like a bug in the petals of a flower, with his head on top of mine, his arm around me. I didn't care if anyone saw us this way. They could look. It wasn't socially acceptable, at all, but I was okay with that.

"Elias?" I said softly, catching the sharp scent of his cologne as I drew his name in like a breath.

"Yes, my darling?"

"Will you kiss me?"

His hand tightened on mine, his fingers at my ribs curling over a little more. "I feel it would make the days waiting a lot harder to bear," he said softly, ignoring the world as another song started around us. "It might be best if we saved that."

Disappointed, but still not ready to let it go, I rolled my face up to look at him. He shut his eyes slowly when he met mine, and I knew I had him. I did that same thing my mom would do to my dad when she wanted something from him. It was a sparkle she put behind her eyes, like she was imagining all the love in the world right there in front of her, and Dad would melt.

Elias fell for it too, and I quietly thanked Mom, as he took my hands and asked me to take a turn with him out in the fresh air which, in old-guy-speak, meant go for a stroll.

We walked for a long time in perfect silence, my hand closed-up safely in his, and when we stopped under the tree where we'd first talked that day, he took off his coat and wrapped it around my arms. It was big, swam on me, but it was warm and smelled like manly cologne, cigars, and rich old books. I pressed my nose to the collar, wondering if he might forget he put this on me tonight so I could keep it.

In the circles of light beaming off the lamps up by the castle, I noticed tiny motes of snow beginning to fall, and smiled. In Australia, we had hot summer sun for Christmas every year, but I loved the snow and it would be so magical if we had our first kiss on the first day of the snow.

Elias stood right in front of me then, both hands on my arms, and I rolled my face all the way up to look at his eyes. He had so much kindness and refinement, and that centuries-old wisdom behind his gaze that made me feel like nothing could ever touch him.

"I've made a fool of myself," he said.

"How so?"

"Holding you that way in front of my colleagues, my king. Your grandfather."

I laughed. "He doesn't mind, or he'd have broken us apart."

Elias looked at the ballroom behind me, his eyes coming back with regret. "I cannot be trusted alone with you. I am no longer a man of integrity."

"Argh, don't be so hard on yourself." I reached over and slapped his arm with the back of my wrist. "I'm kind of manipulating you, you know?"

He leaned back slightly. "You are?"

"Yes. I totally know all the tricks, Elias. I learned from the master."

"Your father?"

"My mother." I smirked.

"You hold such power over me," he said softly, casting his eyes downward. "I'm not a complete man when I am with you, as if I have no morals, no values, no strength."

I pulled my shoulder up to my chin. "Girls can have that effect on guys."

"I've never fallen so hard. Or fast," he added. "I wanted to take things slowly. Learn more about you, who you are, where your heart lies."

"Just because you kiss me doesn't mean that's rushing things. Not in my opinion. And not in my generation, either. People kiss all the time."

"And it has no meaning," he said. "But it does to me. Probably more than it does to you, which is why I cannot kiss you. When I do, it will not be just an electric moment of connection, Aubrey, it will be a promise."

"What kind of promise?"

"The promise of so much more; of eternity, not because it is what I desire but because I know you by that point in time, love you, enough to be certain that we can endure such a timespan," he said, drawing me deeper into his eyes with each word. "It will be a vow that I cannot live without you, that I will not. And that I will fight any cause to keep you by my side. It is a promise I am not willing to swear to you yet."

"Not willing to or not *wanting* to?"

He smiled, his eyes shrinking as he looked away, like a vexed kitty cat. He sat down then on the park bench and exhaled a lungful of regret into his hands, the warmth of it making a cloud around him. "All is lost."

"Why?"

"I am a cretin. A perverted sinner—"

"Why?" I sat down beside him.

"I will be damned for this, Aubrey. You're a child."

"Damned for what? You haven't done anything to me… *yet*." I grinned, leaning closer.

"No, but I'm about to." He clutched the sides of my face, holding me there as though he might be able to stop himself. When he angled his head and the cool air brushed the warmth between us, my lips tingled, and my skin sung with possibility. But as my eyes rolled to a slow close, weighed down by the emotions between us, he drew away.

My attention flicked to the figure in front of me, standing now in a deep bow instead of sitting beside me, as my grandfather marched toward us.

"My King," Elias said, sounding like a medieval knight.

"Mr. Davenport." Drake delivered the words with an air of politeness but a deep undertone of disapproval that was as obvious as it was concealed.

Elias wiped a hand across his mouth then and stalked away quickly, leaving me alone in the shadow of my grandfather's extreme disappointment.

"Aubrey," he said softly.

"I…" A shot of hurt ran through my heart, breaking it a little as I watched Elias walk away. "You ruined my kiss!"

"He made a vow, Aubrey," Drake said, suddenly beside me. "He made me a vow that he would not touch you until you turned eighteen."

"Why?"

"Because it's what I want for you, my dear." He pulled my hand to make me stand, drawing me in for a gentle hug. "Once you begin a courtship with Elias, it will be a very short one that precedes marriage, and I just want you to grow up a little more before then, okay?"

"But it's so intense." I touched my chest, drawing away from his warmth. "I almost feel like my whole body wants to be sucked up into his."

Drake laughed. "Yes, I imagine young love is quite potent."

I nodded.

"Come." He turned us away. "We can fill you with sugar and eggnog. That will help."

"Okay," I huffed. "But… I'll come up in a minute. I just need some air."

Drake hesitated, looking around the yard before he nodded to agree. I gathered that meant Elias wasn't hanging nearby, watching, and I felt empty because of it. Why did he have to go and make a vow! Those were ironclad in this society.

I sat down on the bench and wrapped myself up tightly in his silky-soft coat, looking at the stars. I made a wish on each one then—that he'd come back here now and at least kiss my cheek or hold me again—but he didn't. And I knew that if I didn't go back in soon, Drake would worry. And I would freeze. So I headed up, heels sinking into the new snowfall, finally managing to smile as I thought about how badly Elias had, at least, *wanted* to kiss me. He was so close to breaking his vow. That had to mean a lot. Well, it meant a lot to *me*.

But all those delicious thoughts stopped dead when I saw Beth on the balcony, shivering in her sparkly red dress, with her arms crossed over her waist, tears streaming her cheeks. The smile slipped right off my face and I hopped up beside her unexpectedly, making her shriek.

"Beth, you okay?"

"Go away, Aubrey." She stormed off, wiping her face.

"Why?" I followed her along the balcony, wrapping myself tightly in Elias's coat. "What did I ever do to you?"

"Your mother is a thief," she shouted, wheeling around with tight fists and a red face. "She betrayed my mom, sided with Jason. She doesn't deserve to live with half of my mother's soul, and I want it back."

"How can you say his name like that? With no love. He raised you, Beth—"

"And he's a liar. He's not my father. He abandoned us—"

"He didn't abandon you." I stepped closer. "Lily wouldn't let him see you."

"That's just the story he's giving." She folded her arms, but I could tell from her face that she wasn't entirely sure about that. "The truth is, he left because he fucked your mother and she tainted him against mine—"

"Your mom drugged Jason and my mom, and she drugged my dad too, all so *she* could have him," I yelled, pointing at the giant windows behind us. "She's the evil bitch here, Beth. She did all of this! And now my mom is left caring for a baby she didn't want, to a man she doesn't love!"

"What?" Beth leaned back, a small puff of air escaping between parted lips, forming a foggy circle of regret in the cold between us. "Daniel's my dad's baby?"

"I—"

Her throat made a funny high noise and she spun away, bursting into tears. Lily appeared out of nowhere then, sweeping Beth into her arms and casting me an accusatory glare. "What did you say to her?"

"Is it true, Mom?" Beth cried, looking up at her. "Is Daniel really Dad's baby?"

Lily's head whipped up and her cold, deep-set eyes went even wider, as if that were possible. "Is this true?"

"I…" I shuffled back a step, searching the ballroom beyond the glass for Drake.

"That's all I needed to know," she said grimly and spun away, leaving Beth to fall back onto an empty embrace, alone.

"Look what you've done!" Beth stomped her foot, running after her mother.

Heads turned as Lily stormed into the ballroom and shoved Beth off when she tried to reach for her. And a pocket of dread filled up my stomach, giving me the sense that Lily was the reason my mom had planned to take that secret to her grave. It wasn't to protect Dad, or the illusion of their impenetrable marriage, or even to protect Jase. It was simply to protect us all from Lily's wrath.

I wondered if I should tell Morgana what had happened, if maybe Lily would set out now to make Jason's life hell again or to call him up and scream at him. Or at my mom. But it was Lily's fault. She did this. She drugged Mom. So she had no right to be angry at them.

I decided instead to go back in and enjoy the ball—not let Lily or her melodrama get to me. I did, however, feel immensely sorry for Beth.

JULES

Mia showed me how to thread the daisy into the chain, where we lay under the big shady gumtree in Mike's backyard, with the sour smell of hot grass and eucalyptus etching the moment into permanent memory. Last night, as we sat on his porch drinking coffee and looking across at the bushland between us and the lake, I'd seen a family of kangaroos bouncing past. It was such a surreal moment, like nothing I'd ever experienced before, but this was topping that. I liked this house, this plush grass beneath the rug, and the warmth of the hot December sun. I liked looking up and seeing the big windows overlooking the yard, knowing that there was an abundance of love and kindness and support within those walls like I'd never known before in my life. Not even with Jason in those blissful days before I was stolen and had my memory erased. Somehow, my life here these past three months had slowly gone from being an escape from the horror to a waking dream I couldn't believe I'd been lucky enough to fall into.

Mike came over and sat down hard on the rug beside Mia,

taking her daisy chain and popping it on his head like a crown. "Do I look pretty?" he asked.

I laughed, smirking at Mia. "You're such a dork, Mike," I noted.

Mia rolled up to sit. "I'm gonna get a drink. You guys want one?"

"I'll get it," Mike offered. "I'll grab some sandwiches while I'm in there."

"M'kay." Mia shrugged, sitting back down with me. I sat up, hugging my knees, my failed daisy chain dangling from my fingertips.

"I like this," Mia said.

"What?"

"This." She motioned between her and me. "I know you're not… like… I know you're not *with* my dad or anything like that, but… it just kinda feels like a family again."

Her words went right through my core and sliced me clean open. Holy shit. I wanted to stand up and move away, reset this. I never even realized that my talking late at night with Mike, or chatting with Mia about boys, sitting together on Friday nights and playing board games, might be totally misconstrued. She was falling in love with the idea of us as a family, and it was so far from the truth that I was scared to even speak right now in case I shattered that dream and hurt a probably very fragile teenage girl. I hadn't even had sex with Mike, or held his hand, and yet Mia was resigning me to happy families!

As if the heavens heard my prayer then, her phone rang from inside the house, and she ran off to answer it just as Mike came out with a tray of food.

"You must have prepared that at vamp speed," I noted, taking the tray so he could sit down.

"Maybe." He grinned, raising both brows. He plucked a

triangle of sandwich off the tray then and bent his knees to rest his elbows on them.

"So... um... Mia just said..." I wasn't sure I could say it. This time here with Mike had meant everything to me. And, in some ways, I knew I did love him. And I loved Mia too. They were my family. I didn't want to ruin this, or try to force it to a place it wasn't ready to go. I broke up with Jason a little over three months ago, and I wasn't ready for anyone else to fill that hole yet.

"I know." Mike nodded. "I heard. Why do you think I made these so fast?"

"Oh." I picked one up and pinched the corner.

"It's okay," he assured me, chewing with his mouth open. "She's just grasping at anything to make her feel safe right now after losing Aubrey. They've been two peas in a pod since Aubrey was born, and I'm really pissed at Ara for sending her away. I get it," he added, slightly defensive as though I was going to defend her, "but she could have at least taken Mia into consideration."

"She's scared for Aubrey's life, Mike."

"I know. But now I'm left with a teenage girl, a very sensitive teenage girl, who needs her mom or her best friend. And so now she's latching on to you for that female role model, and..." He shrugged one shoulder, as though it was too heavy. "I'm worried it's gonna scare you off."

"Why?" I grinned, leaning across to bump him with my arm. "You starting to like having me around?"

He smiled to himself, catching my need to avoid anything being established between us. "This doesn't have to be anything, Jules," he said, biting another triangle of sandwich. "Ever. I get that we have a connection, you and I. We get along like we've been friends forever, and I don't want that to change."

"Me neither."

"Good." He nodded, putting his sandwich down and dusting off his hands. "So let's just not… you know."

"Not what? Fall in love?"

"Not give it a name. If it happens. If this…" He motioned around the yard as though it was a feeling. "If things stay this way, if it gets stronger, then I'm cool with that. But let's not label it."

"I'm cool with that," I said, facing the front again and trying really hard to hold back my smile. It was true. I was cool with that. I was still broken and not my whole-self, but Mike, his books, his conversations, his brownies, his piano playing, his long walks and days by the lake… they were slowly bringing me back to life, and I didn't want to admit it, but I could fall in love with him for that. And it made it so much easier now because he wasn't trying to force anything. Didn't even want to give it a name.

We met eyes and smiled then, our grins growing warmer the longer we looked at each other.

"I like this," I said, reaching over to brush my thumb down his stubble.

"Thanks. I like yours too," he joked, running his thumb over my chin.

"Ha-ha." I shoved his hand off, whacking his thigh. The sound of his laughter mingled with the hum of the leaves blowing in the wind and the gentle song of Australian insects, and made the air tingle.

"It's so easy with a place," I noted, bringing my eyes back down from the long, thin leaves and the fat little gumnuts of the tree.

"What?"

"To fall in love." I put the sandwich down and crawled over to kneel in front of him. "I love it here, Mike. I know you think

Mia's overbearing and clingy, but I love her too. And there's only one person in this entire vicinity right now that I can't say that about."

"Ara?" he joked.

"No. *You*," I confessed. "Which means there's a reason I don't want to say it."

One corner of his mouth lifted into a sharp, sexy grin, and he ducked his head shyly. I wasn't sure I'd ever seen him bashful.

"I don't know what this is yet either," I said, "but if I can love this place, your home—"

"It's your home too," he said.

I pouted sweetly, glancing back at it for a moment—at the way it seemed to sit there watching us with a smile on its face. "If I can love that, love Mia, love Rockingham, why can't I say I love you, even if it's not that kind of love?"

"Guess maybe it is that kind of love then," he said, his warm brown eyes stealing mine and trapping me here in this dream. "Because I can't admit it either, Jules. I won't even let myself go there."

"Cool."

His smile grew, pulling up sharply on one side. "Cool."

Mia came out then and Mike laid back, while I sat in my spot, acting like nothing had happened. And it hadn't, I guess. Because nothing had been admitted, and yet everything had.

ARA

I sat down on the swing and sipped my tea, watching Danny run around the yard chasing a magpie, who had adopted Aubrey when she was younger and, now, ten years on, came by in the mornings to play with Daniel. Its pointed beak looked formidable and the trained eye of an Aussie knew the black-and-white plumage often meant “run in the other direction”, since the breed would typically swoop down on unsuspecting cyclists and pedestrians, attempting to remove their eyes, but this bird was a trusted and loyal old friend, and I wasn't worried about Daniel's safety. He'd even named it Corvi, which was much more original than Maggie—the name Aubrey had given it.

The day had that calm, easy feel to it, like I knew Daniel would be a gem today and we'd maybe get to bedtime without a tantrum. I knew David would be home any minute and I could feel a sort of warmth emanating off the trees, like new love was budding somewhere. It made everything feel okay, and I sat back a bit more, relaxing a little deeper than I had in a long time.

My phone rang then, and I almost thought about leaving it to voice-mail, but David was at the store and if I didn't answer, he'd come home with the wrong baby shampoo again. So, I got up, putting my cup down and double-checking the pool gate was shut before heading inside.

Jase's name flashed up on the caller ID, so I stood by the window and quickly answered it. "Hey you."

"Ara?" He sounded panicked. "Where's Danny?"

"Outside." I stepped back out and spotted him going down the glossy red slide, Corvi waiting for him at the bottom. "I'm looking at him. Why?"

"I got a note too. I'm not supposed to call you, but I wanted to warn—" The line went dead. I drew the phone down from my ear, staring at it, replaying the panic in his tone. And when I looked up, my yard was empty.

A wave of panic rolled over my entire body, bringing bumps out on my skin. I dropped my phone and rushed to the cubby hole to see if Danny was in there.

"Danny?" I called. "Baby, this isn't funny. Where are you?"

Even the magpie was gone.

Frantically, I searched every corner of the yard, before running over to the pool and yanking the gate open, checking the water with my hand to my heart, its thumping beat making me shake and then die with relief to see the empty bottom.

"Danny!"

A fluster of wind moved my hair then and a note landed at my feet. I could feel a deep, radiating pull all over my body, like gravity pushing down on me—the presence of witchcraft. I was being watched.

Kneeling down in the prickly wet grass, I tried to open the letter but the trembling in my hands made it take longer. *I have him,* it said. *He's safe. As long as you get on a plane right now and don't tell anyone where you're going. You know where to find me.*

Lily.

The note curled in on itself then, igniting a second later and turning to ash.

"Oh my god," I cried, folding over to hug myself. What if she found out that Daniel was Jason's?

I looked up in panic then as the front door opened. David couldn't find me here like this. She said not to tell anyone. I wasn't willing to risk Danny's life by defying her, and at the same time, David and I had always been stronger when we faced things together, free of secrets. I had seconds to make my decision, the life of my beautiful little boy hanging in the balance, tipped either way by what I decided to do right now.

"Ara?" David called into the yard, but I was already gone, moving like the wind as I placed my baby above the promise I'd made to him to never keep a secret.

I didn't know it in that moment, but as he entered the yard and dropped the grocery bag to the ground, sensing the devastating energy within that place, it was the last time I'd ever see him again… as who he was to me now.

AUBREY

I squealed, folding down to keep the ball from Nate. He reached around my ribs and knocked it out of my hands, swooping in then with the speed of a vampire to steal it. Even though I didn't stand a chance, I darted after him, leaping up just as he tossed it toward the hoop, and knocked it to the ground.

"Nice one, human," he teased. "Let's see you try that again."

I tossed him the ball, and he bent slightly, bouncing it from one side to the other. When I moved in for it, he spun, walking up the court, while a snowy breeze swept into the stadium through the suddenly open door. I glanced over my shoulder for no real reason at all then, seeing Drake march toward us at an unusual speed.

"Uh-oh."

"What's uh-oh?" Nate stopped bouncing and looked up as well. "Oh, uh-oh."

I nodded. "He looks pissed."

"Here." He handed me the ball. "I'll catch up with you later."

"Kay."

Nate took off at vamp speed, and I shrunk under the harsh glare of my grandfather's evil eye. "I need the truth, now."

"Okay... what?" I threw the ball down and let it roll away against the bleachers.

"What did you say to Beth last week?"

"Um... A bit, why?"

He sat down on the bench nearby, head on his hand. "I am told by several of my subjects that Lily was seen storming away in an argument with Beth. It wasn't until now that I'm made aware that you had something to do with that."

How could I have gone from loving Beth like a sister, my whole life, to hating her right now? I totally understood my mom then—to feel so betrayed by Lily. "What did the little dibber-dobber say? Because—"

"She didn't say anything, Aubrey." He exhaled, closing both hands slowly over his face and pinching his open lips between them. "It's what they've *done* that concerns me, or *may have* done."

"What do you mean?" I sat down too.

"No one has seen Jason, David, Ara, or Daniel for a few days—"

"What?" The ground stretched beneath my feet, and I felt suddenly itchy all over my body with no real reason to be. "What do you mean? How do you know?"

"Mike saw Ara out in the front yard two days ago, and he saw David return from the supermarket with bags of shopping later that morning. He hasn't seen them since. They're not answering their phones. Jason hasn't been at Elora's house, and it was just assumed that he'd gone a few towns over to kill."

"Are you sure he hasn't?"

Drake shook his head, looking so human right now—scared,

worried, not a mighty king. “His phone was found near Ara’s house, and when they managed to get into it, the last call made was to your mother. It lasted six seconds.”

“Did anyone check my house? Maybe Uncle Jason is there with Mom—”

“Yes. Her phone was found broken on the back porch. The shopping bags dropped carelessly to the ground beside it.” He turned his electric eyes onto me. “The milk had spoiled in the heat. The butter melted.”

It sunk in then. “It’s my fault, isn’t it?”

“Why? What did you say to Beth that would possibly see Lily abduct four people?”

“Abduct? Oh my god.” I buried my head in both hands, shaking it. “I only told them Daniel is Jason’s baby,”—Drake sighed as I said it—“I didn’t realize… I just thought Mom didn’t want to hurt Uncle Jase with the secret about Daniel. I honestly didn’t know anyone was in danger because of it—”

“No, and how could you know?” he said calmly. “We’ve kept that side of Lily carefully concealed from the children in this family. If anyone were to blame here, it is I. I should have warned you.” He reached over and put his hand on my shoulder as the gravity of this hit me in the stomach. “It will be alright. I will send my men to Loslilian at once—”

“How do you know she’s there?”

“My sister is the queen. It is my duty to know where she is. And if we find her, we possibly find Ara and the others.” He stood up. “I will set this right, my dear. You have my word.”

“Should I come with you—”

“No. If I know Lily, then this news will have shattered her. And knowing what I know now, I am certain she means to harm that little boy.”

I folded in on myself, my entire face mashing into an ugly cube as I cried.

"I don't want you there to see that," he finished.

"You have to save him, Drake. Please, he's only a baby—"

"I will do my best." He nodded once and walked away, slow and heavy, like he carried the entire world on his shoulders right now.

But he didn't need to carry it alone. I stood up, fists clenched. This was my mess, and I would be damned if I let him fix it without me.

HARRY

I drove for four hours, leaving Rochelle at home with the dogs and Grandma Vicki, because I wasn't quite ready to tell Uncle Arthur that she was alive. He'd moved out here, well-away from family—away from the world of the supernatural—so that he could live a life of peace. And we were supposed to respect that. He'd come for family gatherings, Christmas, the occasional birthday—like a twenty-first—but other than that, he just wanted to live a very separate, very human life. Bringing the girl here who triggered fifty years of feuding between Dad and his brother would not be honoring that agreement.

When I pulled up in the driveway of his beachfront home, he appeared in the doorway, arms folded. I knew I should have called, and it was a risk that he might be at the hospital if he was on shift tonight, but if I'd let him know I was coming, he'd have said no straight up when I told him why.

"Uncle Arthur."

"Harry, what brings you to my neck of the woods?"

I ran lazily up the steps and hugged him, noting the humanness of his aging form and how I was now the same height as him. "You look tired, old man." I clapped both of his arms affectionately.

His smile warmed, that eternal familial connection flaring within his almost-matching eyes. "I am tired. I've just spent sixteen hours in surgery."

"Wow. Tough case?"

"Very. Humans are much harder to fix than vampires," he remarked. "Now, what brings you here?"

Here goes nothin'. "Mom's gone missing."

"I beg your pardon?"

"None of us have seen or heard from her or Dad. Or Uncle Jason."

Arthur groaned, running his hand over his face, as if to rub away the exhaustion of this life. "Are you concerned that something is afoot?"

"Yes," I said, holding his gaze so he'd understand the gravity of this next bit. "Arthur… Lily drugged my mom and Jason… about three years ago. And we think, maybe, she found out that Daniel is Jason's son."

He understood exactly what I'd wanted to convey. Not just the fact that Lily was known for her temper, and that my family were now missing, but also the fact that Jason had a son. No one could possibly understand more than Arthur what that had meant to my uncle. It meant a lot to me when Elora told me this morning, and I still hadn't quite stopped celebrating on his behalf.

"Where is the child?"

"Missing too."

He backed inside. "You had better come in."

Sitting at the wide island counter in Arthur's giant kitchen, I explained everything over a few cups of coffee. It felt good to talk with him again. Almost as if everything might be okay if he'd accept my proposal.

After a while, when the most important part of the truth had come out, I tested the waters, addressing the topic of Rochelle. Arthur was surprised to learn of her resurrection, but he also wasn't.

"Ghosts tend to linger near those they were once connected to. In fact," he said, "we should warn Aubrey to be careful who she brings through, now that I think of it."

"Why?"

"There are some enemies we might not want alive again."

I nodded, knowing my parents had many. Ever since I was a little kid with an adorable speech impediment, I'd seen the darker side of the world inside their thoughts, and even I wouldn't want some of those people walking around out there.

"Arthur, without Mom and Dad here, and with no way of knowing what's happened, or what's *happening*, I need to know more about my abilities. You always said you'd teach me when I grew up and… it's time to teach me."

Arthur groaned and turned away, walking over to the fridge. "I don't have time for this, Harry. I have a life—"

"And my mom's life, my *dad's* is hanging in the balance right now. I know you care. So don't pretend that your job as a surgeon—*job*, not *life*—is more important than they are."

He slammed the fridge and sat down on the stool, shaking his head. "We've had seventeen years of peace, and now this," Arthur barked angrily. "Can a man no longer age without the world coming to a god-damn end!"

"I'm sorry, Uncle Arthur. I know you just wanted to live out a human existence, but I need you. I need you to become a vampire again and I need you to show me how to manipulate the minds of a hundred men in one room."

He sighed, cradling his head in his hands. He was so much older now than when he first came through the veil. Ten years had altered him beyond recognition. He was gray in places, hairier, taller and broader, and his eyes crinkled deeply now when he smiled. And his brows, where he pushed them up every time he had to convince a patient they wouldn't die, had formed a row of neat lines across his forehead. If he turned back now, he'd be this older, more mature man for eternity. It would be an easier life than the twenty-five-years he carried in his previous immortal form, but there was a burden here bigger than age.

"Being a vampire again will make it easier to spend sixteen hours in surgery," I offered, flashing him a grin when he looked at me.

He smiled before lowering his eyes again. "And who will turn me? You?"

"Yes."

"Do you know how?"

I laughed once, because I'd done this many times. "Yes. I plucked it right out of Dad's head."

"Very well." He stood up, altering himself now into the tall, wise vampire within his mind, which showed in his lordly disposition. "Turn me back. I will teach you what I know, track down your parents, and then you will all leave me in peace again—at least until the next great family tragedy."

I sat a little taller, laughing out my relief. "Thanks, Uncle Arthur."

"Don't thank me just yet. I may return to the immortal state without any powers at all."

"For my little brother's sake, I really hope not."

HER PHONE RANG OUT TWICE. I TUCKED MY ARM UNDER MY elbow to hold it up, calling the number again as I glanced at Arthur, where he slept away his anguish on the couch. It had been over twenty-six hours since we realized Mom was missing, and nine hours since Arthur began the transition back to vampire. His heart had stopped within the first four hours and he was now sleeping it all off, not breathing, as his cells changed. But I still needed it to go faster.

"Harry! Where are you?" Elora screeched when she finally picked up. "I went to your house—"

"I'm with Arthur."

"What?"

I couldn't hold back my grin, knowing what she'd say. "He's a vampire again."

"What!" Her voice went so high that it hurt my sensitive immortal ear. I held the phone away from it for a moment while she raged in the exact way I'd expected her to.

I laughed. "Chill out, Lors. He's fine with it."

"Mom and Dad are going to fucking kill you, Harry!"

"If they're even alive to do that, Lors," I shot back. "We need him. He was one of the most powerful mind-manipulators of his time—"

"Yeah, *of his time*, but we don't know what he can do now, Harry. He wasn't born, he didn't live, grow, his brain is barely ten years old. There's no saying he will *ever* have any powers."

"Well, I had to try." I sat down on the dining room chair, watching him.

"Look, I know you're scared for Mom and Dad. And I

know... we all feel the same, Harry. None of us can possibly imagine a world where they're not here, where they're not watching over us all. But it was wrong to place that responsibility on Uncle Arthur—to make him immortal just because you need a parental figure—"

"That's not why I did it."

"Come on, Harry. I know you better than that."

A pang of guilt surged through me. *Was* that the reason I did it? Because I needed a father-figure? Elora had Mike, and if Mom never came back, then Mike would raise Daniel, as per their agreement. But I never bonded with Mike the way the girls did. I had Arthur. He was like me.

"Look, I know you were close with Arthur in the early days, when he lived here with us. But... he's not your father. He can't replace your father—"

"You don't know what you're talking about, Elora."

"Then why did you call me Elora just then?" she said smugly. "You only do that when you're losing at an argument."

I huffed, sinking down in the chair to bring my ankle up on my knee. "What if she's hurting them?" I said softly, my voice sounding deeper through the phone. "I know Dad can handle it. I know Mom can come through it. Uncle Jase will be okay. But... what about Daniel?"

Elora sighed. "I can't think about that right now, Harry."

"Why? We have to, Lors—"

"Because Drake thinks she is," she said, and my whole world shrunk, thinking of that little round baby face and the big toothy smile. "Drake says she's a spiteful tantrum-throwing little bitch and he wouldn't put it past her."

A hand appeared on my shoulder then as I broke down to tears, and Arthur, suddenly awake and standing beside me, took the phone.

"Elora."

"Uncle Arthur?" Elora cried, and even *she* sounded relieved to hear his voice.

"Does Drake have any word yet about your mother—"

"Yes. They tracked her at Loslilian a few hours ago. He's sending his men in there now."

"And what about Daniel? And my twins?"

"Dad and Jason are being masked by magic. We don't know where they are. But Daniel is with Mom, from what the witches can tell."

"Then, perhaps, there is hope. Keep us posted."

"I can't. I'm flying out now. You need to meet us there."

"I gotta stop home and grab Rochelle first," I said, a bit louder so she'd hear.

"Bad idea, Harry," Elora said. "If Lily learns who she is—that she was once Jason's great love—she might hurt her."

I sighed, bending over to curl my hands around my face.

"We'll see you soon," Arthur said, and he hung up the phone, looking down at me.

"That was fast," I said solemnly. "Your transition."

"Not as fast as the first time I became a vampire, and a hundred times more painful, I might add."

I wiped my face, feeling heavy inside as I sat up and looked at him. "You were a Drakarian vampire then—"

"And now, it seems, I am a..." His brow pulled, still showing the age that we'd all come to know, to love, on his face, "Harry-ian?"

I laughed once. "I have no idea."

"What about your created?" he asked, pulling out the chair beside me and sitting down at a slight lean inward, his hands gathered between us. "Are they hybrid-feeders, like you?"

"No. Drake says that because I chose to be a human-blood-drinker, my created will be too." Not that I'd ever asked them. And I couldn't even tell Arthur that I'd created before, not without getting in a heaping pile of shit from Mom and Dad, and possibly placed on trial if anyone else found out.

Arthur nodded.

"Would you rather be a hybrid?" I asked.

"I'm not entirely sure." He rubbed his chin, looking over at a giant painting on the wall—one of Uncle Cal's. Beside it, a portrait of our entire family—before Daniel—stared back at us, swathing the conversation in a heavy, grim tone. "I need blood."

"Okay." I stood. "Come on. We'll feed on the way to the airport."

AUBREY

We came by chopper, twenty in my unit, and hovered over a clearing at the base of a slope on the south side of the island, where the trees thinned out between the forest and the ocean. Patches of snow had been worn away by the obvious scuffles, revealing muddy grass, made bloody by battle.

My entire heart rumbled as I stood by the edge of that door and readied myself to jump, but part of the nerves were for hoping no one recognized me and realized I wasn't a member of the team—that I'd snuck in, grabbed an outfit, a weapon, and then marched off with them all as if I were in the army. A few had sniffed at me, curious, which was because I smelled human, but they clearly just figured I was Lilithian, since they pretty much smelled the same.

"Three seconds, from my count!" the chief called. "Break the line of defense at the border, storm the manor grounds, find Queen Ara."

On the ground below us, clusters of men and women pushed

back and forth at each other, long bloodied swords coming up between them. I measured the numbers with a quick sweeping gaze, counting roughly six in the cluster to my right—four good guys and two bad guys—and two more clusters of about ten, the numbers dwindling quickly as Drake's men overcame them. I'd clearly picked the right side to be fighting on. I'd have to tell Falcon that his men sucked. I'd heard great tales about his army —*his*, because he trained them—but they'd really let the ball drop since Lily took over and appointed a new Chief.

At the call of the signal, we all jumped the last meter from the chopper and, when my feet landed on that slippery dead grass, heart hammering, and I saw the big cream fascia of the manor rise up in the distance, I was nothing but ready. I hadn't grabbed a sweater when I'd changed into black cargos and a black t-shirt, but I wasn't cold, even in the snow. My blood was pumping, hot and ready for battle.

The whir of the chopper receded and left me in the dense, wet surrounds of a violent brawl. Real battle looked nothing like a Game of Thrones episode. It was all grunts and clinks, and the screams seemed to come up above a still kind of silence, like listening to the men spar at the training hall when I was little. It seemed otherwise calm; no intense, inspiring battle music, no hero montage. Just people swinging hard stuff at each other, and fleshy stuff being cut open. Oddly, the sound of a sword going through a person didn't really sound like it did on tv either. The grunt they made as it entered them was louder than the sound of flesh popping. But then, I was mortal, so maybe it sounded different to vampires.

With my hand on my sword, and no idea how to use it, I picked a cluster of men to start slicing up, and charged in, hoping no one realized I wasn't even a soldier.

The enemy hit in a new wave of fresh soldiers then, before

we'd even made it up the slope, coming at us with the force of a wave on a rock. Several men tipped backward, and the enemy came over them like a flood. I ducked and rolled as a sword swung at me, even though it wasn't aiming for me, coming up on my hands and knees a second later. The punch and speed of battle was completely unexpected, like standing on the edge of a race track. I couldn't find a spot on the ground that was clear of thick boots, weapons or body parts where I could manage to get to my feet without being knocked back over again.

I grunted and coughed on a hard breath as powerful legs bashed me sideways and something kicked my arm, making me cry out in pain then as a heavy man stepped on my hand, nearly crushing it entirely.

But I flew up onto my feet suddenly then with a hand around my wrist, Elias's wide, shocked eyes staring at me from beneath a bloody face. "What are you doing here?"

"I had to save my mom," I yelled over the roar of a man dying.

He looked at my sword, my cargo pants and my black t-shirt, shaking his head. "You're still human, you could die."

"I don't care! I—"

His elbow went out then, knocking a man in the teeth. "Hang on." Elias let go of me for a moment to chop him up and then bent down, hoisted me over his shoulder like I was some damsel in distress, and turned to march up the hill. I heard the shift and swipe of metal on flesh as he fought his way through the fray. At some point, my sword fell off me, landing among the mess of blood and limbs. I tried to reach for it, but he was moving too fast, the lone soldier breaking through the wall of men and entering the border they tried to protect.

I had to admit, he was good. Even fighting all these faces, these people with names and jobs and lives, with a girl over his shoulder, he did better than most of the men out there who were fighting with both hands.

Elias stopped by a garden wall and threw me gently down, coming to squat in front of me, looking damn sexy in the cargos and black shirt, his arms bulging where the muscle had been pumped all afternoon by sword-swinging. "What were you thinking, Aubrey? Are you hurt?" He lifted my arm, and then my shirt, inspecting me all over.

"Stop it." I shoved his hand away and pulled my top down. "I'm fine. I was only there for a second before you—Ah!" My arms reflexively flew up over my head as a sword swung down at his. He sensed it a second before I saw it though, and wheeled around to fight the man off. But six more came out of nowhere, and I pressed my back into the wall, trying to get away from it. Right now, I could actually see how stupid I'd been coming here. What was I thinking?

I know what I was thinking: I was thinking that I'd seen heaps of battles on tv, and this would be fine. I could fight, as long as I had a cause to fight for.

And suddenly, I could see why Drake wanted me to wait a year before giving my youth away to be with Elias. This was pretty dumb and, admittedly, naive of me. Lesson learned, Drake, lesson learned.

Truth was, even if I'd known it would be like this, I'd still have come. I just wanted to save my mom and my brother—to make up for what I'd done, even if that meant dying. It was *worth* dying for.

Elias roared then and fell forward, his body wobbling as he hit the ground, face down, with the powdery snow puffing up in a dense cloud of cold. The soldier beside him spun his sword and stationed it above his neck, ready to sever him from this world.

"Hey!" I called, instantly regretting it. His steely eyes fixed on me, sizing me up, while mine flicked around, looking for a weapon as I got to my feet, ready to fight him but with no idea how. And as if by some kind of magic, I looked down and noticed a sword at my foot that I was certain had *not* been there a second ago.

Keeping one eye on the tyrant—a guy I'd probably met growing up—I bent and grabbed the shiny spear of metal, casing my fingers around the hilt as if I'd held it a thousand times before. And as the vampire came at me, swinging his blade wide and high, my own sword answered, speaking to each of his strikes with one of its own. The powerful force of them went down through my arms, making me cough, but I held on tight and kept fighting. I had never in my life even held a sword, let alone swung one, and yet this was light, easy to use, and seemed to know how to fight even if I didn't.

Another man came in at my right, and my arms pulled as though the sword was leading me to strike, so I relaxed them and moved my body at the sword's command. But I didn't see the man behind me until I was suddenly on the ground, the sky in front of me.

He pressed his muddy boot into my chest and turned his sword to my throat. The cool of the roughed-up snow soaked through my shirt and I drew a breath of defeat as my death became imminent, but the man gurgled then as a thrush of red liquid burst from his mouth and all over my face and my chest in a warm, wet splash. I coughed down half of it and spat the rest out, rolling up to sit as I watched Elias with my sword, fighting off the bad guys like some action hero in a Viking movie. He nailed it! So much so that I sat up, lopped my elbows over my knees, and cheered like this was a harmless fencing match. The blood in my mouth tasted like rotten meat, salty and putrid, but I tried my best to ignore it and be cheerful, even though the sticky warmth was now making me colder.

"Woo-hoo! To the right. Now left." I shifted like I was playing a video game and trying to get the avatar to do what I wanted. "Yass! Good one!"

Elias flicked me a playful grin, knocking the last man out with the hilt of his sword, then marched over the body parts, crunching the blood into the snow, and got down on one knee beside me, like a knight presenting his rose.

"Are you all right?"

"I'm fine. Better now after watching you kick ass!"

He grinned, that lovely sharp one with the warm edges around his eyes, and presented me with the sword in a very 'King Arthur' way. "Where did you get this?"

I took it gingerly. "I found it. It was just there"—I nodded to where I'd been standing—"when I needed it."

Elias laughed, ducking his head to wipe a palm across his cheek, smearing off some of the blood. "Do you know what this is?"

"A sword."

He aimed a finger down the blade and the Celtic inscription there. "Fragarach—also named The Retaliator. It belonged to a once-great warrior; a sword one cannot simply *find*."

"Then how did I find it?"

"You didn't." He stood, offering me his hand. "You summoned it."

"I did what?" I said, clambering to my feet. A siren sounded then, and Elias exhaled, his shoulders sinking back to their natural position.

I looked up at the high cream walls of the manor behind me. "What was that?"

"That was the signal. We've taken the island."

"Does that mean they found my mom?"

"I don't know." He looked around, growing taller as the sword in my hand turned bright blue and went really cold and then… vanished.

"What the actual hell?" I stepped back as if it was diseased, shaking my hand off and wiping it on my pants.

Elias capped my arm with his big curled palm, staring at the space where the sword had vanished for a long moment before he brought his eyes up to mine. "What, exactly, are you?"

"I don't know." I rubbed my lips, realizing then that I'd just swallowed at least a cup of vampire blood. "I should be Lilithian."

His attention went to the mess all over my face, and he reached over to swipe some away, sniffing it. Then, he closed his eyes. "This is a tragedy."

"Yep," I stated. "That's gonna suck. Being seventeen forever."

When he opened his eyes, they were pooled with deep regret. "I am sorry, Aubrey. I should have done better to protect you—"

"It's not your fault." I tapped his arm to stop him going on. "It was my choice to come out here. And I don't want to dwell on it. I want to go find my mom."

He followed me as I turned and trudged over the stinky body parts in search of someone that could tell me what was going on.

ARA

A war raged on the border of the island—Drake's army fighting to get to us in time—but none of it mattered. Lily had this planned down to the last detail. We weren't walking out of here, and no one was coming to rescue us, unless she let them.

It had been thirty hours since I'd laid eyes on my baby boy, and I couldn't honestly say he was being cared for right now. I'd seen a cruel side to Lily, even with her own children, and that side had been more prominent since everything happened with Jason. There was no saying if she'd been cruel or even just cold to my baby.

As I climbed the lighthouse steps, shivering in a summer dress against the steely winter snow, a guard shoved me every time I stopped, barely able to walk through the weightless agony in my soul. I planned out all the things I'd do to her, readying my hands to strike, despite the cold making them stiff, but when I heard Daniel's cries as I reached the top, shrieking in terror, I ran, forgetting what it meant to fight.

"Come any closer, and he dies," she said loudly over the rush of the wind, beating at the top of the lighthouse. She stood by the railing with Daniel in her arms, his face bright red, his nose dripping with tears that hadn't been dried away. He looked so relieved to see me as I stepped up, screaming and reaching for me, but the guard held me back.

"Give him to me, please," I pleaded, searching for an opportunity, a way to use my powers against her without hurting him or knocking them over the edge—a flicker of light, a moment of thought where she let her guard down and I could knock her unconscious—but she was as powerful as me, and I didn't stand a chance against her while she had my little boy in her arms. I just wouldn't risk it. "I'll give you anything you want, just let me hold him."

"You know what I want," she said, her dark hair whipping out around her face. I looked at Danny, longing to grab him.

"I don't know what you want, Lily. But if you want him dead because he's Jason's—"

"I don't want him dead. I don't care about Jason. I don't care about you. I just wanted David to love me, Ara, and he would have if you'd let him."

"So…" I edged forward, bumps of cold rising out on my bare arms as a new snow fell, making my throat raw with each icy breath I took. "You want a child with him? Is that's why you took Danny?"

"I took him as a bargaining chip," she stated, edging closer to the openness beyond that flimsy rail.

"Where's David? And—"

"I have him. *And* Jason. They're… well, *David* is safe. But he will never love me while you exist—not without all of my soul."

"It won't matter if you have all of your soul," I warned her. "He loves me for me, not my soul."

"*My* soul," she corrected. "And before you came back to life, before I gave you a piece of me, he loved me, Ara. He could have been mine if I'd never brought you back. I saw it in a vision. And I want that. I want that life with him like I need air!"

"If you kill Danny, he will never love you."

"I won't need to kill the child if you just give me what I want."

"Okay, just let me hold him, he's terrified," I cried, watching my little boy reach for me, squirming in her arms, his cries going out, untended, into the open air around us. He was still in a summer t-shirt and shorts, his diaper heavy and hanging down, probably starving and freezing out here. I couldn't think. Couldn't plan out an attack because every instinct in me was just trying to grab him. "Please."

"I want your soul. Release it to me now, and you can have him."

"But I'll be dead…"

"Yes, but you will have time to get him to safety before you die—"

"But without a soul, I won't care enough to get him to safety—"

"Just give it to me, or I'll let him go over the edge!"

My eyes darted around the lighthouse, looking for a path of escape, a way to bargain with her. But in a second of madness, Lily walked to the ledge and dropped Danny over.

I screamed, reaching for him, but she grabbed my arm.

"You have about two seconds before it's too late to save him—"

"Do it!" I screamed, and I felt a rip within my chest, my soul tearing away as she shoved me over the edge too. My heavier adult body fell fast, much faster than Daniel, and I drew on the entire strength of my Cerulean energy, all the elements, to slow his fall.

His cries ripped through the wind, terrified, jerking into a squeal as I finally reached him and closed my arms around his body, pushing back on the power of the wind to slow our descent.

The ground came rushing up in a breath though, and I turned us, wrapping myself around him as my back hit the water. The impact burst through my ribs and spine, opening the flesh on my back and ripping Daniel from my arms. He hit the sand and tumbled toward a rock as a violent wave rushed over me, pushing me under. But I dragged myself through the whitewash and used the forward motion to press back onto the shore.

As I got to my feet to run for my baby, my legs faltered and I went down hard, hitting the ground with my elbows and broken ribs. I could feel the bones were shattered there and in my legs, but I wasn't healing fast enough to get to Daniel, and he was too terrified to come to me where I lay along the violent edge of the ocean.

I reached out to him, looking up at Lily as she landed beside me, her shadow closing around me.

"I won't kill him," she said. "If he can survive here on his own until Drake's warriors make it to his side, he can live. If not… I really don't care."

I tried to speak, but only coughed up a clot of blood instead, thick and lumpy beneath my tongue. Lily arched down then and rolled me onto my back. As I tried to reach out for Daniel and tell him it was all okay, she pressed her fingertips into my chest, a sharp sting meeting a tight, deep pressure within, until her hand reemerged with a fat clump of dark meat. I didn't feel any pain then, couldn't even comprehend what had happened, that my heart was no longer beating, that the cold cavity there was open to the elements. She slipped the fleshy mass into a silver box and turned away, leaving me and my baby to die on this violent beach.

As I closed my eyes, feeling the grains of sand grate my skin with each wave that pushed me back up the shore, Daniel's desperate screams echoed in the empty space where my heart and my soul should have been.

I knew I cared, but I also knew I couldn't anymore.

AUBREY

I heard Falcon's scream rip through the sky like he'd found a thousand children dead in a park. It shattered across the open field by the lighthouse and blast images through my mind, warnings, about the horror he'd found. When I looked at Elias, we both started running.

His eyes went down my body to my feet as we ran through the thick snow and, seeing my slow human steps wouldn't get us there fast enough, bent slightly and hoisted me into his arms, taking off at vampire speed. I closed my arms around him and shut my eyes, holding my breath against his chin so I wouldn't vomit under the g-forces. With my brow against the prickly stubble, I let myself feel safe, until he placed my feet down on the slushy sand, steadying me with a hand at my back.

"Are you all right, my darling?"

I nodded, wishing I could just run away from all of this—to a place where it was just him and me, and nothing in the world was wrong. When I looked up, my eyes instantly found Falcon by the rocks beneath the lighthouse, his body curled around something.

"Stay here," Elias warned, pushing his hand toward me as he walked over. When he got closer, he stopped dead and covered his mouth, looking up at me a moment later. His wide eyes fixed me in place, but he was too late to stop me as I rushed past Falcon and saw the gaping hole in my mother's chest, her eyes fixed, glazed over, her entire body bloodied and bruised.

I cast my eyes to the screaming child in Falcon's arms, breathing a sigh of relief that Danny was alive. But he wasn't okay. How could he ever be okay? What had happened here? Why was mom so broken?

"She can come back, right?" I cried, feeling Elias behind me, wrapping me up in his arms and turning me away from the grim scene.

"Only if Lily hasn't taken her soul," Falcon cried, his voice thick with grief.

"No," Elias said. "Look at her chest. She's taken her heart."

We all looked, and reality set in. Without her pieces, all of her pieces, Mom couldn't be brought back.

Daniel noticed me then and he screamed louder, reaching for me. I broke away from Elias's arms and curled my brother into mine, feeling him go limp with shock as he tangled his fingers in my hair, just like he did when he was a baby and I rocked him to sleep. He sobbed quietly, pointing at Mom, while the rest of the people who came here to fight for her slowly emerged from the world at our backs, falling to their knees as they realized… the queen was dead.

"Aubrey?" said a high, feminine voice. I turned to look at Ali, and she put her arms out to us. Elias helped me stand and I leaned right into her, letting her take Daniel as the grief consumed me.

I didn't tell her. I never got to tell Mom that I understood why she didn't hate Dad for hitting her. I understood now what their love was and why nothing could destroy it. I didn't get to tell her she was right, that I should never have used my abilities behind her back. I'd learned now. I was sorry, and I'd never get to tell her that.

"Mom," I whispered, feeling the weight of everyone's grief surrounding me. I sat down in the sand, my head in my hand, and when I looked up, it was into the queer aqua eyes of the malevolent ghost.

I quickly did a double-take of the stone castle walls and the circle of salt around me, mouth hanging open in utter confusion as a million thoughts about how I got here flicked through my head like flashes going off. The beach was gone, the wind, the rush, and instead there was silence and the ancient chill of an old castle.

I shot to my feet. "What is this?"

"This," he said theatrically, spreading his hands out to indicate my position, "this is a summoning circle. And you, Demon, have just been summoned."

JULES

Every face was expressionless. They hung, long and grave, from beneath haunted eyes. No heart could dare to feel. There was only shock. And fear. And uncertainty that was rattled by disbelief.

A brutal death had taken place. A beloved queen, once a savior to this world, had been taken. The kidnapping and cruelty toward the infant prince had sent shivers down the spines of those who knew. And no one was here to make it better. Every single ruler of this world was gone, missing, presumed dead, or being buried. We were all that was left of an empire.

I walked behind the procession of mourners toward the Enchanted Forest, all in black, with Daniel in my arms, not really sure my heart could take any more. Overnight, Mike had inherited everything of Ara's that I'd never wanted, and all the weight that came with it. And it all became mine too, because I was falling in love with him. It was their plan, from the earliest days when Ara had Elora, that Mike would take the kids if anything ever happened to Ara and David. She hadn't wanted the burden to fall to Elora—to become a mother to her siblings. I understood that, but it would change us in ways I probably couldn't comprehend yet.

Elora, Harry, and Ric walked beside the bed of flowers where Ara lay, so perfect and pretty, even in death. She'd been cleaned and sewn shut, dressed in white, her face flawless, as though she wasn't dead. And I just couldn't make sense of the horror, the sadness. Couldn't bear to look at Elora and Harry, and the eternal expression of loss in their eyes. No one could ever measure up to their mother, her kindness, her grace, and anyone could see that they were struggling to come to terms with the velocity of such a loss.

Mike put his arm around me, giving me strength to keep walking where I just wanted to falter and die. The child in my arms would never be okay again. Not after this. What he'd seen, what he'd suffered, it was too much. He wouldn't sleep. Wouldn't eat. He didn't even cry anymore. He just stared at nothing, all day. And I didn't know how to help him. He needed his mother, or either of his fathers—Jason or David—but they were both missing. Even young Aubrey had vanished from the beach that day, and no one could quite explain what had happened.

The moon hung low in the sky, making Ara's skin glow where she rested atop the bed of roses and other flowers to mark the passing of an Auress, while her beloved people walked behind us with lanterns that would later be set to the night sky, carrying up a prayer for her soul. Her stolen soul.

I didn't know how to do this. How to be this. How to cope with this. I'd gone from kangaroos and coffee on the porch to being a proxy mother to a traumatized toddler, with a missing teenager. They needed me. Mike, Mia, and Daniel. And I couldn't walk away right now any more than I could face this.

The men who carried Ara's body placed her down on a stand

in a clearing by a twisted old tree and stepped back, looking up the path as though something might appear there. And it did. Just a flicker of pink, like a ghost, and several people gasped.

"Who is that?" someone whispered.

"Lilith. The Goddess of the Moon."

The ethereal form wavered over Ara, stunned into absolute shock for a moment before her light turned dark and red, a wild wind blowing around the entire clearing and yanking the branches, tearing the leaves away above us. It was like a storm had suddenly risen out of nothing, violent and determined in its intent to destroy. No one cowered though, no one moved, except Mike, who closed his eyes, darkened to grief by it all, and slowly got down on his knees. With my hair whipping out around me, I knelt beside him, cradling Daniel close to me, as if I might be able to one day love all of his suffering away.

"This is never going to be okay," Mike whispered.

Lilith appeared in front of him then, her eyes scanning every inch of his face before focusing on Daniel. She lowered herself, placing a hand on his back, and the baby looked up at her like he knew her face, like he could tell her his story.

She smiled then, catching a tear that rolled down Daniel's cheek. It balanced on her fingertip for a moment, glowing in the light of her form, then she blew it back against his nose. His body absorbed it, the liquid turning the tip of his nose blue for a moment, then he snapped his head around as though he had no idea where he was, his big green eyes lighting up in a playful grin.

"Mike!" He reached for him. Mike laughed, bursting to tears, and swept him into his arms, cupping the back of his tiny little head in his giant hand.

"He won't remember," Lilith said, giving me a camaraderie nod as she stood. Her hand came softly down on Mike's shoulder then, and she turned her gaze on Falcon, who hadn't lifted his eyes from the ground since Ara died.

"We will find them," Lilith assured him, appearing at his side. "I will not cease my hunt, my vendetta, until Lily is cold in the ground."

"And neither will I," Morgana vowed, stepping up to meet the goddess face to face.

Lilith touched her cheek, smiling into her, then looked over at the freckled red-head beside her.

"I swear it too," the girl said. "She has gone too far this time, blood or none, she cannot be allowed to live."

Lilith nodded, and Mike rose to his feet, along with Falcon and the other people who knelt too. I got up, taking Mike's hand when he offered it, and a sense of revenge, of retribution rolled over us all, filling our hearts with determination.

This would not end here, not like this.

For the first time since I came into this immortal family, I wanted to see Ara's face. I wanted to see David. I wanted them back.

And I would not rest until that day. None of us would.

AUBREY

"Summoned?" The gravity of the situation struck me, scattering all thoughts and worries for my mom and brother to the farthest corners of my mind, and a deep sense of self-preservation settled into my bones instead. "Where am I?"

"Scotland." He presented the room.

The walls here weren't as high as in Drake's castle, but they held all the chill and charm. Exposed beams hung overhead, supported by layer upon layer of unique, hand-laid cream stones, which had been made more homey by tall pictures of angry-looking men in kilts, and two medieval wheels, hanging down with modern electrical globes. There was a wide fireplace to my right, stone cold, and a few rugs laid but pushed back to allow room for the circle of salt I found myself in.

"I had occupied my family's castle in England," he said, "but… for this measure of misbehavior, I needed to be far away from witches. Especially the witches under Elias Davenport's Set."

"Why?"

The man smirked, like it was obvious.

"Who are you?" I asked. "And what do you want with me? I brought you back, what else—"

"Yes, you did. Under great protest and at my expense, I will add." He rubbed his elbow, eyes flicking away to what I assumed was a memory. "Nonetheless, I caught myself a vampire and forced him to transform me—"

"Not Harry?" I leaned forward. "You didn't—"

"Harry is fine." He waved the hand of dismissal. "I sought the assistance of someone who could be bribed for their troubles."

"Anyone I know?"

"Not likely." He stood up from his ancient wooden chair and moved toward me. He was taller than me by an inch, with small sharp-edged eyes and a slight triangular peak to the middle of his eyebrows. Since becoming immortal, he'd taken on an air about him that scared me. His beard was shaved down to styled stubble now, leaving a slender, youthful face framed by a messed arrangement of dark-brown hair, but he looked altogether formidable and cunning. He walked with an edge to his step, like he had something overly smart or sarcastic to say, or maybe like he knew a dirty secret about you, and he'd never tell you he knew, but he'd use it against you behind your back. *That* kind of person, just to give you an idea.

"Do you remember your past?" I asked conversationally, trying to get a handle on what he wanted. "Most of my resurrections don't."

"Yes," he said, circling me slowly, hands behind his back. I turned to watch him as he walked around me. "My name is Cillian Blackwell—"

"The witch?"

He nodded, eyes shrinking with satisfaction. "My name still strikes fear into the hearts of those who remember."

"Why?"

"You will come to understand that soon," he offered, stopping in front of me. "You obviously don't know much about what you are."

I shook my head, feeling grimy and dirty with blood all over my face from the battle. "I'm pretty sure I'm Lilithian now."

Cillian just laughed to himself, casting his eyes down in amusement. "You will never be a vampire—of any kind. You're something so much more powerful."

"What am I?"

He showed me a ring on his pinkie—a great gaudy thing with a pentagram set into the metal, a red stone at its center. "This protects me from you. From anything you might think of to hurt me. It also binds you to me," he advised. "You cannot leave the boundaries of the castle without my permission. Ever."

"What?"

"I am your master now—"

"Excuse me!"

"And you will either obey my every command, or I will torture you and humiliate you until you learn. I will not give the command twice. I do not give second chances," he went on in an eerily calm voice, ignoring my scoffs of protest. "If you please me, I will treat you fairly. If you defy me, you will suffer."

"Why?" I let the word out with all my confusion.

"You're more than just a conduit for the dead. You are a creation of *mine*—brought to life by a spell *I* wrote—which was stolen by a very powerful witch."

"Morgana?"

"Yes." His teeth seemed to set hard in his mouth, making his cheek hollow into his jaw. "She brought you into existence, but you belong to me."

"Why? Why did you want to create me? And what am I?"

"You're a necromancer," he said, and my knees went weak. I sunk down onto them. "But you must forget all myth and folklore, because none of it accurately describes your abilities."

"Which are?" I asked, head in my hands.

"Nice try," he said, coming down to my level. "But I didn't design you so you could use your power against me and then run off to live some human life, enjoying all that I have mastered. I created you as a tool, a weapon. And yes, I did so in the days when my mother—my Irish mother—joined the Jacobite rising, and we had need then of such a powerful ally. But, even then, I do still have enemies in great numbers, despite my magic dying when I was reborn, and I have much use for you."

I lifted my head from my hands, so tired I could just lie down right here and sleep.

"I will not give you the knowledge of yourself," he continued, his eyes warm with kindness, even though his expression and his tone screamed sociopath, "because I will not give my tools the power with which to fight me, defy me, therefore forcing me to teach you a lesson."

"I'll be the one teaching *you* a lesson," I said through my teeth.

He reached into the circle of salt and thumbed a line of dried blood from my cheek. "Your transformation has already begun, and one day, when you have resurrected enough souls and sent them by the hundreds to the Other Side, you will be powerful enough to help me overthrow the Lilithian and Drakarian monarchies."

"Overthrow them? Why?"

"One, because the very woman who birthed you in her

womb also guards the Tree of Life, whose fruit gives a man immortality and power without limits."

"My mother is dead," I said, voice crackling. "Lily killed her—"

"Then that is something we shall have to remedy." He smiled, satisfied. "But when I finally take over, without even tasting of the fruit, I will already be the most powerful man in the Four Realms."

"Four Realms?" I raised a brow at him.

"I suppose you call it the Four Worlds, or is it Three…?"

"No, it's four now. Four Cores," I advised, remembering Drake say that. "We include the humans."

"My definition does not," he said.

"Who's the fourth then?"

"Those from within the underworld."

"There's an underworld?"

Cillian smiled, the sharp corners of his eyes and lips concealing something, and stood up again. "I'm going to break the circle now, and you will be free to wander. But do not go past the castle grounds. The binding ritual will prevent it."

When he kicked the salt away, I felt a sudden retching in my limbs, as if they'd been pulled free from thick mud. I exhaled, gasping for the air I hadn't realized was missing, and crawled out of the circle, turning around and sitting a few feet away from it. Stunned.

"How did you do that?"

"You've grown up believing you're human," he explained. "Your mind is still trapped by human limitations. You have no idea what your master can achieve with you yet. But you will learn."

"You can't be serious," I said, thinking about my family, my home, school, friends. Elias. My heart bottomed out in my chest when I thought about him. "You have no right to keep me here—"

"See, but I do," he said, squatting down, his elbow resting over his knee.

I looked up along his buckled leather boots and tight jeans to his black shirt and the many leather bands and silver bangles and chains he wore, like Ali and Lors—all that witchy protection stuff. He was kind-of cute and stylish, but he had something creepier, ickier about him than the devil.

"I own you," he continued. "And the sooner you come to accept that you should never have been allowed to live a human existence, the sooner you will find a sense of peace here. Not happiness, because I don't believe it is my job to keep my weapons happy, as I would not wonder and muse over a sword, but you will be at peace, serving your master."

"You arrogant fuck!" I shoved him back hard, but he didn't even tip. The vampire in him was powerful and strong, like a wall. When I shot to my feet, he was there already, grabbing my arm like my dad always did to my mom.

"You really shouldn't have done that," he said calmly. "When I have to hurt you, it slows the progress of your transition. And when that happens, it pushes back the time-frame in which I expect to have achieved my goals. So please, for the sake of what your master hopes to attain, do not attempt violence against me, and do not disobey me. You must be subservient, and you will need to remember that."

With my lip stiff, twisted with hatred, I tried to shove his hand off my arm. "You picked the wrong girl if you wanted a submissive—"

"You're not a girl. You're not human. You are an *It*. A necromancer." He shook my arm to get the point across. "A low-level demon. You have no gender, no identity. You will one day be powerful enough to live outside the limits of perception, choose gender, race, form. But you will not ever be free of me. And now, I am going to demonstrate to you, as gently as I can, that you must never disobey me or disrespect me."

"What are you going to do?" I said, keeping the terror from my voice.

"Start by making you ugly. This human form…" He looked me over, picking up a length of hair from my ponytail. "She's attractive, and I'll struggle to be firm with her."

My heart peeled away inside me, taking my soul and all my fears to the back of my body, as if to escape. But there was no escape. He could do anything he wanted to me, and there was nothing I could do to protect myself.

JULES

Mike pressed his hand to the back of my head, where I rested it against the table. There was something so normal about sitting in a kitchen, even if the kitchen wasn't familiar. With its half-door leading on to a manor garden with a hedge maze, I could smell herbs and grasses along the crisp winter breeze, and the ancient, almost country feel of the long cabinets was enhanced by the old dining table, with mismatched chairs from just about every era. But the sound of a kettle boiling, a refrigerator humming, and the smell of bread, could be understood in any language. And it could ease just about any supernatural concern, even if just for a moment.

He leaned down and kissed my head where his hand was, sitting beside me then. "I'm so proud of you."

"Why?"

"Everything you've taken on, overcome, in the last few months is… it's inspiring, Jules."

I rolled my head to look up at him, seeing a warm, loving smile there. "Do you think she's hurting Jason?"

"Yes." He nodded, certain of it. "But I also think he can survive that."

"Why did she do this? Why did she kill Ara—"

"She just wanted all of her soul. That's what we think, anyway. No one can say for sure. But she loved David all these years," he explained. "She fell for him when she first met him, and David was falling in love with her once, when she had her entire soul. Maybe she plans to keep him forever, keep both of them. Maybe she plans to re-join their souls, like she did her own—"

"Re-join them?" I put my head up, hands landing flat on the table.

"You know the twins were one soul, right? Split in two?" he asked.

"Yeah, all the evil and the good."

"Right, so… if you combined the two souls into one body…"

"But then… one of them would die, right?" My eyes instantly sprung tears. "One of their consciousnesses, if that's even a word"—I frowned at myself—"would have to end?"

"Yes, and I think it's likely that person would be Jason."

My heart broke, shattered out into a billion pieces all around me. I still loved Jase. I would always love him in my own way. I didn't want that for him. I wanted him to be happy, to have Ara—the only thing in this entire world that I couldn't be for him—I didn't want *this*.

"I know." Mike put his hand over mine, squeezing gently, as my lungs shook with panic. But his touch brought me back to the kitchen, the boiling kettle, and the smell of bread. "In this world, you're quite often faced with the sensation that you're about to swim into a lake of sharks to save a baby, and that can make you feel like there's no ground beneath your feet," he said.

"But you've just gotta learn to take a breath. Slow your heart. Look around and realize that you're not suffering right now, in this moment. And yes, Jason probably is, but panicking won't help him."

"I just want to run to him," I said, taking a long, slow breath.

"Me too." He got up and took the whistling kettle off the stove, pouring some hot water into a few mugs. We both looked up then as Elias Davenport, the London Set Leader, walked into the kitchen like a man with a thousand rocks in his heart.

"I'm sorry," he said, "I didn't realize anyone was in here."

"Stay," Mike offered. "I'll make you a coffee."

"Thank you kindly." Elias sat down across from me, taking up so much space but… in the way Mike did. Big, bulky, but warm and almost lovable underneath it. "White, with two," he started, but Mike cut him off with a laugh.

"I know, mate," he said.

"How do you know?" Elias narrowed one eye at him, revealing a hint of his ancient wit.

"I uh…" Mike sat down and placed the cups in front of us. I instantly warmed my hands around it. "I don't know if anyone told you this, but Drake once had a vision, and I asked him to show me."

"What vision?" Elias's voice peaked with interest.

"Ara… he was looking for a way to alter her future so she wouldn't have to suffer so much. And he saw one that involved falling for you—Ara falling for you."

Elias tried to hold back a smile. "Interesting."

"Yeah, which is why none of us have been too concerned by the fact that you took an interest in our Aubrey."

Elias's gaze dropped to his giant hands around that mug. "I couldn't do anything to save her…"

"We know, mate," Mike offered. "We'll find her."

"Hey guys," Elora said, joining the party. "What are you all doing up so late?"

"I don't think anyone can sleep until we know what happened to Aubrey," I offered, watching her as she poured a cup of tea and pressed her hip to the counter behind Mike, her long legs at a lean.

"I barely knew her," Elias said, a tormented look in his eye, "and yet I feel... *haunted* by this."

We all seemed to swallow hard then, seeing how obvious that was in his posture, his eyes, his mouth. What had happened between them in the time she was at the castle? With Aubrey at seventeen years and Elias at thirty-six human years and something like five centuries, what had they been up to?

Silence lingered over the room for a moment then, until Elias laughed to himself. "She was at the battle, you know—a stowaway."

"I heard." Mike's voice carried all the impatience of an angry father.

"She fought well. Well..." He smiled to himself, reliving the memory. "After Manannán's sword appeared to her."

"What appeared?" Mike sat forward, suddenly very invested.

"What is she?" Elias asked, looking at Elora. "Because she's not Lilithian. Or vampire. And she's not human."

"Um..." Mike looked at me, and I shrugged.

"We assumed she was Lilithian," Elora offered.

Elias shook his head. "She was splashed with vampire blood, undoubtedly drank some down—"

"What!" Elora put her cup down, standing tall.

Mike groaned, pinching the bridge of his nose.

"But her cells did not begin the change. With my experience, my time spent with Lilithians, I would have been able to sense some changes in her, no matter how subtle, in the minutes that passed after she drank blood. But there was nothing. I watched as she spat the blood out, disgusted by the taste. And… that sword… it…"

"It can only be summoned by Manannán himself," Morgana said, coming in to the room.

Mike stiffened a little, clearing his throat, not sure where to put his eyes.

"Who is Manannán?" Elora asked, taking the words right out of my mouth.

"You say it appeared to her?" Morgana asked Elias, sitting beside him and leaning around slightly to look right into his eyes, almost as if to cut us off from the conversation. She didn't even answer Elora's question.

"Yes. And then it vanished when the battle had been won."

Morgana stood up.

"Where are you going?" Mike asked.

"To pray to the goddess. She might know something."

"We can *pray* to her?" Elora said.

"Yes." Morgana started away. "And I suggest, if you ever want to see your sister again, you do the same."

Elora and I swapped grave looks of concern, while Elias met Mike's eyes, two experienced warriors exchanging knowledge that I couldn't even begin to understand.

When Elias stood, pausing there for a moment with his hands on the table, I got the sense that he would be going to find the nearest punching bag to destroy it. "Well," he said calmly, but his body was like a clenched fist, "I must bid you good night."

Mike bowed his head, and I waved, watching him saunter away.

"He should be at the monthly World Council meeting right now," Mike said, grinning at me. "At Elysium."

"And?"

"Aubrey really got her hooks in him." He laughed. "I've literally never seen him like this."

And I'd literally never heard Mike use the term 'literally' before.

"Well, I don't care what he feels," Elora said. "Aubrey's a child, Mike. He needs to keep his distance."

"She's seventeen. She's not that young. Not if this is what I suspect it is."

"What?" I asked.

"She doesn't carry the First Woman's Curse, not since Ara broke it seventeen years ago. So this connection they have, it's real. And it's intense." Mike smirked, sipping his coffee. "And I don't really wanna admit this, because Aubrey's like my own little girl, but it's possible that it's a soul connection."

I nodded, smiling to myself.

"He'll fight to the ends of the earth for her," Elora said. "Anyone can sense that in him."

"Then I guess it's really lucky they met when they did, because we're probably going to need him," I said.

"Yeah." Mike nodded, sitting back in his chair. "We will."

Elora said goodnight and left the kitchen then, and I looked Mike over, thinking about bed and checking the baby monitor on the table to make sure Daniel was okay. And I liked the fact that, when we went up to bed—sharing a room so we could both look after Daniel—I could lay beside him. Nothing had been established yet, but I really liked sleeping beside him, waking up beside him. He never touched me, but I really wanted him to. And tonight, I decided, I'd make that known.

Mike looked back down from the ceiling and all his worldly problems, and smiled. "What were you just thinking?"

Finally letting him in, I grinned wider, showing him all my

desires in the sparkle of my eye. And he responded exactly the way I wanted him to, standing then to offer his hand.

"Probably time we went to bed."

I got up, closing my fingers around his and imagining them moving down my naked body. "Yes, but… it's hot tonight," I lied. "We should probably sleep naked."

He leaned in and kissed my cheek, whispering, "I was hoping you'd say that."

ELORA

"Lilith?" I called, looking around the clearing by the Tree of Life. My mother's body lay lifeless and decaying on the altar of herbs and flowers in the center, where she would stay, as was the modern custom, for forty full days and nights. Rotting, stinking like perfume sprayed over a dead cat, all so her people could worship her as some shrine. "Are you here?"

The goddess appeared before me, her wavering dress blue, unlike any other time I'd seen her. "I heard your prayer," she said. "Regarding your sister, Aubrey."

"Do you know where she is?" I shot forward, desperate for even a breath of news.

"No. But I know why she suddenly vanished, and I know that only because I appeared to your aunt, Morgana."

"What does she know?" I barked, enraged. "She said she didn't know anything."

"She didn't know much, until we talked just now," Lilith assured me. "All she knew was that the child had possibly been summoned."

"Summoned?"

"When Morgana used a spell—one she stole from a Blackwell Coven Book of Shadows—she knew only that the Child of Ashes would bear the gift to resurrect the dead. She could not and did not know, at the time, *what* she had created."

"Well… what did she create?"

"Aubrey is a creature which has many names. Some may call her a conduit for the dead, others may call her a necromancer. And all names, rightfully, are correct. All meaning one thing: she is a powerful creature, a bringer of life, but also a harbinger of death."

"Of death?"

"Like a key to a doorway, or a keeper of vessels, her responsibility to the natural order is to both restore life and end it—to ferry souls from a place of nowhere and send them back home."

"But… I don't understand. How is she this… necromancer? She's human, no, Lilithian—"

"She is not Lilithian. Nor will she ever be, even with blood."

"Then… but… Mom and Dad…"

"Are not the only parents of that child."

I looked up from the glow of her flowing, living gown, and into her glass-like blue eyes. "What do you mean?"

"You may have heard of the third parent?"

"No."

"In all life, creation requires two parents." She looked over at the corpse of my mother. "They give the being body, mind, heart. And, Nature—the third parent—gives it a soul. But in Aubrey's case, her soul was held back from crossing over, with the use of black magic. And when she was resurrected in her mother's womb at the time of conception, by will of a powerful dark spell, it was with the involvement of a fourth parent."

"Who? And what?"

"She is created with that of the darkest, most impure intention, with a warrior of the Underworld—"

"There's an underworld?"

"There is." She nodded once. "Creatures such as you, and your mother—creatures of light—will not ever lay eyes upon it, cannot even feel its existence until made aware of it. In most cases, cannot even fathom such a place. But it is there, and Aubrey, when she has completed her transition—much like a Lilithian does, by natural means—will be a creature of which lives with one foot in the darkness of the Underworld and one foot in the living realm. Neither light nor dark, neither dead nor alive."

"And… how will she do this—complete her change?"

"Much like with your kind. While the accumulation of blood over time completes your transition, hers will be by the souls she brings over, and those she puts back. Every time she uses her abilities, she will grow stronger until, one day, she will have powers beyond comprehension."

"One day?" I pulled my coat around my chest, cold now as the heat of concern trickled away with new answers. "How long does it take?"

"Several lifetimes," she advised with a single nod. "It will take several lifetimes."

I felt a small pang of relief for that. So she wouldn't be a dark entity of the Underworld for a while then. "Is she immortal?"

"In a sense. Being neither dead nor alive, she is more like an emulation of human existence and the bonds that come with it. A demon in human form—"

"Demon?"

"Yes, she is a child of a demon parent. When she completes her transformation, her blood will run black through her veins—"

"Will she be evil?"

"No more evil than she is already capable of," she advised. "Contrary to popular belief, not all demons are evil, and the Underworld is not a place of fiery hell and carnage."

This was all too much. I sat down on the leafy forest floor, feeling connected to nature here but feeling so torn by it too, because I couldn't come to terms with the fact that my mother's light had left this world, and that Aubrey, my sister, my *baby sister*, was always just an illusion. "What is it then?" I asked. "What is the Underworld?"

"Elysium: a beautiful and glorious place, but with many dark, terrible corners." Lilith smiled, eyes marking out something in the distance, as though she was looking at it right now. "But, no matter what Aubrey is, Elora, she is in the wrong hands as we speak. Whoever was masterful and knowledgeable enough to summon her must know all she is capable of. And if they know that, then they will be training her, possibly torturing her to trigger her abilities much sooner than naturally possible."

My skin wanted to crawl off my bones, to slug away and go find her. I felt powerless. "Can she heal? If they hurt her—"

"She can. If she has learned how. A creature like that has the power to self-heal, much like with vampires, but it is a conscious task, requires meditation, thought, reflection."

"And… if whoever has her triggers her abilities now, will she be a teenager forever, like my mom?"

"No." She smiled softly. "Aubrey, once her power is triggered, will have the ability to age—to take on any appearance she desires. As I said, she is not human and, therefore, this human form is really just a belief she has at this time, given that she knows no other form."

"As in… what? She can shapeshift?"

"Not quite. Not to any creature. But she can alter her

appearance, alter what you see—an old hag, a youthful angel. But her true form, that which you see when she's sleeping, will be a reflection of what's in her heart."

"As in… if she's good or evil?"

"Something to that effect, yes."

"What are they doing to her, Lilith?" I asked, worried now, because Aubrey already had a lot of darkness in her. I'd sensed it all our lives, but it was only as dark as what was in my father—something that made him powerful and untouchable. I never worried about it until now, when it became possible that someone could taint and shape that darkness to make it evil.

"We have no way of knowing, and we never will. Even if your mother were to enter the living realm again, she could not trace Aubrey's energy signature, because she is already too far gone. By the time Aubrey came here to Loslilian to help rescue Ara, she had begun her transformation, and she no longer carries the energy of the living."

"So… what does that mean?"

"It means we can do nothing to save her now. This is her path. One day, she will discover her abilities by pure will alone, and it is on that day that no man, bearing a binding stone or a summoning spell, would be powerful enough to hold her."

"How long? In this lifetime, or…"

"I cannot say. All I can tell you is that we must prepare for war—"

"War?" I rolled up onto my knees.

"Her captors will use her against us as soon as she is ready, and considering her fourth parent—Manannán—was a great pagan warrior, a deity of the sea—that his own parentage was that of a demon—if she possesses even a fifth of his great power, she will one day kill you all or, with hope, perhaps give her captor reason to fear her."

"Deity of the sea?" My brow pulled in confusion, eyes widening then. "Is that why she always goes to the beach when she's upset?"

"Yes." Lilith smiled. "It was her connection calling to her from such a young age. Her demon parent possessed many powers, many gifts, that she may inherit from within the sea, if she is worthy."

"Like what?"

"The power to cloak oneself in a fog of invisibility; to whisper words on a chalice and charm it for truth; and to summon a warrior horse that runs on water." Her gentle blue glow changed back to pink then for just a moment as she said, "Morgana tells me that your sister, in battle, summoned Fragarach."

"What's that?"

"It was Manannán's sword, known also as The Answerer, The Retaliator. It has many names, but it's one most prominent trait is that it answers the swing of any weapon with a strike of its own. Its bearer need have no skill whatsoever with the sword. And if Aubrey can summon Fragarach then, indeed, my assumptions about who her fourth parent is are correct, and she will, if the need arises, be able to summon Fragarach again."

"Can she escape though? You said she's bound—"

"She would be able to, yes."

"But she doesn't know that yet, right?"

"Correct. See, to summon a demon, you must also be clever enough to bind them to a master. But when a demon becomes what we refer to as a High Demon, no summoning spell or binding ritual performed by a man, or a witch, will hold them for long. Until that day,"—she closed her hands together at her front—"we can only wait."

I rubbed my head, exhaling. "Do you think they're hurting her?"

"Yes. Pain will be a necessary tool in triggering an early transformation."

My poor baby sister. All I could see then was her big round eyes when I'd walk into her nursery to get her out of her crib. She trusted me, knew that I could keep her safe, love her, care for her. And yet I'd let her down in the worst possible way. My own instincts to protect, as a mother, flared up within me. "I can't just sit around and do nothing. Can't we summon her—"

"Not while she's trapped by her master, no."

"What about her ability to kill with one touch?" I asked, pushing on my upper thigh to stand up, dusting the wet dirt and leaves off my jeans. "If she uses that on her master—"

"She can bring him no harm, not as long as she's bound to him."

Damn. I exhaled heavily, thinking for a moment. "That touch... what was that? Was it a consequence?"

"No." Lilith smiled. "She inherited that in her blood, from her great-great-great grandfather, Cain."

"Really?"

Lilith nodded. "It will, at first, present itself without warning or conscious desire, much like your mother's Cerulean light in her early years. It will rise to defend her when she's in danger or feels threatened. But, with practice, it will become a tool she can use at her disposal."

"So it's an ability?"

"It is. In mythology, it is spoken of as The Mark of Cain—a gift given to Cain by Lucifer before his imprisonment. But, in fact, it is simply a natural skill that developed with time."

Then there was hope, at least. I wasn't sure what Aubrey

would become in that hell, or what they were doing to her there, but she would be powerful. And while there was little hope of us ever saving her, ever finding her, there was, at least, a hope that she could save herself.

I WANTED TO GO TO ARTHUR'S ROOM, FIND OUT IF HIS powers had surfaced again so he could save us all. He'd once had the skill to freeze an entire room of men, or make a crowd pick their noses at his command. I couldn't think of a better ally at this time. But he'd have told us if anything had changed. I didn't want to risk annoying him and driving him away by asking questions that he'd answer in his own time.

I wanted to run to Mike, tell him everything I knew, but we couldn't help Aubrey right now, and all it would do is make him lose sleep too. And I was pretty sure he and Jules would be getting it on tonight, if their vibe was anything to go by. I didn't want to cut into that. Not when it could actually wait until morning.

The truth was, everyone just needed to go home now, to stop hanging around here waiting for everything to be okay. It wasn't going to be okay. Mom was dead, her soul in Lily, and no one would ever see Dad or Jason again. Lily had Vampirie on her side, helping her, and she was also ancient and cunning. We could waste the next twenty years of our lives trying to track her down, while she was out there, getting on with it.

And then Aubrey…

The goddess Lilith would do anything to fight for family. If she said there was no way to find Aubrey, I believed that. But I still couldn't let it go.

So, instead of waking Arthur or disturbing Mike, I found myself walking to the room of the one man who I had sensed, when I saw him earlier, would go to the proverbial ends of the earth for my sister.

Elias opened his door and his eyes widened when he saw me. "Mrs. De la Rose, what can I do for you?"

I looked in past his body and saw the dresser mirror shattered, the contents of the entire top spread onto the ground. He looked so harmless in his loose-fitted track pants, shirtless, bare feet, but he had the body of a warrior. And seeing how he'd destroyed that dresser, I actually felt like I'd made the right decision coming to him. "Call me Elora, please."

"Very well. How may I be of service?"

"You've been around a really long time," I said, getting straight to the point. "Can you think of a being, any breed of supernatural being, that might have reason to summon a necromancer?"

His big blue eyes popped for a moment, until it all sunk in. He clearly thought about that sword he'd mentioned over coffee, its legend, and then the magical vanishing of my sister from the beach that day. When he stepped back and sat down heavily on his bed, a tight fist to his lips, I walked in and closed the door.

"I shouldn't be feeling this way," he said angrily. "I barely know the girl, and yet I find myself ready to give up everything for her."

"I'm sorry, Elias." I leaned on the large table by the fireplace, feeling out of place in here while he was shirtless, his bedcovers ruffled. "I do actually know how much that sucks."

He glanced over his shoulder to smile softly, eyes straying to the mess all over the floor beside me. "Please excuse that. I… had a moment of weakness."

"I get it." I moved my foot away from a shard of glass. "I wanted to do the same."

He nodded to himself, turning back to face the door. "A necromancer?"

"Yes."

"How do you know this for certain? I researched those creatures and could not affirmatively apply their attributes to my Aubrey—"

"I went to Lilith—the goddess."

He nodded again, breathing into his palms. "I don't know of anyone who would have need for such a creature and… I know little of them myself." With an air of determination energizing the room, Elias stood up. "But I will find out. Whoever it is, they must be a member of the supernatural community, and I am beginning to have my suspicions already."

"Who?"

"A certain powerful family has just resurfaced after centuries of death or, perhaps, living in secret."

"And you think they could be involved?"

"Possibly. But I'd need to tread carefully. If it is the case, accusing them could start a war."

"War? Why?"

"They're a power-hungry family. Always have been. They would stop at nothing to control the entire supernatural community, all for the sake of supremacy, and they'd use any excuse to initiate a war that would be to that end."

"Do they stand a chance though, really?" I scoffed.

"Well, I would not, for a second, underestimate them."

And a family like that, with a weapon like my sister, or even just the sordid things those kinds of people might do to her… they were something to fear. "Well, let's just hope they don't have Aubrey then."

His eyes darkened. "Hope will not be enough, Elora. For what I know of them, we had better pray."

"Why?" My arms flooded with a loose, empty feeling, like I just wanted to grab her and make it all okay.

"There is no sense in me horrifying you with tales, when there is little to be done tonight if it is, in fact, the case." He moved over to his door and opened it. "Get some sleep, Elora. I will leave at once and begin my investigations."

"You'll keep me posted, right?" I asked stepping out.

"Of course." He bowed his head, shutting the door.

I only made it to the end of the corridor before I heard him roar with unbound emotion, as something crashed loudly to the ground.

My phone screeched through the dark and the quiet. I was certain I'd had it on silent—for all callers except those on my favorites list. But most of those people on that list were either asleep here at the manor, or dead, or missing.

Ric grunted as I reached over him to grab it. "Who the hell is that at this hour, Lors?"

"Probably someone back home not realizing the time difference," I said, hopping out of bed. But when my eyes casually passed the screen and I saw Lily's name there, my gut dropped. "Shit."

Ric popped his head up. "Who is it?"

"Lily," I whispered.

He threw the covers back and appeared beside me. I put the phone to my ear.

"Elora," she cried, her voice broken with desperate, sobbing grief. "I need your help."

"What?" I sunk down onto the arm of the lounge chair, and Ric tried to take the phone, but I held tight.

"If you meet me in the forest, send the guards around Ara's body away and tell no one about this, I will bring her back. I swear. I have her heart. I will bring her back."

"Why would I ever trust you?"

"Because I need her help, Elora. I can't do this without her. I need the fruit—"

"What have you done, Lily?" I asked, my voice cutting through a thousand layers of heartbreak and confusion on the way out.

"I tried to combine their souls. Something went wrong."

"Whose souls?"

"Jason and David—"

"Is my father okay?"

"Just meet me there. Promise me," she pleaded.

I looked at Ric, who shook his head to say no. "I promise," I said anyway, hanging up the phone.

Ric moved in and pressed my face against his hip, his cool, solid form grounding me. His hands firmly rubbed my back and he exhaled a long, hard breath. "He's dead, you know that, right?"

"Who?"

"David. She wouldn't be asking for help if Jason had died."

I nodded, just now realizing that. But I had to put it aside until I was certain. I couldn't let the possibility destroy me when there was so much at stake.

"You want me to come with you?" he asked.

"She said come alone." I stood up, looking for my jeans. "I'll go alone."

"Will you be able to get the guards off Ara for a bit?"

"Should be fine," I said, slipping my clothes on. "It's a sacred place. I'll just tell them I need some time to talk to the goddess again."

"Okay." He leaned in and kissed my head. "I'll be on the outskirts. Just call me, or text me, and I'll come."

"Thanks," I said, touching his arm as I left the room, my heart a ball of panic in my throat.

ARA

My eyes flicked open and went straight to the rocks in search of Daniel. But it was dark, and the beach was gone, changed now to high trees and a shocking frost. Snow had fallen in dense layers over the ground, hanging from the trees in sharp dagger-like warnings that this was no longer a place of reflection and solace. Dark things lingered here now, and even the stars in the sky had closed themselves in behind heavy clouds.

I set my attention down my physical form—the soft fabric of the dress I was in, with its laced-up front, my wounds closed, my body full, unbroken—and then sat up, sensing two people. Relief and panic hammered in my chest with equal force when I saw Elora on one side and a very humbled, very chastised Lily on the other, her hands bloodied.

"What happened?" I rolled my legs over the bed of flowers, feeling them crunch and fall away under my knees. "Where's Daniel?"

"He's safe," Elora assured me. "But we need your help."

I followed their eyes then to Jason, sitting against the Tree of Life, sobbing in to his hands. David lay flat on his back beside him, his lips blue, eyes fixed into the eternal stare of death. And every single molecule of air pushed from my body in one sweeping moment of horror.

"No!" I screamed, launching off the altar to his side. As I knelt down beside him in the cold snow, I reached over and touched Jason to make sure he was okay, but he shook his head to say he wasn't.

"Lily, what have you done?" I shrieked, fear and grief replacing rage.

I couldn't undo this.

She'd taken his life while I wasn't there to protect him, and I didn't have the power to fix it. Not this far along.

Not by natural means.

"His soul…" My words came out in a soft breath of icy air, as I felt around his chest, desperate to sense it. "His soul is gone."

"I tried to merge them," Lily explained, kneeling on David's other side and taking his stiff, cold hand. His fingers didn't flex or move, didn't mold to the shape of her touch. They were frozen forever that way, curled slightly, marking the moment of his death. "But I had to make them human first. The one who bore the soul would awaken, restored, but it went to the wrong twin."

"Of course it did, Lily!" I yelled, not knowing where to touch David as the anger finally surfaced in me, a raging storm blowing in overhead and making thunder in the sky. "Jason's the root of the spell. David was the leftovers."

"I didn't think, I…"

"I can't believe you've done this," I sobbed, feeling like I had no power, pushing my hair from my eyes as the wind ripped through the clearing and sent the icicles raining down into beds of snow beneath. "There's no coming back from this. He's human. He's dead. I can't fix this!" I screamed.

"Yes you can," she insisted, placing her hand on the tree. "Restore his body, split his soul, and move it back into him. And then I will go. I will take him, and I will leave this place, and you will never see me again."

"Even if I used the fruit, and he did come back as the man you knew, he won't love you, Lily—"

"He *does* love me, Ara. He's not yours to keep. He was designed for me," she reasoned, like we were arguing over a new toy. "Jason is yours, he—"

"It's out of the question," I yelled. "Even if I would agree to that, I can't bring David back with the fruit. I was warned. Lilith warned me never to let it touch the lips of an impure man, and David is the *epitome* of impure."

"In your eyes—"

"In *Nature's* eyes," I barked loudly over the raging storm, my tears blending with the icy rain. "He has tainted blood from the hex, and from the very spell that created him. What I bring back may not be David at all. It *won't* be human," I assured her. "With the power of that fruit, it would be immortal without need of blood, and I can't guarantee he will be anything of the man you or I love."

Her eyes fixed mine, deep-set and wide with shock, but she just wasn't willing to understand what any of this meant.

I sunk down on my butt then as I came to terms with what she'd done here, feeling my stomach flip with unwelcome butterflies.

"Lily..." I said softly, forcing myself to admit this. "He's dead."

"No." She shoved me down hard and reached up to the tree, forcefully slicing a piece of fruit from its branches. It screamed out in agony, and I leapt up to stop her, but Elora grabbed me and yanked me back.

"Mom, no!"

"What are you doing?" I shoved her off as Lily took the now-human Jason by the shirt and muttered a spell that split his soul in two again. He retched in agony, clutching his chest as the shock of the unethical method blast him into unconsciousness.

"Stop it!" I yelled, trying to push Elora away without hurting her.

"I don't need your permission," Lily said, holding the fruit. "I only needed you awake, present, for the fruit to reveal itself."

"And you need me to split his soul properly, Lily. You don't even know if you have the right piece, or if you just shattered it into a thousand!" I wailed, tears and rain making my entire body heavier. "Even if he's carrying the pure light, that fruit cannot touch his lips. He's been tainted by a dark hex; it's in his bones—"

"Don't fight her, Mom," Elora cried. "I can't lose my dad. You need him right now. You don't even know why yet but trust me… we *need* him."

"It won't be your father, Elora," I reasoned, reaching up to touch her wrist, pleading with her. "That fruit has the power to restore life. *Life*. Not the living. His entire being is dark, not of the natural world. It can only work to exacerbate everything evil he is and—"

"It's too late," Lily said, sinking back on her knees as the magical glow of the fruit's living light illuminated his lips.

I watched the apple roll across the ground and settle at my feet, rotting from the break in its flesh and slowly dying, blackening outward. I felt raw then, felt the entire natural world cave inward, as the darkness seeped inside the roots of the tree and burned it, twisting its branches and forcing shadows along the clearing as it tried to reject the damning energy now connected to it by this impure man.

All the shock and devastation of the tree cut through *me*—like being violated in the most heinous, violent way—forcing me down to my knees as the full weight of everything to come, all the consequences of this, rose up around me like shame. I felt like the heart of all the worry in the world, bleeding out, pulsing the shadows of things to come along the veins of the future, knowing that nothing could change it.

David died when she took his soul.

But he would rise again as something else.

And there would never be a way now to undo that. Lily hadn't saved him. She hadn't saved anything. She'd *created* something. I felt it coming—the death, the devastation.

Elora stood, her face white with the haunting knowledge she saw now as a new future set itself deep within the bones of the earth, changing what was. I shut my thoughts away when I looked into her Seer's eye, casting my gaze across the clearing to David as he rolled up to sit, turning his head to find me here in the darkness.

"Ara?" he said, and he sounded just the same, but his eyes were no longer green. He cast the onyx prisms onto Lily, and she cried into her hand, leaning in to kiss his mouth.

Though he seemed taken aback for a moment, he accepted her lips, bringing his hands alongside her face as he kissed her deeply, making my stomach turn.

"What was that for?" he asked, laughing softly as she drew away.

"I love you," she said. "I'm so sorry. The spell didn't work. It killed you and I had to resurrect Ara so I could access the fruit. It all died when she did."

"Why?" he asked, looking at me.

"She's the guardian."

He nodded, wiping his mouth as he stood up. I lifted my chin, making myself seem taller, as he walked over. "You look worried," he said, his eyes warming with a smile.

"You kissed Lily."

"She kissed me."

I looked at my feet, too brokenhearted to keep looking at his changed eyes. "I don't know what you are now."

"What I am?" He glanced down at his hands then over at his unconscious brother. When his eyes came back to me, it was with the knowledge of the ages—something only those of the fruit's wisdom should bear. "I'm immortal. No longer Vampire."

"Yes," I muttered unwillingly.

He exhaled, pressing his lips in as he nodded, as though something had to be done that he didn't want to face. "I am different," he stated. "Things… it feels different. Not so much physically, but… it's like I can hear my old-self speaking his beliefs to me and…"

"You don't share those anymore," Elora said, tears streaming her cheeks.

David looked at her, bringing his hand up again to inspect it as the rain stopped and the beads of water drained away from his fingertips. "No. I don't. But that's not necessarily a bad thing."

"It is," she whispered in a breaking voice, nodding. "I saw it."

"Don't worry," he said, moving over to kiss her head, like he was still the same David and she was still his little girl. "I do still love you. You're my daughter."

"It doesn't matter." She shook her head, too grieved to speak clearly, crying so hard her face was red, nose swollen. "If you saw what I saw—"

"I'm sorry," he said, not really meaning that. He looked back at me then, and in one swift move, he vanished.

Lily made a wet coughing sound, and Elora screamed, jerking back, as the heart of our once beloved Lily hit the roots of the sobbing, molested tree behind her, splattering the snowy earth with red.

David wiped his hand on his jeans, stepping back to let her fall flat to her face, her dark hair sprawled out like the tendrils of a mythological beast. "Take her soul," he demanded. "She doesn't deserve it."

"This will start a war," I warned. "Her father will come for her."

"Not where I'm taking her," he said, bending to hoist her off the ground.

"And where is that?"

David just winked, walking away. "You have three seconds, or her soul is lost for good."

Without a thought, I reached out with my Cerulean Energy and the words of an ancient language to extract the warm, tingly light from within her, drawing it inside me. And for the first time in almost twenty years, I suddenly felt complete. Whole.

"Take care of my brother," David called, while the strange shadows of a world I'd never seen gradually swallowed him. "I will be back."

"Where are you taking her?"

"To the darkest corner of the underworld," he said, his voice echoing up the crossway between life and death. "Where no one but me will ever find her."

JULES

As a low roll of thunder grumbled in the sky just seconds before it cracked sharply with a bright flash of light, Mike shot up out of his sleep, his big bulky body looking sexy there without a shirt, the contours of his pecs lit up by another flash of blue light.

"Daniel's fine," I mumbled. "He's sleeping."

"It's not that." He threw the covers back and got out of bed, walking toward the window. "It's the energy."

"What about it?"

"That's not a storm…" He opened the curtain and peered out, another flash of lightning making his nose and chin white.

"Certainly looks like a storm."

"It's a Cerulean Storm, and if… I'd know that energy anywhere. I grew up with it."

I hopped out of bed and grabbed the baby monitor as Mike pulled the door open, throwing his shirt on as he darted down the corridor in bed shorts, no shoes.

"Mike, where are we going?"

"Ara's alive," he said, moving at a half-run. "I can feel it. Something's happened."

I ran faster then, and we pushed out through the front doors and glided across the university courtyard, coming out near the hospital. Immortality did nothing to protect my bare feet from the snowy ground, wet and slippery as the icy-cold rain came down in slanted sheets.

"Where are you going?" I called over the raging wind.

"To her body—if it's still there."

Regretting my decision to leave the warmth of my bed, I followed him on aching feet to the forest, slowing my steps when Falcon came running out from the shadows toward us.

"You felt it too?" Falcon said to Mike.

He nodded, and we all ran a little faster. We reached the tree line just as a humble queen in a long white dress appeared, ethereal and stunning in all her immortal, *living* glory. The trees behind her bent and swayed, weeping and crying as a flash of light made the rain sparkle on the crystal-like snow around them. As much as I wanted to hug Ara in that moment, I also wanted to high-five her for being so damn gorgeous after just waking from the dead.

Mike's steps slowed and he exhaled as he closed her in his arms. "For fuck's sake, Ara," he mumbled into her shoulder. "I never thought I'd see you again."

She hugged him back, looking at me as I moved in and wrapped my arms around them. "Don't. You. *Ever*. Die again," I demanded.

Ara laughed, leaning out to look at me.

Falcon stepped in then, as the thunder raged on overhead, smacking the grounds with wind and soft spatters of rain, and he took her in his arms, pressing every inch of himself up against her. She was clearly precious to him, and I hadn't known that until now.

"I found you," he said, his voice muffled in the noise of the rain. "I found you on the beach."

She squeezed him tighter, shutting her eyes. "I'm sorry."

"No, I'm sorry," he said, clutching her face and tilting it up to his.

"For what?"

"For this."

He bent then and kissed her deeply on the lips, angling his head in perfect unison with hers, as though they'd kissed a hundred times before. The hard rain pushed their hair flat to their heads, running in rivulets along their cheeks and into their mouths. When he pulled away, Ara was stunned to silence.

She laughed out a breathy puff of disbelief. "Are you crazy?"

"David can punch me for it if he ever comes back."

"He's back," David said, making us gasp as the shock took the night out from under all of us. He marched over to Falcon and struck him hard, sending him to the ground in a limbless heap.

"David!" Ara grabbed his wrist and pulled him back, while Mike just shook his head, watching on with folded arms and a boyish laugh.

Falcon grunted, wiping his lip as he rolled up. "I deserved that."

"And don't forget it." David leaned down and offered his hand, helping him stand. "Go get my brother. He's by the tree."

Falcon's eyes shot toward the forest. "Is he alive?"

"Barely."

He took off at a run, and Mike's gaze glided after him, small with a knowing smile.

"What?" I said, shivering now from the cold. "What was that look for?"

"There's only one other person on this planet that Falcon loves as much as Ara," he said, heading over to David and leaving that hanging. He hugged his long-lost friend and shook his head as he stepped back. "I thought we'd lost you."

"You did," David said simply. "I was dead. And now my brother is human."

Mike's gaze moved to Falcon then, as he came out of the forest, carrying Jason.

"He's alive," Falcon called. "But he needs medical attention. Now."

"Should we use the fruit on him?" Elora asked, following Falcon out of the forest. I didn't even know she was in there.

"The fruit's dead," Ara whispered, a thousand lifetimes of regret staining her words. All heads turned to her, as Falcon and Elora vanished into the sheets of rain.

"What do you mean?" Mike asked.

"Lily used it on David."

And we all looked at him, realizing what it was we'd sensed in him, the difference, however subtle and subconscious it may be.

"If the fruit touches the lips of an impure being," she said, and then collapsed. Mike moved to catch her, but… David didn't even try. I barely knew him, and even *I* knew that was weird.

"What happened to her?" Mike asked, lifting her, unconscious, off the ground. "Did she get hurt?"

"She's connected to that tree," David advised. "I think a part of her shattered when it suffered that way."

"It's dead?"

"No. But it will never be the same again," he said, and

walked away, leaving behind nothing but a pit of confusion and despair.

ARA

I woke in my old room—the queen's chambers. It still smelled like Lily, like lavender and spite. Still held all of her things, and for a moment, as I opened my eyes, I forgot she was dead. Forgot that she'd done unspeakable things to my David, to Jase… and my little boy.

When it all hit me, it was with such force that I sat bolt upright, moving to launch over the side of the bed. But a hand grabbed my arm.

"Mom."

"Elora." I turned to look at her where she sat beside me, the big open sky bright behind her through the balcony door. "How long was I out? Where's Danny?"

"He's safe," she assured me with a simple look in her eye. "It's midday. You were asleep all morning."

"I need to see him."

"He's okay. Lilith erased it."

"Erased what?"

"Everything. He doesn't remember anything after that morning he was taken."

My heart slowed, eyes coming back in to their normal shape as the fear and worry left them. "Does he know I've been gone?"

"He's been too busy having fun with Uncle Mike and Aunty Jules."

"Aunty Jules?" I smiled.

"She's been amazing, Mom." Her eyelids fluttered a little in emphasis of that. "Danny adores her, and she's been a rock, getting us all through this."

I hadn't expected that, not in my wildest dreams. "Is Jason okay?"

"He hasn't woken yet. Falcon's with him."

My mind rushed along the corridors, searching for Jason, tracing his energy signature, and when I found it in the king's chambers on the other side of the manor, I put my face into my hands, feeling the deep cracks and aches within his soul. "He's so broken."

"Yes." Elora nodded. "He's been badly beaten, from what we can tell. What did she do to him?"

"I don't know," I whispered. "I was never with them. She took us all separately. I got a note," I said, recalling it all. "And Jason called me—said he'd gotten a note and he wanted to know if Danny was safe."

"What happened after that?"

"Danny vanished from in front of my eyes. Lily told me to get on a plane—in the note. And when I left the yard, evaporated so David wouldn't see me go, everything just..." I stared at nothing. "I came into consciousness again almost thirty hours later, being walked out to the lighthouse by a guard."

"She must have had a witch working for her—to shut down Uncle Jase's abilities. Dad's even."

I nodded.

Elora tucked her hair behind her ears on both sides, pressing her lips thin. "What happened then, Mom? How did you end up dead on the beach?"

As much as I didn't want to say it aloud, I knew she needed the truth. So I began my story, and after three sentences, she crawled into my arms and cried while I recalled it all, her slender body shaking with sobs, tightly curled up in the safety of her mother's embrace. I hadn't held her like this since she was a child.

"Is Harry here with you all?" I asked. "Is he safe? Is Cal?"

"Cal's fine. He's at home, but Harry's here. He has a surprise for you." She looked up and smiled, her nose and cheeks red with sadness. "But… there's something I need to tell you."

"Is it David. Did he come back yet?"

"He came back right after you." She sat up. "You don't remember?"

I shook my head.

Elora moved to the edge of the bed and sat with her legs hanging over, her palms pressed between her knees. "Mom. Aubrey's gone missing."

"What?" I appeared in front of her, the air cold and harsh on all my limbs as the panic in the room cooled it. "What do you mean? When?"

"A week ago. The day we found you dead. We didn't know much until recently, but... tell me honestly, did you know what Aubrey was?"

"What she was?" I knelt down in front of her, fixing her gaze with mine. "What do you mean?"

"She's not Lilithian, Mom. She's a necromancer."

I sunk back as that sunk in. It all made sense. I didn't know much about those creatures, but I knew they could raise the dead. But... Necromancers were demons, from what I knew. And Aubrey was human.

Hesitantly, I sat down beside Elora, wrapping my arm around her. "Tell me what you know."

Mid-morning gave way to afternoon as Elora talked, and I went through several stages of fear, numbness, and extreme raging grief. My little girl. My sweet but dark and sassy little girl had been taken, possibly by the most heinous and influential witch family in the history of the earth.

"What are they doing to her, Elora?" I asked rhetorically, rubbing my brow.

"I don't know." She sobbed into her hands, taking jagged breaths between words. "And I'm so scared for her, Mom. I'm so so scared for her."

"Where's Morgana?"

"She's gone to London to help Elias Davenport investigate."

"Good." I nodded. Just days before I was taken, Drake had called to say that Aubrey resurrected an old enemy, but he'd also had a number of interesting things to say about Morgana and Aubrey's relationship. Including the fact that Morgana had referred to her as "Aubs". My sister didn't do pet names, which meant that Aubrey must be very special to her. They'd bonded somehow, and I knew I could count on her, and the ever-knightly Elias Davenport, to do everything within their worldly and supernatural power to find her.

"What do we do now, Mom?" Lors asked, drying her face with the sleeve of her sweater.

"Right now, we leave Aubrey to Elias and Morgana. You saw what comes," I said, my tone grave as I recalled the vision she'd had in the clearing this morning. "We have to find a way to fix your father."

"I don't know if we can, Mom. I've been searching as I sat

here, looking at every possible course of action and every vision that results," she said, staring into the hinged mirror on her necklace. "And I can't find any path where…"

"Don't finish that sentence, Elora." I spun away, standing up. "I don't want to know."

She swallowed hard and stood up too. "Look, I need some food. Some blood. And I need to see my husband. Just… go see Danny, and then check in with Harry, okay? He has something he needs to show you."

"Okay." I reached out and touched her arm. "It'll be okay."

"Mom, you know it won't." She curled her arm up and patted my hand there. "But thanks for saying that anyway."

THE NURSERY HAD ONCE BEEN TWO ROOMS. WHEN LILY had Beth, they knocked the wall down between the two rooms next to ours, and set up a kind of child's playland. There was a crib, a few beds, and an activity area where they could play, watch tv, draw and paint. There was even a rope swing suspended from the ceiling. It was more like a childcare center than a bedroom, and the Peter Pan's Neverland theme made it all feel magical. Of course, Lily didn't know when she painted it that Neverland was a metaphor for the afterlife of dead children, but decided to keep it anyway, because it looked amazing and Lily and Jase weren't superstitious.

When I opened the door and stepped inside, prepared to find my little boy crying, a sobbing mess, he looked up from his train set, sitting on the ground in front of Aunty Jules and said, "Hi, Mommy."

That was it. He nearly died. I nearly died. And he casually says *Hi, Mommy.*

I cried, doing everything I could to conceal it. It was the best I could have hoped for—to have him so calm and so at ease that he didn't even care that I was gone—so why was I crying?

Jules smiled softly at me as I came over and knelt down beside him, examining every inch of his gentle, human little face to make sure he was okay. There were no signs of the trauma he'd suffered, the horror. His bright Jason-green eyes sparkled, and he was happy, and I was so grateful to Lilith for what she'd done—something that would have taken the magic of Life, the magic from our tree—which made me feel so ashamed of myself for not being able to save it from its fate. For not doing the job entrusted to me.

"How's he been?" I asked Jules.

She nodded, laughing once. "Energetic. Full of sass."

"Has he been waking at night?"

Jules nodded again. "But I was glad."

"Why?"

"Because…" She reached over and wiped Danny's nose with the tissue in her hand. "In those days before Lilith erased his memory, I'd have given anything to see him throw a tantrum over wanting the spoon instead of the fork."

I understood then what she had been through. I saw it all play out in her thoughts, and I got up to sit beside her on the bed.

"Thank you."

"Don't mention it," she said, her voice squeezing out as I hugged her tightly.

I took a deep breath then as I leaned back, looking at Danny. My miracle. My marvel. My little piece of Jase that I'd been so close to losing. He was okay, and I was okay, but there was still so much darkness to follow. My daughter was missing, Jason was human and still hadn't woken, and David… if Elora's vision was anything to go by, then we had a very long, very painful journey ahead of us.

Stepping outside of that, I glanced around the otherwise empty nursery, brow pulling tight in confusion. "Where's Lily's children?"

"Vampirie came for them the day of the attack," she said. "Mia and Evie are here though. We flew them out a few days ago."

I shut my eyes with relief that everyone was okay. "I should go see Harry."

Jules smiled mischievously. "He has a surprise for you."

"So I hear." I stood up with lifting curiosity. "Are you okay with Danny for a bit?"

"He wouldn't let me leave if I tried." She laughed. "I'll feed him and put him to bed soon. Mike's on his way back up with some more paint for him."

"Okay." I nodded, taking in this girl with new eyes. She was really something else. And while she may not have been able to work things out with Jason, I was glad she'd become a part of our lives. Our family. Aunty Jules, I said to myself, really liking the sound of that.

I left the room, closing the door on all those worries about Danny, and headed down to Harry's room. But he met me on the stairs as he came out of the Great Hall, running in and flopping around me like a big, goofy teenager. I squeezed him tight, breathing him in, my neck bent up awkwardly where he towered over me.

"I brought you a present," he whispered.

"What is it?"

After kissing my cheek, he stepped away, angling his arm back as Arthur came out from the Great Hall too. And I knew right away. A quivering squeak left my lips and I threw myself at him, hugging him tight and breathing in the deep, familiar scent of his vampire blood. He looked good. Strong and unsinkable. And though his aged face didn't fit the vampire I remembered within these walls, everything else about him was just the same.

"How did this happen?" I cried. "Who turned you?"

"Me," Harry said proudly, big cheesy grin and all.

"How'd you even know how to… oh," I finished when he tapped his temple. So, he'd stolen the method from our minds. I reached over and hugged him with one arm. "Thank you, Harry. You know how much this means to me."

"I know." He patted my back, drawing away, and I hugged Arthur again.

"How did he talk you into it?" I asked. "Do I need to punish him?"

Arthur wrapped his arms almost twice around me. "He happened to catch me fresh off a sixteen-hour surgery." He laughed, drawing out from the hug. "When I thought about how much more energy I had as a vampire, it was a done deal."

"Never mind the fact that he was worried about you guys," Harry added, winking at his uncle.

Arthur cleared his throat. "That goes without saying, I believe."

I smiled affectionately up at him. Right now, Jason was unconscious—human again—David had returned to the living realm with a darkness we had yet to understand, Lily was dead, and Aubrey was missing. But if Arthur were here, it all just felt a little less overwhelmingly impossible. "I'm so glad you're back. We're really going to need you right now, Arthur."

"I'm sorry about Aubrey." He rubbed my upper arm. "We will find her."

I nodded, wishing I could know that for certain. "Then there's David."

"What's wrong with Dad? Elora said he was alive." Harry's arms dropped, his expression catching the concern in mine.

"He came back as something else. He's not a vampire. And he's not… the same."

Harry and Arthur exchanged glances, looking ever like a father and a son. "Look, I can fill you in later. Or maybe Elora can—"

"She did. But she didn't tell us that."

"Maybe she wasn't sure she should, Harry. Go see her now. Ask her for the full story. I need to go see Jason."

"Why can't you just tell us?" Harry probed.

"I don't know what to tell you, I guess." I threw my arms out in a defeated gesture. "We don't really know what Dad is now. All we know is he's different." And that Elora had predicted many cases of extreme violence and malice. Inhumanly malicious things.

"It's all right." Arthur capped my arm, giving me a nod of reassurance. "Go in and see Jason. He…" His eyes darkened. "He needs you right now."

"Why do you say it like that?"

"He hasn't woken, but there doesn't seem to be any logical reason, as far as my medical and vampire knowledge goes," he said. "I'm not sure he wants to wake."

"Why?"

"Think about it, Mom," Harry said, stuffing his hands in his pockets. "From the get-go, his life has sucked. He lost Rochelle. You chose Dad. Aunt Jules left him. And now Lily, the one he married, tried to rip his soul from his body and leave him for dead because she chose Dad too. And, from what Falcon tells me, she beat him pretty badly as well." Harry shrugged. "So what kind of a life is he even coming back to, where he doesn't matter to *anyone*?"

"He matters—"

"No, he doesn't. He's family, we love him, but if it had come down to Jason or Dad in there, Jason wouldn't even be here right now, Mom." Harry's voice cracked. "And I love you for that—knowing that if that had happened, you'd save my dad. Because I can't lose him… *ever*. But if I was Uncle Jason, I just flat-out wouldn't have come back. I'd take my pride, my self-respect, and I'd fucking *die*."

"Harry, language," Arthur reminded him.

"I'm sorry, Uncle Arthur," he said, arms out wide as he backed away. "It's just how it is."

I looked up at Arthur. "He's been beaten?"

His throat shifted, calm blue eyes shadowed by regret. "Badly."

"I can heal him."

"Then do so. But… while you're there," he said, as he went to walk away, "do something for his soul."

"What do you mean?"

"He's been through an ordeal. He probably feels like the most unloved, unwanted man in the entire world. Say something, *anything*, that will bring him back."

I nodded, walking away, not really sure there were any words with that kind of power.

The room had a kind of reverence to it, like the space where mourners gather. The lone man by the bed looked up, lifting his mouth from a curled fist as his eyes met mine.

"Ara, you're awake."

"Yeah." I moved over and hugged Falcon as he stood, then we both looked down at the sleeping human. He was breathing softly, seemingly peaceful, but every few breaths, his chest caved a little deeper and he stopped for a moment. "What's she done to him?"

"Based on the damage to his body," he said, and I realized then that he'd been crying. For a really long time. His voice was dry and tender, eyes red and his tears had dried in salty layers beneath new ones. "She wasn't planning to bring him back, Ara, so she just went all-out. Went to the darkest depths of all her sick desires, and punished him for ever being alive."

I looked down at Jase as Falcon fell into his seat again. He leaned over and plucked a thick lock of hair from Jason's brow, gently and lovingly sweeping it into the dark wavy mass. When I sat on the bed, Jase didn't even stir.

Slowly, making sure I didn't dip the mattress, I reached for the blanket covering his bare chest and rolled it down, revealing several bluish bruises and the half-dozen tattoos he'd gotten over the years—both the inked ones and the Marks of Nature.

I'd loved him once. Touched this chest, kissed it. It had held my tears, my fears, my worries, and now it was damaged, as if none of that had ever mattered. As if the love within it had never filled Lily up, made her whole. How could she do this to him, when he'd never been anything but the man any woman deserved?

Falcon leaned in again, pointing to Jason's chest. "He has three cracked ribs." He drew the blanket down a little more and showed Jase's stomach and the curve of his waist. "Internal bleeding. And extensive bruising."

I covered my mouth as he drew the blanket all the way down to reveal his entirely naked body. And there, in a place no man should ever be hurt, was the worst of it. It was swollen and black with bruising, dotted with tiny cuts.

"She hasn't cut him, but she must have kicked him or hit

him with something pretty fucking hard." His voice broke away and he started crying as he tried to get his words out. "Look what she did to him!"

Thick fat tears spilled over my hand and into my mouth. I drew my fingertips away and pressed them to Jase's waist. "I'll start the healing here," I said. "But I'll need some of my stones. I won't have the energy to heal him properly while we're inside, and it's too cold to take him out."

Falcon nodded, standing up.

"Falcon." I stopped the healing for a moment, grabbing him as he went to walk past me. With the warmth of his hand curling around mine, my face close to his hip, eyes on Jason still, I felt comfortable enough to ask him this without worrying about offending him. "What happened between you two? And when?"

"What do you mean?"

"I mean…" I nodded at Jase. "Come on, Falcon. I know you're in love with him. When did *that* happen?"

He swallowed hard, looking Jason over. "When I left you. Just after you had Aubrey."

My eyes rolled to a slow close as I exhaled the deep concern, because I knew their lives wouldn't have been easy with Lily around. "Did Lily know?"

"Yes. And she toyed with us."

"Did… was the feeling…"

"Mutual?" he scoffed. "Not really. Not in the way I needed it to be."

"In what way then?"

"We talked over whiskey every night." He squeezed my hand a little, as if the memory sunk through him and he didn't realize he was doing it. "*Every* night. Until midnight. And I told him everything. And he did the same. I knew about the abuse long before any of you did, because I was helping him through it."

"Does he know you're in love with him?"

"Yes."

I smiled, wishing it had been reciprocated. Maybe, if Jase did love him, he might have a reason to come back. Falcon would be that one guy who would always fight for those he loves. And then, in the end, Jase would lose Falcon too, I suppose, if history were anything to go by.

"I'll get the stones," he said, his familiar, soothing voice deep and sad with remorse.

I nodded, watching one of my tears as it fell onto Jason's stomach and rolled down his waist, then I leaned in and kissed the fine dark hairs around his navel. He was warm, his flesh soft, pressing in with the touch of my lips, and I just wished I could make it all better. But I wasn't sure anything would. Ever again.

When night time rolled around, I was glad Jules and Mike were taking care of Daniel. I hadn't wanted to leave Jason's side, and I hadn't yet managed to heal him. After dying, and with so little time passing since I came back—so little blood consumed—I wasn't strong enough to make him better without the help of Nature. I needed to take him outside to the forest, but the mercury had dropped, and it was snowing right now. Hard. I wouldn't risk taking a fragile human out in that, not when the tree was also sick and there was a possibility that its magic might not have the strength to support mine.

For the longest time now, Falcon hadn't said a word. He sat by Jase's bed, hands clasped where his forearms rested on his thighs, leaning inward. Every now and then, he reached over to touch him, as if he could possibly ease away his suffering, apologize in some way for everything that was true about his life.

I sat staring at him, wishing I knew what to do, until eventually the door opened and a column of yellow spread across our darkness. David stepped in, shutting out the light again.

"How is he?" he asked.

"Damaged," I said. "Heart, body, mind, *and* soul."

He nodded, turning on the lamp beside the bed. It took Falcon and I a moment to adjust to the light, while David pulled the blanket off Jason in one swift move and looked over his naked body.

"What did she do to him, David? You were there. What did she do?"

"I would say that's pretty obvious, Ara," he sung in a factual, emotionless tone. "Do you need details?"

"I'd like them, yes."

"Why?"

"So I know how to help him when he wakes."

"You can't help him," he stated, folding his arms. "She made sure he knew just how unimportant he was to anyone. And people don't come back from that, Ara."

"I can help him."

"How? By telling him you love him?" He angled his shoulders around so he wouldn't have to unfold his arms to look at me. "Oh, wait. You don't love him. You love *me*."

"Well…"

"So, I reiterate," he said, dropping his arms and stalking over to me. "Why would he come back at all?"

I sighed, looking over this dark stranger in front of me. "Well, if he wants to die, then he can do that. But he has to wake up first and tell me to my face. He has to break it to his son."

"His son is two. He won't even know."

"That's not the point." I moved over and covered him with the blanket again.

"No, the point is that you love him, and you don't want to let him go." David grabbed my wrist to stop me. "But you don't love him enough to either give him the peace of being with you or to put him out of his damn misery."

I drew my wrist away from him, pushing a hand out to tell Falcon to back down.

David searched my eyes, groaning in the back of his throat. "Fine. I'll heal him, and you can look him in the eye and tell him he has no reason to live."

"He has Danny."

"A child is not, nor will it ever be, a reason to live. A noble ideal, I'm sure, but you need to face reality—"

"How can you say that? He—"

"Because it's no life, living for another. But…" He drew the blanket away again and pushed his sleeves up. "If you want him back, I'll do it. But you can face the consequences of his death being a *choice* he makes when it comes to that. Or…" He looked at Falcon. "You can let him die now, peacefully."

"I won't let him die. And what do *you* hope to do about healing him?" I sneered, aiming a hand at the damaged body. "You don't have the power to heal."

"I do, actually," he stated, and my mouth dropped. "When Lily fed me the fruit, I was instantly connected, or perhaps bound to, the natural and spirit world in the same way you are."

"No, not the same way," I said firmly. "I am Light—"

"And I am a part of that tree, of its magic, of its life, as much as you, as much as Lilith, and as much as the once-powerful stone that we worshipped in the forest," he said a little louder over my voice. "Except that I'm connected by my darkness and you're connected by the light. But I am still connected."

"Meaning?"

"What you can do, so too can I. But without your limitations, because the magic within the Dark Veins does not live by the same strict rules as the Light."

"Dark Veins?"

"Where powerful magic pulses from within the Underworld."

"What underworld?" My eyes flicked off, seeing the memory of him entering a shadowy realm with Lily in his arms—one I could feel but not see—with its cold, its emptiness, its darkness.

"I can hear my powers speaking to me, Ara. I don't need to discover them, learn them. It's as if all the knowledge I need is right here." He brushed a hand up his arm, his lips parting, ears lifting as if he were listening now. "I can heal him. I will need your body, or Falcon's—the power you both have inside to heal—but I can do it much more effectively than you ever could."

"Then do it," I demanded. "I'm tired of sitting here watching him suffer."

"Fine. Undress," he said.

"What?"

"You heard me. I can't perform this ritual while the energy is blocked by your clothes. Undress."

Without hesitation, I kicked off my shoes and reached up behind me to unzip the dress I'd been dead in. It slipped down my body, and I stood naked before my husband, who was like a stranger to me, and Falcon, who'd seen me naked a hundred times.

"Press your body to his."

"How?"

"Lie flat. Your chest to his chest, stomach to his, as much flesh touching as possible."

I crawled onto the bed and drew a breath before I let my naked skin fall against his. The last time we laid like this, Daniel was conceived. And so many memories ran through me then of that night, making me realize how badly I'd miss him if he died.

Careful not to hurt him more, I pressed my breasts against his warm, human chest, feeling him breathe softly against my cheek as I laid it to his. His beard had grown in while Lily had him, and it scratched at my skin pleasantly, the hair on his chest, belly, and groin tickling me where our bodies met. I hooked my toes around his feet and rested my arms along his ribs, exhaling and relaxing into him. I did feel a bit exposed with my naked butt facing the two other men in the room, and I just hoped that David really could do what he said and that this wasn't some sick, twisted joke.

"Jase," I whispered, my breath coming back warm off his ear. "If you can hear me, you come back, okay. You come back to me. There is a life here for you. I promise. I'll make sure of it."

"And how will you do that, exactly, considering you can't give him the only thing he wants?" David grunted, leaning over us. He exhaled his annoyance then and pressed his hands to my waist. "Just lie still."

A cold, tightening sensation went down my body, tingling and making my skin itch all over. I could hear Jason's cells changing, responding, could hear his bones lifting and knitting back into place, and I could hear the clean, flowing rush of his blood beneath the healed skin.

"There," David said, drawing back.

I wanted to move too, but Jason's arms closed around my waist and he held me tight, breathing me in until I leaned back a little, looking down into his hurt green eyes. "I'm dead, aren't I?" he asked.

We all laughed.

David helped me get up, and Falcon covered me with a sheet as David covered Jason with the blanket. He sat up a little and rubbed his head. "What happened? How are we both alive?" The agony in his eyes came clean then as he looked at his brother. "I *saw* you die."

David sat beside him on the bed. "Lily brought me back."

"Then why aren't I dead?"

"A lot went down, bro." David pushed his brother's chest to make him lie down. "I'll fill you in later."

Jason pressed a hand to his beating heart. "I'm human."

David nodded. "And you will remain so, until you're ready to decide if you want to live or die."

Jason cast his eyes downward in a sorrowful gaze. He looked over at Falcon then and smiled. There was an exchange within that look that made me wonder if whiskey and late-night conversation had gone beyond at some point, especially since Jase had once wanted to blood-share with Falcon.

"Gross," David said, standing up. "Did *not* need to see that."

"Stay out of my thoughts then." Jason laughed, and so did Falcon, sitting back down on the chair beside the bed.

"Did you guys have sex?" I asked, catching on.

"Lily drugged us," Jase advised, looking over at me. "She wanted a blood tryst with Falcon and…" He couldn't finish. I watched as years of hurt and shame stuck in his throat.

"After what Hans did to him, Jason couldn't face it," Falcon explained. "But she wanted her own way, so… one night, when we sat for our usual whiskey and conversation, she drugged the bottle."

My shoulders sunk with regret.

"She came in, joined the fun for a bit, then got bored anyway," Falcon added in a very matter-of-fact tone. "We woke the next day, having… finished on our own. And… that was that."

I nodded, wetting my lips a bit as my mouth dried. "I'm sorry."

"It wasn't all bad." Jase grinned. "The thing about that potion is that it makes you think you had the best sex of your life."

David pretended to retch and cover his mouth, laughing it off as he reached the door. "I'll catch up with you later, bro," he said, his face bright and happy. "Gotta go do a few things."

"Kay." Jason nodded, then he looked at me as David left. I thought he wanted me to stay and make him all better, but he said, "Can I get a minute—with Falcon?"

"Sure." I frowned at Falcon, a bit confused, and he looked at me guiltily. I wondered how long ago all of this happened. And what had happened since.

Then it occurred to me: he probably hadn't seen Falcon since he came back from New York. He was held captive here for a year while Jules had no memory—forbidden to see anyone—and then he was with her in New York, then with us. This must be the first time he'd had a chance to speak with him about it.

I backed out of the room and closed the door, hearing Falcon break down to tears on the other side before I walked away.

AUBREY

My captor led me to a long and wide room with one entire wall of windows that overlooked a slope of snow-clad grass, leading away to the calm ocean down below. The sky went on forever out there, endless in all its freedom.

At the head of the room was a stone altar and a set of three tall banners with family crests in maroons and golds, while two pillars at the other end parted way for entry and exit. Down the middle was a shallow indent in the stone floor, like a bath. No deeper than my ankles and about as long and wide as two small cars, with manacles of varying sizes and lengths hanging above it from a sturdy wooden frame. I noticed large square drains at both ends of the tub, with shackles open and ready on the ground, and shuddered. I didn't have the senses of a Lilithian, but I knew the red stains on the edges and around the overflow was blood.

Out beyond the giant window, an orange sun was beginning to set, making the snow pink and the ocean a deep blue. I could almost hear the waves calling to me, guiding me home, and it made the fear inside me raw and unbridled in comparison. I didn't know what he planned to do to me, but just being trapped here, bound to my master, was enough to make me want to break.

He took my arm and positioned me in the stone bath. I didn't dare speak, afraid I'd cry. I'd been stripped naked already, while four women shaved me all over, cleaned me, and cut off all of my beautiful thick hair, leaving me bald but stubbly. My eyebrows were gone, all hair except my eyelashes. Standing here now in a black cotton tunic, the fabric scratchy and stiff, I wasn't brave enough to question anything he asked. There's no telling what he'd do next. And yet I still felt my defiance raging inside me, like a storm.

"Before you get any ideas about using your ghosts to send messages to your family, know this," Cillian said, standing in front of me, only slightly taller but so much more commanding. "I may not be a natural witch anymore, but I am a very practiced one. No ghost is getting past my barrier without my say-so. I will bring them in as I need them, and you will resurrect them and kill them immediately after."

"Wait, what?"

"You cannot become a powerful demon without feeding your hunger. You're not a magical being put on the earth to ease the suffering of those who are grieving. Your job, Necromancer, is to set right the balance. To ferry the souls from within the gaps in the veil, and then put them back where they're supposed to be."

"The Other Side?"

"Yes." He moved away from me and walked to a door on the opposite wall to the window. When he came back out, he had the same items Morgana had used in her ghost-summoning spell. After laying the pillar candles out at five points, he then drew a pentagram in the middle with red chalk.

"It will take many years of this tiresome task to make you as powerful as I need you to be, but… we have all the time in the world."

"My family will come for me. They will figure this out." They already knew the evil Blackwell family was back. If they were smart, they had to put two and two together.

"Considering that my family are working *with* your family to find you, as we speak, I highly doubt that."

"What?"

His forehead furrowed in the middle, studying me, its two vertical lines capped by a curved one that gave clues about his every thought. "One of my descendants infiltrated your family before I was even brought back from the dead. Granted, that wasn't her intention, but it works in our favor. And now that I have returned, and made it my mission to restore magic to all in our bloodline, she will follow me to the ends of the earth—do anything I desire."

I shut my eyes, worried for my family, for Elias, if there was a spy among them. "Who?"

"What?"

"Who is it? Who's your spy?"

Cillian stood up from the drawing on the ground, his seedy eyes shrinking in a calculated set. "My great-great-great niece, Anandene."

I sunk down, my knees bent, head in my hands. Did that mean Morgana was a part of this? Only a few years ago, I'd lifted Anandene from within a fissure. I gave her life. I was responsible for this! "My aunt is her daughter."

"I know," he stated, as though it was ancient history. "We have tried, tirelessly, to get Morgana on side. But she's faithful to the queen. So, she can die along with the rest of them."

Internally, the sun in my heart rose, lighting up hope deep within. Cillian himself had told me when I first arrived here two days ago that Morgana was a powerful witch. If she was still on our side, even if my mom really was dead, Cillian didn't have as much hope in hell as he thought. And Anandene didn't have any powers. She was just a shameful disappointment of a woman to her daughter. She could spy, infiltrate, but she was no real threat against my bad-ass witch aunt.

I knew I could be strong then, endure what he put me through, because I knew, without a shadow of a doubt, that my family would save me.

"I will call one spirit at a time," Cillian said, kneeling by the pentagram with his hand to the dagger at his belt. "You will bring it back quickly and then you will kill it without thought. Do you understand?"

Reminding myself that I would one day escape this, I nodded, readying my heart for what was coming.

Cillian shut his eyes and whispered something, and a spirit appeared like a wavering column in front of me. In the form of a child. She looked at me with curious eyes, and I felt my soul pull backward, his words "Kill it without thought" ringing through my darkest nightmares.

She was someone's little girl. Someone's child that had—if she was in a fissure—died a tragic death. How could I kill her?

I reached for her hand, drawing her to this side, and as she took her first breath, I decided that it didn't matter if my family were trying to find me. I was wrong. I couldn't face any task just to be whole when they got here, because if I did this, if I killed this little girl, there would be nothing left of my soul anyway.

"Kill her," Cillian said, and the girl huffed, whipping her

head around to look at him. She backed away, her small feet clean on the mucky blood-stained stone, as her innocent round eyes tried to understand her captor.

"Just let this one go," I pleaded. "I'll kill an adult, but—"

"I warned you that I would not give second chances." Cillian turned to me, making my heart leap uncontrollably into my stomach as he grabbed my arm. "You haven't saved this soul by refusing to kill it. You've merely subjected it to more suffering now as it waits in a dark cell, without food or comfort for its human form, while you endure your punishment."

"No. Please." I sunk my knees down and tried to break from his grasp, scratching up my bare foot on the stone floor. "Please don't."

The little girl wailed, running for the window, but there was no way out. For either of us.

"There is a better place for her to go, Aubrey. Better than this world that she will now suffer because of you," Cillian explained. "Remember that when I come to ask you to kill her again, and if you defy me then, I will torture it and make you watch."

He led me away, snagging the child by the hair and dragging her, screaming, along with us.

A SMALL DOT OF LIGHT APPEARED IN THE COOL, PUFFY DIRT. It was white, the light of the sun, channeling down through a thin hollow in the cell wall. After a while, it moved up over the bars and then, eventually, vanished. It did that six times as I lay here, marking the days that passed. I hadn't eaten since I was last at the castle with Drake, and my stomach had protested painfully, loudly, at first, but now it had given up. I hadn't showered, and the only toilet in here was a bucket in the corner that I, shamefully, had used several times. It hadn't been emptied, but with the agony ripping through me every time I breathed from the foul, debased things he did to me, I couldn't hold my pee. I had to go, and the smell in that bucket—like boiled potatoes with lemon and unwashed vagina—was enough to make me want to vomit now.

Cillian had left the little girl in a cell right beside mine. I couldn't see her, but I heard her whimpering. She'd tried to talk to me when he first delivered me back here after my punishment, but I physically couldn't speak. And I didn't want to give her hope or get to know her. Already, I knew she must have been only eleven. But Cillian was right: the kind thing to do was to send that girl to the peaceful place on the Other Side. The place my mom talked about. I would just have to look at it as though I was opening a doorway for her to go back where she'd fallen from, and not look at it as though I was killing her.

I had to accept it.

I'd accepted it as he beat me, as he kicked my stomach over and over again with his heavy boot. He never once showed anger or aggression, never sweat or grew tired—just kicked over and over, like he was performing a task. And I'd decided then that I had to kill her. That I had to kill them. Any ghost I brought back, any task he ordered. I had to do it, because he was so cunning, like my dad. So evil. Anything he could think of to squash my defiance, it was worse than what the original task would do to my soul, my will to live.

I was already dead. I'd been humiliated, stripped, shaved, had my body touched in places no one had a right to, as they cleaned me and removed all my hair. I'd been kicked, slapped, and when I was curled into a ball on the ground, cut from the steel-cap of his boot on my human flesh, he told his men to piss on me. The stink from it still made me shudder, still stung my open cuts, got into places I didn't want to feel it, taste it. It was in my clothes and on my face, and the dirt only stuck to it as he threw me in here on the floor.

Now, six days had passed, my bruises were swollen and festering, and I was so sick with fever that I couldn't stop shaking.

But I would not cry. I wasn't completely powerless. Cillian could hurt me. Force me to do terrible things. But I would never satisfy him by crying. I would make my parents proud by refusing to let this break me.

As the little ball of light appeared for the seventh time, the cell door opened and Cillian stepped in, looking me over.

"Your time has been served. Get up."

My hands moved, afraid to defy him, and pushed into the ground. All of my bones ached like they'd been stretched. I limped as I followed him out of the tunnel and up to the stone room again. The girl was sitting on a chair, pale and thin, her lips chapped and her hair scraggly. She didn't even look at me as I came in.

Cillian handed me a dagger, and I did my duty, sending the girl back to the Other Side, this time, hopefully, at rest. At peace.

"Now, we do another." Cillian took the dagger and slipped it into his belt. He knelt then by the pentagram and lit the candles. The once homey scent of a struck match didn't bring me peace today. I glanced over at the blood dripping down from the child's once-clean foot and then turned my eyes away. I would not cry.

I brought back and killed ten souls that day before the exhaustion, the hunger, the thirst swept over me and I collapsed, waking then in a bed, clean.

ARA

"I found him sitting in the middle of a busy room. He was just staring, his eyes were completely fixed with worry, and he had his thumbnail rested between his teeth," Morgana said through the phone. "I've never seen Elias like that. Ever."

"He's in shock," I noted.

"Yes. But he is *not* sitting on this, Ara, believe me. He is as committed to finding that girl as I am."

"I know. I'm sorry." I sighed, sitting on the blanket box at the end of the bed, because I just felt too hollow in my limbs to stand. "I shouldn't have doubted him."

"It's natural, I guess."

"Oh god, what are they doing to her, Morg?" I cried into my hand, so weak with worry. I just needed answers. I'd called her, hoping with all my heart that they knew something, anything, and it only made me ripe with rage to find they'd learned nothing.

"To know that, we'd have to know who has her."

"And you're sure it's not the Blackwell family, or the Blackworths?"

"They're working *with* us, Ara. They've been very helpful."

"Your mother… has she…?"

"She's reconnected with the family. Went in there at my request to spy for them, but she's adamant that they don't know anything about Aubrey?"

"Do you believe her?"

"In all honesty, I have no reason not to. But when it comes to the safety of my niece, I will never truly trust anyone, Ara," she assured me. "Every single person is a suspect, in both mine and Elias's educated opinion, until I've laid eyes on that girl myself."

I nodded, glancing across at David as he came into the bedroom. I'd wanted to ask Morgana if she knew anything about what David had become now—in the catalogue of darkness she understood—but I couldn't do that with him in the room. It would have to wait. "I have to go. Keep me updated."

"Okay."

I hung up and took a deep breath, trying to relax my shoulders.

"No word yet?" David asked.

"Not yet."

He leaned on the back of the lounge across from me and folded his arms, looking right into me. With his eyes a different color now—dark and black, reflective—he didn't look like him. He almost had more depth, more 'to him'. Which *was* the case, I suppose. He was more powerful now, and had knowledge about things I could never even comprehend. But he also didn't connect the way he once did. I'd not seen him be cruel or unkind, despite the darkness I could sense in him, flaring within but he wasn't loving either. He hadn't even touched me.

Hadn't kissed me or come to see Danny, after everything we went through. Hadn't even asked me if I was okay. Then again, four days had passed, and I hadn't been in to see Jason again either. I just couldn't face him—couldn't listen to him tell me he wanted to die.

My eyes narrowed at David's hand then. At first, I thought the muck there on the back of it was blood from a feed, but it was darker, and had a white layer over it. And he also didn't need to feed off blood anymore.

I moved in and inspected it. "What happened?"

David drew it away, rolling off from his lean and hiding the wound against his body. "It happens."

"What is it?"

"It's a side-effect."

"Of what?"

"When you mix dark and light. There you go,"—he showed me the now-healed skin—"fixed."

"How did you do that?" I said in a breath, eyes wide. "Can you self-heal?"

"Yes. My body doesn't do it in the way it did when I was a vampire. I need to concentrate on it, similar to the way I healed Jason." David examined the healed skin for a moment, then looked over at me, making himself taller, his shoulders straighter. "You can do it too."

"I just don't need to." I grinned proudly.

"No, I suppose you don't, being Lilithian." His raven eyes moved up and down my entire body in a brisk evaluation, then he turned away and walked across to the bed. "I need the room for a while."

"Why?"

"I just do."

Pinching my thumbnails together, I stared at him, as he

busied himself digging around in a trunk by the door, moving things aside and sifting through its contents. My David had always dressed in the kingly attire of a navy blue uniform, with the high collar and the sash across the shoulder and chest that distinguished him from the men in the Knight's Core. Jase had always worn the black one. But now, kneeling there by the trunk in the black uniform, it felt almost like he was making a statement. Jason was human now, and after his and Lily's legal divorce through the House a few months ago, he was no longer the reigning monarch, so why had David gone as far as to wear Jason's colors? Was it a statement? A provocation?

The air and even the energy around him seemed to shift divergently, like a wavering cloud of heat emanating off his form and being swept the other way by an icy breeze, making all who passed curious about him, even if they didn't know why. He moved with a graceful yet calculated cadence, as if he had all the time in the world, taking care to evaluate every possible gesture before it became action. And all of his new mannerisms and the secretive air layered atop my fears because he wouldn't tell me why he needed the room, and yet he was sifting through Lily's trunk of sex toys and torture devices.

"David, enough time has passed now," I said carefully, testing the waters. "I've given you space to come to terms with everything, but… please don't shut me out like this. You're my husband. I love you, and—"

"You don't even know me," he said, frowning back at me, but his lips smiled. "I am an entirely different man to the one who died on Lily's altar."

"Yes, but…"

"Look." He rose slowly to his feet, smoothing his hand down black silk rope that he took from the chest. "I may have the life, the same interests, mostly, but not the same values. I just see things… so much more clearly now. And I'm not sure you'll like me this way."

"What does that mean?"

"Not what you think it does, sweetheart." He appeared before me, gently tucking a strand of hair behind my ear. "I just don't feel love the way I used to. And… love… it doesn't make sense to me in that way anymore."

"Meaning?"

"I would die for my daughter, my son. And I would fight for you. But you're not the only girl in the world. I appreciate your love, and I'm looking forward to stripping you naked and fucking you, but I'm just not as consumed by it." He tapped his chest, nodding at me as if he wanted me to acknowledge that feeling, as if I understood it. And he said it all so gently, with so much kindness, that it was like he was joking. But he wasn't.

My eyes went to the rope, imagining only the worst. "Is there a way to fix you?"

He smiled, probably knowing that was about to come. "To some degree, yes."

"How?"

"I'd need the other half of my soul."

"What?"

David nodded, moving over to the windows to look out on the day, his hands behind his back. "I won't *take* it from him, if that's what you're worried about. But… if you want me to be like the David you love… the one you lost, then I will need my soul intact. There's too much darkness in me."

I knew that. I'd seen it. Felt it. It just amazed me that he was calm about it, so upfront. It was almost scary. He wasn't fighting to keep his darkness, and he wasn't trying to stop us from fixing him. It was like he really didn't care either way. Which, I realized, he didn't.

"You can't stay this way," I said softly, meaning it.

"Then you know what has to happen."

I nodded, turning away. "The room is yours, as you requested. You have an hour."

"That's not long enough, Ara," he called sweetly, moving to the bed post to loop the rope around it. "If you come back before that, don't get upset by what you see."

"But..." I stopped by the open door. "You don't drink blood, so you're not feeding in here. What are you doing?"

"Well, I'm not having sex, if that's what you're implying." He smirked, pulling the knot on the rope to check its hold.

I studied him, catching a dangerous wave of energy off his body that made me want to get out of here immediately. "I don't want to know, do I?"

"Nope." He laughed, his sharp eyes alight with a glittering grin.

I walked away, knowing *my* David would never do anything that I would be upset by. But that wasn't my David. He was still him, still caring in some ways, but there was something altered that I couldn't put my finger on, couldn't trust.

When I reached the kitchen, in search of some brownies, I found Jason there instead. He looked up with wide eyes, having just run into the very person he was clearly trying to avoid.

"Hi," I said unapologetically.

"Um... hi." He leaned on the table, crossing his arms, a half a grin lighting up the corners of his eyes. But it slipped away then and his brow furrowed, the muscles beside his lip twitching with grief. "I can't do this."

"What?"

"I can't be around you, Ara. Pretend that I'm not ripped apart inside."

"What do you mean?"

"You know what I mean." He looked up from the ground, shutting his eyes tight as he fought with his pain. "All of this is your fault."

"What is?" I asked, his words cutting into my chest.

His eyes opened, darkened now around the glare of his disapproval. "You were warned. We were all warned by Lilith that our fates were entwined and that we couldn't fight it. And look what's happened because you didn't listen."

"So it's my fault?" I jerked forward, pressing my fingertips to my chest. "Just because I chose to honor my vow?"

"You chose to honor it at *any* cost to me, Ara. I didn't decide this. I fought for us, I would have dropped everything at any point in my life to be with you, and you rejected me. Over and over again." His voice got louder as he spoke until it cut off completely on a sad break, and then came back weak and quiet. "I can't make you be with me. I have no power. I never have, and I never will."

I understood then why he was so upset. And he was right. It was my fault. I did sacrifice him, at any cost, to be with David. But I'd just never viewed it that way before. Yet, when he put it like that, I could understand if he never wanted to see me again. I could finally see myself for the insensitive, selfish beast I truly was.

Jase lifted his hurt green eyes up to mine, clear and focused, looking so far into my soul that I felt like he was standing right beside me, touching me. And there was so much love in that gaze as he looked over my face, but when he spoke the next words, it was with all of that love shut away, like an iron door slammed over it. I'd never seen him like that before, except for when he first kidnapped me and tried to destroy me.

"I hate you because of that, you know," he said, exhaling so deeply after that his posture changed. "I don't say it to hurt you,

I just… I don't even know why I'm telling you, except maybe that the truth won't hold so much power over me if I let it out, but"—he shrugged, as though it just didn't matter anymore—"I hate you for what you've done to my life."

The truth ripped a new vein through my heart, sucking the air out of me too quickly. I sat down on the chair right beside his hip, shutting my eyes and resting my brow against his waist. "I made a promise to David—"

"Is that really all? Is that really why you've tortured me all these years?" His voice cracked. "How little I must matter that you'd let me suffer just so you can honor a stupid fucking promise."

"It's not that you don't matter—"

"It's that he matters more. And I have to live with that. You all expect me just to live with that." He put both hands over my head, as if he meant to push me away, but just didn't have the strength. "Do you have any idea how much it hurts?"

"Jase, please—"

"Lily hated me so deeply that she *killed* me, Ara. She beat me. She ripped my soul out of my body and tried to place it in my brother."

"I'm sorry." I put my hand up on his hip, sliding it around to hold him.

"No. Don't do that. Don't touch me like you can make it okay." He shoved my hands off and stepped back. "You can't make it okay, because that's just it: you're the *only one* that actually can. And yet you *won't*." His human face turned red with the anguish, his voice so shattered with the weight of it all that every word changed tone. "So don't comfort me, don't try to make me feel like there's hope for me, because there's not—"

"But I—"

"Just stop. Okay? I am the soul that *nobody* fought for, ever, and I don't even say that to pity myself, Ara. It's just a fact—proven and ingrained repeatedly over history," he stated, suddenly free of all emotion from it, as though he'd accepted this truth and just needed me to see, to know that he knew now. "And you know what?"

I shook my head, watching as the emotion slowly trickled back into his eyes, his voice, his curled fists.

"For the first time, Ara, this hatred is real." He pressed his fingertips to his chest, rubbing the center. "For all that you've cost me, forever now, I will *hate* you. I *have* to hate you."

Jase walked away then, and I didn't dare reach for him. When I looked up, Harry was standing in the doorway, his eyes lensed with tears.

"Harry, I—"

He put his hand up, backing from the room. "Just don't, Mom," he said, turning around to run after his uncle.

David found me later. I'd given him all the time he needed to do whatever it was he was doing, and when he came into the kitchen and looked at my tears, he sat down beside me, his legs open, and dragged my chair between them.

"Everything okay?" he asked, sounding just like his old self.

I looked at him, at those creepy black eyes, his pointed nose and defined lips, and shook my head to release the haunting trap of the awe he stirred in me. Evil or not, he was more strikingly beautiful now than he'd ever been. He was like a cup of dark liquid, filling up my heart.

"What happened?" he asked, and when he reached out to touch my wrist, I noticed a line of blood under his cuff. Not his blood.

"Jason hates me," I told him, fighting hard not to ask him who he'd killed. "I saw it in his eyes, David. He's never looked at me like that before. In fact, I don't think that guy has ever looked at *anyone* like that before."

"It takes a lot for him to hate," he noted. "But if it's any consolation to you, I understand it."

"I do too."

"Do you though?" he asked gently, cocking his head like a curious creature from another world. "Because it's not what you think, sweetheart. It goes deeper than just feeling unloved and unwanted."

"Then what is it?"

"He and I are one soul that was split in two. When we were born, it was split by much gentler means. But, when he carried both parts of the soul for that time while I was dead, he started to understand what it was like to feel complete."

Like I did with Lily's soul, all of her soul, in me.

"And, that sudden emptiness he feels now without my soul," David went on, "well, he needs to fill that with you—with his soul mate."

"But—"

"I'm not saying I want you to be with him. I'm just saying that we *both* need to fill that hole now." He glanced over my face, smiling softly as he swept my hair behind my ear and wiped a tear from under my lashes. "And, while I fill my emptiness with depravity and pain, his way is to find the light, the good. He's not even aware of it—that he seeks *you* out—or that he needs to hold *you* to feel complete."

I didn't miss the word, or the inflection on the word 'depravity'. "What do you mean?"

"By what?"

"By… you fill your missing pieces, your holes, with *depravity*?"

"It makes me feel complete, the things I do," he explained, lifting his shoulders to draw a deep breath, then he let it all out in relief. "When it's done, I get a sense of… satisfaction, fleeting as it may be. And I feel whole for a while, until it needs to be filled again."

"I don't understand."

"Charity work. People who do charity work do it because they get a sense of being filled up. It ignites them," he said, and I thought about that warm feeling you get when you do a nice thing. "Yes, that feeling right there." He pressed a finger to my chest. "I feel that when I experience suffering, pain."

"What kind of pain? Your own?"

He laughed, sitting back, and crossed an arm over his body, looking so lovely and so innocently human as he did. "No. I don't really enjoy hurting myself."

"Then… do you mean… on tv?"

His smile changed, eyes getting smaller as a wash of sympathy moved over it when he realized I could never comprehend.

"David?" I slid forward on the chair, my knees between his, bringing both hands onto his arms. "What have you done?"

"Sweetheart." He cupped the side of my face. "You're so kind, so filled with light. You wouldn't be able to cope if you knew of the things I've done here."

"Have you killed someone?"

The corners of his lips pulled outward like daggers, eyes lighting up. "Many, sweetheart," he said with a soft laugh. "I've killed many someones."

I sunk backward, hand to my mouth.

"Look, don't get upset, okay? It doesn't matter anymore because they're dead. What do they care now?"

My eyes traced the blood on his wrist. He covered it, as if he were ashamed.

"If you're so *fulfilled* by it, why do you hide it?" I snapped.

"Not for the shame, my love. It's just that people don't understand. I have to fill this hole; I *have* to feed this need. And if I don't keep it a secret, they'll all try to stop me." He reached over and affectionately swiped his thumb at my chin, winking at me. "But I knew *you'd* understand."

I covered my brow, fighting hard not to fall apart as I thought about every soul on this island—the only place he'd been since he came back. I was responsible for every single one of them, held accountable by multiple divisions of the government if anything were to happen. "How many people have you hurt?"

"It has to be this way, Ara."

"It can't be, David!" I reasoned, hard and stern, like he was a naughty kid. "You can't just go around killing people—"

"Perhaps it will stop once I've taken my brother's soul—"

"Do you really think that's the only way?"

"That rotting flesh you saw earlier, it's Nature's way of eliminating the anomaly. *Me.*" He pressed both hands to his chest. "With only half a soul in me—an evil one at that—my body cannot sustain the goodness from the fruit's power."

"And that's why you kill?"

"No. I kill, I hurt, to ease the burning, the calling in my soul. And it only calls to me, whispers those needs because it's empty. Missing a piece now."

"And why can't you fill that hole with me, like Jason tries to?"

"I'm connected to this world by my darkness, Ara. And darkness feeds on misery and pain—"

"So it has domain?"

"Yes, and I rot now because you can't have two forces equally great, dark and light, in one vessel. They fight against one another, a power struggle. And eventually, one of them will win out."

"And then what?"

"I will cease to exist," he explained. "Because my dark blood, my body, is alive by the magic of such pure light, I now need balance. I need something good in me. And when I take my brother's soul, that should fix my body for a time."

"For a time?" I shoved my chair back, throat opening with cold worry. "Not forever?"

"Not likely, but I suppose I have to try."

"You can't just kill Jason."

"What do you care, you never wanted him anyway?" He waved a dismissive hand at me. "Put the poor sod out of his misery."

"I can't let you do that.

"Then I will die." He shrugged, as though it was my problem. "And that's all there is to it."

Damn him. I shook my head, looking him over. Dark wavy hair, so full and thick, and those oil-like eyes that screamed evil but softened on the corners still, showing kindness. His golden skin beneath the rolled cuff of his black sleeves, and the hair on his knuckle, right under his wedding ring, just made him so real and so human. I still loved him, and I would go to the ends of the earth for him, kill for him. So if he needed Jason to die so we had even a small chance of saving our future, he knew, everyone knew, that I'd press the knife into Jason's heart myself if I had to.

"How long?" I asked, choking on that a little because the question carried the truth up from the prison of lies in my heart —the truth I wanted to deny but no longer could: Jason was right to hate me. "How long until you have to take him?"

He studied his wrist, scraping his fingernail along the flesh. "Maybe a year."

And that was it. I knew what had to be done. I would never allow David to die. I just wouldn't.

"What if it doesn't fix you, and you both end up dead?"

"That won't happen. I *will* live—even if it's just for a few more years," he said, the corner of his eye twitching. "But I don't know if his soul will restore me to the man you love."

I loved his honesty. I looked into his eyes for a long time, trying to find my David in there, somewhere. This new David was impassive, sociopathic, and yet he was somewhat charming as well. Could I love him even if he was never my David again?

"Look, I know you don't want to do this to Jason, and I'd do it myself to spare you. But I don't have that power. I need you." He leaned forward and took both of my hands. "I saw the memory—how Lily tore the soul from him. She fractured it. Broke him. Broke me. If you do it, you'll be kind. He will go peacefully to sleep and that will be that. He will live on then, in me."

Tears welled in the corners of my eyes as I came to terms with what had to be done. "So, a year then?"

"Roughly. I would say now, but…" David sighed, sweeping my hair back off my shoulder. "His soul is fractured. It's not much good to me in that state—so damaged and hateful. I need you to repair it."

"How?"

"You need to love him—"

"What?"

"Just for a while. Just make him believe there's hope, and—"

"He'll never believe I love him like that, David." I drew my hands from his, face mashed inward around disbelief. "And I can't just lie to him, pretend—"

"You can if I go," he reasoned. "I'll leave—fulfill my dark needs out in the human realm, where no one will catch me; get it out of my system before his pretty soul makes me into a fluffy rainbow unicorn"—we both laughed—"and you can pretend to be with him. Give him the life, or even just the friendship that he always longed for. Just for a while so his soul can knit back together."

"I couldn't betray you that way."

"I'm asking you to—for his soul's sake. For my sake. Let's just put this to rest, my love. The entire mess."

"And what if he doesn't want me now? He hates me, remember."

"One of his only dreams—something that keeps him awake at night, longing—is as simple as a family life with you and Daniel." He raised a brow in mockery. "Offer that to him, in love or merely in friendship, and he will be content."

"I can't betray him that way. It'd be a lie—"

"You can." He stood. "I'm going away. I will leave in the morning—"

"But—"

"You can either help me or not," he said, shutting me down with a hard glare. "I don't care. But when I return in, say… six months, it will be for his soul, and if it's not healed by then, it will do nothing to help me and I will die with him."

As David left the kitchen, I sunk my head down onto the table, barely able to catch a breath as it all came crashing down on top of me.

David never came to bed. When I woke in the minutes before dawn, it felt like I could sense him out there, with the tree. His connection to it now meant that, where I once traced him by his energy signature, I could now simply close my eyes, think of him, and know where he was. What he was feeling.

I grabbed a coat, slipped on some boots, and headed out into the freezing snowy morning just as the sun was beginning to light the horizon. All around me, *shadows* and *light* fought for control, and as I broke through the barrier of the forest and came upon the clearing, I could see why that feeling—of things being out of balance—was so prominent this morning.

David stood staring up at the tree, its weeping branches hanging low, like it had lost the will to go on. I stood beside him and looked too.

"Does it speak to you?" I asked.

"Not like the one in my world does."

"Your world?"

"The place Beneath."

He didn't move his eyes from its upper branches, and I watched him, looking down his squared jaw, his stubbly cheeks and neck, to his shoulders and then his hands. All over him, I could sense death. Not just death coming for him, eating his body away, but death that lingered near him, like a scent from the things he'd done as the night passed in secret.

"It's dying," I said, looking back at the tree.

"Yes. Like me."

"*Because* of you."

He nodded once.

"Will it live when you take Jason's soul?" I asked.

David hesitated, turning his head to see into my eyes. "You're the guardian of this tree, the one who set it free, and yet you seek that answer from me—a mere branch within its greater reach?"

He was right. I looked back at the tree, hugging myself, because I didn't want to admit the truth. Over the many years we'd been together, I'd quietened my own knowledge of magical things in order to make David the strength, the pillar within our relationship. Even if I knew things, I looked to him. It had become a habit now. My first instinct was to always listen for his words of wisdom instead of to ask for my own.

"It will die if you live," I said with a horrible, sinking feeling in my bones. "There's no saving it now."

"Because you won't let me die," he stated.

I nodded once.

David drew a deep breath through his nose and turned to me. "I spoke with my brother last night—told him what must be done."

"How did he take it?"

In the stillness of a morning without a breeze, without the whispers of life bleeding beneath the tree and the chirruping of Nature's morning song, the silence felt dense, connected too deeply to a realm I'd never known existed until David walked there, with Lily in his arms. This world now sounded like that one, felt like that one, as if his connection to that darkness had leaked into my realm, tarnishing it, changing it.

"He would not accept my offer to live his dream with you. He's angry. He's filled with hatred and hurt. But he has agreed to give up his soul." David looked back at the tree, reaching down between us to take my hand. "And yet it is no good to me in that state."

"What do you want me to do?"

"Find a way," he said, kissing my hand. "Find some way to reach him and alter it. For my sake."

"And what about the tree?" I looked at the rotting black roots, sensing its agony. "That magic left a curse in its roots, and the only way to repay the debt is—"

"You let it die," he stated. "Because our love will always be more significant than a magical tree."

"So you want me to lie to Jason, turn his heart to me and then betray it by taking his soul, and then you want me to let the tree die, all so we can live our lives together?"

"Yes," he said simply. "And our love deserves that."

"No love deserves that."

"Ours does," he demanded, turning to me. "Because you promised me, Ara: you swore nothing would do us part. Not even death."

"But this…" I looked at my tree, feeling a great sense of responsibility and shame. "This is too great a cost."

"For the greatest love you must make the greatest sacrifices."

"I made a vow—to protect this tree."

"And it will die for the vow you first made to me," he stated. "It is one of two trees, Ara. There is another—its twin on the Other Side, the Spirit Realm. You will not end all life by letting this tree die here in the mortal realm. But you will end our future if you do not."

I shook my head, not sure if he understood the gravity of what he was asking. "If this tree dies, then so does the connection to Light Magic on Earth—the Cerulean Energy."

He nodded once, looking the tree over. "But we will live."

AUBREY

He said I wasn't human. I had no gender, no self. I was an *It*. A thing. A weapon. And yet he'd given me a bed. I'd been here for three weeks, slept on the dirt, with only a gentle hum in the back of my throat to comfort me, and now he'd put me in a bed. In a room that was warmed by a fire.

I opened my eyes fully and rolled up to sit. The plain black tunic was still in place, no underwear or bra beneath, because something with no gender has no private parts, but I was covered with a blanket, the flames in the stone hearth across from me roaring. The gray, drafty room had one tiny window in its ancient rocky grip that revealed a rainy, miserable day. I could sense that I was high up, and since the room was round on one side, with a heavy wooden door, I could only assume this was one of the turrets.

Beside me, a small wooden nightstand with two drawers housed a lantern for darker days, and an iron ring held four unlit candles above me, dangling down from rotting exposed beams. It wasn't much, but it was a hundred times better than a cell.

I flopped back on the flat pillow, exhaling. All over my hands, though they were clean, I could feel death. I could almost smell it, taste it. It tingled like holding a phone on vibration.

Curling my fingers and shutting my eyes tight, I relived every moment when I took a life that day. It was changing me. I could feel it. I just didn't know how, or what the consequences would be yet. All I knew, from the deepest, most knowledgeable part of my soul, was that I wanted to be immersed in water. I wanted the fizz, the rush, the cool of the ocean's waves to conceal me, caress my skin. Carry me under.

When I hopped up and stood by the window, my eyes shot back to the bed and a hard breath of bewilderment expanded my throat, because I hadn't taken any steps to get here. I'd *appeared.* And it wasn't like Mom or Dad using vamp speed to shift through the atmosphere at a greater speed than a human. This wasn't conscious. I didn't move my feet, or my legs. I aimed my mind at the window and then appeared. Even now, where my bare feet touched the ground, it didn't feel like I was standing. It felt like I was hovering just above it, walking on the energy that surrounded things.

Glancing out the window, I hugged myself against the cold morning and the tightness in my chest, refusing to call it panic. It worried me to feel this way, and yet there was no place for worry when changes were occurring. I couldn't control them or predict them. I just had to go with it.

On this side of the castle the ocean wasn't visible, but it was out there, calling to me. Maybe, if Cillian had given me a room for obeying him, pleasing him, I might also be able to earn the right to walk outside by the sea. Or maybe even a pair of underwear. I touched my heavy breasts. Or a bra. If he kept me here for ten years without one, would I end up with really saggy boobs?

I laughed at myself. How was *that* my concern right now, after everything I'd just been through?

With a sigh, I cast my gaze to the world beyond, wondering about my old life—about Mom and Dad and Elias. I knew Drake and Morgana would never give up the search for me, but I hoped it didn't take away from the search for Lily—to find her and make her bring my mom back. I wasn't afraid of that. It was like I knew Mom would be okay. I knew Drake wouldn't rest until he had his daughter in his arms again. And I knew Daniel was okay. He had Lors and Harry, and Uncle Mike. Nothing was ever that bad when Uncle Mike was around. Nothing was ever that bad when Elias was around either. Or, at least, it hadn't seemed that way.

Since I'd been taken, I hadn't had a chance to think much. At all. I'd wanted Mom when I was left in the cell after being beaten, but I didn't let myself think about her arms around me. And reflecting back on the battle now, how Elias swooped in to save me, I also remembered the sword. I didn't know much about what I was or what I was capable of, but I wondered if maybe I could summon that sword again now and use it to escape.

But if it hadn't come to me when I was being kicked, shaved, pissed on, or forced to kill innocent humans, it wasn't coming now.

I lifted my hand to the glass and blew a circle of hot breath onto it, drawing a smiley face. It was the strangest thing, to feel so miserable and alone that all you needed was to see a smiling face, and even stranger that a simple drawing could make you feel better. I wiped it away and blew another circle of heat there against the cold glass, this time writing, *Dear Elias.*

I couldn't write any more than that, couldn't tell him about the humiliation I'd suffered here, because I wasn't sure he'd still want me after. I wasn't even sure I'd ever see him again. But if I did, he could never know. Those memories… they were my greatest shame, and I would take them to my grave. So I wiped his name away, in case he somehow saw me, saw into me, and turned around as the door opened.

Cillian smiled, folding his hands closed in front of him. "Are you ready to begin?"

"Yes, Master."

"Good." He nodded once, but as he went to turn away, his eyes flicked to the bed and he sniffed the air, moving over and yanking the covers back. My eyes widened in horror when I realized what that feeling was—the slight ache in my tummy and the wetness between my thighs.

He appeared beside me, lifting my tunic so quickly I couldn't stop him, and pressed his cold, thick finger between my legs. I gasped, whimpering once before I got control of my emotions, as he drew his hand away and rubbed his thumb across the blood there.

"It's a period," I stated, insulted and so violated. "It happens once a month."

He studied the blood, his eyes changing.

"Still think I'm not human?" I said snidely.

"Necromancers bleed too," he said, bringing the bright red blood to his mouth to taste it. I shut my eyes, angling my head away. "Come."

"Where?"

"Menstrual blood is extremely powerful in witchcraft and, oddly," he said with a laugh, "very hard to come by."

"Why is it powerful?" I followed him out of the room.

"It's the ultimate sin, the darkest betrayal: the failure of life."

"Oh."

"Now, when it's the blood of a necromancer, it will be even

more powerful, and worth quite a bit of money on the black market."

I smirked to myself, walking along the wide, pitch-black corridor at two steps behind him. If he took my icky period blood and tried to market that, my parents would find out. No one knew that the monarchs profited and benefited in the black market as much as the criminals, or that we had spies operating in there. Elias was researching my genus of immortality, which meant he'd figure it out eventually. And when my parents heard the words 'necromancer blood', they'd know where to find me, so I welcomed it.

But a roll of dread washed through me when I thought about what that would mean: they'd *know*. They'd imagine me here, see it in their minds, they'd worry about what else he'd done to me if he'd taken my period blood, and my shame would be made public.

Elias would find out.

When we reached the stone room with the long bath, Cillian led me to the center and brought down a pair of shackles.

"What are you doing?" I asked, backing away.

"I won't waste a drop of this." He put both of my wrists in scratchy iron cuffs and I felt my skin pull under my arms as he tugged the ends of the chain, raising them above my head. After fastening me in position, he walked to the storage room across from me and returned with a large silver bowl, lifting my tunic up a little and placing it between my feet.

"I'll bleed for seven days," I said, refusing to let the emotion out in my voice. "You can't leave me like this for seven days."

"I can."

"But it's painful. I need a hot water bottle and ibuprofen. I can't be chained up like this," I reasoned.

Cillian stood, pressing the bowl a little closer with his boot. "I'll see you in seven days."

"Wait," I called. "I need food. Water. Cillian!"

He kept walking.

"Cillian, I'm human. I won't have the strength to go another week without food." I pulled down hard on my chains, cutting in to my wrists a little. "Cillian!"

A big door slammed shut out there, taking me back to my grandfather's castle when I'd slammed the door on Nate and how it'd echoed the rage behind it, had satisfied me so much. But it all built in me now, churning and boiling, as the small ache between my lower pelvic bones wailed at me, slowly getting deeper.

By this afternoon, I'd be doubled over in pain, and the bleeding would be so heavy I'd normally need baby-mama napkins, because tampons just wouldn't hold it all. I'd need Mom there to give me a day off school and stroke my hair, bring me hot tea and watch sappy movies.

But instead I'd be here, chained with my arms above my head, my legs shaking, bleeding out into a silver bowl for the black market.

I shut my eyes, but I didn't want to be trapped in my own mind with the pain, so I cast them out to the ocean beyond the large window and spun my body to face it, keeping my legs apart over the bowl. If I wasted a drop, he'd probably make me do this again next month.

As I looked out at the ocean, I sighed though, because I realized that if my blood fetched a high price, there's no way he'd take just one month of it. He'd do it every single month for the rest of my eternity.

In that, I knew I had to find a way to cope.

He'd told me when I first got here that when they torture a

person, they begin with the smallest, most harmless acts, because what a person can survive, sustain, will build. One day, he'd told me, I wouldn't be bothered by a beating, or by piss in my cuts. One day, I would laugh at that kind of pain.

If that was true, then I had to start right now. I had to start reaching deep within myself to learn how to feel *beyond* it. So, I stared at the ocean, trying to connect to the water, and let my arms relax as much as possible, accepting this as my new normal.

One day, I would be strong. One day, I would not notice pain as much. And there was peace in that. But there was also peace in knowing that, one day, I would find a way to overpower him.

And on that day, he would suffer everything he did to me, tenfold.

ELORA

I came in through the front door of the manor, with the university awake and buzzing at my back, and as I closed the door, set eyes upon my father. And a suitcase.

"Dad?"

"Good morning, Elora," he said, always that little bit too chirpy and yet… there was something underneath it, like dissatisfaction or resentment.

"Are you going somewhere?" I nodded to the suitcase.

"I'm leaving for a few months," he stated.

"Why?"

"My body is dying." He revealed a decaying mass of black flesh on his arm, and my eyes widened in response when he waved a hand over it, healing it with his touch. "My soul and my blood are rich with darkness, and the power, the life within that fruit, is slowly winning a battle against it."

"Meaning?"

"I'm going to die."

"What?" I rushed in to his side, taking his hand. "Is there something we can do? We—"

"Yes. I will need the other half of my soul—the light," he said, glancing back as Mom started down the stairs with Daniel in her arms. "Jason is going to give up his soul but it's far too damaged to be of any use to me. So, as a gift to him, to heal his soul, I'm giving him six months to experience joy—a life with a family, the woman he loves."

"And Mom agreed to this?" I looked up at her. She stopped about six steps away from the bottom, staring down at us as if she just didn't know what to say. As if her entire world were falling apart right now, and she had no power to change it.

"No." Dad glanced at her, coming back to me with a smile on his face. "And my brother refuses her affections. But I trust your mother to do what must be done in order to win him over."

"Daddy." Daniel wriggled in Mom's arms until she put him down, then he slid over each step on his belly quickly to get to him.

Dad watched on curiously for a moment, but his eyes were void of any love, any connection or even familiarity at all. And the childhood memories of my loving, funny, playful father died right there in front of me, taking all the light and the joy of the past years and stamping it out, changing those memories for good, as he turned, picked up his suitcase, and walked away without saying a word to that little boy.

Danny got to the bottom, racing after his dad. He didn't understand that he'd turned his back deliberately. He probably just thought Daddy didn't see him, didn't hear him.

"Daniel," Mom called, trotting down after him. I watched, my mouth agape, as Dad opened the door and walked out, shutting it on Danny's face.

"Daddy!" he cried, grabbing the handle and hanging off it. "Daddy… wan say bye."

"It's okay, Danny." I grabbed him, ripping the door open and tossing my gaze down the steps to the cold, heartless man. "Dad!"

"David," Mom cut in, pushing past me to get outside. "Daniel wants to say goodbye."

He looked at the crying child. "Ara, there's no part of me that wants that sniveling creature hanging off my leg. Take it inside."

"How can you say that about your own son?"

"That's just it. He's not my son."

Mom's heart shattered. I saw it in the look on her face, the way her shoulders came around like she'd been punched. "You never used to feel that way."

"Yes, but I'm not me anymore," Dad said simply, glancing at a few students from the university as they passed. "I'm me two-point-oh."

"Daddy!" Daniel cried, hitting at me to let him get down.

"I can't be okay with this." Mom hugged herself, her face paling to a gray-white.

"Look, Ara." Dad put his suitcase down and walked up the steps to stand before her, and Danny stopped crying, arching his body in Dad's direction because he thought he was coming back to say goodbye. "Love doesn't mean the same thing to me anymore. I care for those who are connected to me"—he looked down at both hands as though they were branches on a tree—"and your son just doesn't fit there. You do, but not as much as Elora, Harry and…" He said the next name with a deep look of regret. "Aubrey."

"Look at him, David," Mom pleaded, pointing at Daniel. "He's screaming for you. Don't you feel any pity?"

"No." He didn't even look at him before saying that.

Uncle Jase appeared then and closed his hands around Danny's ribs, sweeping him into his arms. Dad walked away, and Mom and I just stood watching, stunned, as he exited the university courtyard and disappeared.

Uncle Jason calmed Danny down almost instantly, showing him a bird in the sky and making him laugh when he told him the scientific name, and I was grateful to him for that. I looked over to watch him—one arm under Danny's body, pointing off at random things with the other. He'd always been a good man, a good uncle, and like a father to Aubrey as she grew up and spent time here with Beth and Lily, but I would never forget this. He may have been human right now, hurt and weak from what the world had done to him, but in that moment, he was ten times the man my father was.

Mom looked over at me, holding back a thick well of tears, casting her gaze then to Jase and Daniel. I knew she was grateful to him. I knew she was hurt on Daniel's behalf and just wanted to wrap him up and protect him from the truth. But he wasn't the one who needed protection right now, and yet, as I moved in to hug her, she shook her head and backed away, heading inside.

"He's okay," Uncle Jase assured me in his deep, gentle voice.

"I'm not so sure she is though." I nodded to where Mom wandered up the stairs, her steps slow and heavy.

"To be honest," he said, handing Daniel to me, "I'm not sure I care."

ARTHUR AND HARRY LAUGHED, LIFTING THEIR SHOULDERS, opening their mouths and tipping their heads back in the exact same way, which made me laugh. It was so adorable to see them together, see the relationship they had, and it made what happened this morning hurt a little less. I knew Harry would be okay, and I knew Danny would be too. When Uncle Jason was dead and Dad had his soul, even if he never loved him as his son ever again, Uncle Arthur and Harry would fill that void. Even just a little. It put me at peace somehow.

But, with Lily gone and with Uncle Jason's death just months away, it occurred to me that life was going to change, no matter what. Mom would be forced to move back here and become queen again, and I knew how much she'd hate that. This isn't the life she wanted for Daniel, for any of us.

"What's on your mind, Elora?" Uncle Arthur asked kindly.

"I just can't believe how much our lives have changed… so quickly," I said, lost in the mundane thoughts of the week I *would* have had ahead of me if I were at home, with my daughter and my normal life. "I had plans. This weekend. And I was supposed to host an Australia Day barbecue next week, but… it's all just…"

Harry got up out of his seat and landed beside me, wrapping both arms around my body. "Same here, sis. Rochelle and I were gonna drive down south for the hotter part of summer and I had to cancel a meeting with a new producer looking to buy my songs." He drew back from the hug, keeping a hand on my shoulder and an empathetic look on my face. "It's insane, but this is family, and we are right where we're supposed to be right now."

"Mom's not," I said. "She…" She was so fragile already. She'd been at breaking point for years, but it had compounded over the last six months and I'd been so worried about her, watching, almost every day, for signs that she might just leave this place and return to the Spirit Realm for good. Harry didn't know her like I did, he didn't see the signs, and Arthur had been gone for so long that he probably wasn't even aware of how depressed she'd been. They just couldn't understand the gravity.

"Don't worry about your mother, Elora," Arthur offered in that calm, wise voice, making everything seem like it could be okay. "No matter what happens, I will be here to help her through it, even if that means I step up and rule the monarchy while she returns to Australia."

"You'd do that?" I rolled my gaze up to meet his.

He bowed his head. "As would many more who love her."

"Hell, even I'd be willing to," Harry suggested, winking at me. "I'm older than Mom was when she first took over."

I smiled at him, the expression slipping away when I felt a stir of very nervous energy behind me, as Ric moved into the room like a solid shape appearing from within a receding shadow.

"What's wrong?" I put my coffee cup down and stood up.

"I was down in the kill suites. A room's been cordoned off and the House are investigating the contents," he said, eyes wide and fixed in horror.

"Why?"

"A human…" He swallowed hard, as if he'd carried the saliva in his mouth all the way from the kill suite and hadn't even thought to swallow it. "*Several* humans have been killed in there."

"That happens every day."

"Not like this," he said. "They haven't been drained. Drank. They've been murdered."

I glanced back at Harry, about to tell him to wait here, but he'd already seen it all in Ric's thoughts, clearly, because he shot to his feet, shoving me off as I tried to grab him.

"Harry." I ran out of the kitchen and into the hallway after him. "Where are you going?"

"I have to help them—"

"You don't need to see that," I called, jogging to catch up. "Let Uncle Jason handle it. He's the king."

"He's not the king anymore, Elora."

"While Dad's gone—"

"And if that's true"—he stopped dead and pointed at Ric, his voice breaking under tears—"if my dad did that…"

"Dad?" I looked at Ric, who shook his head apologetically, too struck to speak.

"I… he's gone now," Harry added, pinching his eyes, "so that makes *me* the man of the house."

Arthur snapped ahead of us all and cut Harry off at the end of the corridor. "No, son, it makes *me* the man of the house," he said, relieving Harry of his burden with a gentle hand to his shoulder. "It is our job to protect humans, especially those that reside here, but we must handle this case very carefully to avoid an all-out war with the human faction. We cannot get emotional. And if it is true, if David killed them"—he looked at Ric, who nodded, his eyes wide and hollow—"then we must act to cover up the king's crime immediately."

"This isn't right," Harry said, looking down at his shaking hands. "We're vampires—among the most dangerous, sordid beings on the earth. And I've never seen anything like *that.*"

"It's not uncommon for vampires to murder humans," Arthur advised. "I've put many away for that crime myself—"

"Dad's not a vampire anymore. And that wasn't just murder. You didn't see what I just saw, Uncle Arthur," Harry yelled, but he wasn't yelling at Arthur. "He tortured them! Why would my dad do that? What is he—"

"It's okay." Arthur turned Harry by the shoulders and led him away in the other direction. "Come on. I'll make you a stiff drink."

I looked at Eric. "What happened to them? Why is Harry so upset?"

His words couldn't give me the details, but the look in his eyes told me enough about the magnitude of the suffering.

"Men or women?" I asked.

"Both."

"How many?"

"Six."

I slowly closed my lashes over the dread. "Does Mom know yet?"

"No. I don't think she should."

"Why?"

"Because she doesn't need to know what your father is capable of. Even if he comes back and even if Jason's soul cures him of the evil, she won't be able to forgive this, Lors."

"Then you don't know my mom very well."

"But…" He put both hands in his pockets, his shoulders coming up. "Lors, he…"

I stepped closer, breaking his hesitation with a hard glare. "What? What is it?"

"He cut the *dick* off one of them," he said with measured, tightly-contained rage, looking me square in the eye. "And… we found it…"

"Found it where? Just say it!"

"In the…" Those warm brown eyes that I loved carried away from mine to hide the shame, his chin trembling. "He used it to fuck one of them."

"While it was cut off?"

Ric nodded, hiding behind a mass of blonde curls that covered his face in the tilt of his head. I tried to think about how that was possible, forcing the sickening rise of bile away from my lungs with a breath through my teeth when I realized.

"He's not a vampire anymore, Ric—"

"I know." He put his hand on my back and pulled me in to hug him. "But he obviously still feels the need to kill."

"Is that the worst of it—what you just told me?"

"No. I'm a vampire, Lors, and… I threw up," he stated, wetting his lips. "I didn't wanna tell you. And you know me, I tell you everything—give it to you straight. But this was bad enough that I actually didn't want to tell you."

I nodded, understanding the severity with that one statement alone. "We have to tell Mom."

"Don't you think she's been through enough?"

"Yes, and it's not my job to protect her, Ric. She's a big girl and she needs to know this." I hugged myself and stalked away. "She needs to know what she's fighting for."

"You know what she'll say," he called after me. "She'll say it's his darkness. It's not his fault. She'll say he'll be different when Jason's dead and he has his soul."

"Then let's hope she's right," I said, heading in to see Mom.

Uncle Arthur sat forward on the leather armchair, the familiar library, with its aged-book smell and shiny gold titles on hard spines, offered a sort of calm to me as we broke the news to Mom, giving her every sordid detail of what Dad had done, while Uncle Jase leaned on the table across from the circle of conversation, his arms folded, head down.

We all knew Dad had a dark side, was twisted and shaped by it, and that he enjoyed pain—had done some awful things to humans in the past, even before he consumed the magical fruit. But those humans we found today hadn't just been killed, choked, cut, and abused, they'd been victims of something tainted by a being that's connected, like he said, to both the living realm and the underworld. He'd hurt in order to induce the highest amount of pain, terror, and he'd done it in secret. Which means he had to understand that it was wrong.

Now, we had unleashed him on the human population. And we had a moral obligation to do something about that.

"We need to find him," Mom said softly, still lost deep within the nightmare she'd seen in Arthur's memory just now. "We need to bring him back and get Ja…" Mom looked over at Jason, as though she'd forgotten he was in the room, forgotten, by what she said next, that he was a living, breathing man with feelings. "We need to give him the other half of the soul *now*."

The words moved across the space between them and blast Jason's chest open. I watched as they almost visibly hit him, and his arms fell to his sides. Arthur stood, sensing it too, but he stayed back as Jason sauntered away.

"His soul isn't ready," I reminded her. "How can we fix Dad with a soul that's so broken?"

"We don't have a choice, Elora," she said. "We have to do something before he brings more pain to the world."

"I'll track David down," Arthur offered. "And we'll discuss this when I return."

"There's nothing to discuss," Mom stated, looking him square in the eye. "This is David's ruling, and Jason agreed, so I'll take his soul—"

"I will not lose the only decent one between them," he commanded in a gruff voice, one fist curled tightly by his side. "My son, for God's sake."

Mom pulled herself up taller. "And I will not lose my husband."

"Then, as I said, we will discuss it when I return," he concluded, bowing to his queen as he exited the library.

Mom looked at me. "You know I'm right. David can't be allowed to roam freely in the living realm. Every act of sin he commits sends a shockwave through that tree, through the veins of life, Elora. We need to find him today and—"

"But do we need to kill Jason today?"

"Look, I don't want this either," she said. "You know I love Jason. But it's not about losing one brother to save another. It's beyond that now. It's about saving the world from that darkness."

"How can you say that?"

"Because that's how it is. Go to the tree." She shook her head impatiently at me. "Touch it. Feel it. You'll see it's no longer about saving David or putting Jason out of his misery. It's about preventing the Light from enduring anymore of his pollution, for the sake of all that is pure and good in this world."

"But—"

"That tree is Life," she reaffirmed, tucking her dark hair behind her ear. "Its magic runs through the veins of the earth. It's the peace, the goodness, but it is also Cerulean Magic," she reasoned, stepping closer to me with every line of explanation, as if to draw me into the words. "It is what binds your crux, your soul, to the earth. Every time he kills, he taints that. Taints the goodness in the world."

"And when he has the other soul, when he's complete, a balance of light and dark, the tree will heal?" I asked. "The magic will be restored?"

Mom pressed her mouth into a line, growing an inch taller. Then, she looked away. "It will never be restored, but at least it will no longer endure the suffering from the fulfillment of his dark needs."

"Never?" My neck jutted forward, a thin rod of shock jabbing into my core. "The tree will *never* be restored?"

"Not while he lives."

"Then why would you let him live?" I squeaked.

Mom folded her arms, lifting her nose as she looked away. "Because I can't live without him. I *won't*."

I took a deep, shaky breath, and backed out of the room, no longer seeing my loving, pure-light mother there. Instead, seeing a monster that was tainted by her love, her connection, to my evil father.

The tree was dying. She said it herself. And it would take its power with it, but she didn't care about that. She'd save my dad even if it meant letting the tree die, and I had to wonder, even after all the sick things he'd done to those humans, if she wasn't just as twisted and amoral as him.

ARA

Danny built a tower with his blocks, while Toy Story blared in the background of his nursery. I walked in to find Jason sitting on the bed, his forearms on his thighs, while deep pools of regret gathered at his feet.

"How long do I have?" he asked.

"We don't know where David is," I lied. Because I did. I knew exactly where he was. I could feel the earth screaming under his feet as if it couldn't stand the connection any longer, like its hand had been placed on a hot coal. I just didn't want Jason to know that he had hours, if that, before my men reached David and told him to come back. Or before Arthur reached him instead, and probably killed him himself so that Jason wouldn't have to die.

"You don't have to worry, Ara." Jason stood. "I'm okay with dying."

I followed him over to the window, my arms folded to make me seem like less of a threat. "No one is okay with dying."

"*I* am."

"Then why do you look like you just lost everything?"

"Because I have," he yelled, and Danny looked up, shocked. "Are you really that effing stupid," he added in a quieter voice, eyes flicking sideways to make sure our baby went back to his game. "I'm hurt, Ara, because I feel like nothing. No, I *realize* now that I *am* nothing, to anyone."

"Jase—"

"I'm disposable, that's the truth." He sat down on the toy box behind him, the sun streaming through the window to light up his grief. "It just hurts, that's why I look like I've lost everything. It hurts that I don't matter." He pressed his chest, choking on the word. "My soul is the only important part of me, and everything I am, everything my life was, or ever could be, means nothing to any of you because my brother will *always* mean more."

I knelt down in front of him, but his energy screamed at me to back away. So I removed my hand from his knee and just sighed.

"I'll give the soul to him," he said, looking at me regretfully. "I'm ready to die. But I don't want your pity. I don't want your love. Because we both know you're not here, right now, comforting me for *me*. You're doing it to repair what's broken so you can fix that fucking monster."

"Fucking," Danny said casually, but he didn't even look up. He kept playing with his toys as though he hadn't registered saying that.

"Can you not swear around our son, please?"

Jason scoffed, eyes coming up to mine, thick with tears. "*Our* son, huh?"

"Jase, don't..."

He got up, pushing past me, so I followed.

"Is David going to love him?" he asked, whipping around to face me. "*Can* he? After what I saw this morning?"

I glanced over at Danny. "I can't honestly say."

Jason put both hands in his pockets, accusation thick in his tone when he asked, "But you won't leave him if he doesn't, will you?"

"I—"

"Right." He nodded, his jaw set hard. "So Daniel has to grow up with that? Being nothing in his father's eyes?"

"It won't be that way—"

"And what if it is?" He held my gaze, not letting me escape this, escape the possibility of that truth. I tried to hide from many truths that I'd have to accept in order to save David, but he would not let me hide from this. "What if David is just the same with my soul as he is now? Would you leave him for Danny's sake?"

"Yes," I said, and I meant it.

"Good." Jase nodded once. "Because I want better for my son, Ara. I want better than what I had growing up."

"Me too."

"No. I think you just want David, and I actually think, no…" He looked up at me, pushing his hands deeper into those pockets. "I *know* that it comes at any cost."

"Not the cost of my children."

He wet his lips, his eyes narrowed conceitedly. "I hope that's true."

"You know me, Jase—"

"No, Ara. I thought I did. But what I saw today…" He shook his head.

"What about what you saw today?"

"You can't hate him," he said, laying one hand across his gut. "*I* felt sick listening to what Arthur said—what my brother did to those humans. That's in him, Ara. That's not the darkness tainting him, that's the darkness giving him permission to let loose."

"He's always had that in him—"

"And you can love that?" He leaned forward, eyes wide with disbelief. "You can love him knowing that's in him?"

"I have no right to love him if I can't love all of him."

"You're sick, Ara." He folded his arms, stepping back from me. "You changed. Ever since..." The words ended with a short huff and a shake of his head.

"Ever since what?" I moved closer, daring him to say it.

"Ever since that vision Drake showed us, where we were together in another life, you... it's like you took some of that on board—the beaten down woman you were in that life. It's like you took *her* on. And you were never the same again."

"In what way?"

"There's this..." He touched his chest, right in the middle. "Column in here. And when I looked at you after I saw the vision, I got a rush of cold and heat through it. And I knew it was my soul. I knew you, in that instant, wanted to run away with me."

I swallowed hard, remembering that day.

"You promised David forever, I know. And you love him more than you will ever love me," he said, like a broken record. "But you wanted me after that vision, and that changed you too —the fact that you wanted me. This woman you became after you saw it, she wasn't beaten down by her husband. She was beaten down by *herself*, forced into submission."

"I don't break my promises..."

"But he gave you an out. On that day, after you saw it, he gave you an honest-to-god out."

"And what would I have done?" I shrugged. "Left him? Had you leave Lily?"

"I don't know." He looked down at his feet, hands in pockets again. "Maybe, just maybe, admitting the truth and not burying it might have been enough."

I exhaled, my lungs tight and heavy. "It is what it is..."

"No. It is what you made it. And you just accept that now, using that statement, because it's safe for you. It's what you know—"

"I won't lose David—"

"I'm not asking you to," he said, his voice slightly raised. "I wouldn't dare, for even a *second*, ask that you let me live. I know to the deepest part of my core that you'd never do that if it meant he'd die. And to watch you deny me would shatter everything that's keeping me together right now. But you can"—he stepped into me, his eyes sharp and dangerous, his voice low and determined—"at least, just once before I die, admit to me, out loud, that you love me. That you wanted to be with me and that you wished you could."

I felt the words on my lips, and I knew they'd cleanse his soul, even a little, and ease its passing over to the next life, but I physically couldn't admit it aloud. I'd built a wall around that emotion after thirty-seven years, and it felt cursed, dangerous. Like if I opened a hole, looked inside, the world would come crashing down. I knew why. But I couldn't admit it to myself, much less him.

"I'm going to die," he said, lifting his arm to look at his watch, "in as little as a few hours, and you can't even..." Jase bit his lip, casting his eyes away as his tears filled them. "I really mean so little to you that you can't even say those words to me?"

A fat tear rolled over my lashes as I fought with myself. If he was a vampire, mind reader, he'd know. He wouldn't need me to say them aloud. I could put him at rest. But something deep inside me, something stronger and more powerful than my own heart, just wouldn't let me.

Jason nodded to himself, his fists balled up by his sides. "Can you go?" he said, sitting down beside Danny. "I'd like to spend my last few hours alone with my son."

I nodded, pressing the tears into my lips as I turned away.

TWO DAYS PASSED, AND MY MEN DID NOT RETURN WITH David. In fact, they hadn't returned at all. I sat by the tree, my hand against it, reading the tales within the pulses of its life-force.

Everyone assumed the men were on his trail, trying to find him, but I knew better. They were dead, killed in the same slow, disgusting way those other people were in the kill suites. He took his time. He relished in it, feeding his soul with their pain, their humiliation. Poisoning my tree with it too.

He was sick, and his sickness was weakening the Light Magic in the world a little bit more every day. I needed to find him, make him come back. So I drew my phone from my pocket and dialed his number. To my surprise, he picked up.

"What's wrong?" he asked.

"You need to come home," I said, feeling weak sitting here in the radiating agony of my tree. "Your darkness, your nourishment, it's killing the good in the world. I need to try to fix you."

"And I need to feed," he stated. "I'll return when I'm satiated."

"You never will be," I whispered, hearing that truth for the first time in my own bones. "It's a disease, David. And I need you to come back. If you die before I—"

"I know how scared you are," he said softly. "I know the tree is a part of you, of this world, so deeply-connected that everyone with an empathetic heart can feel it right now, can feel its sadness. And I know that if it dies, so too does a lot of the magic, the light in the world. I know all of this, and still, I can't return, Ara. I will kill anyone you send to find me, so please… just wait for me. Just stop listening to the tree's cries and get on with your life. Go back to finding Aubrey. I will return when I've had my fill."

When he hung up the phone, I shut my eyes tight and cried. He would never have his fill. Nothing would ever satiate this hunger. Which meant he was never coming back. He would die out there, and in his death, he would take the tree with him. I'd need to bring Jason, and I'd need to do the ritual there in the human realm. If he didn't kill me when I arrived. And if Jason agreed to come with me.

A familiar pink glow appeared then and reflected off the tree, glistening, as though that light had all the answers.

"How do I fix this, Lilith?"

"With this." She presented the Blade of Eden—a weapon cast from the branches of this very tree, forged to take the life of a being but keep their soul here, until it was time for rebirth. "You cannot go to him. This must be done here."

"Why?"

"His blood, tainted and dark, must return to the roots of the tree. Like with a curse, or like when Anandene used the stone for evil, blood must be repaid to put it right."

"I already know that, but…" I stood up, my knees sore and covered with mud and snow. "I can't let David die."

"It is the only way to restore the damage that's been done." She pressed a hand to her heart. "Listen to the soul of the world, Ara. Listen to what it's telling you."

I closed my eyes, my heart breaking when I heard it. Evil for evil. Blood for blood. To end a curse, the life of the one who bound it must leave this world too.

"You know I can't do that, Lilith. There has to be another way."

"That man is not David—"

"It will be. With Jason's soul."

"If you truly believe that…" Lilith shook her head, sighing then as if she didn't see the point in saying anything more. "It's up to you. You are, after all, the guardian of this magic, and you decide if it lives or dies."

"You can't put that on me."

"You accepted it on the day you birthed this tree into the mortal realm to save your daughter," she said, her cold disappointment trickling around the clearing.

My hands fell into the earth, holding me up as my knees hit the ground. I had thought all this time that I was killing Jason to save David. But it wasn't the case. I'd be killing this ancient connection to the other side if I let David live, even with Jason's soul, and yet I couldn't imagine a world without him.

I'd heard Elora's thoughts earlier today. I knew what she thought of me. I knew she wondered if I was as dark as David now, and I had to wonder if that was true, because in my heart of hearts, maybe a heart of darkness, I actually contemplated the death of the tree to let David live.

"Can this world survive if the tree dies?" I asked.

"Only you know the answer to that, Auress."

"I need to find him," I said, wishing I could just talk to him about all of this.

"He will not return here until he reaches a critical point," she said, appearing beside me, her cold hand on my arm. "Stop sending men out for him to kill, and just wait for him to come.

The instinct for self-preservation will not allow him to stay out there and die. He will return."

"When?"

She looked up, looked into the nothing, seeing the future. "When his brother wants to live."

My eyes widened as she faded away, and I looked down at the knife she'd given me, regretting my entire life.

Jason's soul had been damaged. When Lily carelessly and brutally ripped it in half to return a piece to David, it had shattered. I could feel it, even if I tried to ignore it. He was darker, sadder, angrier and colder than I'd ever known him to be, and I could feel that a lot of the light in him had gone out.

But it wasn't detrimental. It wasn't the kind of damage that couldn't be undone, reversed, healed, loved back. For David's sake alone, if I had any chance of saving him, he needed a soul of light. I had to get through to Jason, or I'd lose them both.

When I followed Jase's energy signature, it led me to the oak tree. These days, it was less than sixty feet out from the university walls, but still just private enough anyway to feel like we could talk. I wondered if there was some underlying emotional message there in the fact that he had come to sit under *our* tree, even if he hated me.

"Hey," I said, sitting down beside him in the muddy brown snow.

He looked around to see if anyone was nearby. "Ara, you're the queen again now, you can't be seen sitting here with me."

"Why?"

"Because queens don't sit on the floor. In the mud."

"Maybe not *your* queen." I smirked, because Lily would never have been so casual with him.

He sighed, brushing a few flakes of snow off his thigh.

"So… I was just at a meeting with the Upper House," I said.

"And?"

"And, I told them David isn't coming back—"

"What?"

"He's killing anyone that comes to find him," I stated, to his shock. "So we're going to stop sending them."

"But… I thought his sins were poisoning the tree."

"They are." I nodded, not letting it bother me in an obvious way. "But Lilith says he'll return before the darkness eats his body—self-preservation, I guess—but that won't be for a long time."

"How long?"

"I think about five, maybe six months."

"Right." Jase swallowed hard, visibly relieved.

"So, we need a king."

He angled his head to the side and slowly looked up at me.

"And that has to be you," I advised.

"I'm human."

"It won't matter. They accepted David as a human—"

"But they love him."

"They love you too." I caged his icy hand and gave it a squeeze. "Come on, it'll be fun. Safe to say you and I have never ruled the monarchy together before."

He smiled at my cheer, examining my entire face with his pretty green eyes. "You're in a good mood."

"I'm just trying to make the most of a shit situation," I said, meaning it. "My tree is screaming out for help, and I can hear it *all the time*—"

"I'm sorry." He pouted, looking at my chest where it hurt the most.

"It's okay. Well, it's not, but it will be. I can fix it"—or kill it —"but, for now, I need to shut that voice out and I need to spend some time with you."

"Before I die."

"Yes. And I'm sorry." I waited for him to look at me, but he wouldn't.

Silence hovered around us like bad news then. I looked down at the snow stuck to his jeans and the thick layer of it gathering in the tree above us, and grinned mischievously.

"What?" he said, catching on a second too late. The clump came tumbling down in a giant heap, making a wet sound as it turned to slush over his head, missing me completely.

"Ara!" His face opened up in a huge, Jase-like grin, with all of his beautiful personality shining out in it. He hopped up on his knees to swipe it all off his lap and his dark hair, and then I jerked back, laughing hard as he tickled my ribs, his icy wet hands going under my sweater and against my skin. When he stopped, beautifully breathless and smiling, his cheeks and nose all pink, I leaned my head against the tree, turning my body to his, and he did the same.

"I'm freezing now," he noted. "No thanks to you."

"You're so human," I mocked.

"No kidding," he said in his deep, rugged voice.

"I'll warm you up. Here." I took his hands and held them in mine, pressing the heat of my Cerulean light into them—magic that would, one day soon, be gone.

"Do you remember when we were learning how to use that light?" he asked softly, resting his head on the tree right in front of mine, our noses almost touching.

"Yeah." I thought about Winter Falls and how I'd swam with

him, playful and fun, in our days of absolute innocence. "A lot of what I am, what I became, is because of you." I reached up and smoothed my hand down his sweet face. "Because of your brilliant scientific mind and your refusal to take things at face-value."

He smiled shyly, and I could see a little light start to come on in his soul. But it went out, and he glanced over his shoulder. "Do… what did Eva say about me going to my death? I heard you telling Morgana about it on the phone. She must have told Evada."

"She threw a fit. She said it's not fair. That you deserve better. And Drake isn't happy either. He rang me as soon as he found out."

"What did he say?"

"Oh, the usual," I said with a casual wave. "That the entire balance of the universe is at stake right now and if we don't set things right, the world will change in ways we cannot yet understand."

Jason laughed, hugging his knees. "So… not happy?"

"Nope." I threaded my fingers through his and held his cold hand with a firm, loving grip. If I was honest, I'd come out here to find him and start bringing him back, loving him back, I guess, so that his soul would have even a smidge of value when I harvested it for David. Yet, in sitting here, actually connecting with him again, I'd realized that wasn't true—that I was lying to myself, just so I'd have a decent excuse to spend a moment with him. I felt like I'd needed to justify it.

But he was right before. I did owe it to him to admit out loud that I had wanted him after that vision, and that I denied that love again. That I had denied it, shoved it down, put it away every time it'd surfaced over the years, and most importantly, that it *did* surface; that it had never stopped; and it never would. Even when he was gone, I would miss him, miss who he is.

"Jase?"

"Yeah."

"You're a good father," I said. "A really good one. And I love you for that."

"Only for that?" he teased.

"I'm sorry."

"For what?"

"I should have admitted it." We locked gazes, but he looked kinda scared. "When Drake showed me that vision, I should have told you the truth. Even if I didn't tell David. I shouldn't have cut you deeper by lying about it, especially when I knew that you'd seen it in my eyes."

He nodded, opening his fingers out in mine and tracing a line over the back of my hand, concentrating all his thoughts on that one spot. "Do you ever wish Drake had chosen that life for you?"

"Do you?"

"Yes. Every day."

"Even though I suffered?"

"Yes. Even then." He smirked, laughing at my expression. "I'm sorry, I know that's awful."

"Well, not as awful as me choosing to be with David when I was warned that the universe, Nature, would work against us," I confessed, bringing my shoulder up shyly into the tilt of my head. "I was naive and arrogant, and I honestly thought I could make it all okay by defying nature. And I'm sorry, Jase, because, in the end, it was you who was made to suffer the most."

"We've all suffered, Ara—"

"Not as much as you have. And now you're dying for it—for that choice *I* made." I sighed. "Eva's right: it isn't fair."

He let go of my hand and brought his knees up again, hugging his ribs as he faced forward.

"Are you cold?" I asked. "Should we go inside?"

"You can. I wanna sit for a while with my thoughts. Danny will be up soon."

I nodded. But I didn't walk away. Instead, I sat with him and his thoughts, reliving our entire existence up until this point, and looking in on all the ways it might have been changed. All the ways it might have been set right if I'd, just once, put him first. He didn't deserve to die, but I certainly didn't deserve his love, and David didn't deserve his soul.

JULES

Even though our engagement had been put to rest, I still loved Jason, and I always would. Except, now, because of his love for Ara, I would never see him again.

I'd leave today, fly out to Australia—back home with Mike—and Jase would stay here, and he'd die. Unloved. Unwanted. And I loved Ara. I did. She'd grown on me since we arrived at Perth, but I hated what she was doing to him. I hated that she could just so easily accept this and not be a wreck.

When I hugged Jason one last time, I just wanted to squeeze him into me and keep him safe. He was so different as a human. He'd always been so gentle and sweet, but in this form, he was also fragile. I wasn't sure I could've loved him if we'd met when he was human. I was attracted to the vampire, clearly. But he still felt so familiar to hold onto, and I fought hard to let go, knowing what I was letting him go to.

"This isn't right," I whispered, Heaven forbid an official might hear and step in, stop the tyrant queen. They couldn't know. No one but our family, our small circle, could know, because it was wrong, and Ara knew it. Yet she was doing it anyway and forcing us all to go along with it. "You deserve better than this."

"So people keep telling me, and yet, it means nothing." He shrugged, drawing away. "There's nothing I can do."

"You could *not* die, how about that?"

He glanced over his shoulder at Ara, where she stood in a group by the helicopter with Ric and Lors as they said goodbye to Mike, Mia, and Evie. "If I say no, if I keep my soul, my life, Ara loses him. And I've been down that road with her, Jules. She couldn't love me. She never could. I would be left here in a life I don't want anyway—one that's without her—and she'd be miserable, hate me."

I cocked my head sympathetically at him. "I hate that I understand that."

He smiled, hugging me one last time.

Harry moved in then and hugged him at a lean, just slightly taller than him now. "I love you, Uncle Jase," he said, such a warm, overgrown lank of a young man, but with a heart as big as Jason's, worn in plain sight, on his sleeve. "I'll take care of Danny, okay, when you're gone."

Jase nodded, and I saw him falter, saw the emotion shake his mortal coil, but he'd composed himself by the time he leaned back from the hug. After having said goodbye to Mike and the kids already, he stepped back and waved again, just one last time. Arthur would be staying here, along with Lors and Ric, in the hopes that they could find Aubrey, while Mike and I would take the eldest kids home to Grandma Vicki and let them get back to school.

Ara stood between Jason and Arthur, and we climbed into the chopper, shutting the door. I didn't want to look back and see them walk away, because I couldn't stand the idea that it'd be the last time I ever looked at Jason. I was in love with Mike now, and nothing would change that—his love was clean, honest, unwavering, and totally worthy of mine—but I'd spent so much time with Jase that it seemed too final to have hugged him for the last time.

I was angry. And sad. And hurt. Especially because he was giving his life up for a man who'd done unspeakable things, all for the love of a woman that had never loved him back. And as the chopper lifted off, rattling me around, I fought hard not to burst into tears.

Mike put his hand on my knee, so I forced a smile, focusing hard on the way ahead instead of looking behind.

"They'll figure it out, Jules," he said.

"Figure what out?"

"I don't think she can go through with it," Evie added, smiling out the window at nothing.

"With what?" Harry asked.

"Killing Uncle Jase."

Mia shifted uncomfortably in her seat beside Evie. "But then that'd mean David… your grandfather, would be dead," she reminded her, probably so she could wipe the smug grin off her face.

"Maybe she won't let either of them die."

"But then the tree would," Harry reminded her.

"Yeah, and I heard Aunt Ara say it could mean there'd be no more immortals, because we're all made by the magic it brought to the earth," Mia offered.

"So?" Eva shrugged. "It wouldn't be that bad. Not if it meant they both got to live."

"Yeah, except my sister, your *mom*, would die," Harry pointed out. "Because her crux is magic."

Evie clearly hadn't thought of that. The grin washed off her face and she folded her arms, looking out on the hopelessness with the rest of us.

"Maybe it shouldn't be her decision," Mia snapped. "She's not in her right mind, Dad, if she can even think about letting him live."

"I heard about what he did," Evie added, and Harry shifted uncomfortably in his chair. "He's sick and evil—"

"And it isn't fair to the rest of us if he lives and we lose our magic, all because she doesn't want to live without him."

"I know, Mia," Mike said softly.

"Well, what are you gonna do about it, Dad? Someone should step in, take the choice away from her, lock her up and just kill Uncle David."

Mike looked at me. I shrugged, because I loved Ara, even David, in my own way, but I completely agreed with Mia.

"I'll talk to Arthur," Mike said. "But if we did that... Ara would die too. And Daniel would be left without a mother."

"Too bad. He'll survive. But the rest of us won't if she does this, Dad. If she kills that tree because she's too weak to live without love, then we all stand to lose a lot more than she does."

"I agree with you," I said, trying to simmer things down for Harry's sake. He didn't show it, but I could see he was at breaking point. This was his mom and dad they were talking about. "And like your dad said, we'll talk to Arthur, okay? It's not for us to decide."

"Then whose choice is it?" she asked.

No one said a word, because the truth was, it should have been everyone's choice, voted on by the greater population, and yet it was covered up, swept under a rug, left in the hands of the one person who couldn't possibly make an informed decision on what was best.

"Should we go back?" I asked, ready to turn this chopper around.

"No." Mike squeezed my hand. "There's still time. David won't come back for a while. Let's just hang back and see what happens when she's had time to think, process."

I bit my teeth together, looking over at Mia, who was doing the exact same thing. This family was nuts, and her and I were the only sane ones right now that could see it.

AUBREY

Yesterday, I was given one cup of water. The woman then shoved a hard piece of bread in my mouth—a small piece, about half the size of my open palm—and left me to chew it down with a parched, dry tongue. I'd tried to ask for more, but she walked away, leaving me angry and hot with rage all over my limbs.

My wrists were cut deeply from where I'd hung from the binds as I'd slept, and my armpits were aching, my fingertips numb from the blood flowing downward for so long. And I couldn't even think about the cold, gooey wet mess down my legs, dripping intermittently into the bowl beneath me. It smelled bad, like rotting pig's blood or meat left out for too long, and the pain in the deep bowl of my pelvis throbbed, as if my insides might fall out through my vagina. If Hell were a place on earth, I'd found it. All I wanted was to lie down, snuggled into a pillow and a blanket. I didn't want my mom or my dad, or even food as badly as I just wanted to lie down.

When the woman came in again today with another round

of dry bread, I realized where I'd seen her before, but I don't think she remembered me from when I pulled her through a fissure a few years ago. If she'd just meet my eyes, listen to me for one second, she might have some compassion when she realized who I was and maybe get me something with protein or any kind of vitamins. A piece of chocolate certainly wouldn't go astray right now.

Squeezing my cheeks to pop my lips apart with all the compassion of an angry bear, she shoved the food in my mouth and lifted the cup to make the bread soft with water, but it dribbled down my chin, wasted. I was given one cup a day. One! And she wasted it.

"Open your mouth!" she demanded.

I tried to pull my chin away from her slimy hand and tell her I couldn't swallow yet, but she forced the water in, impatient and mean, and the entire cup tipped down my chest. I gushed out at the cold, soaking through in the wintry chill of the Scotland air, and the bread projected from my lips as I coughed.

"Well, you'll be getting no more now," she said sternly, her mean black eyes stabbing me with hatred.

"Fuck you, bitch!" I spat on her, hungry and angry and ready to kill.

After a flick of a gaze around the room, clearly checking for onlookers, she slapped me. I squealed, breathless from the shock. But as it simmered down, it gave way to a roiling grumble of heat and rage. My teeth caged and I reared up inside, daring her to do that again.

When she caught the defiant look in my eye and tried to squash it with another slap, an old friend of mine, who hadn't surfaced since its first murder, injected her skin with a deathly toxin the second it connected with mine. In that first instance, as she peered at her hand, the touch of death racing up her arm and over her shoulder, I understood everything about this ability. And she understood what it meant too, her feet carrying her swiftly from the room.

I turned my head to watch where she slipped through the stone columns, making it only a foot farther before she fell face-down, and someone screamed. A loud clatter of dishes followed, and Cillian appeared in the openness of the entrance then, shoulders straight, like a dad checking in to see if the kids would stop fighting before he had to intervene.

With gliding, calculated steps, he skulked over and inspected my cheek, reaching up to swipe a small dot of blood from my lip. "She hit you hard."

I nodded.

"What did you say to her?" he asked, licking the blood off his thumb.

"I called her a fucking bitch."

Cillian laughed once, eyes flicking off to the side as he clearly thought about how to handle this. "You've interrupted my meal."

"She spilled mine." I nodded to the water down my front.

Cillian's eyes went there, considering the wetness. "Do you know who that was? Who you just killed?"

"Anandene," I said, jaw tight, not one shred of regret in my bones, even if he punished me.

An audible breath came through his nose, then he turned away. "You will have no more food for the duration of your isolation."

I shut my eyes and rolled my head down, so bitter and angry I could scream. But also overjoyed. Because I knew now what that touch of death was. I knew it was a toxin. I knew it discharged from my skin, all over. And I knew how to call on it. I just had to want someone to back off—to want to push them away bad enough. That was it. And they would die.

If only Cillian wasn't protected by his stupid binding ring. Then again, he was a vampire and that woman, and Sawyer, were both human, so Cillian might not die. But at least I knew now how to call on that power. I may hate Cillian for what he'd done to me, but no matter the route he took to get there, he was teaching me about myself, and he was making me into something greater, something more powerful than my parents would ever have dared.

As I'd slept on and off, dropping down through layers of consciousness out of pure exhaustion, my lips chapped, arms and shoulders numb, I'd managed to cut the deep gashes from where the cuffs held me up all the way down to bone. I'd gone three days through this torture so far, and already, it was enough to break anyone.

I just wouldn't let it do that to me.

I'd focus, hold my breath when I was about to cry, and think about how other people were suffering way worse than me, and surviving. The first rule to refusing to break is refusing to pity yourself.

It was never so bad when the sun was up and it wasn't as cold, because I could see the ocean, watch life happening out there, despite the snow. Birds moved across the sky, and the trees that had leaves left would flicker them in the wind. It was pretty, almost magical when the snow would glisten, and if I wasn't being held against my will, mistreated, starved and hurt, I would maybe be able to love this place.

But, at night, when the candles burned behind me and the black turned the window into a mirror, there was nothing to see but the skeletal form hanging by chains. My skin had sucked inward onto my bones, and my cheeks were sunken, my eyes like hollow caves in the reflection. Cillian insisted that I wasn't human, that I didn't need food. But if that were the case, then why were my lips cracked to bleeding, my skin flaking, and my entire body so weak with hunger that I'd vomited twice? They cleaned it up, thankfully, when they came to change my blood bowl, and when I retched now, nothing came up at all. I was dying, slowly, painfully, and he didn't believe me.

I closed my eyes and imagined Elias for a while. But when I tried to see his face, it was gone. I knew he was tall, and that he'd had blue eyes, but I couldn't see the length of his nose or the way his eyes changed when he smiled. Of all the things Cillian could have taken from me, pride and comfort on the top of the list, the memory of Elias was the most damaging.

As I tried to open my eyes again and see if the sun had come up yet, a pulling sensation drew me backward. I felt myself falling through the earth, arms outstretched, until I landed hard on crunchy black grass.

I pulled my freed hands around to rub my cuffs, but the wounds were gone.

All around me, a green-gray sky hung low, and the silence was so pronounced it sounded like I was in a small room, not laying by a large lake, in a clearing that went on forever. The water there looked silky in its blackness, and I wondered if I could drink it, but when I wet my lips in thought, I realized I wasn't thirsty.

A very small island sat at the center and a lone black tree stood there, looking at me. Its branches were bare and wiry, with hooked fingers arching downward, like an old man who'd died in a sudden shot of agony. But there was something curious about it, as though it was waiting for me to notice.

Getting up, I felt light and capable. There was no exhaustion, as if I'd never felt it to begin with. I moved toward the lake, casting my eyes along the horizon for another tree, a building, a person. But there was nothing.

"Hello," I called, cupping my hands around my mouth. My voice didn't echo, or even carry very far, and when I lowered my hands back to my sides in a large, dramatic movement, the tree across the water shifted its branches down.

Standing motionless, waiting for it to move again, I could feel the presence of things beneath me, behind me, hear whispers. But they weren't the kinds of whispers my ears could hear; they were like words along my skin; a feeling, a sensation of being watched and also spoken to, but I didn't know how to speak back.

So I waved.

And the tree did the same.

Laughing to myself in disbelief, I raised one hand and held it there.

The tree copied, its limbs creaking like an old door, its movements slow and stiff.

I raised the other arm and closed my hands together over my head, and the black, twisted branches of the tree moved upward and folded into a V shape at the top.

"Wicked," I said, lowering my arms.

A clearer vision of something appeared for a blink in my eyes then. I rubbed them, shaking it off, but it looked like Cillian's face within the gap between the slits. When I shut my eyes again, I saw him looking at me, crouching down to touch my face.

Then, I woke up to the stone room and to Cillian, with his arm under my head.

"She's back. I got her, tell him not to worry," he ordered. "Get me some water."

"What happened?" I coughed.

"You left us for a moment."

"Left?"

He looked to his right as he reached up, and a cool rim touched my lips a second later, the refreshing salvation of clear liquid running in to my mouth. I rolled up to sit, my spine searing from being straight for so many days, and drank the water down hungrily. It felt like my limbs were lifting themselves up on their own, my brain unwilling to acknowledge that they were free now, comfortably by my sides.

"Better?" he asked, raising a mocking brow.

I wiped my mouth on my arm, noting the horrid deep cuts as they stung. "Please don't chain me up again."

"Aubrey, you are not human. Your mind is struggling to come to terms with that," he said, reminding me of a wise young teacher I had once—in the way he squatted at my level, forearm on his knee. "Being chained that way, even without bread and water, should not have caused you to die."

"I died?"

"For a moment."

I wondered if that place I saw, the tree, was the Other Side. If so, it wasn't very peaceful.

"If you keep fighting against this, if you can't get it into your head that you're not a human, I will need to be harsher with you."

My eyes strayed to a woman nearby, the silver bowl in her hands, ready to take more blood from me. "Please don't."

"Also, you will need to wear this." He slipped a leather chain over my head and tucked it into my dress, the rock on the end cold against my sore, thinning skin.

"What is it?"

"A spelled object. It will prevent you from using your touch of death on any being, so don't even try."

I shut my eyes, fighting hard against the pitiful being inside me that wanted to feel sorry for herself.

"Now, up you get." He launched me to my feet and dragged me by my arm to the iron cuffs. When he looked at my wrists though, he thought better of it, choosing a larger ring instead and fastening it around my neck. I gagged for a moment, fingers wedged between the iron and my throat, readjusting my chin to angle it up a bit and stop it touching my neck the wrong way. Then I stood still, defenseless but not emotionless, while he positioned the bowl beneath my feet again, standing up and walking away after.

And that was how it would be.

I faced the window and looked down at the ocean in the pink dawn, wishing I'd stayed dead.

Raise the dead. Kill them.

One piece of bread.

One glass of water.

Into my room to sleep for a week.

Repeat.

I did that until the break in the month when I'd bleed, and then I'd be strung up by that window over a silver bowl.

This had gone on four times now, and still, no one had come to save me.

The hope died when Cillian said Elias had arranged a meeting with his agent to buy some of the blood of the necromancer, which meant word had reached my family. They knew what I was. And they knew what Cillian had done. Which meant I could never face them again.

Elias wouldn't have found what he was looking for when he

met with the agent. Cillian was too smart for that, and I didn't want him to find me now. Not if he knew. I was just so ashamed. What would my mom say, if she was even alive? Or my dad?

My hair had grown back in since I got here. And Cillian let it. As long as I did what he said, and he didn't have to punish me, I was pretty sure I'd be allowed to keep it.

I was given one bath a month, after my period finished, and I hadn't heard music or laughter since my last night at the castle. I missed my family and my friends so much it hurt me in my chest, and the anger and sadness had just balled up in there with it, dying. I hadn't cried yet. Hadn't yelled or screamed. Hadn't even fought Cillian again or argued with him. I just existed, like a good little weapon.

One day, very soon, he had plans to teach me how to fight so that he could use me to take over Loslilian, kill everyone who wouldn't bow to him, and have ownership of the Tree of Life and its guardian—my mom. If Lily hadn't given her soul back by then, Cillian would find her and he'd make her, because that tree couldn't grow fruit without my mom there, apparently. So, at least, in that sense, we were fighting toward one cause that aligned.

I got out of bed and appeared by the window without walking again, hugging myself. It was spring out there now, and the grass was a yellow-green, the sky violet-blue this morning. My hair was touching my chin now, and my eyebrows were back. I hadn't put weight on, but I was no longer deteriorating either. I wondered if Cillian was right: that I wasn't human. And if that were the case, could I be capable of things no human would be?

But I never had time to think about it, because almost as soon as I ever stepped out of bed, he was in here, leading me away to start our day.

"Good, you're awake," he said, standing there in my doorway. See what I mean?

I followed him, without need of invitation, and when we walked into the stone room, I took a deep breath to prepare myself. But Cillian kept walking. I wasn't sure if I should stay put or follow him, so I stayed put.

"Come," he said, walking backward for a moment, his eyes warming with a smile.

I followed, heart in my throat, afraid of what he'd do to me. Through the stone columns at the other end of the room, I looked up and around at the hall, with a throne at one end and hard wood floors. I barely felt the sensation of ground beneath my feet these days, but I made a conscious effort because this was better than being on cold stone. The room was more decorated here, with shields and swords on the walls, banners hung in bright colors, and a giant empty banquet table down the middle.

When we walked out through two heavy wooden doors and into the sun, my arm came up to shield my eyes. I felt small and fragile out here, like a bug in an open field of birds.

"You may wander outside for an hour a day," he said. "Displease me, and the privilege will be taken away."

"Yes, Master," I said humbly, keeping my head down until he was gone.

I hadn't seen the sun without it being through glass in months, and I couldn't smell the ocean, the grass or the trees from inside. But out here, it was like all my senses went into overdrive. I moved down the stone steps and planted my foot to the prickly grass cautiously, letting my more human form walk here, really feeling my feet and my legs for the first time in a while as they connected to the earth and all its life. I wondered if my mom would be able to sense me, if she were alive, like maybe the earth would find me and tell her where I was.

The sun moved over the peak of the stone room wall then and splashed warmth along my skin. I hugged myself, looking out past a stone footbridge that led away to freedom, then down to the ocean, where it crept in a thin rivulet beneath that bridge. I could spend my hour under a tree, shaded from the sun, or maybe down by the water, soothing the longing sensation in my skin.

The sea had called out to me many times in my captivity, begging my return, and I wondered if a part of that was simply because that's where my two lives met: the ocean was the one place that, right now, touched the shores of my home. Maybe Harry would be standing there, thinking about me. Maybe Elora would look up from the tables she was clearing and wonder if I was wondering about her. Maybe Uncle Mike would stand on the jetty and whisper something to me, and I wouldn't hear it, but the sentiment would carry on the sea. Maybe I could tell my dad how sorry I was for what I said to him, and those words, the meaning, would live in the waves like a message in a bottle, and he might one day duck beneath the cool and understand, even without ever hearing me say it.

I wandered slowly down the wide sloping plain, past a small garden, and smiled when I met a white horse there by the calm, lapping waters. It looked up at me, blinking its eyes, and mine filled with tears. I'd never been much of an animal kind of person. Never asked for a dog or a cat. Didn't ask to ride horses at the town fair. But something about this creature, its soft white mane and gentle eyes, just made me want to cry. I sucked the tears back in and held my breath, afraid I'd scare it off.

"Hello there," I said, and it made a noise at me, shifting sideways as if planning to run. When I looked around, there were no other horses nearby. He was all alone.

Before I approached him, I glanced up the long slope to the

castle to make sure Cillian wasn't watching me from that window. But the glass was reflective, and I couldn't be sure.

I'd never seen the castle from this perspective before, didn't even know the exterior was built with cream bricks, like Loslilian manor. From here, I could see that the room I spent all my time in was just a big rectangle hulk of stone, with that one big window and several smaller ones above it that must have been bedrooms. The bricks were grubby and grimy with age, and there was a greater part of the castle behind it, but from this far down the slope, I couldn't see much, aside from one turret. I could tell that the castle sat out on a small island-like circle of land, with the thin rivulet of sea cutting it off, but for as far as the eye could reach, there were no other buildings.

I didn't want to go back in there. I wanted to stay out here with the plush grass and the lapping water, but the time would come, and Cillian would make me, and there was nothing I could do.

Since he didn't seem to be watching, I turned back to the horse. "What's your name, boy?" I asked.

He, of course, didn't answer. He just looked at me for a long time, and I looked at him, feeling the hour pass behind me.

"It's okay," I said encouragingly, extending my hand and rubbing my thumb and fingers together. "You can come out of the water."

He shifted back, going deeper, so I stopped advancing.

"Don't be afraid. I won't hurt you."

"Aubrey!" I glanced back as Cillian approached, coming fast down the slope. "Come away from the water."

"I wasn't going to run."

"And I don't ask twice." He slapped me across the back of the head, so hard my legs buckled and I rocketed forward. I fell into the sea with a splash, my hands out, and when I looked up, the horse was gone. But he hadn't run down the beach or into the water, he was just gone.

"I'm sorry, Master," I said, getting onto my knees, head down.

He grabbed my arm and pulled me to my feet, the burn of his strike reverberating deep within my skull.

"I saw a horse," I added, looking for it.

"We don't have horses here," he said offhandedly, dragging me along, dripping and wet, but then he stopped. His cunning eyes took me in, head turning to the sea.

In a flash of madness then, he lifted the dagger from his belt and grabbed my wrist, making me yelp as he cut a line down my flesh.

I cupped my palm instantly around the pain, but he shoved my hand away, inspecting the blood. And if it could have run cold throughout my entire body, it would have when I looked down and saw a black oil-like substance flowing from within the wound.

"What is that?"

"You're getting stronger, becoming less human and more demon."

My throat made a shuddering noise as I thought about what that might mean. I wasn't sure I'd ever be free of this place, not if Cillian had anything to do with it, but I was certain no one, not even Elias, would ever love me if my blood was black and tainted. Ugly.

"Come." He lifted my wrist and showed it to me. "Heal it."

"How?"

"Imagine it healed."

I looked at the cut, swallowing the lump in my throat, and imagined the skin knitting together like it would when Mom healed me up as a kid. She was so magical, so powerful, and if this darkness, this demon power, could do even half of what she could, then I would one day have a renewed hope of escaping this tyrant.

"Try harder." Cillian squeezed my wrist, pushing the black substance up and over the thin wound like bath water in an over-filled tub.

I shut my eyes and felt a moment of peace in my heart when I saw the tree there—black and twisted. Misunderstood. Like my dad. But not to my mom. She loved him no matter his darkness, and I knew she'd love me too. It was enough. I could love that tree, ugly and black as it was, because it had been my friend. For that split moment where we met and it waved, it was my friend. And when I thought about warm things, love, light, friends that hug you when you're sad, I could feel that magic tingle in my skin.

The voices that whispered to me that day by the black lake moved up my feet, over my legs and through my core, crossing paths in patterns along my wound.

When I opened my eyes, the tingle of whispers still on my lips, the cut was closed and Cillian nodded, satisfied. "Very good."

I smiled, and though I wasn't smiling at him, he returned it. Just for a moment.

ARA

It's like a sliver. Like something moveable and hard—oily metal. It slithers inside your heart, dragging vestiges of pain behind it. It never went away—just slithered in and out of my core like the agony of life raping me over and over again in my soul. But as I sat in my throne, with Jason beside me and no promise made between us except to rule the monarchy together, that pain magnified when I heard that my daughter's menstrual blood was being sold on the black market.

I was supposed to be a strong queen. I sat in front of my people every day and made decisions and did the hard things, and I never showed my tears. They saw compassion and empathy, joy, light, anger, but never tears. We hadn't allowed the people to be present for this, only the Upper and Lower House, but even they hadn't seen me cry before.

My father stood in the back corner of the room, his own grief shaking out of him and into his fingertips, while Elias davenport stood with his hands closed in front of him, staring at the ground as though he might rain all hell down on it.

"Jase?" I cried, the word coming out like 'jakes' through the sobbing. He slipped off his throne and knelt beside me. "What are they doing to my little girl?"

I felt his heart squeeze, tightening with the agony mine was in. Because Aubrey had been his little girl too. She'd loved him like a father and found comfort in him when she spent those long summers here with Beth. He loved her as equally as I did, and there was no denying that.

"We'll find her, Ara. We know now that the Blackwells *are* behind this—"

"But they're not at the castle—"

"We will find them. They wouldn't sell that blood in the country they're residing. It'd be too obvious." Jase patted my hand and stood up. "But we'll find them."

Elias moved over then and knelt before the dais. "I vow to put an end to this tyrant, My Queen. And I vow that I will not, on my honor, sleep until I have found your daughter and brought her home."

I smiled down at him, remembering the vision and how I'd called him Eli. "She's lucky to have a friend like you," I said, drying my tears as I stood up to move toward him. I took the step down and sat in front of him on the platform. "She won't be the same girl when we get her back. But from this, just this"—I motioned to the vial of her blood on the table by the window; the vial that Elias had brought with him from Mississippi, where he'd tracked down the agent who was selling it—"I know my Aubrey will feel angry, bitter, violated. And she had darkness in her, Elias. She won't be the same girl."

"I know," he whispered regretfully, closing his eyes tight.

"Knowing this, I'm giving you a chance to walk away, because if—"

"I'll not take it." He lifted his head, shaking it. "She wrote to me while she was living at Drake's castle, did you know that?"

I shook my head softly, so in awe of this unexpected romance.

"Drake was kind enough to pass those letters on after she was taken." He nodded over at him up the back of the room. "If the girl in those letters is still alive, then I will never give up on her. Not until she tells me that her heart has changed."

"Okay." I smiled, patting his arm to say thank you. "And please stand up. You're family. And family do not kneel."

Elias stood, humbled, and I walked back up to sit in my throne beside Jason. He offered me a smile to say it would be okay, but until my daughter was safe in my arms, I just wouldn't believe that.

"Go," I said to my men. "Find out what you can. And bring me Cillian Blackwell's head on a fucking pike."

They bowed and moved backward until they were halfway down the room, then turned and set off on their mission. Elias bowed once and followed them, carrying his solemn vow on his shoulders with him.

FOR THE LAST FOUR MONTHS, JASON HAD BARELY SPOKEN to me. We held court sessions, ever the united front, and we were often playful and conversational in those sessions, showing the community that everything was all right. But behind the curtain, he was merely civil to me. He was *living out* his days now, instead of living them.

But after the news about Aubrey, a very different Jason came to my room that night with a bowl of popcorn and a block of chocolate. I wanted to turn him away, but he was wearing a big grin and a white long-sleeve shirt, the kind without buttons, and he looked so sweet and so human that I didn't have the heart. When in his kingly attire—the uniform he wore to court—you'd think he was a different man. He stood taller in the straight black jacket, which went all the way up to his chin with its high collar, a sword on the belt, and I liked that I knew the Jason underneath that. *This* Jason, who was standing in front of me with his heart on his sleeve. Jase.

I stood back as he came in, and we flopped down side by side on the pillows. Jason handed me the popcorn while he pressed the remote to bring the tv up from within the floor, and neither of us said a word. He chose something to watch, and straightened his arm out along the top of the pillows for me to lay in. Then we watched a film, eating popcorn and saying nothing.

We'd been given permission to be together while David was gone, and yet neither of us had accepted that offer. But we needed this. Just a bit of friendship. Companionship. To not feel so alone and scared right now.

Jase took a deep breath as the end credits rolled to the final words, and let it out slowly. "Aubrey's strong, Ara."

"No one is that strong."

He nodded, curling his arm around my shoulder. "We can make her okay again. If she comes back before David does, I'll become a vampire and erase her mind—"

"I can do that, you know—"

"Yes, but you'd have to look into her suffering to do it," he stated, and I nodded. He squeezed me tighter, kissing my head. "I'm sorry I haven't been here for you."

"I don't expect you to be. It's cruel and selfish of me to expect that."

"No, it's cruel and selfish of you to let me die to save my

brother, but expecting me to be your friend, to be the man who has always loved you and cared about you, that's just… human."

I rolled onto my side and put my hand on his chest, listening to his heart. I'd known him as so many versions of himself: the strong king, the soft human boy, who was way too young in his mind, even for me; the sad, hurt vampire; the angry kidnapper; the one who tortured me to save me; the scientist; the painter. Now, he was a human king. Just as strong as when he was a vampire, and every bit as formidable, but he still had this softer, kinder side that he rarely showed people nowadays. And I loved him in each of those forms. It was sad to think that would be lost forever. His soul would live on but, as we saw with Lily's soul in me, a soul wasn't the same. It wasn't me; it wouldn't be him.

"Did you ever figure out how to explode heads?" I asked.

"What?" He laughed, because I didn't give him context.

"In that vision—the other life—you could explode heads. So you're clearly capable of it. Did you ever figure it out after you saw it?"

He cleared his throat. "I may have. Why?"

I sat up a little. "Really?"

Jase nodded, smiling in a way that reminded me of David—before he became the thing of evil. "I learned many things, especially in that year where Lily held me captive, torturing me."

My eyes hooded themselves from the grief and the shame of that, since it was me who brought him back here. "I'm sorry, Jase."

"It doesn't matter now," he said, and he meant it. Because he'd be dead soon.

"This whole thing is a mess," I said, falling back down with my ear against his heart.

"I'm trying hard not to dwell on that right now."

I nodded, trying hard not to think about my daughter. She

left me seven months ago. I'd dropped her at the airport, and she'd refused to hug me, still so mad. That was the last time I ever saw her.

"Will you stay with me tonight? I don't want to sleep alone?"

Jase shuffled down on the bed and his shirt came up a little as he did, revealing his hairy stomach. I pulled it over his abs and laid back down on him, closing my eyes as he closed us into the blanket, pressing the remote to turn off the tv.

I was finally ready to just enjoy this for what it was—this moment of freedom to love him like I'd wanted to for so long—knowing that when my husband returned and Jase was gone, I'd never have the chance to hold him again.

I WALKED IN ON A PIRATE BEING STABBED BY A TINY LITTLE Peter Pan, in costume and all. Both of them.

Jase got up, still hunched over his pretend wound, and tucked the treasure chest under his arm, so adorable in the pirate hat and eye-patch.

"The treasure be yars, ya wee scar'vy dog." He handed the small box to Danny, who rejoiced, sitting down to open the chocolate coins within.

"Hi," Jason said to me, hobbling over on an imaginary peg leg.

"You are adorable," I stated, lifting the eye-patch to kiss his cheek. He took off his hat, laughing.

"Kid really knows how to handle a weapon," he joked. "And this parenting thing is a lot more exhausting in human form."

With my arms folded, I scanned his red face, the slight sheen of sweat in the heat of spring, and his breathless smile. I was going to say it'd be easier when he was a vampire again but… I let that thought die with the agony it brought.

"It would be worse if *all* the kids were here," I said, thinking back to how it used to be. But it just didn't sink in that my comment would cause him pain until I saw the look on his face. He sat down on the small table, shifting the play-dough aside. I could see he and Danny had had an amazing day of creative play and adventure, and I felt left out. I hardly spent any time with Daniel lately.

"You must miss them like crazy," I said, sitting beside him.

"The kids?"

I nodded, referring to his and Lily's children, who weren't his blood children but had been raised that way.

He toyed with the hat in his hands, looking down at the big pink feather. "It hurts like hell, Ara."

I leaned on his bony shoulder. "Vampirie… he was a good dad to me. He'll love them—"

"But they lost their mother, and I'm the only father they've ever really known. They must be wondering why I haven't come for them."

"I'm sorry." I touched his knee, meaning that, because I was the one that did this—forced the hand of the universe.

"Anyway"—he looked behind him, marked a spot on the hat rack, and tossed the pirate hat on exactly where he'd aimed —"did you get those documents signed for the Lower House?"

"Yeah. Can you look over the proposal for the new primary school in the village later though? Because I had a pile this high of new vampires to approve and I just didn't get to it."

"When does Jackson need it?"

"Five." I flashed him an apologetic grin. "If you can."

He groaned, rolling to stand. "You get him bathed. I'll be back for dinner and story."

"Kay," I said, pressing my head into his kiss as he bent to say goodbye.

I sat watching Daniel play then, oblivious to the troubles around him. He hadn't asked for his sister Aubrey, and he'd only asked for his dad twice, but I think he was asking for Jason then, because he hadn't asked again. When I thought of Aubrey, I could still see her in the nursery, with fiery hair and that sassy personality, in the corner there talking to invisible things while the other kids played. She'd always had a lot of spirit, a lot of fight, and people often remarked that she got her darkness from her father, but I think she got it from me. Because only David really knew the depth of my darkness, but if Aubrey had even a fifth of me or her father in her, then she'd be okay—if we ever found her.

Elias had called this morning to say that he'd been out to the Blackwell castle in England many times and found nothing, but there was word of another castle in Scotland, that might once have belonged to them. Even if it was a few centuries ago, there was a chance they could be there now. And it was worth looking. If he found her, he'd take her to London with him, being closer than America. And I'd fly out there to be with her, bring her home. But I couldn't shake the feeling that something bad was about to happen. And it had something to do with Aubrey and death.

I looked at Danny, and he wandered over to give my leg a hug.

"Hey baby."

"Where's Daddy?"

"He's gone to sign papers," I said in a singsong voice. "He'll be back. Wanna go have a bath?"

"Five minutes?" he asked, putting his little hand up, looking so much like Harry then, all cheeky and cute. I smiled, saying okay, and he ran off.

It filled my heart up to know that he was Jase's little boy. It had cut, at first, been so hard for us to come to terms with the fact that I'd have another man's baby, but David had handled it with grace and love. He'd never once said Danny wasn't his or that he couldn't love him. And a part of me wondered if this darkness he had now made him feel that way, or simply made him feel okay to say what had truly been in his heart all along.

I bit my lip, looking away so Daniel wouldn't see my tears. This would be a very long journey. Mourning the David that once was, the David he may never again be, that was one thing. I was halfway into that journey, it seemed. But it would begin all over again when Jase was gone, when his body, his mind, his… heart was gone forever. And if David couldn't be the same loving guy he was before all of this, then I would mourn all over again. And I just felt tired. I didn't feel prepared to cope with that—with a headstrong toddler, a missing, probably very traumatized daughter, and a husband that couldn't love my son, all while contending with the death of Jason.

And yet I had no choice. This was happening whether I liked it or not. Which made me empathize a lot more with Jase's plight —with having no say.

All of this family drama had been kept very quiet. People knew that Aubrey was missing, and that I had become queen again, with Jason at my side while David was "searching for our daughter", but no one knew about what David had become. No one knew that I planned to take Jason's life. Because if they did, and the truth about the dying tree also came out, the decision would be taken from my hands. It would be put to a vote, for the greater good of all.

I'd been tense, just waiting for Jules to speak up and say

something in the hopes that she might save Jase, but everyone seemed to be standing back, trusting me to either do the right thing and kill David to undo the curse on the tree, or find a way to save it without his blood, his death.

But if the tree died, and Light Magic went with it, that meant my daughter, with her crux of magic keeping her soul here, bound to the earth, would die too.

I'd been through every single book and scroll within this place, looking for a way to save everyone. That's why I hadn't had time to go over the proposals, in truth. I spent too much time reading, researching, whispering to the tree to find its wisdom. But it was too sick to care now. And I was starting to realize, with each day that I spent searching for a way to save the tree without killing David, and to save David without killing Jase, that David may, in the end, have to die to save Elora.

I locked that thought way in the back of my mind though, somewhere deep and shadowed, hooded. I would keep looking for a way to save them all, and I would never give up. It was too early to accept defeat just yet. And it was too soon to even mention it to Jase. I couldn't give him hope, even though there was a small chance that things may just work in his favor.

AUBREY

"Good," Cillian said, standing back with his arms folded, reminding me a bit of a horse trainer, watching it go around a ring. "Bring it up out of the ground."

I drew a long breath and pushed a calm wave through my body, focusing all my energy on the hot soil beneath my bare feet, where I could feel a thread—a vine of nightshade. As it passed through the earth, it would slowly become solid, harden into a thick branch, and with the magic it brought from the Underworld, it could then turn into an impenetrable cage.

As the vine snaked up around my ankle, caressing me like its master, I opened my eyes and commanded it to crawl into my hand.

"Good," I whispered, stroking it. I could feel the darkness, the power within its silky shell, and I thought about sending it through Cillian's eye, but that stupid ring on his finger prevented me from doing anything to bring him harm. Many times, over the last eight months here, I'd thought about appealing to his obvious attraction to my human form. My hair had grown out and, it turns out, he was right, I didn't need food. I could survive for weeks without even a glass of water. I could still drink and eat for pleasure, not that I had, but I didn't need it. I looked healthier now, almost as if I had control over it. And sometimes, I felt like I could be beautiful, more beautiful than usual, in his eyes, simply by willing it. I wanted to use that to get myself into his bed, take off his ring when he wasn't looking. But in those moments when he found himself attracted to me in an obvious way, he'd usually find some excuse to hurt me. It wasn't worth it yet.

"Good. Now, send it back." Cillian took a wide step away and nodded to the vine.

I leaned down and stroked its head, whispering to it softly, "Go home."

The nightshade obeyed, twirling and sinking back into the earth like a pet snake, closing its hole completely, as if it had never come through.

"Defense is the most important skill to learn," Cillian said. "You cannot attack if you cannot stand somewhere safely."

I nodded.

"You have the power to command the forces of the Underworld to rise up at your discretion," he said. "But it will require focus and concentration."

"Where do they come from—the army?" I asked. "As in, is there a gateway they come through? Because my mom, when she went to the spirit world, had to pass through a gate."

"No. She could enter that world through light. Columns of light. She only used the gateway to the Other Side when she needed to go to a particular corner of that world."

My brows pushed up. "Oh, really?"

"Yes."

"So…" I looked around for a beam of light. "Can I do the same with the Underworld?"

"Not consciously, no. Not yet. And you enter through the shadows," he said, nodding to the shadow of the castle that we were standing in, where I'd just brought the vine up from the place Cillian called the *Beneath*. He was divulging so much more these days, and sometimes it almost felt like we were friends. I did appreciate that he was teaching me how to be powerful, but not enough that I wouldn't turn it on him first chance I got. And he knew that. He still held back so much, and quite often told me things only to realize that he shouldn't have said it.

"I would teach you how to fight, hand to hand, but you should never have need for it, unless you wanted the enemy left alive," he said, moving in and putting his hand on my waist.

I looked up at him, the warm sun highlighting the reds in my darkening hair, where it rested in a pretty curve over my shoulder, making him look at me twice. When I arrived here, my hair was a dark auburn color but now, as I grew stronger, it was changing into a rich brown with red hues, getting darker every day, like my blood. He liked it. Liked my darkness. Liked putting his hand on my waist. One day, I would win him over without needing to try.

"Soon, when we attack the London Sets, I will need you," he said, and my eyes widened a little. Elias and Quaid's castles. "I want you to learn how to summon Fragarach—the sword—at will."

"You want *me* to fight?"

"You won't need to. With that sword, you can answer the swing of any man's weapon. But with your power and that sword combined"—he grinned proudly—"you can answer them all at once."

I turned to face him where he moved away to lean on the rock wall that bordered the path to the footbridge. “Really?”

“Yes. You could stand at the helm, command an army from the sea”—he nodded to the ocean—“or simply aim your sword to the ground and command all opposition dead.”

“All who oppose *me*?”

“No, your master,” he said, narrowing his eyes in a sly smile.

“I didn’t mean it like that. I just meant…” I moved over, appearing beside him by a thought only, “I could will them all dead, and all that would be left is the people who were willing to switch sides?”

“Yes.” His smile warmed and he hugged his arms casually, leaning with his legs out long. “Why do you think I wrote the spell which created you?”

“Did you know I could do all that stuff when you wrote it?”

“Some of it, yes, but there are things I’m still learning.”

“Like?”

He glanced over at the ocean, the curved furrow of his brow indicating that he was going over every possible angle of conversation before revealing anything. “The horse you saw when I first let you outside…”

“What about it?” I looked too, seeing it there now but not willing to tell him that. “I take it you can’t see it?”

“No.” He laughed, his body jerking so casually with the gesture. “Do you know who it was? Did it speak its name?”

“No. Horses don’t speak, do they?”

“That one does.” He looked down at his shiny brown shoes, nodding to himself. “When you know his name, it will be time for us to go to battle.”

“Why then?”

“Because he will bring his riders, his army, by the thousands. A force that will roll in over any enemy and decimate them all.

While you, my necromancer," he said, picking my hand up and looking at the palm, "will wield that sword and win me my first castle. From there"—he traced a line over my wrist—"we will take the Castle Elysium and kill Drake, and then we will overthrow Loslilian."

"And what about my mom? Will you find Lily and—"

"She is alive," he said, letting my hand go. "And Lily is dead."

A column of pure light entered my heart and warmed my entire core, forcing me to smile. "How do you know?"

"I'm not held prisoner here, Aubrey." He indicated the grounds as though there was freedom out there. "I have a life outside of these walls."

"Oh." A part of me wanted to jump up and down and scream with relief and happiness, but weapons didn't display emotion. I kept it locked away. "So, what do you do—when you're not here?"

"Work my magic. I network with others, form bonds with those who are powerful enough to assist me, and crush those whose power only serves well to be mine."

"So, you… what? Quietly and secretly infiltrate the enemy?"

He laughed affectionately. "Yes. Something to that effect."

I looked away. He reminded me so much of my father sometimes—the corrupted mind, not his appearance. If he hadn't been so cruel to me, I think maybe we could have been friends eventually, because I saw the same darkness in him that was growing every day in me, and it was like a kinship. Those shadows, carrying that raw maleficence, was like being a child in a room full of adults and then suddenly seeing another kid. There weren't many of us, but when we came across a kindred shadow, it was hard not to feel like you could relate, get along.

"Did you end up getting much money for my blood—on the black market?" I probed.

Cillian's clever mind ticked over, analyzing everything I ever said and churning it around, finding the truth beneath every vowel. His fingers curled tighter around his arms, where he hugged himself, and his eyes shrunk, smiling off at nothing. "Are you asking if I made money to support my cause, or if your family found out in the process?"

"It's not like I think they'll come to save me," I said. I'd lost all hope of that. "And it's... I'm not even sure if I want them to—"

"Why?"

"Huh?" I was taken aback, because Cillian rarely ever cut people off when they were speaking. And he expected others to extend the same courtesy.

"Why would you not want to be rescued?" he reiterated.

"It's... I don't like being held captive," I said. "I want freedom just as much as any other creature. But I'm learning things here that they could never, *would* never have taught me. Even if I were free," I started, but I realized, as I said it, that it was only half a lie, "I'm not sure I'd leave."

If he set me free, I'd stay. At least long enough to learn about my powers. Of course, I'd also kill him after that, and there's no way I'd fight for his cause, which is exactly why he wouldn't set me free.

Cillian cleared his throat, readjusting his seat there on the wall, in the great dark shadows from the looming castle. "Your family did get word of your blood being sold on the black market, and they tried to track down the source, but they failed. They know I'm involved but they don't know where I am. And while they're scrambling around trying to follow my red herrings, they're not watching the proverbial 'other hand'."

I hugged myself and looked off to the hills in the distance, green and hot with a wave of heat, dotted with the occasional big tree. But something caught my eye by the water, and I turned my head to see the horse raise his, bowing it again. Beside him, another one appeared, its long mane majestic and shimmering, like water sparkling in the sun.

Cillian looked too, and I could feel his eyes on me long before I brought mine back to his.

"You can go to him," he said.

"Who?"

"The horse. Strip naked and swim in the sea to cleanse your skin, then ask him his name."

"Do you think it's time?"

He hesitated. "How many do you see?"

"Two."

Cillian stood. "Then yes, the time is drawing near. Come." He took my hand and walked me down to the water. I wanted to shake it loose from his smarmy grip and vomit all over his shiny brown businessman shoes, but I was also so used to being touched by him. We'd spent almost every day together training, learning. He had become my teacher, but not my friend, and yet there was something about that relationship that made me feel sometimes like his touch, his voice, was a part of me. Second nature, I guess. Which may have been a symptom of Stockholm syndrome.

When we stopped by the water, the horses looked up. I expected them to run. But they just watched on curiously as Cillian stood in front of me and reached around, unzipping my scratchy cotton tunic and pushing it off my shoulders. I didn't cover my breasts or my pubic hair, like I would have once. I stood with my arms by my sides, unashamed of my human form, and let him look at me. I knew what his eyes wanted as they passed each inch of flesh, and I gauged the distance between his ring and my grasp for a moment, while the horses stared, curious.

"Go." Cillian gently placed his hand on my back and pushed me toward the sea. "Don't go too far though. I don't want to have to punish you."

"Yes, Master," I said, touching the water with a toe.

Immediately, the sensation of coming home enveloped me, and the horses responded, looking down at it as if I'd just touched them.

It was cool and refreshing in the thick summer heat, and it had been two weeks since my last bath, making my skin sing for the touch. I didn't stink, because I didn't really sweat like a human, and though I needed the bathroom and still made bodily fluids, it was on a much lower scale. I probably only peed twice a week and that was if I'd had water to drink.

I walked in up to my knees, while the cold water lapped gracefully along the shore. It reminded me of the tree in the black lake—my friend—making me want to dive beneath the depths of the ocean and swim into its arms.

Cillian watched from the shore as I swam out up to my chin and called the horses to follow me. And they did, stopping when the water touched their throats. I waddled over, reaching up slowly, carefully, glistening beads of liquid dripping from my fingertips, and pressed one hand to each of their bodies.

"I'm Aubrey," I whispered.

A voice came through my head then, speaking a name. Just one name: Enbarr.

I bowed my head. "Nice to meet you."

Do you need help? the voice asked.

I wanted to answer, tell them my master had me bound here, trapped. But I couldn't say it aloud. He was watching very closely, listening with his vampire ears.

I understand. The horse bobbed its head.

Can you hear my thoughts?

Not thoughts. But we speak, and you speak with us, in the manner in which all creatures of our world do.

I thought about the whispers on my skin: The Knowing.

Yes, the horse said. *The Knowing. That is what we call it.*

Which made sense, because, you know… you just kind of 'knew' stuff.

On the shore, Cillian stood with my dress tucked into his folded arms. He came right up to the water's edge, his body facing me, and I could feel his darkness ripple along the water where it washed just under his shoes. It scared me to feel connected to that darkness, to like it. I was running out of time. Soon, one day very soon, I could feel it, I might be completely consumed by the captive's curse, and I might want to fight with him, alongside him, as he killed my entire family.

Can you help me? I asked.

When you need us.

I need you now.

Not yet, Enbarr said. *You're not ready.*

But I know your name.

And you are ready to fight, to win. But that does not mean you're ready to be set free.

"Aubrey?" Cillian called, his voice changing with mild, concealed panic. "What are you doing?"

In an effort to stop his suspicion, I smiled over at him. "I know his name. He just told me his name."

Cillian smiled, pleased, bringing his arms back into a fold over his chest. "Return to me. We will make plans to attack the castle."

"When?"

He drew a long breath, lowering his head as he nodded. "Three weeks?"

I looked at the long lashes of the horse, its kind eyes, which were completely black and hollow, as if it didn't have a soul and yet connected with me as if it did.

I can't let him kill Elias, I said.

Then stop him, he said, and vanished.

ARA

When I reached the cliff drop, I could smell cigarette smoke wafting up from the beach cove. But before I had a chance to take the steep steps, violent sprays of sand and tiny bits of rock carried on a huge rush of wind and scratched my cheeks. I looked down at Jase sitting on a rock, hands at rest on parted knees, looking like James Dean in his jeans and a white t-shirt. And I smiled, watching as he drew one last puff on that cigarette and tossed the butt into the sand, aiming his gaze off to a boulder nearby. It burst open a second later with impressive force, and I almost fell over.

How could he still do that now? He was human! I knew that he'd redeveloped his skills after a few years of being human the last time, but surely not to this degree, and surely not this quick.

Taking the moment were he wasn't exploding things, I trotted down the steps, loudly, in case he didn't see me coming and managed to explode me. "Hey you," I called.

He sat a little taller, balancing the heel of his palm on one thigh, waiting until I'd trudged across the sand to his side before saying, "Hey."

"Daniel's awake," I said, jumping up to sit on the rock beside him. "He's asking for you."

Jase nodded. "I'll go in soon."

"So…" I folded my arms in and smirked at the pile of dead rocks. "When were you going to tell me you still had your telekinetic abilities?"

His lovely straight teeth showed in a guarded grin as he released that breathy laugh. "Why'd you assume I'd lost them?"

"I just… you're human," I pointed out, and he shrugged. "Got any other cool skills I haven't seen yet?"

"Plenty," he said sweetly. "But we'd have to be naked for me to demonstrate."

I laughed, shaking my head.

"Okay, I got one." He slid forward on the rock, pulling his jeans up his legs a little as he did. "So, this will look ridiculous, because I've found that I need my hands to do this. It's a confidence thing," he added shyly. "I feel like I need to be making an impact on the environment in order to control it."

"Control what?"

"You'll see." He swallowed hard and bounced his shoulders, as if to get comfortable. Then, he put both hands out and made a large ball shape between them. And there, in the sand, a swirling vortex rose.

I jerked back with a gleeful clap. "Wow."

"That's not all." He raised a cheeky brow at me. The sandy vortex modified itself then, taking on shape. I leaned forward and narrowed my eyes in disbelief as it gradually became a horse, moving and walking toward us. "Impressed yet?"

"Holy cow, Jase!"

He smirked, like it was obvious just how cool he was, and

released his hold on the sand, letting it all fall back down into a shallow heap.

"How did you figure that out?"

"Many hours sitting by myself," he said, reaching in to his back pocket to pull out a silver case full of cancer sticks. He popped one in his mouth, offered me one, to which I replied with a raised lip, and then he laughed and put the case back in his pocket. As he reached for his lighter, I obliged—being an enabler—and used my Cerulean light to do it, with just one touch from the tip of my finger. He drew the smoke out, examined the lit end, impressed, and shrugged as he popped it back between his lips.

"You shouldn't be doing that," I warned. "And I shouldn't be encouraging it."

"You encourage it because you think it's sexy." He winked at me, looking way too cute.

"It still can't be good for you."

"I'll worry about it when it can kill me."

"Um, Jase…" I raised a brow at him. "You're human, remember? It *can* kill you."

His lips arched downward in thought, then he just shrugged again. "Didn't think of that."

I drew it from his mouth and snapped it in half for good measure, tossing it away.

"Litter bug," remarked the guy who'd just done that five minutes ago.

"I'd rather kill the planet than kill you," I stated, but we both realized at the same time, innocent as that was, just how inaccurate it also was.

"Nice one, Ara." He hopped down off the rock.

"Jase." I followed him. "I'm sorry. I…" Didn't mean it?

But I did. Because that's exactly what I was doing: killing him to save something more important to me.

I'd rather kill the planet than kill him? What was I thinking?

Truth was, he *did* mean so much to me that I'd rather save him than the planet. But somehow, my decision to come out here and spend time with him had just turned into another opportunity for me to make him feel like he didn't matter. It would always lead back to that, somehow, some way. We couldn't just be in the same space without it coming up. I was starting to wonder if it might just be kinder to get it over with.

When he suddenly turned around and walked toward me again, I was taken aback, thinking he'd read my mind. My eyes widened as he reached out, took me by the shoulder and drew me into his lovely firm chest, wrapping both arms tightly around me. I breathed in the cologne under his arms, rich and sharp with the warmth of his gorgeous human body.

"Listen to me, okay," he said, voice coming through his throat in a comforting hum. "I know you didn't mean that. I know you never do when you slip up like that. But the reason I get so cut is because I can see it, Ara, when I look into your eyes, I can see the love there, and it kills me that it's *so* restrained."

"It has to be, Jase—"

"I know, but just tell me one thing." He exhaled, looking around as he stepped away and pulled his jeans up a bit where they slipped down at the back, making his chest and arms look bigger as he did. I loved how human he was now, squinting in the sun, slightly breathless. "If it were between me and the planet—take David out of the equation—would you fight for me? Is there any conceivable path where you would fight for me as hard as you're fighting for him?"

"You're asking where you rank?" I said, catching on. "Who would I put you before?"

"I guess." He shrugged, throwing his arms out dramatically and then letting them fall to his sides.

Obviously, I wouldn't put him before my children. Or David. But… "Kids aside, and David, I'd put you before Falcon. Or Mike."

"Arthur?"

I laughed. Arthur was one of my oldest and dearest friends, but Jase was the love I was designed for. He still owned a way larger portion of my heart than I would ever freely admit. "Yes, Jase. Before Arthur."

"So"—he wiped a hand over his nose, sticking his thumbs in his pockets then—"Me and Arthur, right now. World's going to end if one of us doesn't die. You'd let me live?"

"Of course."

"Why?"

"Because the love is different."

"Yeah, but… you won't be with me any more than you'd ever be with him. So what does it matter if the love is different? Wouldn't you be better off keeping your good friend than a man who spends his days longing for you to notice him?"

"Aw, Jase." I cocked my head.

"Answer the question, Ara."

"Um…" I knew he wouldn't like the answer, because it would only confuse him more. "No. I'd choose you. Every time. Even if I can't be with you."

"Why?"

"Because I…" Love you. It was that simple. And I would always hold out a hope that, one day, there'd be a way to ease this burn in my soul, my heart. One day, I might finally get to be with him. "Hearts can change," I said. "We both know that. Maybe David and I would—"

Jase laughed over that. "No, you wouldn't. You swore 'nothing do you part'. Ever."

"Yes. But… even then…" My eyes drifted downward slowly.

"What?"

"I'm only human. And David… with the hex," I explained, carefully, because I didn't want to vilify David. "He begged me to leave him."

"He what?"

"I needed a break. I needed some time away from it, and—"

"You were planning to leave?"

"No. I just… I just needed a break from it all."

"I don't understand."

"I would never leave David. Will never. But, just before he was kidnapped by Lily, I was a nervous wreck a lot of the time. I wasn't sure when he was going to turn—"

He clicked his tongue, shaking his head. "I hate that you lived your life like that."

"Hey, it wasn't like that all the time, Jase," I said sharply. "No one ever knew about it because it wasn't what you think. I didn't live this horrible, abusive life."

"Maybe not the entire time, but—"

"Not even a very big portion of it," I explained. "If you flatten our life out into a long red ribbon, a meter long, the abuse was maybe only a centimeter of time, okay? And it all only came to light, suddenly became *everyone else's business*, because Aubrey was worried. But… what she saw… it didn't get like that until *after* we conceived Danny."

"What changed?"

"I don't know. And everyone just assumed I had postpartum depression, but I was just tired of the abuse, Jase," I said, exhausted now just thinking about it. "And I couldn't say that to him, couldn't even talk to him about how it made me feel, because it killed him inside."

"Did it though?"

"Don't be an ass, Jase. You *know* David. He was destroyed by what this hex had done to him, and he couldn't take anymore either. It wasn't..." I sighed with frustration. "I need you, no, I need *everyone* to understand that the last forty years hasn't been this horribly abusive relationship, like you all seem to think—based on absolutely nothing but your own assumptions! There were moments. Just *moments*. And it wasn't him."

"Oh, right, it was the *hex*?" he scoffed. "Just like it's not the fault of the alcoholic."

"He's not the villain here, Jase. And I'm not a victim. You just don't understand."

"I want to, Ara." He moved in and hugged me again, closing his arms around my head. "I'm trying. But it's hard. None of it makes sense—"

"That's because you're all thinking of him as this horribly abusive man that beat me over the years, and it wasn't like that. The surges started out happening only every year or so, and they were nothing worse than a snappy David who could say really mean things," I said into his chest, my own breath coming back warm off him. "I went to Drake for help as soon as I realized it was the hex, but he said there was nothing he could do. We had to live with it if we loved each other but..."

"Easier said than done."

"Sometimes, yeah. I mean, I loved our life—without the surges. But..." I fought really hard not to cry, feeling myself shrink with shame. "I just wish someone could have helped us, because I love David, but he's always been so commanding," I added, my tone rising up in question, as though Jase might not know what I meant. He nodded though. "I love that about him.

I do. But when he was suffering a surge, that commanding air became dangerous and impossible to compete with. And I was so alone in it. And so was he. After it ended, he was always just… *so* utterly devastated, and so was I, but I couldn't let that show. I…"

"Show *me*," he said, sliding his hands into my hair to hold my head. "Take me back. Show me what it was like. Make me understand so I know I'm not about to leave you in the hands of a man who doesn't deserve to live."

"Even if you were, that's none of your business or your concern," I demanded, curling my fingers around his to draw them away from my face, but he held on tighter. "You don't own me. You don't get to decide what's best for me."

"Yes I do. Because I'm the one giving up my life for your future, Ara, and because I have loved you since the day I met you. I've never stopped," he reasoned. "So don't tell me I don't have a say—"

"Your stance in this relationship is at my discretion—"

"Don't do that. Don't shut me out. I care about you." He shook my face affectionately. "I need to know I'm not dying for nothing—for a future where you end up leaving him anyway after he does something unspeakable."

"That will never happen," I said, and I meant it.

"Why?"

I sighed, closing my eyes. He wasn't going to let up. He needed to see why no amount of abuse would make me leave David, even if I got so tired of it that I had to walk away for a while. This love was eternal. After everything we fought for, not even a hex would destroy the unbreakable bond.

And yes, if I was in a relationship like this with a man who was abusive just because he was a dick, I *would* leave. But without that hex, David would never be this way. How could I abandon him because he had a disease, a sickness that changed him sometimes?

I just needed everyone to understand that he was a king, a father, kind and loving and respectful. He brushed my hair, he bought me tampons and hot water bottles when I had my period, he took Danny to the park when I needed five minutes, and he made lunches for Aubrey for school. That was the man I married—sandwiches at the kitchen counter and ironing the school uniforms when I forgot—and the hexed version was just someone I had to tolerate now and then because it wasn't right to hate him for something he had no control over.

"Before I show you this, you have to understand that I love him, and that I am happy with him. I haven't been miserable my whole life, Jase. Only when he surged for long periods of time."

He drew his bottom lip up with cynicism. "He's not the villain, is that what you're trying to say?"

"Yes," I snapped back. "And you'll understand that in a minute, and then you'll owe me an apology for that smug grin."

"Then, by all means, enlighten me."

Pushing the thoughts into his mind, in case he couldn't read them as easily while he was human, I took him back to the first time David was nasty, before we understood that it was a hex. Jase needed to see it in progression to understand how I got to the point where I decided I could never leave David; why he had to die to save a man, a relationship that, by any other standards, would probably be doomed.

"Do you remember your first human birthday party?" I said. "Right after Safia damaged your brain and you came back to us, human but not the same."

"Yes. It was by the lake. We played football, and Sam and I were buddies back then."

I smiled, thinking back to the autumn sun and the orange

leaves, the picnic blanket and Jase, so young then as a human. "David could be unintentionally mean sometimes. He would snap, or grab my arm, but underneath that, there was always a look of affection and playful annoyance. It was just who he was, and he loved me enough that he never really meant anything by it. But that day, that was when I saw the first of it. I just didn't know what it was."

"What do you mean?"

"I had so much faith in our love that when Morgana told me the hex would never leave his bones, I honestly thought it wouldn't be a problem. I brushed it so far to the back of my mind that it actually took me some time to realize I wasn't always dealing with the same David." I laughed, in spite of myself. "I, stupidly, thought love could actually conquer anything."

"If only."

I showed him how we'd left the party in a hurry because we thought there might be a way to resurrect Drake. When we arrived back home—to Vicki's house, in the bedroom that was once Mike's—I started throwing things into a suitcase. David reached across and snagged my wrist, holding it there, so I turned my head to smile at him and ask what was wrong, but his eyes were cold. He looked at me like he didn't even know me. There was no love there, no affection, and it was an empty, piercing sort of look.

"What's wrong?" I asked.

"Are you some kind of fucking idiot." He reached into the suitcase and pulled out his jeans. "We're going to Loslilian, Ara. I won't wear *jeans* there. I'm the fucking king."

I looked at the jeans in his hand, my heart sinking. "Just put them back then. What does it matter?"

"What matters is that I should be able to rely on you—for

everything. But if I can't even turn my back while you pack a suitcase, what good are you?"

He stormed out of the room and the door closed only slightly. I watched his shadow in the bright afternoon light as he walked down the stairs, and a lump formed in my throat.

"I figured he was just stressed about Drake, because he was so invested in my happiness that the idea that I'd lose hope was too much for him," I explained. "When I went downstairs with the suitcase, he acted like nothing had happened and so I thought maybe I'd overreacted or misread it."

"But you were crying," he said, swiping his thumb along my cheekbone as he looked into the memory.

"I figured I was being melodramatic. That maybe he'd meant it playfully and I just didn't catch on because I was worried about Drake. I mean, this was David. My loving, sweet, caring David. He would *never* treat me that way."

"And yet you were afraid to ask him, weren't you? You were afraid to ask if he was joking because you didn't want him to make you feel silly."

"Yes, but I asked anyway."

We both looked back on the memory.

"Did you mean that… before?" I asked David, pulling my seatbelt on and adjusting my visor in the front seat of the car.

"What?" he said, turning his head as he looked both ways down the street before taking the corner.

"In the bedroom, you were kind of a bit… nasty."

"Nasty?" he scoffed, laughter and disbelief taking over his expression. "What do you mean? When?"

"You snapped at me when I was packing the suitcase. Called me an idiot," I reminded him.

"Oh, come on, Ara. That wasn't snapping!" He shook his

head with annoyance. "And I *didn't* call you an idiot. I wouldn't do that."

I thought back to that moment, when those words had shattered me and, suddenly, I wasn't actually sure if he did say them.

"Maybe you're about to get your period, sweetheart," he offered. "You know how you get."

I did. He was actually right about that. I did get very snappy and sometimes even I called people names if they asked me the wrong question on the week before my period. But I wasn't anywhere near my period, and yet, I felt like maybe I'd just misread the entire thing. Now, I felt stupid.

I nodded, looking out the window, and let it go.

"I didn't know what it was then," I said to Jason, coming back from the memory. "I didn't even know what gaslighting was. I'd heard of it but didn't understand it. And that same sort of thing happened again a few more times, to the point where David even started apologizing, but things didn't get bad until a few years later when we went out to Loslilian for an annual House meeting."

"What happened then?" he asked, his hair lashing into his eyes in the fierce wind, but he didn't move it away. He didn't take his hands down from my face, not even for a second.

My mind left this world as my eyes left his lips, where they sat slightly apart, revealing the small white teeth there. I went back to a moment in bed, seeing David's lips, exactly the same as Jason's. In that time, life had been good. We were so in love, living this perfect dream that we'd always wanted. The sun was bright, it was spring, and we left two-year-old Elora with her nanna while we took some much-needed time away at the manor. Two whole weeks of him and me. We finished with the meetings and all orders of business, and closed our bedroom door on the world. They brought our food to us, we made love over and over again—"Didn't need to see that," Jase said with a laugh, lifting me from the memory for a moment—and we were actually dreading going back home, even though we missed our baby.

"God, so many memories here," David remarked, pulling my naked body to his chest as he looked up at the plain glass dome above us, the morning sun shining brightly through it. The stained glass had been destroyed and then replaced after Drake rescued me in here that day when the House were going to lock me away for adultery.

"Everywhere we look there's a memory," I said, but my mind went to a moment with Jason, where we sat on the settee—my legs over his lap—after spending the entire night on the lighthouse talking. It had been a magical night, and I'd never felt that close to anyone before, like the whole world was out in front of us and we only had to take it. I didn't mean to reflect on it that way, but in a flash moment of unguarded thought, David saw it.

He sat up, pushing me away from his arms. "How can you think like that when you're lying naked beside me?"

"As if you care," I remarked with a small laugh. "I've thought about worse than that a hundred times lying naked in your arms and it never bothered you before."

As I reached out to touch him and bring him back to me, he jerked away, and the same cold expression I'd seen several times before looked back at me in place of the loving husband—the one who, in his eyes, no words or thoughts I could say or think would ever be wrong. Our love was so solid that I could openly admit to wanting a blood-only threesome with Jason and he would only ever try to think of ways to make it happen for me. So why did this suddenly bother him?

Unless it wasn't him in the room with me right now.

My mind flashed back to Morgana standing right there by the door, her words:

"I give no guarantees that he makes a full recovery," she'd told us when she lifted his hex—the one she placed on him to make him hate me.

"What? Why?" I'd asked.

"Because the spell I used was an expansion spell."

"What does that mean?"

"It means it gets worse as time goes on," she explained. "Starts out mild, takes a while to fully possess the host but, when it does, it's permanent."

"Permanent?"

"Yup, and I'd say he was about…" She sung the last word while she considered David. "Seventy-percent consumed. So, yeah, good luck getting the old David back."

"Oh God." I folded my lips in to stop my face crumpling, but my chin quivered horridly as my eyes filled with blinding tears.

"That's enough taunting, Morgana. Will he be okay or not?" Falcon asked.

"No way of knowing. Yet. I mean, at seventy percent, chances are he'll always have some niggling pocket of hatred for her, and I can't fix that."

And it sunk in, shocking me back to my room and to David with his cold eyes. I'd seen the effects of that hex while he was bound by it. It was nasty. And he was nasty along with it. He had that same look in his eye now.

Could that be it? Could that be what she meant when she said it would never die? Could it be that the mean man who had surfaced over the past few years wasn't David and his dark personality at all, it was just the hex taking control?

This changed everything.

I shifted back, trying to think and trying to gain control of the situation. If this was like some kind of flourish, surge maybe, where the hex laid dormant and then bubbled up, then I wasn't dealing with my David right now. And that David—the dark personality, all the bad of Man in one soul, mixed with a nasty blood hex like that—he was dangerous.

The only way to find out for sure was to do what I did last time: take him to the forest and see if he was in control or if it was the hex.

"So you're devaluing my emotions right now by stuffing them all under an umbrella that you want to call the hex?" he said with a disdainful snap to his tone. "You can't backswing the blame for what you did with him by making this about me."

"David, it's just… you've never been bothered by it before. You understood that I'd always love him—"

"And maybe now I'm tired of it!" he yelled, snagging my arm in a pressing grip. He pushed up so quickly and dragged me out of bed that I didn't have a moment to get my footing. I struggled to bend my knees under me and stand up, but he hauled me across the hardwood floors and shoved my ribs into the settee, my bare skin scratching against the rough fabric. "Is this what you want? You want to go back to that night and fuck him!"

"David." I tried to turn around, but he grabbed my head and shoved my face into the cushion so harshly I hit my nose. It didn't bleed, but it made my eyes water.

"Answer me!" he shouted, coming down to my level, his dick and balls hanging there out in the open as I looked at him, too afraid to meet his eyes. He grabbed the back of my head, scrunching my hair up tightly in a fist, and my heart just broke. This wasn't my David. That hold, the hex, it was getting worse.

"I said, answer me," he stated with an eerie calm, reaching across to pinch the flesh on my ribs. He closed it tightly between his thumb and forefinger, twisting it so slowly the pain built in layers until I started crying. I shoved his hand off when I couldn't take anymore and hid my face in my arms, sobbing uncontrollably. I didn't want this. I didn't want to live like this. If this is how it would be, if this was the hex and it was getting worse, what was I supposed to do?

"What's wrong?" David asked. "That can't have hurt you—"

"I'm not crying because you hurt me. I'm crying because I miss you."

"Miss me? I'm right here." He turned and sat down with his spine against the edge of the settee.

"No, you're not. My David would never do this. My David would never be upset by a thought I had. He'd never pinch me!"

"You could have pushed me away."

"I shouldn't have to. The man I love would just never do something like that."

"I am the man you love, and I did," he stated. "Or are you trying to say *Jason* would never do that?"

My brow and mouth folded into a tight mesh of unspeakable emotions. He stared at me like I was the ugliest face on the planet, so I dropped it into my arms again and let the tears fall down over my nose and chin, dripping on to my inner thigh where it rested under me. "I love you," I whimpered. "Just know that, okay? Just know that I love you and I know you don't mean any of this."

"Argh, for God's sake." He stood up, his leg creasing under his butt as he walked away. "Nothing worse than a whining, self-pitying little slut."

I bit my lip, holding back everything I wanted to say. There was no point arguing because he didn't even mean that. It needed no defense because it wasn't a real statement.

"I couldn't convince him to come with me to the forest and show him it was the hex," I said, coming back to the beach with the hard wind and the grains of ice-cold sand making my ankles sting. "And even after he calmed down, he wouldn't speak with me about it. It became a forbidden topic. And I think he just didn't want to understand, as if maybe it would go away. Which is because it usually did. He surged, and it ended, and life went on."

"But it didn't."

"Not for good, no. He only surged maybe every six months at that point—and it was short-lived and usually only involved nasty words or a snappy comment—and when we went five years without one, I actually thought maybe it had run its course. We were really happy, Jase."

Jason shook his head. "I had no idea this was going on, Ara. Not back then. It wasn't until I came back and opened Knight Labs that I caught on—"

"And you were the only one who ever did, aside from Falcon—"

"No I wasn't. People knew, Ara. They *still* know." He shook his head, his sharp fangs showing with an arrogant smile. "Even though you directly told me, and Lily, that he's *never* hit you."

"That's because he doesn't. My David…" I said regretfully. "He never hit me—"

"But the other one did—*does*? The hexed version of him?" he asked sarcastically.

I nodded. "Look, Jase, this all needs to stop. None of this is anyone else's business, and no one would be any the wiser if it weren't for Aubrey, and yet now, I feel like I have to explain something to people that's so complicated I can never expect you to understand. I get it, I get that you want to rise to my defense, tell me to leave him, but he's the victim here. You don't know what this does to him."

"Says every abused woman ever—"

"You don't know anything about it."

"Don't I?" he said, his brow raised and ready for a challenge, because he'd come from an abusive relationship too. He knew. He knew better than anyone.

"But yours is different Jase, because Lily abused you simply because she was heinous. David would never do that. You know that. He would never hurt me."

"But he does. Hex or not, you should have left."

"You're only saying that because you want me to. You want me to leave him, maybe even kill him, and be with you."

"The last thing I want is my brother's death, and since meeting Jules and finally gaining some self-respect, I certainly don't want *his wife*," he said, narrowing one scornful eye at me, "a woman who will never love me. I deserve better than that, Ara. But so do you."

"I have better than what your uneducated opinions are painting my relationship to be. You have no right to comment, Jase, because you're not in it. David has a lot more control now since he admitted to himself that it was the hex—"

"But I bet it took something pretty bad for him to finally admit it," he said sharply. "He's always been an arrogant prick—"

"Yes, okay, if you must know. He went too far one day, and he hit me. And I'm glad he did, because that changed everything."

"How?"

"I'd asked Drake and Morgana for help, and to her credit, she went through every book, talked to every witch, read every scroll, looking for a way to help, but she never found anything," I advised, brushing the sea spray off my cold cheeks. "That year, when all this happened, when I finally made David understand that it was a hex, we were at Loslilian again. And I'd just spent an hour talking to Drake the night before about it all, telling him it didn't seem to be an issue anymore, and he was overjoyed—"

"But you celebrated too soon?"

I nodded, taking Jason back to a morning when I stepped out of the forest after my dawn walk to find David waiting for me. His arms were folded, my cloak tucked in with them, and he smiled as I walked over, holding it out for me to step into.

Falcon came out behind me, though, and when he nodded his greeting, David's eyes darkened. He drew the cloak away and wouldn't let me cover myself. "Were you fucking him?"

"What?" I laughed, reaching for thc cloak.

David jerked it back. "Answer the question, Ara."

"Why would you think that?" I smirked, looking at Falcon.

Falcon just shook his head and walked past us with a long sigh. "I don't know what this is about," he said, turning to walk backward as he said his piece to David, "but you know better than that."

He left us to it then and I closed both hands over my breasts, pressing my thighs together. "David, give me my cloak."

He balled it up and tossed it with the arm of a vampire into the middle of the clearing, where the construction workers had stopped laying bricks for the new university and were sitting down for bit of breakfast.

I looked at David, slinking back into the shadows of the forest a little, both where I'd be safe from the eye of any onlookers and where the grasp of the tree's power would keep me safe from this hex magic. "You're going to have to go get that," I demanded. "That was a really shitty thing to do."

"So was fucking another man."

I clenched my jaw, exhaling through my nose slowly so I wouldn't start a fight with him over this. He was baiting me. He wanted it. I could feel how hungry he was for a fight—to release the buildup of this energy after he'd played with it for a moment.

But not feeding into that was probably worse.

"Say something," he demanded with that unnerving calm. "What? You walk out here, naked, fuck another man, and you have nothing to say for yourself?"

"I'm not going to let you drag me into an argument, David."

His eyes went down my naked body so slowly I felt ashamed, stopping on the dark patch of hair between my legs. He took a calculated step toward me and reached into the shadows of the forest, taking my wrist. "Do you think I like sharing my wife with Nature's perverted eye? Do you think I like the fact that you walk naked, where anyone can see you? You're a slut, Ara," he said, yanking my arm. With a hard gasp, I jerked out of the forest in one swift move and hit the ground as he struck me across the head. It jarred me, stopped my heart and made me want to scream and cry, unable to believe it, but the part of me who'd been through this before knew better. I rolled as I hit the ground and spun my knees until I was on my feet, darting into the forest before he could grab me.

David followed, stalking along like a serial killer with all the time in the world. Morgana had removed the magic in the hex, but it was still in his bones. I wasn't even sure that the magic within this forest would protect me from him now, but I had to try.

I stopped by the tree and turned to face him, covering my exposed parts, my ear bleeding where his hand had struck me, and watched his eyes as he stomped over to me. My heart thumped like a fist in my throat. If he was still consumed by this hex in here, he'd hurt me right now. But that wasn't what worried me. What worried me was that I'd have to fight him back. My sweet, loving husband, I'd have to hurt him to stop him from hurting me. He wasn't himself right now. Any idiot could see that. It wouldn't be right to hurt him, not even in self-defense.

"David," I said, putting both hands up as his lashed out.

But he grabbed my arm, and when I looked up from his soft dark lips, hanging open in shock, to his tear-struck eyes, I knew I was safe. I relaxed my shoulders and closed my eyes, stepping into his arms as I felt them close around me.

"What have I done?" he whispered, cradling my bleeding ear against his shirt. "I'm so sorry, my love. I am so, so sorry."

"It wasn't you—"

"The hex," he said, squeezing me a little tighter. "You tried to warn me. So many times. You've been saying it for *years*! Why didn't I listen?"

"You're listening now."

David nodded, swallowing so hard I heard it. "We have to do something about this—"

"We can't. I've had Morgana working on it for years, David. There's no way to undo a curse in someone's bones."

His chest caved with a ragged breath and I cried as he did, feeling the weight of the truth sink us down to the ground. I sat there naked in his arms, with the warmth of the tree around us, and worried about the future, not sure what to do or where to go. All I knew, all that was clear to me, was that this wasn't his fault. It wasn't mine. He didn't do this, and we couldn't undo this.

"I hate myself, Ara. I've… for years, I've asked myself why I treat you that way and I promise to do better. But it wasn't me." He squeezed me tightly, pressing his jaw to my head. "I need you to know that. I would never do those things. Please, please understand that. I *love* you, mon amour—more than anything in this entire world, and every single one of those times I hurt you… it just feels like a dream, like it didn't really happen." He cried into my hair for a moment, his voice broken. "I wish it didn't happen."

"This won't ruin us. I vowed once before to stay by your side no matter what, and this is just one of those no-matter-whats."

"No, I'm sorry, Ara, it can't be," he said, spit flaring around his lips as he spoke in his grief, his brow and eyes screwed up with the weight. "I feel like I'm in this endless nightmare now, I —" He coughed out as he broke down crying again, his mind going back over the times he mistreated me, even the ones where it wasn't that bad. But he knew; he knew he would never be that way and he just couldn't believe it, couldn't fathom a world where he treated me like that, or where I, his sweet, beautiful girl —the girl in the yellow dress—had to endure it. "Do you know what you are to me? Do you understand that you're my reason to exist? How can I possibly live with this—live in a world where I abuse you?"

"You don't. It's this hex—"

"No, it's *me*. Even under the hex, a man like Falcon, like my brother, would never do this." He reached over and swept some blood from my ear. "This is my darkness, who I am."

"It's who you were as a man before you met me. I know you treated women this way in the past, but you would never have done this to me if the hex didn't make you justify it."

"But if the hex is incurable…" His eyes searched mine because he didn't want to finish that sentence, but he needed to see that I understood. "It's getting worse. You've seen it. So what does that mean?"

"It means we have to endure it. For love, we have no choice," I said firmly, holding his gaze with a thousand lifetimes of determination. "I won't let this ruin us. If it does, she wins. Morgana wins. We can't let that happen."

David shut his eyes, dropping his head. "I'm sorry, Ara, but I won't live like this."

"What are you saying?"

"If you won't leave me, I'll leave you." He looked up at me. "I can't live in a world where I have to hurt you."

"And you can't live in a world where I'm not a part of it either."

"I will if I have to—"

"But we just got that life, David. Everything we ever wanted! We got it, and for the sake of a few moments of pain, or suffering, I won't give up on it. I won't!" I demanded, breaking to tears. "And if you try to leave me, I'll die. I'll—"

"You can't." He grabbed my arms. "You have Elora—"

"*You* have Elora. *We* have Elora. There is no me without you, David. There never has been. Never can be. And maybe that's twisted, sordid, stupid, I don't care," I cried, seeing eternity expand around me, trying to imagine for even a second if he wasn't there within it, beside me. "I won't lose you over this. I can't. Otherwise, what was the point of any of it?"

He leaned forward and swept my face against his shoulder, wrapping his legs around me next and closing me up within the safety of his entire body. "Shhh, it's okay, my love. We'll figure it out. I promise. I won't leave until you tell me to."

"Don't make me leave either, okay?" I cried, my voice barely audible. "I can't live without you. Not after everything we fought for."

"Okay, I won't make you leave. I just—"

"Don't say it. Don't say you just can't handle hurting me—"

"But I can't," he affirmed. "Do you have any idea how I feel right now, Ara? Imagine our little Elora. Imagine her soft blonde hair and innocent green eyes, the way she looks at us, trusts us. She is everything to us. We'd die for her. Now imagine hitting her. Imagine looking at her coldly—that little girl—looking at her like she means nothing, and then imagine how she'd look at you if you hit her."

I nodded, crying into my hand because it hurt just to think about that. "But I'm not a victim, David. *You* are—"

"No. I'm a monster, and I want to tear myself apart for what I've done here." He looked at my ear, smoothing away the blood with the tip of his thumb. "What kind of man am I if I can hurt you this way?"

"One I love. One I vowed to stand by, protect, for all time. And I will protect our relationship now as fiercely as you would if this were in reverse."

I slipped out of the memory, the tears from that time staining my cheeks in this one, and looked up at Jason as the sun dipped behind a cloud and made it easier to see.

"That's hard," Jase said, pressing his brow to mine, his hot breath coming across my lips. "I don't want to, but I *can* understand why it is the way it is with you now. I understand why you can't hate him or fight him back."

"That's not why I don't fight back."

"Huh?"

"I don't fight back, but it's not just because he's a victim as much as me. It's because I did fight him. I raised my hand to stop him when he tried to hit me. I even hit him back once. And it would only make him hit harder and then regret it all so much deeper after."

Jase clucked his tongue. "I can only imagine."

"And I tried running away," I told him. "I tried hiding until the surge passed, but it only made him angrier, and he'd hunt me down and hit me until I couldn't breathe—"

"Aw, Ara." His hands tightened on my face.

"Until one day, I learned that if I just took a hit in the first few days of a surge, it simmered down," I explained. "It went away. If I fought back, it fed it. If I ran, it fed it. If I just accepted one hit, not too hard, it eased it. And it would go away, and things would be okay again, and David wouldn't bleed in deep regret for weeks after." I sighed to release all the tension. "I didn't have a choice."

"What about when he was human? After you had Aubrey? Was it as bad then?"

"No. I mean, he fell under that stupid First Woman's Curse, but once I undid that, he was lovely. Really lovely. And I think, without the vampire as his first nature, David's not really as dark."

"You think being a vampire magnifies it?"

"As being a vampire does for many human traits, yes," I said. "So those human days were pretty blissful and even after that, when he entered the vampire world again, things were okay. Maybe once every six years he'd have a surge. It's not like my whole life was miserable."

"I know," he said with a soft, kind smile.

"Until Daniel came along."

Jase looked up from his wandering thoughts with white shock. "What do you mean?"

"After Lily drugged us, it started happening every few weeks or even days?" My eyes widened, a feeling of breathlessness taking me back to those haunting days.

"And it was worse than before?"

"Yes. But as long as I didn't fight him, as long as I let him, or sometimes *pushed him* to hit me within the first three days, that's all it would ever be. Just a hit. Usually across the face. And then he'd be over it."

"He hit you while you were pregnant! With *my* son?"

"He only hit me across the face. Never anywhere that would hurt the baby."

Jason rubbed his brow, exhaling. "Hex or not, I can't honestly say I think he did the right thing by making you stay with him."

"He didn't *make* me."

"Yes he did. Whether you believe that or not is irrelevant. He made you stay."

"No, I could have left so many times, Jase. He begged me to—"

"I doubt that."

"He did. Look." I grabbed his arm and pulled him closer, reaching up to touch his stubbly cheek. He closed his hand over mine and shut his eyes, going back with me to a dark night outside a university just a few years ago.

Jason saw his own face through my eyes, and gasped because it was such a leap from one place to another, so unexpected, that his mind couldn't make sense of the two versions of life for a moment.

He stepped out of his car, his mind on the evening ahead, and I froze on the spot, watching him. He wasn't the Jase I knew a year ago. He was thicker, heavier and broader, as if he'd been eating, sleeping, as if he was happy.

His jaw dropped when he sensed me, eyes sweeping up a moment later to find me standing here in the darkness of the cool night.

"What are you doing here?" he barked so aggressively I drew a breath, ready for a fight.

"Jase," I said, my heart breaking and then swimming across the decades of love I'd carried for him, where it knitted back together as soon as I looked into those eyes. "We've been looking for you for a year—"

"Well, you've found me." He spread his arms out and then pressed the button to lock his car, pocketing his keys, voice thick with annoyance. "What do you want, Ara?"

"I want you to come home—"

"I'm not going back."

"Jase, we can work it out—"

"Work what out?" he demanded, his voice high as he fought to restrain the emotion. "Lily has been cheating on me since we met, Ara—"

"I really think you've got it all wrong, Jase," I said, hoping I was right. Even if I wasn't, Lily loved him. If she had made a mistake, they could work it out. "Elora saw it, remember? She's seen you happy with Lily."

"Elora's visions can't be trusted. When has she ever been right? Ever! She was wrong about Lily—"

"She's desperate, Jase," I told him, hoping he'd understand what this meant. If I couldn't convince him to come back... "She'll go to any lengths to get you back."

"I'm not going back, Ara. Ever!" he yelled, his eyes wide and his body screaming at me to back off as he turned away.

It wasn't working. If he wouldn't listen to reason, listen to me, then I'd have to leave it to Lily. But he couldn't avoid this any longer. It wasn't getting any better by allowing it all to fester. For everyone's sake, they needed to argue this out.

I walked forward and moved to drop him under a deep sleep, but he wheeled around so fast I thought he might hit me.

"Don't. Touch. Me," he warned, the intention of a madman flaring in his gaze.

"I don't want to, Jase, but if you don't come with me, Lily told me to drag you home. You're family and we have to work this out—"

"If you move… if you blink in so much as a threat to put me out, Ara, I will kill you—"

"We both know you better than that—"

"Stop it!" His hands thrust out onto my arms and he shook me hard, his teeth caged. "I am warning—"

"Whoa!" A small blonde girl came shooting out from behind a tree like a little rebel warrior and wedged herself between us. Jason let go, dread filling his face. "Hey," she roared. "Don't you touch her. You don't get to touch her like that!"

"Juliet." Jase sighed, rubbing the bridge of his nose like he did when one of the kids asked him a difficult question.

"No. Shut up and don't say a goddamn word, Mr. Knight!" she yelled, hugging her books so tight her fingers were white. She glanced back at me. "Are you okay? Did he hurt you?"

"I… I'm fine," I stammered, still completely shocked by this fearsome little wolf. But I had someone on my side right now, and he couldn't stop me from putting him out if he wanted to protect her, which, clearly, he did. I folded my arms, smirking at him.

"Jules," Jason began, his pleading eyes reaching for her mind, as if to warn her to run.

"Don't you 'Jules' me, Jason Knight," she snapped. "Call me the crazy feminist, call it an overreaction if you like, but when I see a guy manhandling a woman, I will step in and whoop some ass. I may be small"—she lifted her chin, pushing her glasses back on—"but I know kung fu."

Jason's mouth popped, his eyes warming with a smile. And it all sunk in. He'd fallen in love. He'd come here to get away from Lily, but that wasn't the reason he couldn't come back. This little firecracker of a girl, with her glasses and silky blonde hair, had captured his heart, and in one cute move had won him over for good. Kung fu.

Jason wanted to tell her to go away, to run as far as she could, but he was too shaken up by the sudden realization that maybe he was falling in love with her.

"I get it," I said, backing away. "That's it, isn't it?"

"Ara," he said, coming after me, but the girl moved between us.

"Jules, I'm not going to hurt her. Do you really think I'd hurt her?" he asked, cut because he knew she did think that, and he just wasn't, nor would he ever be, that kind of guy.

"That's what it looked like from where I was standing," she said.

"Just…" He showed his hands then gently grabbed her upper arms and shifted her aside, coming to stand before me. I felt his connection to her fade as he looked at me, felt him cry deep within his soul as his mind flashed back for a moment to the night we made love. The night he left. "Ara, I know you all want me back. Okay? But there is more to the story than what she's telling, and that's why I won't return."

"Jase." My heart broke as I saw something there in his eyes—something I thought, until now, that I had only imagined. "I miss you. We all miss you. But… Just…"

She's good for me, Ara, Jase said in thought. *For the first time, I found someone good for me, who's never loved anyone else in her life. I'm not second to her heart like I am with you, with Lily. I can't go back to that.*

I fought hard not to think of the baby boy in the hotel room with David, waiting to meet his father, who didn't even know he existed. Jason was happy right now, and no one had a right to take it from him. Not even me. Daniel would destroy this, and I had to protect it as fiercely as I'd protect our baby boy.

"I'm just glad to see you're okay," I said, fighting back tears.

"Then please go," he pleaded, and as his hand touched mine,

I thought about how right it felt on my body when we made love, when we made Daniel. Everything had been ripped apart by what Lily did to us that night, but something so right had come from it, and I still loved Jase in so many ways. Walking away right now, I knew I was letting him go for good.

"'Kay." I leaned in and kissed his cheek, wishing so hard that I could tell him about his son and that he'd still stay here and fall in love with this girl if he knew.

But he wouldn't. And yet he needed to be free. He needed to be away from Lily. So he could never find out about Daniel.

"I love you. I'll talk to Lily."

When I backed away, I felt him hold onto me with his heart too. He sensed the ache, he sensed the words I wanted to say to him, but he was afraid to ask. He was afraid that whatever I came to tell him would make him want to go home, and he just couldn't do that. But he didn't want me to leave either. He just didn't want me here messing up this new possibility.

"I'm glad you didn't tell me then," Jase said, closing his eyes regretfully as we lifted out from the memory. "I learned a lot about myself while I was with Jules, and I needed that. I needed someone to love me like I was the only thing that mattered."

"And now you've lost her as well," I said sadly. "I'm so sorry, Jase."

"And I stand to lose my life, too—for a brother that's been abusing you," he snapped. "So tell me, how does this have *anything* to do with my brother being an honorable, deserving man?"

"I'm getting to that."

I showed him next how I went back to the hotel where David was waiting for me. I took off my cardigan and set it on the bed, peering into the cradle to check on the baby.

"Did he need anything while I was gone?"

"No. He was fine. Did you find my brother?"

"Yes." I looked up at him, eyes thick with tears. "I couldn't do it."

"Couldn't do what?"

"He's happy. He found someone, David. I was right there"—I looked back on the moment I reached out to put him under a sleep, how he stopped me because he knew what I was going to do. He was mean, cold. And it broke my heart a little because he'd never been that way with me. "I couldn't do it."

"Ara." David sighed my name out, moving backward to sit on the bed. He cradled his head in his hands for a moment.

"I'm sorry. I know how badly you wanted him back—"

"It's not that. That's not why I'm upset."

"Then what is it?" I asked, sitting down beside him, the smell of hotel hand soap and cheap floral air freshener filling my senses.

"I saw it all, Ara. Just now. I saw it all." He rubbed the left side of his chest. "Do you have any idea how intense your love for him is, and his for you?"

"I know—"

"No, you don't. It's like toxic gas, like a chemical that soaks the air. It's always there. At every family event, every Christmas, birthday. I ignore it but…" He looked up at me, a tear slipping past his lashes. "Now I wonder if I should."

"What do you mean?"

"I should walk away. If I am any sort of man, if I have any love for you, I should leave."

"Why?"

"I hit you, Ara," he said, kneeling down in front of me, tracing his hand over the last place he'd done it. "I can't control it even if I try. And you will eventually leave me for it. I'll push you away. This is only getting worse. And if you wait, and he does fall for that girl, you'll lose your chance to be with him."

"David, I'm not ever going to be with Jason over you. Ever." I tossed my head back, laughing.

"See, you said it all right there are: *over me.* But it's not a him-or-me decision. It's you. *Alone.* You being abused. You suffering, miserable."

"I'm not miserable."

"Yes you are. And my brother, the only other man you love, is finally free of Lily. And this tired old argument will never end, because the fact is, you *will* leave me eventually—even a hundred years from now, after I do something worse to you—and if you didn't have me, you'd be with him. That has *always* been the case. Since our early days, Ara. It's not an either-either situation. It's… without me," he said sadly, "there's him."

I grinned, taking in his kind green eyes, swarmed with worry, and thought back to the moment the little boy in the cradle beside us had come into the world—the look of both immense pride and love that had shone within David's eyes. *That* was love. Pure and unadulterated. It was David, who he is at his core, without a hex or any interference, and *that* was the man I married. The man I made promises to. The man I would fight for, or die.

"You're an idiot," I said.

"What?" He frowned, but it was atop a half smile.

"You idiot." I grabbed his cheeks and leaned in. "I am never leaving you. You can beat me brainless and I will still be here, right up until it's no longer the hex making you do it. Right up until you, my sweet David, are the one who hits me."

"That will never happen."

I leaned in to kiss his soft lips, ignoring the stale taste of coffee on his breath. "Then I will never leave you."

"Do you think that's true?" Jason asked, bringing us back to the present. "Do you really think you will *never* leave him?"

"I can't say. I know I can if I want. I know he'd support my decision with all of his heart. But I still just don't know if I ever could."

"I think you need therapy. You may be immortal, but that's a classic case of beaten wife syndrome."

"It's not." I laughed to myself. "I'm not, nor have I ever been, the type of woman to be beaten down by someone. I will admit, I was at the end of my tether before all of this nightmare and kidnapping began, and I had spent maybe a millisecond thinking about taking a break from him, but only because it was so frequent at that point, but…"

"You're afraid of being alone," he said accusingly. "You always were. That's why you haven't left him."

"Oh, that's bullshit, Jase," I asserted calmly, because I didn't need to fight over something that wasn't true. "I haven't left him because I love him. It has nothing to do with being alone."

"I think it does—"

"I can be alone," I assured him. "I don't like it. I'm the kind of woman who needs that *one close person*, a life partner, I guess, or a best friend. And there's nothing wrong with that. It doesn't make me needy or diminish my sense of independence—"

"I know. I wasn't saying that. I just… I think it was a major factor in your decision to stay."

"But it wasn't, because…" I looked up into his caring green eyes, feeling mine sparkle with tears in the sun. "I wouldn't have been alone, and we both know it."

"What do you mean?"

"After I saw that vision of our alternative life, and I saw how you reacted to that future too, I knew that if I ever did leave him, if it ever got that bad and I couldn't stand one more day, I'd have you," I said boldly. "I knew you'd leave Lily for me."

At first, his eyes sparkled with love and affection as he heard that, but then it all burned away with cold frustration. "Then why are you giving him my soul? You love me so much its intoxicating to others when they feel it around us. And you know David will eventually wear you down and make you leave—"

"I don't know anything, Jase." I looked down at my feet, stepping back from his arms. "I don't know what will happen between me and David in the future—if we maybe do break up for a few decades, get some space, clear out the hurt and then come back to each other—but it has to be me and him. It will *always* be that way, unto death."

"*My* death." He pointed to his chest, leaning forward, and then sent that finger off to aim at nothing. "Not his."

"It's not like you're not willing, Jase."

"I'm willing to do it in a world where *I don't have you*, Ara." He gently took my arm, drawing me closer to make his point. "But after what you just told me, how can you expect me to just lie down and die!"

"And how can you expect me to love you if you won't?" I said, and the honesty struck him right in his heart. "You'd be forcing me to kill David—"

"No. I didn't do this. Lily did! This is not my fault."

"It's not mine either, or David's."

Jase sighed, running his hands over his silky brown hair and flattening it down before it all stood up against the wind. "You know what, fuck my fucking life," he said in a breaking voice, turning away. "I fucking give up."

"Jase?" I called. "Jase!"

But he didn't turn back.

We could fight. We could scream and yell and cry, but within a few hours, we were always friends again, as if nothing happened. I felt like maybe we should talk about it all, but what was the point? We were both trying so hard to just live out these days, enjoy time together, and not get caught going around in circles with the same argument.

Jase sent me an easy smile as he hopped up out of his chair, almost knocking a pawn down on the table between us.

"Careful." I straightened it.

"Sorry." He laughed. "I'll be right back."

"And bring milk," I called. "You can't have brownies without milk."

"You're lucky you can eat your emotions and not get fat," he noted, hugging the doorway of the common room, that gorgeous brow furrowed in mock irritation. "I'm human now. If I keep eating like you, I'll get fat."

My eyes strayed to his tummy, a brow arching. "You mean 'fatter'?" I joked.

He shot a straight finger at me, eyes wide with playful insult. "You're lucky you're so adorable."

I laughed, smiling up at Arthur as he came in. "Hey you."

"Hello." He stood in the doorway with an air about him that had me looking up from the game I was trying to win—or cheat at.

"What's wrong?" I asked.

"Lord Eden has contacted me."

"Why?"

"He has always fought to protect the humans from great harm—stepping in during the wars, or when serial killers are left to roam without intervention."

"And?"

"And…" He came all the way into the room in a sweeping long step, his head down, and sat on the chair beside me. "Word has reached him about David."

"What about him?"

"There is an epidemic out there, Amara, of missing persons." He cleared his throat, sniffing once. "My nephew, it seems, is no longer acting with discretion—"

"He's leaving the bodies to be found?"

"The fact that he's doing the killing in the first place is enough to have turned Vampirie's head. But, add to it that several children have gone missing—"

"Children?" I turned to face him, sliding forward on the seat. "He's killing children?"

"We don't know for certain. All we know is that sixteen children have gone missing in the last week. If it is, indeed, at David's hand, he cannot be allowed to bring any more harm." He put a hand firmly over mine. "Lord Eden has requested my assistance in bringing David in."

"Will he kill him?"

"I asked that he does not. And he is allowing us to instead lock him away, if we can hold him, until Jason is ready to pass on his soul, provided you are certain that it will alter David's evil state and restore the tree."

I brought a hand up to cover my mouth. Jase wasn't ready. *I* wasn't. I hadn't found another way to save the tree. And Daniel wasn't ready to lose his dad. He loved Jase, and I knew it would be traumatic, for both of us, to lose him right now. How could I look in to my little boy's eyes when he asked where his daddy was and tell him Jase was dead? That he was gone and never coming back? Danny would lose his shipmate, his storyteller, his airplane ride, and instead trade it in for a piece of that man inside the body of a dark, evil one who would never call Danny his son. A man that had possibly killed children.

"Can I ask you something?" Arthur said carefully.

I nodded, sweeping a tear from my chin.

He slid a little closer, bringing his head in and keeping his voice low. "What if you let David die—"

"Arthur, I just can't even think like that. I—"

"Yes, but… just imagine for a moment," he said softly. "Imagine if it was okay to love Jason. Imagine if I gave you permission, right now, if Mike, Elora, Harry—what if we all gave you permission to love Jason the way your heart has eternally longed for him—"

"I—"

"Don't deny it, Amara. I may have been living away from you all for these past ten years, but I knew you before that. And I know it killed you to make the decision to stay with David." He put both hands on my upper arms, bringing his eyes in line with mine. "You loved David, which made that decision easier, but you never stopped loving Jason, and no one ever told you that was okay."

"But David—"

"Is dead, my dear. He died when Lily turned him human and took his soul from his body," he stated, his own voice breaking. "How can you rightly bring him back when both you and Jason are happier here, in this moment of time, than you have ever been?"

"But—"

"Don't deny it. You *are* happier," he insisted. "And that's with a missing daughter, and the death of your old lives hanging heavily off your hearts right now. How can it be that you are happier now, when all is lost, than you were when you had everything?"

"I was happy then—"

"But not like this," he said, a knowing glint in his eye. "I am not asking you to erase David. I am not asking you to kill him. I am simply asking you to analyze the what if. Analyze the possibility of letting Jason live. Just look in on the way it might be and realize that there is another option. That you could continue on this path of friendship with him, maybe something more, but certainly something that lifts you both up. And you could save that tree. Not all is lost if David dies."

"But it is—"

"Because you love him. You have lived a life, a very long life, with him, and there will never be a way to replace him. Ever," he said kindly, with a century-worth of understanding, because he'd lost someone he loved too. "But you are lucky in that you have another piece of his soul. You have Jason, and you do not have to do this alone, unlike so many of us when we lose a loved one."

I thought about Danny, and what he'd want. And then I thought about Elora, and her life and Evie's. If the tree died, and Elora's soul was taken by the Silas, her daughter would forever mourn her. Her husband would forever be lost, wandering again without his soul mate. There was more to lose here than just David. This wasn't just about me losing my husband, and I had not been ready to face that until now.

Finally, the blinders were off, the truth stepping out of shadow, and I couldn't deny it any longer.

I nodded. "I can think about it, but… I have wanted to. Sometimes, when Jase looks across at me while he's playing with Danny, or when I come into the kitchen late at night to find him there, having practically read my mind and started making coffee… sometimes I do want to think about what it'd be like, but my heart won't let me."

"Of course it won't, my dear." He patted my hand. "You have

loved David for almost forty years. And it was a deep, all-encompassing love. But things change," he added, and his tone changed too, "life in this long eternity never stays the same, and you *have* had a lifetime together. If you choose to let him go, it would not be the end. For any of you."

I drew back and turned away, leaning my elbows against the table and looking out the window. "How will you bring him in? He's powerful, Arthur. Even more than me, because he uses the darkness."

He grinned, standing up and offering his hand. "I'll show you."

I walked with him along the corridor to the front entrance, wondering what he was up to. Outside, he let go of my hand and we stood on the front steps overlooking the university courtyard.

"What are we doing?" I asked.

"Just… watch." Arthur folded his arms and leaned on the doorway, looking at all the people going about their day. In that moment, every single person walking, sitting, standing, reading, drinking coffee or laughing with their friends, subtly put a finger into their nose and had a dig around, drawing the digit away then with embarrassment and shame, some wiping it on their jeans, others laughing and pointing or looking around, unsure what happened.

I laughed, turning to Arthur. And it wasn't enough just to say wow. I launched into him and threw my arms around his neck. "You're back. When did this happen?"

"Almost immediately after I was turned," he confessed. "I've been strengthening my abilities every day, but I didn't want to tell you—"

"Why?"

"Because you've been so happy." He affectionately swiped his thumb down my cheek, his eyes glinting with pride. "I knew that if you saw that, your efforts to track Aubrey down would be renewed and you'd not rest. We will never find her, Amara, and I know that. Lilith herself believes it," he said sadly. "And I just didn't want you to waste these last few months with Jason fighting for something we have little hope of achieving."

I nodded, stepping away. He was right. These last few months had been some of the brightest of my life, but it hurt to admit that, so I cloaked it away in the place where I'd always kept Jase. "When are you leaving?"

"Immediately. Vampirie is meeting me at the helipad in New York, and we will bring David back here to await your decision."

"Do I have to make it now?"

"No." He shook his head, smiling sympathetically. "We will have time. Between the great Lord Eden and myself, we should be able to contain David in a cell. For now. But a decision will need to be made."

"And you think I should let David die?"

Arthur straightened, unfolding his arms. "I think that there are times in life when we have to admit that something has come to an end. I don't want to lose my nephew, my son, but I am strong and wise enough to accept that he has had his time."

But I wasn't. And I wasn't sure I would ever be.

FALCON FLEW IN FROM HIS SET WHEN HE FOUND OUT THAT David was being brought back in, probably afraid I'd kill Jason and he wouldn't get the chance to say goodbye. He and Blade guided me down through the tunnels of the cell block to where David was being kept, both completely without words to say. Everyone had been told now. They all knew what David's dark soul had done out there, what Arthur and Lord Eden found when they subdued him, but, so far, no one had said a word to me about it. I told them I didn't want to know. I fought against them when they tried to call a Private Council meeting to discuss what to do next, because I knew what they'd say. Even now, I was afraid they were leading me down here to lock me up so they could take matters into their own hands, do what had to be done.

"Is he awake?" I asked, approaching the cell.

"No. Vampirie has put him under somehow," Blade said, his voice cold and angry.

"Is Jase coming down to see his brother?" Falcon asked. It sounded so weird when he called him Jase.

"No." I walked into the cell when Blade opened it, hugging myself. "He's with Danny."

Falcon nodded. "Is it okay if I go up and see him?"

"Sure." I smiled, reaching over to rub his arm. He placed his hand on mine, holding me there for a brief exchange of everything he wanted to say, and then turned away, sucked up by the shadows outside the cell.

"Did you know about his relationship with Jase?" I asked Blade "You were here when it was going on, right?"

Blade smirked, leaning on the wall with his hands in his pockets. "Yeah. I knew."

"Lily drugged them," I said, moving to sit on the steel-framed bed beside David, looking him over in the darkness to make sure he wasn't hurt. "But… was there anything between them besides that? Like—"

"Did they have sex outside of the potion? No. Not after that one time."

"Falcon's so…"

"Hung up?" Blade laughed. "Yeah. But Jason's like that, I

guess. I'm no pole-hugger, but I think Jason's personality makes him easy for someone like Falcon to love."

"What do you mean?"

"Falcon's manly. Jason's… not." He laughed.

"He is," I assured him. "He's just also a gentle soul, very creative and poetic, I guess. The last of the true romantics."

Blade scoffed. "You got *that* right. You know, Morgana stole Jason's journals once—"

"What?"

"She read them. And because we used to date, we got to talking one day and she told me about them."

"What about them?" I swept a lock of hair off David's brow, watching his mouth press in with his restless dreams.

"Jason said in them that he didn't have to be a man. That, with Falcon, he didn't have to be strong or hide his emotions. He could be hurt, crushed by the world, and—his words, not mine —Falcon would be the man that held onto him until it all went away."

"So he held him while he cried?" I glanced back at him.

Blade shrugged an affirmative response. And my heart peeled open and wilted. Was that all Jase needed? All this time, he'd been there for me, and I knew he was hurting too. I'd talked with him, laid with him, but he hadn't cried. And I thought maybe he was numb, but… he just didn't feel safe to cry with *me*. To be anything but a strong, capable man. A knight.

And yet he clearly needed to so badly. I wondered then if he'd spend the evening with Falcon tonight—talking in the study like old times—his chance to finally have someone hold him who wouldn't make him feel weak, who didn't want him to die or be someone else.

After I was killed by my sister and then rose from the ashes, living without my memory, David had just wanted me to be *his* Ara again, no matter what. So I completely understood how Jase felt to be second to someone's love. And it hurt.

Blade suddenly stood up off the wall then and dropped his arms to his sides, bowing his head. A second later, Lord Eden emerged from the darkness, floating into the room. His youthful face took in the scene, fixing with hatred on David's unconscious body.

"Leave us," he said firmly to Blade, who bowed to me, then left.

I didn't know why he was here or what he wanted, so I turned my attentions away from him and swept David's hair back again, running my hand along his cheek. "How is he more beautiful now, with all this darkness, than he was when he was my David?"

"If you had seen what I've seen, you would not touch him that way." He grabbed my wrist gently and moved it away, as if I were about to touch a hotplate.

"When he's his old-self again, all of this will kill him, you know?" I advised, snatching my hand back and laying it to David's cheek. "My David was nothing like this."

"The David you loved would never have done this, no. But this darkness did not taint him; it merely made him feel righteous to commit such sin."

"I don't think—"

"Your David would have changed with time, Amara. Over the centuries that passed, his darkness would've overtaken him, and you knew this." He nodded, holding my gaze. "We all knew this."

Yes, as it slowly had already, every year layering atop another, just as his surges of hatred from that hex had become stronger, happening more often. It mixed with his magically dark soul, and gradually tainted him. I could understand that he might have eventually been gone, beyond repair. But…

"He wouldn't have become this—"

"He would have. You forget," he said, holding both of my arms and making me stand. "I see all. I have looked into the future of every single possibility within the circulating energy of this world, and though it takes time, that darkness in him eventually takes hold, and he, more with each decade, becomes a man you despise."

"But with Jason's soul, he…"

"He is still the darkness of all Man, even if he carries the light. As you have seen these past months."

"But he wouldn't do what he's done if he had Jason's soul."

"Yet." Vampirie turned away.

"Then, if Jase had his soul, would he become dark, like David?"

"No. Because he is not born of darkness. It is not only the soul of a man which defines him, but what is in his blood."

I didn't want to believe that. It was safe being ignorant to it. I wasn't ready to look into David's darkness and see it as a disease that would one day take him away from me. But it had already begun to progress. And I had ignored it for the sake of love.

"I do not need to defend my knowledge, Amara. It serves only as a warning. And you will make your choice either way but hear this"—he turned back and looked me square in the eye—"it will be on your shoulders and you will get no help or pity from me. Or from Lilith."

"What's that supposed to mean?"

"In his darkest hour, one day, thirty years from *this moment*, he will do something unspeakable. And you, as a mother, will kill him for vengeance."

"What does he do?" I asked, mind racing.

"I will say no more." He lifted his head, placed his hands behind his back, and walked away.

He'd once predicted the death of his son Sam—at Elora's hand. And we'd done everything in our power to prevent that. Yet it happened anyway. As a being that was surrounded by prophecy and premonition all the time, I had come to learn that there were few cases in which the future could be changed. And Vampirie knew that. He wouldn't have told me that unless it was one of those cases.

I turned my gaze away and let it fall on the sleeping, almost innocent face of David, afraid, because I could so clearly see the monster now beneath the lies I'd always told myself.

And yet my heart only wanted to defend him, protect him from his own dark truth.

AUBREY

Cillian trusted the supernatural bind of me to his ring enough to take me into battle—outside the grounds of this castle, where he had no wards, no barrier spells. I would be able to see ghosts within the fissures out there, and he couldn't stop me from passing messages on to my family. I didn't know where I was, what this castle was called, but I knew it was in Scotland. That's all I needed to know. They'd figure out the rest.

But if we took the London Set tomorrow, Elias would be dead. Nothing could survive me. I hadn't tested my power yet, but I had trained endlessly over the past year, and Cillian had a lot of faith in it all. Enough that he was only bringing an army of two hundred vampires—all of them his own creations—to fortify the castle once we'd taken it. I was excited about a battle, excited to test my skills, but if I killed Elias, I'd have nothing left to fight for.

There was also a chance I might see him. I was probably only a few months short of eighteen now—not that I could really say

—and it would have been drawing closer to the time when he would come to 'court' me.

I smiled, thinking about that word and how he'd reacted when I teased him for it. I missed simple things like that now—like laughing at words, and his knightly manners.

As I'd laid falling asleep beside Cillian tonight—the only place he felt safe having me the night before battle—I thought about how it would feel to leave this castle tomorrow. He'd fly out by chopper in the morning, and I'd be summoned by magic later when he was ready for me. Then, I'd be standing in the very place Elias had lived since he became a vampire, so close to a breath of freedom, and I couldn't slow my heart enough to make myself sleep. If Elias saw me, he'd fight for me. I might not be able to overpower my master, but he could. Could I possibly be one sleep away from freedom?

Cillian stirred beside me, his deep, restful breathing halting for a moment to listen, and when I turned my head a little and opened my eyes, I was in front of my tree. The living realm just slipped away, as if I'd fallen upright through a gateway in the darkness.

The tree waved to me, and I waved back, moving to sit on the ground just by the water's edge. There were things in that lake that couldn't be seen but could definitely be felt, and I knew not to step in there, no matter how badly I wanted to touch my tree. Whatever those things were, they guarded it like my mother guarded hers. They were mean and evil, I sensed it, but the tree… it was alone out there.

"What is this place?" I asked. "Am I dead again?"

The whispers of this world, The Knowing, moved along my arms like wind and crawled into my ears. I couldn't understand the words, but I knew what they said anyway. Underworld. This is the Underworld.

I looked up then at the sky. It never changed. I'd been here a few times since that first day and, I'd come to realize, many times before that. This was the place I'd seen in my nightmares as a child, scared, because I understood its darkness, its sorrow, but didn't understand that I was a *part* of that. I was home here. Safe. In love with all its darkness, enough to see its beauty.

I heard a voice then, tuning my ear to it. And when I caught it properly and remembered his name, I spoke it aloud and appeared a second later in front of a long wall of gilded picture frames.

From somewhere in the distance, I could hear the drip-drip-drip of a faucet that hadn't been turned off, and there was the distinct smell of pancakes frying in butter here, but I didn't know why.

Off to my right, the corridor went on as far as the eye could see, with no ceiling above, only a sky of stars. It was papered in a rich, deep red with gold embellishments, and behind me, there was another wall just like it.

The paintings there were larger than me and spaced evenly apart, with mismatched frames. All the images were moving and living, showing worlds beyond—corners of the Underworld, I realized. But I didn't need to be told, didn't need to learn, I just knew.

I brought my gaze back from the endless line and looked to my left, meeting with a familiar pair of eyes. Where once they were green though, a colorless dark shone out from within now, like with the horses. Empty, blackened with evil, but beautiful beyond comprehension

"Dad!"

"Aubrey?" He frowned at me, the spark of recognition fighting to complete itself. Something had happened to him—

something that washed his skin with a sickly pallor and stripped his wits away.

"Dad," I cried, reaching across to touch his wrist.

His eyes went down my body, coming back up again to my hair, and he picked up a knot of it to run his thumb over. "You're different," he said.

"Dad, what happened? Why are you here?" I shook his wrist, breaking him out of his stare. "How are your eyes so dark?"

He seemed to remember where he was then and looked down at his hands. They were patchy with black and blood, and the putrid smell of off meat was almost unbearable.

"Are you dead?" I asked, voice crackling.

"No. But I'm close. I need to go back. I just…" He looked along the wall. "I can't remember which doorway."

I took his hand, ignoring the oily puss and the sticky wetness of the rot, and led him to the right door. I didn't know how I knew it was the right one, but it seemed like everything here, even this, was just… an understanding.

"Dad," I said, taking his cheeks to get his attention. "Tell Mom to get Elias out of the castle tomorrow."

"Why?" He touched my hand and drew it away from his face.

"Because everyone is going to die."

I shot up out of my sleep then with Cillian's arm across my waist, cold and heavy. At some point, he'd taken my clothes off me and pressed his naked body alongside mine. With that, and after the shock of seeing my father and the hope of saving Elias, I couldn't calm my heart. But if I didn't then Cillian would wake, sensing it, hearing it, and push for me to tell him why.

So I closed my eyes and imagined his touch was Elias's. Imagined his naked body was big and strong, not small, thin and weedy, like it was. I always thought Cillian looked like a choir boy: soft in the middle—the kind that was secretly a serial killer and later went on to become a priest so no one would know his darkest desires. And it sickened me that I had to lay this way with him. But imagining he was Elias helped. It was hard, but it helped.

I couldn't understand what had happened to my dad—why he was in that place—but I could only hope he remembered what I'd told him and did something to help.

With that in mind, I shut my eyes, drifting off to sleep with the hope that tomorrow brought a new turn of events.

DAWN CREPT IN TO THE LARGE SPACE, MAKING A THIN LINE of orange light over the cold fireplace. Cillian's room was really nice, and it was on the side of the castle where the sun rose not set, so it escaped the afternoon heat that made everywhere else just too hot. Like cooking in a stone pizza oven. But this room stayed cool, and it had a lot of charm, even if it didn't really fit his personality.

Over by the windows, a solid oak table sat behind a Victorian lounge suite that couldn't be seen from here in the bed, because the room had an L-shape to it and the heavy red curtains around the canopy bed were concealing it. All the furniture in here was heavy handcrafted wood, save for the gothic mirror, but with that, and a bunch of witch stuff like pestle's and herbs and little potion bottles around the space, it didn't look like a room in a castle. It looked like a witch's lair. Old books laid on almost every surface, but the biggest one—bigger than the top half of my body—sat on a stand by the fireplace, given pride of place.

I pulled my arm away from Cillian when I realized it was

under his floppy dick, but he felt the movement and shifted closer, wrapping his leg over mine and resting his cheek on my breast, squishing it flat under his slightly open mouth.

Nothing could have been more disgusting to me.

Maybe I got it from my mom, but I just never liked the idea of guys laying on a girl's chest. It was too… I don't know. Maybe it wasn't manly. It left me feeling icky and I just wanted to push him away.

With him sleeping, his arm around my waist, his hair tickling my chin and his icky wet mouth pushing tepid air over my nipple, I tried pressing my hand to his back to see if he'd die—if my chemical toxin would shoot into his vampire skin and kill him.

But it did nothing. Nothing except make him think it was a touch of affection, to which he responded by snuggling down even deeper into my chest, smiling behind sleepy eyes as he gawked up at me. So fucking creepy.

"Mmm," he hummed, wrapping his other arm under my spine and joining them. "You're so soft and warm. I should have allowed you into my bed months ago."

I didn't know what to say to that. But I knew him well enough to know I would never again sleep in my own bed. And from there, it would progress to more than just sleeping. I would be his slave now in every way. His tool, no longer just a weapon.

But if I wanted to get out of this alive, survive, be free, I had to play his game. And I could. I had it in me. I could open my legs and let him fuck me if it meant I'd be free. I'd be out in the real world today, and I'd seen Dad in the Underworld. It was only a matter of time now before I sensed him there again, like a spider feeling a bug in its web, and I could get him a message if I didn't manage to get one to a spirit today. I finally had hope.

"How about we make a deal?" Cillian said, lifting his head to look at me.

"Okay."

He got up, the sheet falling away to reveal his thin, spindly body. He was muscled but he wasn't all built and sexy like a real man. He reached over and touched my breast. "It's your birthday today—"

"What?"

All the air stopped before entering my lungs. I wanted to cry. I wanted to throw his hand off me and tell him that part belonged to Elias! How had so much time gone by without me realizing? I thought I'd been here for maybe eight months, but when I thought about it, that would make it pretty much a year since my last birthday. I'd wanted this year to pass quickly after I first met Elias, and I once couldn't bear the torture of having to wait, loving him and not being allowed to have him. But I was wrong. That wasn't torture because torture actually made time pass faster. I was eighteen today. Eighteen! Old enough for Elias now and not free to have him. It wasn't fair. It wasn't right. And I wondered if he'd wake today and think the same thing, or if maybe he'd moved on.

"You didn't realize?" he asked

"Time passes differently here, I guess," I said with a smile, shielding him from all the raging agony inside me. "Or maybe time flies when you're having fun."

He laughed, running his thumb in gentle circles over my nipple. No one had ever touched me there before. It made my skin pinch in disgust and shame. "I will grant you anything," he said. "One wish, if you give yourself to me. We can stay here in bed, all day—"

"But we're supposed to attack the castle."

"We'll put it off for one day." He moved in and pressed his tight lips to my breast, and my skin tightened all down my arms, his hair brushing my jaw and my heart. We *had* to attack today. If we waited, they wouldn't know it was coming. They'd drop their guard and Elias wouldn't get out on time.

"I was looking forward to stretching my limbs, testing my abilities," I lied, shutting my eyes tight as he sucked my nipple like a man-baby. "I really wanted to see what I was capable of."

He brought his head up and smiled, cupping the side of my face. "What's your one wish?"

He had me. I didn't want anything so much as I wanted to go to that castle today. I didn't want anything so much as I wanted to get word to my family or attack when we said we would. I couldn't have all my plans unravel now. "I want to attack today," I said. "That's my wish."

His eyes sparkled and he leaned in to kiss me. His lips, though they were full and really quite nice for a guy, they felt thin and cold and tight. They didn't relax as they touched mine; they ate at me, snapped at me, disputing the natural order of things.

This would not be my fate. I would not have him as my first. I didn't even care about virginity or anything stupid like that. It's just that I'd wanted Elias to be the first one.

As he laid me back, crawling between my open legs, his floppy penis dangling against my hip for a moment, I looked up at the heavy red curtains, praying for something to happen, for someone to intervene.

But they didn't.

He batted at his ugly length of skin until it was hard, then shoved it inside of me, exhaling as though it was the most pleasurable moment of his life. When he curled down and sucked my nipple again, bile rose up in my throat, but I forced my hands onto his back and moaned out his name. And the dream of having Elias as my first died and burst into flames.

Happy birthday, Aubrey, I thought to myself, just wanting to scream. Happy fucking birthday.

ARA

I woke to a screeching ring through the room, darting over to my phone so fast I tripped on the rug and hit the table, bashing my hip.

"You okay?" Jase laughed, sitting up in bed.

"Yeah." I winced, swiping my thumb across the screen as I rubbed my sore hip better. "Blade, what's up? Is David okay?"

"No, he just shot up out of his sleep, and… hang on."

"Ara?" David said in a deep voice, strained with agony.

"David, are you okay?"

Jason got up and came over, sitting beside me where I collapsed onto the arm of the chair. It'd been so long since I'd heard his voice. I never thought he'd come out of that sleep Vampirie had locked him in, and to have him wake, today of all days, was the best gift I could've asked for.

"It's time," he said. "I can't sustain the light any longer."

Jason sighed, and my mouth dropped, a cold gasp of air filling my heart with regret.

"David, it's Aubrey's birthday today. I…" I couldn't do this today.

"It's either now, or else, by the time the sun is down, I will be dead." He grunted, and I heard Blade in the background, asking if he was okay. "And, Ara… there's something else."

"What?"

"Aubrey."

"What about her?"

"I saw her—"

"Where?" I stood up.

"No time to talk. I'll fill you in later, but for now—"

"No, if you know where she is—"

"I saw her in the Underworld—"

"Why was she there? Why were *you* there? Is she dead—"

"I don't know. All I know is that she guided me back to the passage home. I was nearly dead." The gravity struck me. "She said there's going to be an attack—on London. She said to get Elias out."

The world rocked unsteadily under me as several plans rushed into action inside my thoughts. "Okay. I'll call him now." I glanced back at Jase when he shifted away suddenly and sat on the bed, looking at the floor between his hands, and my throat tightened as the next question formed there. "How long do we have until we need to…?"

"A few hours. I need to do something first—"

"What?"

"I'm hungry," he said, and I knew instantly what that meant. "Have Jason ready."

"David, you can't—"

"Ara," Blade said. "He's gone."

"Gone?"

"Vanished into thin air. Should I get Arthur to help track him down?"

I sighed, pressed upon by too many consuming worries. "No. Leave him. And get on the phone to King Drake. Tell him there's going to be an attack on London Castle. I'll call Elias."

"On it." He hung up. I wanted to sit with Jase and hold onto him, comfort him through his grief in his last hours, as he'd never let anyone but Falcon, but I had to warn Elias first.

He picked up his phone on the second ring, the noise of a party going on behind him. "Queen Amara, what can I do for you?"

"There's going to be an attack. You have to get everyone out now."

"Attack? From what enemy?"

"I don't know. But… Aubrey—"

"You've found her?"

"No. David slipped into the Underworld," I explained. "He's near death. He saw her there."

Elias let out an audible squeak of grief, and I could almost see him sitting down on something, pinching his nose. "She's dead?"

"No. David didn't think that was the case. She is connected to the Underworld, like I am to the Other Side, so I would say she can walk there," I offered. "But she told David to get everyone out. Elias…" I paused, hoping he understood the magnitude of this news. "We know what she is. We know only half of what she is capable of. If Cillian is using her as a weapon, no living soul in that castle stands a chance. And it won't even be a battle. It'll be…"

"Decimation," he said for me.

"Yes."

Elias sighed again. "Did David say if she was okay? If she—"

"He hasn't said anything. He… it's time for them to merge. David's dying."

"So soon?"

"I don't have a choice."

"Then there's little more to be said," he offered in a kind, supportive voice. "You know where I stand on the matter, Queen Amara. Do what must be done, and I will evacuate the castle immediately."

"Okay. Good luck, and… be safe."

"I will, My Queen."

I hung up and dialed Elora.

"Mom," she said groggily. "What's wrong?"

"Something's happened… it's Dad. He's close to death. I have to…"

"Now?"

"In a few hours. And… Aubrey contacted him—"

"What?"

"Just call Mike. Tell him to leave the kids with Vicki and get here as soon as he can. We're going to need everyone on this, even Harry."

"Okay." I heard her moving about, heard Eric ask what was wrong. "I'm on it. Where's Dad now?"

"He escaped Blade," I said. "But he'll meet me at the forest when he's ready."

"When?"

"You can't come with me, Elora." I caught on then, realizing she wanted to be there. "When I go to the tree, I have to do this alone."

"But—"

"Non-negotiable, sweetheart. Just rally the family," I demanded softly. "I'll see you back at the manor when it's… done," I finished regretfully.

As I hung up the phone, Jason exhaled.

"I'm sorry," I said, turning my body to face him in the darkness.

"It doesn't matter," he offered. "No one can ever be ready for this sort of thing."

I moved over and knelt in front of him, breathing in his human cologne and the oils in his skin. I had wanted to build our friendship up from falling asleep beside someone you trust to eventually making love. I think a part of me even wanted one more child with him—one last piece of him. But we just hadn't gotten there yet. I hadn't kissed him, hadn't really told him how much this time had meant to me—watching movies after Danny went to bed, running the monarchy as a team, a hilarious and energetic team. There was so much light in our days together, and our nights were spent sleeping as though we hadn't a care in the world. Danny had started sleeping through the night since Jase entered his world too, and it felt like everything was just perfect. That it would all fall apart when he was gone.

What would this do to that little boy, who loved him, cherished him more than he ever had a chance to with David? David had worked so often when Daniel was little, and in this last year, my baby had really come to the age where he needed, wanted his dad more than his mom. He wouldn't know David. And he'd eventually love him, but this transition, missing Jason, would hurt. I just wasn't ready for that. Not today. Not on my missing-daughter's birthday.

"Let's not talk about it." Jason stood up. "It has to be done. You know you won't be happy ever again if he dies."

"Where are you going?" I asked, when he moved past me.

"I've got a few loose ends to tie up," he said, coming back to kiss my head. "I'll meet you by the forest later."

As he walked away, I wanted to reach out and grab him. But

what would I say? I couldn't say that I loved him, because that would be salt in the wound. So I said nothing, knowing what had to be done and accepting that, as a shard of my heart broke off forever and lodged itself inside of my soul, damaging it irreparably.

IN A POWDER-BLUE COAT AND JEANS, SAFE FROM THE nearing autumn cold that I couldn't possibly shelter this tree from, I sat with it in its sick, dying state, like it was a child in need of its mother. In ways, all the love I couldn't send to my Aubrey was being given out into the tree right now, as it neared its final breath. David would arrive at any minute, and I would meet Jase at the edge of the forest and lead him here with the intention of killing him. No, with the intention of saving my David.

All my life, ever since I met David, I'd made choices, both right and wrong, to be with him. He met me in a time when I'd lost so much, when I needed something strong and safe to hold me down and stop me floating away, and when I thought about all I'd come through, I felt scared. I felt sad. I felt like I couldn't take anymore.

But those people I'd made my life about now made it okay. David made it okay. Mike made it okay. And even with David gone these past months, Jase, miraculously, had made it okay.

After this, after today, no one would ever make this tree okay again though. David had someone to fight for him. But, just like Jason, the tree was collateral damage. And the truth was, I never deserved either of them.

I wasn't sure what the world would become without it, but

the sadness, the pain I felt in my heart right now screamed at me that it would be more than just Elora's crux that would fail.

Could I do that, face that? Face my eldest daughter being hunted by the Silas? Face fighting for a way to keep her safe?

With David beside me, I could face the absolute worst of life… but a mother choosing her husband over her daughter? Even choosing a husband over the greater good of the world, for a love like mine and David's, I could forgive myself for that. But a daughter?

David appeared behind me, folded slightly with a hand across the bloody path on his shirt where his rotting flesh soaked through. I could smell it from here. It was thick and putrid, like days-old blood.

"Hey." I got up and moved over, supporting him with both hands as I led him to the tree to sit in its roots. There, I could see he felt a sense of coming home, of being at peace. "Are you okay?"

"I'm so close to death that…" he strained, sweating and shaking, "I fell through to the Underworld. I'm only alive right now because of Aubrey."

"Tell me everything that happened?"

"She's changed. She walked there as an equal to the fourth-highest power, Ara. And her hair…" He shut his eyes, wincing as a new sweat broke out across his brow. "Her hair had changed."

"Do you know where she is? If she's okay?"

He shook his head. "But I know what she is."

"She's a necromancer—"

David shook his head again. "She is *so* much more than that. She's like you. You're a Light—you walk the souls to the River for rebirth. But you're also an Auress, a guardian. You have many names, many titles, many occupations in the greater good of the natural world. And so does she."

I smiled, kneeling down in front of him with my hand to his arm. "What do you mean?"

"She's a High Priestess of the Underworld, Ara. Like an Auress, maybe soon to be a queen. She has power she probably can't even comprehend yet. I felt it." He tapped his chest. "With my connection to the tree, to the darkness, I felt it and it whispered to me."

"What did it say?"

"Her fourth parent… she carries a royal title because of him. She can raise the dead, ferry them back to the Other Side, but with her connection to her fourth parent, she can summon great armies, wield a sword that had been lost for thousands of years, and make people speak the truth at her command."

My heart warmed with hope. "Does she know this?"

"No." He coughed, shaking from the pain it derived, and readjusted his seat. "But, like you, how you spoke with the stone before it was a tree, she'll learn. Every time she enters that realm, they speak to her. It's only a… matter…"

"Of time?" I finished for him. "So, if it's the Underworld, is she evil? A demon?"

He laughed, shutting his eyes and leaning his head back on the tree. "No. She's not evil."

I leaned in and kissed his cheek. He'd just given me a gift he probably couldn't comprehend in this state.

"Where's my… brother?" he asked, barely able to get the words out.

"Waiting at the edge of the forest. I can sense him," I said, touching the ground to feel his energy. "I'll go get the dagger and then grab him on the way back."

David snagged my hand before I could move. "I know what this means to you, Ara."

My eyes strayed up past him to the tree, its leaves blackened and hanging with regret, weighed down by all that his dark soul had put it through and all that we stood to lose now without his blood to undo its curse.

"No you don't," I said softly.

Jason walked behind me toward the tree. I held onto the Blade of Eden tightly, my hand sweating, feeling a pull against my soul, my body, trying to make me stop. I didn't want this. I didn't want any of this.

But then, I didn't start this. Lily did. She kidnapped them and she tried to erase Jason for good. I was merely the one that had to finish it now.

When we reached the tree, the raw pain in my stomach felt like a bleeding tendril from my soul, made me want to take my own life instead. I couldn't picture the moment the blade would pierce his heart, severing the connection of his soul from his body. The moment he'd look at me one last time and then, like a light going out, never again.

Behind David, the faint, broken whispers of Life's magic here cried for the end. Alive or dead, it no longer cared. The tree, this sacred beauty of a tree, it was the magic in all of us. It was Cerulean Light, it was Elora's crux. Without it, all of that would die. Would the power of vampires go with it? Would the world return to a state of normal, no more witches, no more unnatural death?

No more Light?

For all the magic in this tree, for all the power it gave the earth, it also brought kindness and empathy in new measures when it was born. What would be lost when it died because I couldn't spill David's blood, his life, back onto its roots to cure its curse?

I looked up at Jason, edging toward me in my grief, and tried to smile. "It'll be quick," I told him, barely able to meet his eye.

He pressed a hand to my shoulder blade and tried to draw me in. "It's okay, Ara."

"No, it's not." I looked over at David where he stood by the weeping, blackened tree. "It's never going to be okay now."

"You'll find a way to bring the tree back," he assured me. "You always do."

I loved his faith. I loved his trust in me. I loved his heart for giving up his soul.

I wrapped both arms around his neck and held him tight, pressing every single inch of my body into his. "Thank you."

He just sighed, squeezing me.

"Just take care of him, okay?" he said. "Daniel. And tell him every day that his daddy loves him."

"I will. But… in ways…" I glanced over at David. "You'll kind of be telling him that yourself."

"I guess." He looked too, and David nodded as if to say he agreed. But he was lying. Jason's soul wouldn't change David. Nothing would. Not now.

"You should say goodbye," I told Jase. But when he moved over to his brother, David shook his head.

"He'll be a part of me soon enough," David said. "It's not goodbye."

"But it is."

David just rested his head back on the tree, tucking a foot up where he stood, looking like a zombie in a rotted corpse.

My hands and wrists shook violently now with what was coming, but I grabbed Jason's shoulder and turned him to face me, hugging him again one last time. "It doesn't make it okay. I want you to know that," I whispered. "I may have chosen to be with David all those years ago, but I need you to understand that I still wished every day that you were with me. It was never okay in me, Jase, and my biggest regret is that I let you believe I was happy without you."

"It's okay," he said sweetly, patting my ribs. "I know now, and we'll be together forever, in David."

"No we won't. Because it was never your soul I was in love with." I squeezed him tighter, allowing myself to admit that freely in front of David, the magic of the living forest, and my own open heart. He drew back to look into me, waiting for me to say what he needed to hear.

"I love David. That will never change," I confessed. "But I need to make it clear that, when it came to you, it was always the *person* I loved. Not your soul." And I meant that. And the confession carried with it more than thirty-five years of torture, for both of us, because if I could have just let David go, then Jason would never have suffered all that he had.

He closed his eyes as that truly sunk in, and I stepped back, readying my knife.

"I'm sorry," I whispered. But as he went to say it was okay now, it ended in a gasp. His head whipped around, finding me instead across the clearing, the dagger in David's chest. His flesh split open around a cough of surprise and his blood spilled out in a wide gush onto the tree. I withdrew the blade and dragged it quickly across his throat to spill every drop, beginning the process of reversing the curse within the roots and restoring all that was undone.

The liquid seeped into the earth and sparkled there, turning blackness into light before my eyes. And the pain split me like a thousand knives through my midsection as David dropped to his knees, fixing my eyes first with a look of horror, betrayal and regret, until it faded slowly away to acceptance.

He nodded as he folded over, and I gently guided him down to the soil, to the tree's roots, leaning in to kiss his head.

"I understand," he grunted.

"I know," I cried, sobbing then as his mind slipped away, eyes fixing on nothing, in the same state they'd been that day he truly died.

The ground soaked up the last of his blood and, like the beat of a baby's heart before it's even born, I could hear the tree healing, hear it returning to what it once was. As his life bled out under my hands and my tears, the magic of the world, of Life, was finally set right.

But it would never be right again in my heart. He was dead.

That last moment when he walked into the backyard with the groceries, when he called my name, that was the last time he would ever be that beautiful. The last time he was my David. The last time I saw him.

"Lily did this," I cried, rocking back and forth to move the pain through my core. "Lily did this. She killed him. She ended it all when she killed him."

Jason landed behind me, gently cupping my ribs to pull me back, and he inspected the body of his brother, as the last breath that he held in his lungs finally exhaled and it all came to an end.

A sad, tragic, waste of an end.

As I howled my agony, my rage, out into the world around me, igniting the skies and bringing the heavens down on top of us, the tree stretched its arms widely and reimagined the life around it, reaching for the rain, everything restored.

"Ara?" Jase tried to touch me, but I felt stiff all over. I couldn't breathe. Couldn't loosen the twist in my stomach. Until

I remembered the soul, attached now only to the magic in the Blade of Eden.

"Your soul," I said, shaking as I got up on my knees and tried to turn around. I fished for the dagger, but it shifted away with my careless reach, so Jason picked it up for me, his face frozen around the shock as our eyes met. I touched my fingertips to the blood there on its shiny silver surface, my own cold, raw shock settling in to the airlessness in my throat.

Taking Jason's cheeks in both hands, I looked into his eyes. He was so confused, so conflicted right now because he didn't understand. He thought I did it for the tree, for the Light, the Cerulean Magic in all of us that would have died with it, but I didn't. I wasn't that selfless when it all came down to it. And he would just never be able to comprehend that I didn't just do it to save Elora; I did this for him too.

I shut my eyes and whispered the words to guide his soul back from within the blade, turning away then because I didn't want to see David's life in his eyes. I didn't want to see the truth of what I'd done.

I folded over David again and cried out loudly, as if it were a song from deep within my soul. It all happened then on replay: the moment Lily pressed that fruit to his dead lips, and he awoke as something else.

His fate was set in stone from before that. He'd died and she brought back what should never have been brought back. And now it was gone. My David, my rock, my knight. He was gone.

Lilith appeared beside me then, casing my body in her long, cool arm. "My darling."

"Lily did this," I cried. "She did all of this."

"I know," she whispered. "Come on. Get up. It's time to go."

"Go where?" Jase said, stepping in protectively.

"She needs to go away for a while," Lily warned. "Her soul is shattered, Jason. She will need to heal, or she will die along with him."

Jason nodded once, his fists tight by his sides.

"Take care of Daniel for her."

As I stood up to follow Lilith, my legs aching, just wanting to buckle out from under me and take me down to the ground, I glanced back at David. He wasn't there anymore. His body was, but he wasn't, and I had never seen anything so empty and sad in all my life, until I stole one last glance at Jase, where he stood in the middle of the clearing, with his entire world changed, and closed his eyes.

JASON

Conflict was born in me in that single moment.

Ara pressed the soul of my dead brother into mine, and a warm swell of completion expanded inside my core. I felt more whole than I had since that second before Lily had ripped it out, but more dead inside than I had since Ara approved of my death for David's sake.

I couldn't make sense of what happened, what she'd done. Why she'd done it. I knew she'd acted to save her daughter's crux, to save the tree and all of its magic. But I couldn't make sense of the look in her eye in that moment before she passed his soul on to me, like she was sorry for what she'd done to me. Not to him. To *me*.

As I walked from the forest, struggling with the weight of my brother's dead body, Falcon appeared, making it safe to falter, safe to fall to my knees and let him take the burden. He settled David onto the ground and wrapped himself around me, as several people came flooding from nearby, wailing out the agony as they saw their dead king. As Elora saw her dead father.

I could hear her sobs, hear her scream, but I couldn't look. I knew she had Eric to comfort her, and that she'd be okay. And all I could think about then was that final moment, thirty minutes ago, as I'd hugged my baby boy and said goodbye. He didn't understand why I was crying. He didn't know I was supposed to leave and never come back. And I thought about his small, floppy little body as he'd thrown his arms around me and said, "I love you, Daddy," and how I thought I would never ever feel that again.

Now, all I wanted was to run to him. To hold him and absorb all that love into me, because I was crushed beyond grief that my brother was dead, but so grateful that I would get to hold Danny now every day of my life. I couldn't think of anything else.

Falcon moved back as I stood. "Where are you going?"

"I need to hold my son."

He ran up behind me and followed, keeping a step back, and I left my brother there to the care of my uncle, whose shock could be felt but not heard. Left him there so Elora could touch him one last time and grieve his passing. Left him there because there was nothing left in there now. He was in me. And I would always carry him with me, an ever-present reminder now to the woman I loved of what she'd given up.

When I opened the nursery door, my little boy looked up from the story he was reading with the nanny. He didn't show much interest in my sudden appearance because he couldn't comprehend the fact that I was never supposed to walk through that door again.

"You can go," I told the nanny. "I got it from here."

She smiled softly, bowing her head as she left the room, and Falcon closed the door.

"Hey, buddy bear." I sat down on the bed, reaching over to

lay my hand on Danny's ankle, just needing to touch him. "Can Daddy get a hug?"

He grinned playfully, putting his book down, and launched himself up and into my arms. And everything in the world settled, all the broken pieces of my life coming together there in the love between my arms. It didn't matter to me now if Ara hated me, if she couldn't ever look at me again, because this little boy was all that mattered. I squeezed him tightly, shutting my eyes and breathing in the soft soapy smell of baby shampoo in his silky brown hair.

My little boy. The first child that had ever survived.

Ara hadn't just given me my life, or my brother's soul. She'd given me hope, restored my faith in everything. Set the balance in the world right, for once, at the cost of her own heart.

AUBREY

Seven choppers flew out from the main castle grounds this morning, carrying Cillian and some of the men who'd fortify the castle after we overthrew it. The rest were already stationed in London, awaiting orders.

But as the day passed with me pacing back and forth, waiting to be summoned by magic to Elias's castle, it ended with all seven choppers coming back in. I stood with my nose pressed to the window in the stone room and watched them fly over. They landed on the opposite side of the castle, so I didn't see Cillian until he came into the room, his face tight with rage.

"What happened?" I asked, pressing my hands behind my back and moving guiltily away from the window.

"Someone tipped them off." He marched over to the stone altar and leapt up to sit atop it, his arms folded. "Which means we have a mole in our midst."

"Shit." I leaned on the altar beside him, my arms folded too. "I knew something was up. I was worried."

"About?" He turned his head a fraction, eyes lighting up with a hopeful smile, but it didn't reach his lips.

"I thought maybe they'd won," I lied.

"Did you now?" he asked, but the undertone reeked of disbelief. He grabbed my wrist and hopped down off the altar. "Come."

"Where?"

"I need you to do something for me."

Cillian led me to the table in the hall on the other side of the stone room and sat me down. He took a cup from the sideboard, an ordinary wine glass, and put it in front of me, pouring some water in.

I looked at it, not sure what he wanted me to do. "What's this for?"

He dragged a chair right beside me, leaning his elbow on the table to bring us into a close circle. "You could possibly have an ability I've never taught you."

"What?"

"In the fourteenth-century texts, the demon with whose name I created you bore a gift from the gods, they say: a magical chalice that, when drank from, could make any man speak the truth."

My mouth popped, hoping to the gods that wasn't true.

"But the truth of the fable is actually that he had the ability to whisper Truth over the glass, any glass, and the liquid within would have that power."

"And you think I can do it?"

"I created you in his likeness. So, yes. I think you can."

"But, how will that help?"

"I will line up every sniveling excuse for a follower and ask them one question: did you betray me?" he said.

My eyes widened but I rolled my head down to look at the glass so he wouldn't see. "Should we try it?"

"That's why we're here." He pushed it closer with one finger, the energy in the room dense with tension. My tension.

"So, I just say the word 'Truth'?"

"And it is done," he said, taking the glass. He threw back a sip, and his wet lips sat parted, waiting. "Ask me something, and I will try to lie."

"Like?"

"A generic question. If you ask me anything that results in an answer I wouldn't otherwise give, I will beat you," he warned.

"Okay, um…" I scratched my head, looking around, but my mind shot back then to a tale of two birds and a door to Heaven and Hell, and Elias. "What color are my eyes?"

His jaw pulled tight, tongue sitting at the entranceway to his mouth, fighting some deep urge. "Blue," he said finally, shooting the word out in a breath. He looked at the cup, smiling. "It works."

And now I was really scared. One sip from that, and he could know all my secret thoughts. He slid it over to me.

"Drink."

I didn't wait for him to ask twice. The consequences of that would be worse than telling the truth. I wiped my lip dry and looked up at him, knowing exactly what he was going to ask and trying, in vain, to find something likeable in him.

"You've flirted with me on numerous occasions," he said. I wanted to crawl away, knowing what he'd do to me when I answered this. "Are you attracted to me, or are you doing it so I might one day drop my guard and you can escape?"

"All I want is to escape," I said, the dread running stale down my throat like all the air had been sucked out of the room.

Cillian didn't react. He didn't explode and yell, didn't strike me or even show signs of being upset.

"Fool me once," he said to himself, his lips pressed flat as if he should have known better. "You've made me a stronger, wiser man for it."

Saliva gathered under my tongue with the fear, and when I swallowed it down, it made a gulping sound. He stood up.

"I have news," he said, drawing a regretful but dutiful breath. "Of your father."

I looked up, hiding the fear in my eyes, even if I couldn't hide the thumping in my chest. "What about him?"

"He's dead."

"What?" The thump doubled, exploding in my core with a wave of shock.

"Your mother killed him."

"I know you're lying." My voice shook, and a raw, unwelcome emotion took root in my soul, pushing a lens of tears into my eyes. I blinked them back. "She would never do that—"

"Apparently, Lily fed him fruit from the Tree of Life and, in that, he became connected to it. With his evil blood, the magic became tainted, and the only way to cure it was to repay the debt—"

"In his blood, with his life," I said, the words leaving my lips in a shaky whisper as I recalled the tales of Anandene and her curse being repaid—an act that started centuries of war for my grandfather and resulted, in the end, in my dad and his brother even existing.

My mom loved that tree like I loved mine. I understood then what had been at stake, what had been lost—what its life had cost her.

Cillian squatted down by me, sweeping a line of tears from my cheek. He inspected them carefully, bopping his head in amazement. "I wondered if there would ever be a way to make you cry."

My lip stiffened and I sat taller, shoving all my emotions back down into that hole in my stomach. I turned my eye on him then, cold and hateful, no longer caring about anything. He stole me. He took me from them, and I wasn't there to protect them. I wasn't there to say goodbye to my father.

Oh God. I wanted to sink down, but I held his gaze firmly, even as the truth ripped through me: my last true words to Dad were hateful, shattered his heart. He saw a truth in my eyes that day, saw that his little girl hated him. And he believed it. And I was sorry. Because I understood all about his darkness and I understood why Mom never hated him. And now he was gone. And I never got to tell him.

"I want to punish you for your lies," Cillian said, standing up. "I want to force you to give me your body in front of a room filled with your family—humiliate you the way you have done to me. But I have a mole to uncover, and there isn't time."

He tugged my arm until I stood up.

"You will sleep in the cell until I'm ready to deal with you." His eyes went down my body. "Naked."

ELORA

No one knew. Mom vanished that day, and no one knew what had been done until a rolling wave of relief washed over the world, making those sensitive to it take a breath suddenly.

My phone rang a moment later and it was Morgana, asking me if Dad had died.

I knew then.

I'd dropped the phone and run for the forest, my legs falling out from under me when Jason came through the shadow of the trees with Dad in his arms, a deep look of regret and confusion eternally etched within his eyes. I didn't run to him. I didn't hug him. I knew what my father was, that his death was the only option if Mom were to fulfill her holy duty and protect that tree. But I couldn't face it.

Ric had come up behind me a moment later and cradled me in my grief, as I let go of the man who did those horrible things and instead mourned the one who'd been kidnapped by Lily.

Now, with days having passed since Mom vanished, we were

given no choice but to bury my father. I stood at the lectern and looked down at the faces of our closest friends and family around the coffin, set to rest just above a hole in the ground—beside the graves of the children who'd died here once—where his body would now lay for all time.

In the village, not far from here, the people would mourn and farewell their once-great king in their own ways, setting lanterns off into the sky at dusk. Each one was to represent a part of him, a side of him, that would be truly missed. *Truly*, and eternally missed.

"His death saved more than just my uncle—our beloved King Jason—and the tree. My mother sacrificed her greatest love for the good of *all*. For my crux magic, for Cerulean Energy, for the immortality that runs through our veins," I said, reading my speech from the page in front of me. I glanced down at Dad's coffin, white, with flowers over the top, and cried for a moment. "My dad—the man he was before that fruit ever touched his lips—would not have let her save him if it meant losing me or breaking her vow to Nature."

I looked down at Uncle Jason to drive that point right into his guilt and make him see that Dad would have wanted this, but he couldn't look me in the eye.

"I will never see my father again. And in this eternal life, that's something I can't even fathom right now. But he *is* gone, and even though he will live on in the king, it feels like my soul went away with him." I placed my speech on his coffin, resting my hand there as though I could kiss his head, see that warm look in his eyes that would make everything all right. "I love you, Dad. For forever. And I'm sorry for what Lily did to you."

Ric came in behind me then and held me up as the pall-bearers lowered his coffin slowly to the ground. Harry dropped to his knees in front of it, Rochelle wrapping her arms around him, and Uncle Jason just stood staring at the empty vessel of his brother, knowing he was gone but not yet able to comprehend what that meant—how eternal and how unending this pain would always be. It took almost twenty years for the world to get over the death of Arthur, but this would take a lifetime. And mine, my lifetime, was eternal.

Mom wasn't here to say goodbye, but then, neither was Aubrey, and it broke my heart to imagine what she'd feel if she found out, wherever she was, all alone. I sobbed out my anguish loudly into the rain as it all came down, purged out its pain on top of us, wetting the flowers and running in rivulets over his coffin.

The last rain that would ever touch him.

The last moment he would ever be present in this world.

Mom would die. When she returned from the Other Side and she realized how much time had passed, that Dad was buried and the world had moved on, she'd carry her grief inside of her and her guilt, for choosing to let him go, and it would slowly kill her like the darkness that killed my father's body. Like the darkness that turned him into something I hated. The darkness that made me want that version of him dead.

I couldn't mourn him in that capacity today. I had to mourn the father who bashed pumpkins with me on Halloween, who taught Harry to read minds and move things with a thought, that playful, loving man who'd played piano at Christmas. I couldn't mourn the beast that killed those humans. I couldn't even call on that hatred now to get me through. My dad was gone. And Mom was right when she cried out into the world that Lily had killed him. She *did* kill him. And all she brought back with that fruit was a monster, and a near endless trail of pain and suffering for so many others in the world.

"We will get past this, Lors," Ric said, kneeling down in the mud beside me. I glanced over to make sure Harry was okay, but Uncle Arthur had him. The poor boy was shaking, wrapped around Arthur like a tight cage that would never let go. I wanted to hold Aubrey. I wanted to hold Mom. I wanted someone to walk over there and hold Uncle Jason. None of this was his fault. He didn't ask for Dad's soul. He went there to die, to give up his own, and Mom made this choice. The right choice. And yet I think everyone blamed him. But there was just no way in this entire world that we could find him at fault.

"Help me up," I whispered.

Ric guided me to my feet, staying close as I walked toward Jason. He wiped a hand down this nose and drew his eyes away from the coffin as the shadows in the dirt swallowed it.

"I'm sorry, Uncle Jase." I hugged him, and Ric joined the hug too.

As if he was so broken that he couldn't move, it took him a moment, but Jason slowly brought both hands up around us, his grief so deep, so tight that he held his breath. Harry entered the huddle a moment later, and Arthur closed us all in his mighty, safe embrace. The overseer, the guidance, the one who understood our pain better and more deeply than anyone.

When I looked back up, everyone else had started to head inside, leaving only Morgana and Drake, Falcon, Vicki and Cal, Mike and Jules, and the kids. And when my gaze slipped past Jason to a lone figure standing in the shadows, the pouring rain slating in sheets and sticking his hair to his head, I smiled, thanking him for staying.

Elias felt welcome to approach us then, and the others broke from the hug or walked over, coming together in a circle. I took Uncle Jason's hand, and Drake took Morgana's, the circle closing by one hand to another, with almost every single person that mattered to me right here. There was comfort in that, even if I wanted to ignore that feeling and just die with grief, but it was there. And it helped.

"I'm so sorry," Elias said.

"I know." I nodded, shutting my eyes, and as Drake began a prayer to send my father's memory away with, because his soul would live on forever in Jason, another hand appeared, breaking the circle between Jason and me.

"Mom!"

She tried to smile but her pain melted it away. Her skin was radiant and glowing, as if she'd been dead all these years and we hadn't noticed, and only the time spent on the Other Side had healed what was so terribly broken in her.

Jason squeezed her hand a little, and we all closed our eyes, igniting the pain with the magic of Nature that my father had died to save.

When we looked up, the rain had stopped, and a cool wind swept in to chill our bones. But up there in a clear, sorrowful sky, a thousand lanterns took to the heavens, lighting up my father's memory.

Nothing would ever make this okay. But I suppose everyone buries their father before they're ready, it's the way of life, even if you're immortal, and knowing the future I had seen with him in it, it was better this way. As much as it killed me to close the book on this chapter of our lives, there was peace in knowing *that* future was finally, once and for all, over.

Don't miss book nine, because nothing is what it seems.

No one knows where we go when we die.

But I do.

Life after death isn't something a mere mortal is supposed to know about. It's something we're aware of, but it's like a ghost. You see it from the corner of your eye but as soon as you turn your head, it's gone.

My world is much the same, but I'm going to show it to you and ask that you keep an open mind. Because the afterlife, for me, is not the good place. It's the bad one.

CPSIA information can be obtained
at www.ICGtesting.com
Printed in the USA
LVHW111931230719
625023LV00003B/524/P

9 780648 525837